MVFOL

Annie Henry

and the
Birth of Liberty

D1019752

Adventures of the American Revolution Series

Annie Henry and the Secret Mission
Annie Henry and the Birth of Liberty

★ ★ ★ ★ ★ ★ ★ ★ ★ ★ ★ ★ ★ ★ ★ ★ ★ ★
ADVENTURES OF THE AMERICAN REVOLUTION
★ ★ ★ ★ ★ ★ ★ ★ ★ ★ ★ ★ ★ ★ ★ ★ ★ ★

Annie Henry

and the

Birth of Liberty

Susan Olasky

CROSSWAY BOOKS • WHEATON, ILLINOIS
A DIVISION OF GOOD NEWS PUBLISHERS

Annie Henry and the Birth of Liberty

Copyright © 1995 by Susan Olasky

Published by Crossway Books
a division of Good News Publishers
1300 Crescent Street
Wheaton, Illinois 60187

All rights reserved. No part of this publication may be reproduced, stored in a retrieval system or transmitted in any form by any means, electronic, mechanical, photocopy, recording or otherwise, without the prior permission of the publisher, except as provided by USA copyright law.

Cover illustration: Tom LaPadula

Art Direction/Design: Mark Schramm

First printing, 1995

Printed in the United States of America

Library of Congress Cataloging-in-Publication Data
Olasky, Susan.
   Annie Henry and the birth of liberty / Susan Olasky.
      p.   cm. — (The adventures of the American Revolution ; bk. 2)
   Summary: In 1775 in Virginia, Patrick Henry's ten-year-old daughter,
Annie, tries to concentrate on her day-to-day activities but is increasingly
caught up in her father's role in the colonists' growing unrest.
   1. Henry, Patrick, 1736–1799—Juvenile fiction. [1. Henry, Patrick,
1736–1799—Fiction. 2. Fathers and daughters—Fiction. 3. United
States—History—Revolution, 1775–1783—Fiction.] I. Title.
II. Series.
PZ7.0425Ad 1995   [Fic]—dc20   94-45739
ISBN 0-89107-842-8

03		02		01		00		99		98		97		96		95
15	14	13	12	11	10	9	8	7	6	5	4	3	2	1

For my sons:
Pete, David, Daniel, and Ben

CONTENTS

A PICNIC

ANNIE HENRY LOOKED UP AT THE BLUE SKY. THE MAY air felt warm on her skin as she hurried through her morning chores of gathering the eggs, feeding her chickens, and putting fresh hay in the nesting boxes. Normally, Annie dawdled over those tasks in the hope of delaying her lessons, but today she wanted the morning to fly by because she had planned an outing for the afternoon.

It was not common for girls in 1775 to have regular lessons. Once a girl could read and do arithmetic she was excused from school. Annie, however, was no ordinary girl. Her father, Patrick Henry, expected all his children to be well-educated. As a lawyer, politician, and gentleman farmer, he had enough money to hire a tutor to live on the plantation and teach the Henry children.

Mr. Dabney, the tutor, was a stickler for lessons. Everyday at nine o'clock he rapped his willow cane on his desk and called the class to order. The class consisted of Annie, age ten, and her two older brothers, William, fifteen, and John, thirteen. Andrew Thacker, a thirteen-year-old neighbor, came some days if his father could spare him from his chores. The class met in Patrick Henry's library, among bookshelf-lined walls that made it look as though learning was going on. But that wasn't always true.

The boys were hopeless students. They suffered through Greek and Latin, sprawling lazily in their chairs until Mr. Dabney, in frustration, issued a reminder with his willow cane. Then they straightened up and were attentive, at least for a while until the lure of a bird's song or a scent on a soft breeze drew their attention back out the window to the pastures and woods beyond.

Annie liked her lessons, although she didn't like Mr. Dabney, a distant cousin of her father. He could turn an interesting subject like history into a grand bore. Great battles waged by brave soldiers for glorious causes became dried up facts on brittle paper.

Today the boys were supposed to recite a poem in Latin. When it was Andrew's turn, he stood clumsily in front of the class, shifting his weight from leg to leg, never raising his eyes to meet Mr. Dabney's at the back of the room.

Annie stared at her desk wishing that Andrew could just sit down and be spared the embarrassment, but that was not Mr. Dabney's way. He let the boy suffer for five minutes before excusing him with the words, "Why your father wants to educate you is beyond me. You're the thickest boy I have ever had the privilege of knowing. Sit down."

As Andrew slunk to his seat, he avoided meeting Annie's eyes. William stuck out a long leg, and Andrew tripped over it, nearly falling to the floor. He glared at William who assumed a look of complete innocence. Mr. Dabney looked up from his ledger book and scolded Andrew. "Surely it is not too much to ask you to walk quietly to your seat. Please sit down."

When the boy finally reached his seat it was John's turn to recite. He stood in front of the class and recited the first line of the poem flawlessly. Mr. Dabney smiled and John flashed a smile in return. Annie relaxed in her seat. For a minute she daydreamed as her brother continued to recite in Latin, but a giggle from William brought her attention back to the classroom. She looked up at John who was still reciting and over at Mr. Dabney, whose angry face was as red as a British uniform.

"Stop this instant," he bellowed.

Next to her, William hid his face in his hands, barely containing his laughter as John stopped and looked innocently at his tutor. Andrew looked as puzzled as Annie. What had John said?

It didn't take long to find out. Mr. Dabney stood in front of the class, his willow rod in hand, looking as though he might explode. "So you think it amusing, young man, to alter the words of a famous poem. And you think it amusing to compare your tutor to a donkey." Even speaking the words caused the timid Mr. Dabney to blush, which set John and William into another round of laughter.

What had come over her brothers? Annie wondered. How could John have insulted the tutor? What would their father say? But that was easy. Patrick Henry wasn't home. The colonies were close to war, and he, as one of Virginia's leaders, was often away.

Just when it seemed as though the tutor had lost control of his small classroom, he glanced at Andrew and Annie. Clenching his jaw, he glared at John, saying pointedly, "If you were attentive like your sister, you would be fine scholars. But instead, you are loafers with heads full of sawdust."

Annie squirmed uncomfortably with the attention, sure that it would bring her brother's disapproval on her head once they were beyond the watchful gaze of the tutor.

Without letting up, the tutor continued his tirade. "You may be excused, Annie. Your brothers will be staying for a while yet. And you, Master Thacker, there is surely no reason to prolong your evident dislike of my classroom. You too may be excused."

The boy didn't hesitate. In two swift strides he was

out of the room with Annie close behind. The two tiptoed out of the house so that Patsy, Annie's older sister, would not hear them.

"What will you do now?" Annie asked.

"Don't know," Andrew muttered. "Blasted tutor. Why should I have to learn Latin? Give me one reason a farmer needs to know an old, dead language nobody uses anymore."

As they reached the stable where the boy had tied his horse, Annie asked, "Did you study the poem?"

He shrugged, flashing a smile. "Nope. Didn't study it a minute."

"Then you can't very well be angry that you were embarrassed, can you?"

"That's the kind of thinking that separates boys from girls," Andrew said scornfully as he mounted his horse. "You care about old Mr. Dabney, and I just want to hunt."

Annie waved as her friend rode away. What kind of trouble would he be in when he came home hours earlier than expected? she wondered.

As for Annie, she was pleased with the early dismissal. She walked briskly to the kitchen, a small building behind the main house where several slaves cooked for the family. Earlier in the day, before her lessons, she had asked one of the cooks to fix a picnic basket for her.

She found the basket in the kitchen, full of food.

There were fresh current scones—a kind of sweet bis-cuit—and some slices of ham. It also contained a jar of cold cider and a piece of mince pie. Although Annie had planned to walk, she could barely manage under the weight of the fully packed basket. She lugged it across the yard to the stable where Joseph, the stableman, saddled her small horse. She loaded up the saddlebags with food. Then, with his help, she mounted the horse and rode out of the yard toward the beech woods.

The Henrys owned about 1,000 acres of prime farm-land in the middle of Virginia. The land was rolling hill-side, but on a clear day young Annie could see all the way to the mountains in the west. The largest town was a village about ten miles away called Hanover. It had a courthouse, a tavern, and a small store, but the Henry plantation, Scotchtown, did not need to purchase much from the store. It produced most of its own food and even had a blacksmith who could shoe the horses and make nails.

She had lived there for nearly five years and loved it. Even though her mother had been sick for many of those years and had died just a month earlier, Annie still thought the plantation was a happy place. She particularly liked walking and riding around the familiar grounds. Today, she had picked a special place on the bank of the creek for her picnic lunch. It was a hidden place, blocked from view by a grove of trees and shrubs. The young girl tied her horse up to a sturdy branch and pushed through the shrubs until she reached her secret spot. Except for the horse's presence, Annie knew she was invisible to the world.

As she lay back on a blanket and watched the wind-blown clouds drift across the sky, she daydreamed about her recent adventure in Richmond. She had been lying in her special place for a short time when she heard a noise on the other side of the bushes. Raising herself up on one arm, she felt with the other hand for the saddlebags. They were not there! Annie realized she had left them hanging on the horse.

Beyond the bushes, the horse nickered softly. Rising to her feet, Annie listened, sure that someone stood beyond the dense stand of shrubs.

"Who's out there?" she demanded.

When no one answered, the girl felt the first twinge of fear. Her father had said that these were "unsettled times," and that his children had to be careful about strangers. Shaking off the fear, the girl pushed through the bushes. "Nothing to worry about," she assured herself in a voice that was calmer than her feelings.

There was no one around, and the horse was grazing contentedly. Annie was about to go back into the hide-away when she remembered her lunch. That's when she noticed that the saddlebags were missing. "Great," she muttered with a little stamp of her foot. "Just great. Now someone has taken my lunch."

When Annie drew near to the horse to investigate she saw a crudely written note. "Another way that boys think differently than girls," it said. That's when Annie lost her temper.

"Andrew Thacker," she yelled. "You bring that lunch back now."

She knew she looked ridiculous. Even if Andrew could hear her, and Annie thought he probably was hiding someplace to see her reaction, how would a slightly built ten-year-old girl take back her lunch from a boy who was almost four years older and weighed probably forty pounds more? Impossible.

But Annie didn't always think logically when she was angry, and she was angry now. Tired of being teased, she let Andrew know it, but his only response was a peal of laughter. Without thinking, the young girl ran towards the sound. She was slowed by long skirts that twisted around her legs. "You'd better not eat my lunch, Andrew Thacker," she shouted as she ran.

When she finally caught up to Andrew in the beech woods, she found him sitting on a log and grinning at her as he stuffed the last of the scones into his mouth. Annie glared at him.

"I hope you enjoy that scone, Andrew Thacker," she said. "I will never, and I mean this, share my food with you again."

She held out her hand and marched forward, expecting Andrew to feel remorseful and hand over the rest of the lunch. But he just grinned, clambered to his feet, and began running once again. Annie knew that she could not outrun the boy. He was taller and wore breeches. She was slowed down by her long skirts and petticoats that caught on branches and dragged in the dirt. She tried anyway, but the boy's swifter strides soon carried him out of sight. She was following his trail by the sound of crunching leaves and snapping twigs when suddenly there was a thump, followed by silence, followed by a scream.

A few more steps and Annie saw the strangest sight. There was Andrew dancing about, awkwardly hitting himself on the face, arms, and shoulders. The girl began to giggle but stopped laughing when she saw that her friend was no longer running away but running towards her, his hands continuing their wild motions. He drew closer, and Annie saw the problem. A swarm of bees surrounded him.

Without thinking, she turned and ran, ignoring the branches that tugged on her skirts and scratched at her skin. When she reached the clearing, she slowed down to catch her breath. Behind her came Andrew, and Annie yelled, "Run for the creek," as he streaked passed. She didn't need to worry, her terrified friend had already reached the water and plunged in.

Like a turtle stretching for air, the boy lifted his head out of the water, warily surveying the air around him.

"They're gone," Annie yelled. "You can come out."

He rose up and walked shakily to the bank. Annie's first reaction was to laugh. The boy looked ridiculous. His clothes clung to him, and water ran down from his hair into his eyes and mouth. Her laughter turned to fear, though, when she saw how hard he was breathing and watched him lower himself painfully to the ground. She thought he was reacting to the bee stings. She had heard that bees could kill a man. But after a minute's rest, his breathing went back to normal, and she gave a sigh of relief.

It was hard not to stare at the welts forming on the boy's face and arms. His white knee-high stockings were mud splotched, and Annie couldn't tell whether there were stings under them as well. He groaned, and the young girl bit her lip nervously, not sure what she could say that wouldn't provoke him to yell at her.

"Andrew?" she whispered.

He opened one eye and glared at her.

"Are you hurting?" she asked.

"What do you think?"

"Do you want help getting home?"

Andrew groaned louder.

"What's wrong, Andrew?" Annie asked worriedly.

"Pa spared me from some plowing this morning because Ma insisted that I go to school. Now how am I going to explain how I got wet and bee stung at school this morning?"

The tension of the last fifteen minutes dissolved, and Annie hooted with laughter. "What a sight you were," she said, tears streaming down her cheeks. "Serves you right for stealing my lunch."

"How can you laugh when I feel so miserable?" her friend groaned. "Do I look as bad as I feel?"

"Other than a fat lip, a swollen eye, a couple of unsightly red marks, and torn and dirty clothes, you look fine," she answered honestly.

Groaning again, Andrew rose slowly to his feet. "I wish it was just my clothes. But I hurt bad, and there's no way I can hide this from Pa," he said ruefully. "I guess there's no reason to postpone my lickin' any longer."

"Do you want me to take you on my horse?" Annie asked.

"No, thank you. Pa will be mad enough," he answered.

With shoulders hunched he walked slowly in the direction of the Thacker farm. Annie could picture Andrew's father, a stern-faced, hard-working farmer who had only Andrew to help him in the fields, and she didn't like to imagine what Mr. Thacker might say when he saw his son. She watched until she could no longer see the boy, then she gathered up her saddlebags, retrieved her horse, and rode back to Scotchtown.

CHAPTER 2

PATSY'S WEDDING

PATSY HENRY HAD BEEN ACTING STRANGELY FOR weeks now. Annie would find her seventeen-year-old sister sitting in the ladies' parlor weeping, but when the younger girl would ask what was wrong, her sister would smile weakly and say, "Just happy, I guess, to be marrying John Fontaine."

At supper time Patsy picked at her food. "Where's your appetite, Patsy?" John asked one day, but she only smiled and toyed with her food some more.

Several days after Andrew's adventure with the bees, Annie found her older sister in their bedroom, sitting in the midst of a pile of dresses.

"What are you doing?" Annie asked.

Patsy burst into tears. "I have nothing to wear. Nothing at all. Father doesn't care about it at all. He promised he would come home. The wedding is tomorrow, and where is he?" she sputtered.

"Father will be home. He told you he would," Annie said with more than a touch of annoyance. "And what do you mean you have no clothes. What are those?" she asked, staring at the array of dresses.

Turning toward her little sister, Patsy cried, "I can't wear these. Look. Just look. These silks are faded, and the cottons are out of style."

Annie looked more closely at the dresses. Patsy must have owned a dress in every color of the rainbow. They all had full, layered skirts. Some were lace-trimmed, others decked out in beautiful ribbons and bows.

"If Father had been home, I could have ordered new gowns from the dressmaker."

"But Father wouldn't let you buy silk anyway," Annie said.

"He would have made an exception. Father knows how important clothes are. It isn't right for me to take all these old rags into a marriage."

"Fiddlesticks," Annie said, slightly annoyed with her sister. "Father isn't going to break the boycott of British goods so that you can have silk dresses, Patsy. Not especially when you have all these dresses already. And it isn't like you are moving to Williamsburg. You are just marrying cousin John Fontaine. He probably wouldn't care if you wore old flour sacks."

Patsy flushed. "You just don't understand," she said, shaking her head. "Why I even bother to explain it to you, I don't know." With a sharp jerk of her head, the older girl turned back to her dresses, and Annie slipped from the room.

There was confusion throughout the house as servants hustled to clean and prepare Scotchtown for the wedding. The sweet smell of baking cakes and pies drifted through the yard from the kitchen. Inside, the house smelled of lemon-and-oil polish. The table had been set with the best linen and dishes, but all the fancy preparations couldn't cheer up Annie. The house was too lonely when her father was absent.

Grabbing a tart from a tray of pastries, Annie munched on it as she wandered through the house, dropping little crumbs behind her. Glancing out the window, she saw a cloud of dust in the distance. She hoped it would be Father returning from his week in Richmond. She had to wait as the rider came around the bend in the road. As he drew near, she could see that it was, indeed, her father.

He scarcely had dismounted and turned his horse over to Joseph when Annie threw herself into his arms. Staggering back, he said playfully, "My, how you've grown, daughter. Have you eaten all the potatoes?"

Annie laughed, squeezing her father in a tight bear hug. "I knew you'd come back in time," she said.

He disentangled himself as they walked towards the house. "Of course I came back. Was Patsy worried that I wouldn't?"

When Annied nodded, her father smiled. Chuckling, he said, "Let me wash up and get a bite to eat. I've had a long ride. While I'm doing that, you find your sister and brothers. I have some news for you all."

They gathered in the family dining room, where Patrick Henry was eating a plate of cold ham and biscuits. He was a tall, slender man, whose long face, deep-set eyes, thin lips and penetrating stare gave him a serious expression. It was offset, however, by his wig, which was often askew.

When he finished eating, he wiped his mouth with the linen napkin and cleared his throat. "The Virginia Gazette carried a disturbing story today," he began. "There has been fighting in Boston, although the British have not declared war. Nearly three weeks ago the king's troops fired on the militia at Lexington and Concord, and our militiamen returned fire. Altogether, nearly 100 colonists were either killed or wounded. According to the reports, the British tried to take the gunpowder from the storage magazine in Concord, but they were prevented."

"Didn't they already take our gunpowder?" William asked.

"Yes. Governor Dunmore did steal Virginia's gunpowder. And the militia in Virginia let him get away with it. Our leaders said we must be cautious and not risk war. But now we know that the plot to steal our gunpowder was part of a larger plot to steal all the gunpowder in the colonies."

"What will you do?"

"I'm proposing that the Hanover County militia go after the powder. If war breaks out, we will need all of it we can get. Tomorrow the committee will decide what course to take. I expect the men will agree with me that we must go after that gunpowder."

"Tomorrow, Father?" Patsy asked, a stony expression on her face."

"Yes, tomorrow," he answered. "We must not let any more time go by. We've waited too long as it is."

Annie looked at her sister apprehensively. If her father had been more observant, he would have noticed Patsy's clenched hands and tight angry mouth. But because he was thinking about gunpowder, he didn't notice. Now, Patsy's voice shook with anger as she spoke. "Do you remember what tomorrow is, Father?" she asked.

He started to answer, but Patsy blurted out, "It's our wedding day. John Fontaine and I have been waiting months to marry. First mother died. Then you went off on business. Now you go chasing after gunpowder and then back to Philadelphia. You won't be back until August, I imagine. Am I supposed to wait?"

Patrick Henry shook his head apologetically. "I had

not forgotten. And I don't want you to wait. But your party will have to be postponed."

"But why?" Patsy challenged. "Isn't there someone else who can go chasing through the countryside after gunpowder?"

"No, Patsy, there isn't," her father said patiently. "I have a responsibility to the militia and to Virginia. I can't ask men to risk their lives and then refuse to go, no matter how good the reason."

"Frankly, Father," Patsy said boldly, a spot of color emerging in her cheeks. "I don't care about this matter with England. I want my party." She looked at him defiantly.

"I can understand that," he answered. "But you have not been blessed to be born in a period of tranquility. Sometimes we have to sacrifice our dreams. Going after the gunpowder cannot wait. Your party can."

Annie knew that her sister had been dreaming of a wedding ball. She had talked of little else the past months. Preparations had been made and invitations sent for the dance to be held the day after the wedding. Those plans would all have to change.

Patrick Henry looked at his daughter. "Come, Patsy. You may still marry tomorrow, but we will have to postpone the ball. This is not the end of the world."

"But what is a wedding without a party?" she asked, disappointment written on her face.

"You'll soon see, Patsy. A party is nice, but it pales in importance when compared to many other things."

Grudgingly, the girl gave in. "All right. Tomorrow I'll be married. The ball will have to wait."

☆

The household rose early on Patsy's wedding day. Annie dressed carefully, paying particular attention to her hair, determined to tame its wiry curls. When satisfied, she went looking for Patsy. She found her trying to put on her dress.

"Annie, come help me," the older girl gasped as she wriggled into the tightfitting bodice of her dress. Annie helped her pull the buttery soft fabric over her head, then finished buttoning the last of the twenty, tiny buttons that ran up the back of the gown.

"You're finished," Annie announced proudly, stepping back to view the result. "You look beautiful!"

Patsy examined herself critically in the mirror. "It will have to do," she said. "Do you like the bows?"

"It's perfect. Everything is perfect. But can you breathe?"

"What do you mean, can I breathe?"

"Those bones that hold in your stomach. Don't they hurt?" Annie asked.

"They don't hold in my stomach. They just make the

bodice of the dress fit nicely. Of course I can breathe," Patsy laughed.

"Well, I won't wear bones," Annie announced, looking at her own skinny reflection in the mirror.

"I don't think you need to. Not for a while anyway, Annie."

As Patsy pinned her own hair, she told her little sister to run out to their father's office to see if the committee meeting had ended. "It is nearly noon," she added anxiously.

Annie found her father walking back from his office. Dressed in a new blue coat and white silk breeches that reached just below his knee, with his wig on straight, he looked every bit the gentleman farmer. Bowing low to his daughter, he said, "What a lovely lady. May I have the pleasure of your company?"

She curtsied, and he guided her across the yard and into the house. "Patsy sent me to find out if Pastor Sampson is here."

"Yes. He is in my study, and the groom is getting dressed. Tell your sister that we will be ready in fifteen minutes in the ladies' parlor."

After telling Patsy, Annie slipped down to the parlor. It had been decorated with flowers, and a light apple blossom fragrance filled the room. She sat down on a sofa which had been moved against the wall and looked around. In the corner was a massive stone fireplace, and above it hung a portrait of Sarah Henry, Annie's mother. Her mother's eyes gazed out over the room, and Annie wondered what she would have thought about this wedding. It was hard to imagine, because Annie didn't remember her mother very well. Although she had died in February, she had been sick for years.

The room began to fill with other family members and a few close friends, including Mr. Dabney, the tutor, who played the harpsichord. The groom stood near the fireplace looking slightly uncomfortable in his stiff, Sunday best clothes. Like Patrick Henry, he seemed most at home in the fields or woods. Despite Patsy's best efforts to dress him up, he'd never make a polished appearance.

Finally, the bride entered the room. All eyes turned to her as she walked toward the fireplace where the pastor stood with John Fontaine. Her dress, despite her complaints, looked beautiful. As the pastor spoke, Annie wondered what Patsy was thinking. Was she scared? She'd certainly acted nervous as a cat all month. Or was she sad that the wedding wasn't fancier? Annie's mind drifted off. She wondered if the committee had decided to go after the gunpowder?

A rustle next to her brought her attention back to the ceremony. John, seated next to her, was standing up. He leaned down and spoke to her, "You missed the whole thing, daydreaming Annie."

Annie was surprised to see the family standing around

hugging and kissing. Her father caught her eye and winked before leading them to a table loaded with turkey, ham, and various sweets and breads. After eating, Patrick Henry pushed his chair back. "The committee has decided to go for the gunpowder, and we have a great deal to do before we leave tomorrow," he said. "I apologize for having to interrupt such a pleasant and blessed occasion, but I have a job for Annie and John." Turning to the two young people, he said, "You must alert all the farms between here and the village. We'll have other riders going farther out. Do you understand?"

The two children nodded solemnly at their father, but they made no move to leave. Then nodding, he said, "Let's toast the bride and groom, and send these young ones off with a blessing. Pastor, will you do the honors?"

They all bowed their heads as the white-haired pastor stood to pray. "We thank you, Lord, for this couple, recently wed, and ask your blessings on them and on their children to come. Give them the grace to persevere through hard times, and the ability to take joy in your works of providence. And bless these young children as they go out today. Keep them from harm, and bring them back safely to their father's house. In Jesus' name, Amen."

After they had prayed, Patrick Henry sent Annie to her room to change and John off with an admonition to look after his sister.

ANNIE'S RIDE

BY THE TIME ANNIE REACHED THE STABLE, HER brother was already mounted, and Joseph eased the girl up into her saddle. John was quiet as they set off down the road.

"Why so quiet?" she asked finally.

"Just thinking," he answered.

"Thinking about what?" she persisted.

"Thinking that if Father were in his right mind he would have sent William instead of you."

"That's silly," Annie said, determining that she wouldn't get angry. "William will surely ride with Father tomorrow. "Why would Father send him today?"

"That just shows how little you know," John muttered.

"I think you are jealous because William gets to ride with Father, and you have to stay home."

"Don't be foolish," John said. "If Father was thinking straight, he'd have you stay home with Patsy . . . where girls should stay."

Annie ignored her brother. *She who holds her tongue is wise,* she thought to herself. They had ridden about ten minutes and Scotchtown was well behind them, although its freshly plowed fields stretched out to the right and the left. Already rows of tender, green shoots marched in straight lines in the loose dirt. Early wild flowers bloomed along the road and fences, and their scent gently tickled Annie's nose.

Suddenly eager to be on her way, she said, "I'll see you at the courthouse."

"I'll be there first," John answered. "Don't be stopping to pick flowers or have tea parties," he added as he gave his horse a kick and galloped away.

Annie laughed. The day was too nice, the errand too important, to let John's teasing bother her. She slowed her horse to a trot, not wanting to tire him out too soon. Already she was well out of her brother's sight, surrounded by nothing but rolling farmland and meadow.

The first farm she reached was the Thacker's, and she saw Andrew out in the field with a plow and a team of oxen. Annie hadn't seen him since the bee incident several days before. She was glad to see him up and able to work. As she reined in her horse, she caught a glimpse of the boy's face under his tri-cornered hat. With an eye nearly swollen shut and a fat lip, he looked as though he had been kicked in the face by a mule.

"What happened to you?" she asked. "Your father didn't strike you, did he?" Annie couldn't picture Mr. Thacker hitting his son. He was a gentle, although stern, man.

Andrew shook his head. "Of course not. Although I almost wish he had. It's the bees. I must be sensitive to their sting. I'm swollen all over my body. That's why we couldn't come to Patsy's wedding." He rubbed his arm gently, wincing slightly as he touched a sore spot. "And it itches like the dickens. I think I'd rather wrestle a bear than be covered with bee stings."

"Why aren't you inside resting?" Annie asked.

Andrew laughed. "Pa said there's work to be done. He can spare me for school but not to go tease little girls, so I have to suffer the consequences."

Annie was silent. Then she remembered why she had come. "Andrew, I can't stay. I came only to tell your father that the militia is going after the gunpowder tomorrow. They're riding at eight o'clock from the courthouse. Will you tell your father for me?"

Andrew looked enviously at his friend. "I don't suppose he'll let me go," he said. "He'll tell me that I have to learn responsibility at home before I can do such things."

Annie felt sorry for the boy, so she tried to make him feel better. "John's not going either," she said.

"And William?"

When Annie said, "Father's taking William with him," she saw the envy and disappointment written on Andrew's face. Not knowing what else to say, she mumbled, "I'm sorry," before riding away. After riding a few hundred yards, she turned and saw him attacking the field with a hoe.

For the remainder of the afternoon, Annie visited neighboring farms. In some, she was invited into warm kitchens for a rest and a cup of cider. At a few she was met by scowls from farmers who said they were too busy to go chasing after some gunpowder. But that reaction was rare in Hanover County where the farmers respected Patrick Henry and were eager to serve if he called. Annie didn't spend much time in any place because she did not want to be caught away from the village in the dark.

She drew near to Hanover just as the sun began to set, painting the western sky orange and causing the temperature to drop. Annie was glad for the gloves that her father had made her wear. She pulled her cloak, which she had loosened during the heat of the day, up tight under her chin. Weary with riding, she wanted to be off the horse and in front of a cozy fire with John. But when the girl rode into the square, she saw no sign of her brother.

There was a rail and a water trough near the tavern, and Annie walked her horse over to it so he could drink. Once she had tied him to the rail, she stood uncertainly.

Was a tavern the place for a young girl to be alone at sundown? She cracked the door and peeked into a nearly empty room.

Hearing the door open, the tavern keeper, Mr. Lewis, looked up and smiled at the small girl framed in his doorway. Nodding in recognition, he said, "Mistress Henry. Hallo. What can I do for you?" As he talked he walked toward her across the well-worn wood floors.

"I could use a warm drink," she answered. "And have you seen my brother?"

"William?"

"No, not William. John. He is supposed to meet me here." Annie looked longingly at the fire crackling in the large brick fireplace. "Father sent us to alert the militia to be prepared to ride tomorrow morning. They're going after the gunpowder."

The tavern keeper's eyes sparkled. "I'd heard that news already. I'm glad to know it is true." He regarded Annie kindly and asked, "Are you a wee bit hungry, child?"

She smiled gratefully. "I'm starving, but I don't think I should eat in here. Not alone," Annie answered apologetically.

"Of course not. Come back into the kitchen. My own Molly is there. She'll make you a plate and keep you company until John comes. But I don't think you should ride back tonight. It's too dark. Too dangerous. Stay here with us, and I'll send word back to your father. You can see him in the morning."

Annie bit her lip. "Would you wait to send word until John comes?" she asked.

"Of course. We'll wait, and when the lad comes, I'll find a place for both of you and get word to your father. But come ahead. Come see Molly and have a bite."

In the warm kitchen, heated by another large fireplace, a kettle of thick stew hung over the fire, baking potatoes peeked out from the embers. Molly Lewis, a quiet girl of 12, sat at a table lit by a lantern, reading a Bible.

"Molly, I've brought you a visitor, Annie Henry. Make her some food, please, and set a place for her brother. He'll be here shortly."

Molly smiled shyly at the visitor. She moved quickly to the fire, and Annie watched as she dipped out the stew and poured it into a pewter bowl. She cut a thick slice of bread, spread it generously with butter, and set the meal in front of Annie.

Molly sat down also. She moved her book to the side, closing it carefully over a ribbon bookmarker.

When Annie looked up between bites, she caught Molly staring, but the older girl quickly averted her eyes. She was taller than Annie and bigger boned, and she wore her straw-colored hair pulled back without any ribbon or bows. But her clear, gray eyes and pug nose gave her face a friendly look.

"This is delicious," Annie said, wiping her mouth. "I guess I was hungry."

Molly blushed and murmured a thank you, but she kept her eyes on the table. For several minutes, the two girls sat in an uncomfortable silence, neither one knowing what to say to the other. Finally Annie blurted, "I've been taking messages around the countryside for my father. He leads the militia. They're going to ride tomorrow." She stopped speaking as quickly as she had started, embarrassed to have been bragging, but Molly seemed not to notice.

"And your brother? Has he been helping, as well?"

Annie nodded, remembering John suddenly. "Where do you think he could be? He was supposed to meet me here so that we could ride home together. Of course, it's too late now. Your father kindly said we could sleep here. But John should be here by now—unless something happened to him," Annie said, frowning.

Molly stood to clear Annie's plate. "I'm sure he's fine. If he's at all like my brother, he probably stopped to fish or hunt—or maybe play a game of dice. Come sit closer to the fire and don't worry about him."

Annie let the heat from the fire warm her face and hands. Sitting in this bright, friendly kitchen it was hard to imagine danger, but Annie knew the night could hide robbers and other threats. She knew her father didn't approve of gaming and didn't think John would play dice, but would he stop to hunt? Annie didn't know.

As she sat before the fire, Annie could feel her eyes grow heavy. She felt a gentle hand on her arm. "Come, Annie. You look tired. There is an extra bed in my room. You can wash there."

Annie nodded and let herself be led to a soft, cozy bed.

4

MOLLY LEWIS

THE NEXT MORNING, ANNIE FELT A HAND ON HER shoulder shaking her and heard a voice saying, "Wake up, Annie. The men are gathering."

She struggled to surface from her dream of horses and fire. She found herself on a small cot in a room not much bigger than a slave's room at home. Sunlight poured through the one window, and Molly, already dressed, was standing next to her with a confused expression on her face.

"Can't I sleep a little longer," Annie said as she stretched her legs. "I swear, every part of me aches today."

Molly shrugged, turned her back to the girl as she made the other bed, and filled the basin with fresh water. After she finished those chores, she turned back to Annie. "I musn't stay any longer. There are too many men needing breakfast downstairs. They say your father should be here soon."

Annie sat up. Of course! She had forgotten that the militia was riding this morning. Hopping out of bed, she washed at the basin and then put on her dress and braided her hair. Glancing out the window, she saw a large crowd of men gathered in front of the courthouse across the street. A few were on horseback but most stood in dusty boots, their worn coats buttoned tight against the chilly morning air. There wasn't a uniform among them, and Annie thought they looked too scruffy to be an army. Although she searched the crowd, she could not see her father or brother.

Downstairs in the kitchen, Annie found Molly rushing back and forth between the kitchen and the dining room, carrying plates of sausage, ham, and hot griddle cakes to the hungry men who filled the tavern. She looked hot, her face was flushed, and tiny beads of sweat dotted her forehead. Seeing Annie, she said, "Help yourself to breakfast," and then rushed out the door again.

Annie took her food to a corner where she would be out of the way of the bustle. At home, the kitchen was in a separate building, and she rarely saw all the activity that went into preparing food for so many people. Here, she was in the middle of it. When the ham ran out, Mr. Lewis sliced another. Molly pulled fresh griddle cakes from the pan over the fire. They worked steadily until the

men were fed and began to drift outside to wait for Patrick
Henry. Only then did Molly sit and begin to eat her own
breakfast.

"I'm sorry to be such a bother," Annie apologized

But Molly shook her head shyly, "I like having you
here. It gets lonely sometimes with no one to talk to."

Annie thought for a moment. At Scotchtown, there
was almost always someone to talk to. She didn't think she
had ever been lonely, except when missing her father.

After stuffing one last bite of sausage into her mouth,
she rose to go. "Did you recognize all the men outside?"
she asked.

Molly shook her head. "I don't think they are all
from our county. After you notified folks, they rode out
and told others. My pa says that there could be as many
as 300 riding from here. And others will likely join as
they go."

As Annie got ready to leave, she looked into the dining room at the mess left by the army of recently fed men.
The floor was thick with dirt carried in by their farm
boots. The tables were sticky with syrup, and soiled
plates and mugs still waited to be carried to the kitchen.

In the kitchen, along with piles of dirty dishes, sat
Molly, staring sadly at her now cold, half-eaten food.

"I wish I could help," Annie said impulsively, "but I
have to find my father."

"Father wouldn't hear of it," Molly answered, dismissing the girl with a wave.

As Annie turned to leave, the older girl called out in a soft voice, "There is something you could do. . . ."

Annie turned back to her friend, curious as to what that something could be.

"Promise you will tell me all the news," Molly pleaded. "It will make this easier to bear," she said as she pointed to the mess. Then she clapped a hand over her mouth and turned her eyes away, surprised and embarrassed by her own words.

Annie caught her arm, understanding suddenly how she could help her new friend, and said, "I promise."

Outside, the young girl set off to find John. He hadn't come in last night according to Mr. Lewis, and Annie was worried about him. But before she could find him, she saw her father astride his black horse, surveying the crowd. Annie waved but he did not see her. She pushed her way through the crowd, trying to keep her skirts up off the dusty ground and keep the men from backing into her. As long as her father stayed on his horse, she had no trouble keeping him in sight.

It wasn't until Annie drew close to her father that she saw that he wasn't alone. Both William and John were at his side. Upon seeing Annie he dismounted and gave her a hug. "Thank God you are all right," he said.

"Of course I'm all right," Annie said. "You did get the message, didn't you?"

"Yes. Mr. Lewis kindly sent a messenger to us," her father said in a voice that indicated anger. Annie glanced quickly at her brothers but they turned away. When she looked back at her father, he had an expression, dubbed "thundercloud eyes" by the children, that meant trouble for the one at whom it was directed. It was clear that the look was directed toward John.

Patrick Henry broke the silence by pushing John forward keeping, Annie noted, a tight grip on her brother's arm. He said in a voice that demanded a response, "Tell your sister where you were last night."

John muttered something so softly that Annie couldn't hear, but her father interrupted. "Speak clearly, son. Tell your sister where you were."

Directing his gaze studiously at a point over Annie's shoulder, John said, "Horse rode off," as a blush stole across his cheeks.

"Your horse rode off?" Annie repeated, not understanding.

"Shh," he said through gritted teeth. "I stopped for a short time at Peter Glenn's house. I was nearly finished and almost here. He had a new gun he wanted to show me. We rode out a bit so I could shoot it some. I wanted to try shooting on horseback. But the fool horse was startled, threw me, and then ran off. I had to follow him—

he'd gone clear back to Scotchtown—and that's when Father found me."

Annie could feel her father's glare. She wished there was something she could say to make his anger go away, but she didn't know how to make the situation better. Just then her father spoke. "I've told John how deeply disappointed I am. I gave him a man's job to do, and he did it like a boy. Plus, he abandoned you because of a fool notion. That could have been dangerous."

"But Father, Mr. Lewis took good care of me," Annie protested.

"Yes, he did. But John was responsible, not Mr. Lewis."

As her father talked, John stared at the ground, and Annie could tell he was working manfully to keep from crying. Finally, he relented and loosened his grip on John's arm saying, "Go to the tavern and get provisions for William and me. Some jerky and biscuits, please."

With John gone, Patrick Henry's anger faded. He turned and watched his son crossing the square. "You know this tavern is my old stomping ground. I worked here while studying the law," he said, glancing over at the building. "Those were good days," he mused. "We were poor, but we always had food to eat and your mother. . . ." His voice broke, and Annie could see him struggle to control emotions. Finally, he said, "Well, enough of that.

There's a job at hand." Turning to his daughter, he asked, "Did you have any problem yesterday, Annie?"

"Everywhere I went, the men seemed eager to come. But I didn't know there'd be this many," she said, pointing to the crowd.

Her father smiled at the men gathering around him. "It's freedom, Annie. We are about to see the birth of liberty. And once we have freedom, men will die to keep it. But let us pray to God that none will have to die today."

As more people saw that Patrick Henry had arrived, the crowd began to push against him, until Annie feared that they would be crushed. Her father mounted his horse, and the nervous animal praced skittishly until the men moved away a bit. "We are going to recover the powder that Governor Dunmore removed from Williamsburg," he said. "Some ask, 'Is this necessary?' Just look at what happened in Lexington and Concord. You've heard the news. You know how the British fired upon the colonists. We want only to have our gunpowder for self-defense. We hope and pray for a peaceful outcome. Let us be men of good order."

A lusty cheer went up throughout the crowd before the men fell into line and began to march out of town.

Annie watched them parade by. In their shabby clothes, worn boots, and farmer's hats, they were a ragtag band with an inexperienced lawyer/farmer at their head.

Would freedom really depend on an army that looked like this?

Patrick Henry's horse pranced impatiently. Leaning over, he hugged his daughter. "Be good," he said. Then he turned to William, and his voice trembled as he said to his eldest son, "Time to fall in."

Annie hugged her older brother. He looked too young to be going out to fight. She blinked back tears as he joined the marching column.

Her father then turned to his younger son, who said with a breaking voice, "I'm sorry, Father. I failed at my job. Please forgive me."

"I forgive you. We all have failed at one thing or another," his father said. "Learn from this, son, that the world is full of temptations. You must learn to resist them." Then he shook John's hand, saying, "I love you."

To both of them he said, "Don't dawdle on your way back to Scotchtown. Patsy will wonder where you are, and she will worry about you."

As they spoke, the men continued to clomp noisily by, raising dust until Annie's eyes watered. She looked wistfully after them, knowing suddenly that she didn't want to go back to Scotchtown. Not until the men came back. Without thinking, she blurted, "Couldn't I stay here at the tavern, Father? Just until you come home. I wouldn't be a bother. I promise. Maybe I could even help. Please don't make me go home just yet."

Patrick Henry looked at his daughter's serious young face, her eyes pleading to be part of the adventure. He said with equal seriousness, "Mr. Lewis works very hard, Annie. And Molly must work with him. They have no time for play."

Annie nodded solemnly. "I know, Father. But I could be a help. I would learn and work hard. I promise."

"But you are not used to hard work, Annie. What if you tire of it?"

But Annie would not budge. "I promise I will be a help. Please let me."

She could see her father pondering the question. She held her breath, willing him to say yes. When he got off his horse and walked across the square to the tavern, Annie allowed herself a smile. John kept his face fixed stonily on a distant tree. A few minutes later Patrick Henry rejoined them.

"Mr. Lewis has agreed. Apparently he thinks it would be nice for Molly to have a friend for a few days. But I have told him that if you are any bother, he is to send you home."

Then turning to his son, he said, "Now is your chance to prove yourself responsible. You must ride back and let Patsy know that Annie is staying here until I come home."

"How long will you be gone?"

"Could be a week. Maybe longer. If Patsy gets anxious, you remind her that I've promised no shooting unless the British shoot first." The last of the men had marched down the road toward Williamsburg, leaving silence in their wake. Patrick Henry remounted his horse, and waved. "Be good, children. Mind those in authority over you."

"We will, Father," Annie said. "And God be with you."

"Indeed. And God be with you."

☆

After the noise and dust of the militia, Hanover seemed a desolate place. There was an occasional traveler at the tavern, but the daily business was slow. All the local men were gone. Molly said it was unnatural, the way business had dried up, but Annie thought it grand. Although Molly did not have to work constantly doing laundry and dishes and cooking for guests, she still had chores to do. But Mr. Lewis also allowed her to spend time with her guest.

Annie was surprised that Molly wanted to do lessons in the morning. Although the older girl had no tutor, she wanted an education, so each day she worked through her lesson book. Sometimes Annie tried to draw her away, but Molly was adamant. "I can't play," she'd say crossly. "I want to learn to read better." Since it was more fun to study with Molly than to play alone, Annie studied also.

On washday, the girls carried baskets of dirty linens down to the river where they scrubbed them on boards until they gleamed. Together, they struggled to carry the heavy baskets of damp sheets up the grassy slope to the tavern. At the top of the hill, Annie flopped down in the grass, but Molly set to work hanging her sheets out to dry in the warm spring sun.

"Don't you ever get tired?" Annie complained. "You never just do nothing."

"I guess I don't have time to do nothing," Molly answered, taking a wooden clothespin from her mouth and putting it on the sheet. "Before my mother died, I had more time. But not now. If I don't help Father, who will?" Molly spoke matter-of-factly, without self-pity.

Annie rose wearily to her feet. Grabbing a sheet, she struggled to hang it on the line, but when she tried to pin it, the other end fell to the ground. Just then Molly looked over and said, "You must keep it up out of the dirt. Or we'll have to wash it all over again." Annie could see a smudge of dirt on the sheet, but she hoped Molly wouldn't notice. The older girl, meanwhile, had finished her basket. She came around to Annie's and said, "Here, I'll help you. We'll get it done quicker that way."

Not all Molly's chores were hard work. She taught Annie to milk the cows, patiently demonstrating where to sit so the cow wouldn't kick and how to gently but firmly squeeze and strip the milk into the bucket. Annie's first attempts were awkward. Sometimes she'd squeeze too gently, and the exasperated cow would flick a tail at her. And it was hard to remember to place the bucket just so, in order to keep the cow from kicking it over.

On one particularly warm day, Annie, with sweat streaming down her cheeks, pushed her stool away from the cow with anger. "This dumb cow has no milk. I've been sitting here for ten minutes and the bucket is empty. Why don't you have good cows?" she complained.

Molly stood up from her own stool. Her own bucket was filled with warm, foamy milk. Wiping a stray piece of hair out of her eyes, she said, "Look at the udder, Annie. It's full. It's not the cow's fault if the milker is clumsy. Here, let me do it."

Pushing Annie aside, Molly soon had milk streaming into the bucket. Annie sulked in a corner of the barn, muttering to herself that Molly had all the luck. Soon the bucket was full. Molly untied the two cows, slapped their flanks, and sent them back out into the pasture. She turned back to Annie.

"You can pout, if you want, but I don't have time. Father said we need butter, and it won't make itself."

"Why can't someone else do this work?" a grouchy Annie asked. "Why must you do it all?"

With a scornful glance, Molly said, "Not all of us own slaves to do our chores. Some of us wouldn't own them even if we could." Embarrassed that she had spoken so bluntly to a daughter of such an important man, the older girl turned back to her work. She knew that Patrick Henry was a lawyer and famous politician, while Molly's own father was only a tavern keeper.

Flushed with anger, Annie thought of all the unkind things she could say but caught herself. She knew Molly was right. The only reason Annie did not usually milk cows or churn butter was because someone else did it for her. Determined not to show Molly how much her words had hurt, she said, "I guess I am clumsy. But I can learn as well as you. I'm sorry I gave up on that cow. What was I doing wrong?"

The older girl was eager to be friends again. "Oh she's a tough old cow. Sometimes you really have to yank hard," Molly said. "I'm sorry I spoke harshly to you."

As the girls walked from the barn, each carrying a full bucket of milk, Annie sighed. "There's truth in what you said. We do have slaves. Father doesn't like slavery, but he can't picture life without them. I guess I'm the same way. But maybe if I learn to work, I'll be better able to."

They had reached the dry well, a small building built over a deep hole in the ground—like a well, but without water. It was cool at the bottom, and things that needed to be kept cold, like milk and butter, were stored there.

After skimming the butterfat off the two buckets of milk, Molly poured the rest into a metal jug and lowered it to the bottom of the well.

"Come on," she said to Annie. "Let's rinse the milk buckets and then make the butter. You carry the cream, and I'll wash the buckets."

It was cool under the roof of the porch. As she waited for her friend to return, Annie stretched out contentedly and thought about her father. It had been seven days since the militia had gone out. *Where are they now*, she wondered. When Molly came humming across the grass, Annie turned to her and said, "Don't you worry about war, Molly?"

The older girl shrugged. "Not too much. My father is too old to fight, and my brother lives out west. I don't see how war will bother me?"

"But, Molly, war won't be short." Annie protested. "Father says with the strength of the British navy and the skill of their troops, we could fight for years. Doesn't that scare you?"

The older girl smiled. "You know much more than I do, Annie. But my father always says not to worry about what tomorrow will bring. Today has enough worries of its own. And I know that one of my worries is getting this butter made before my father takes a paddle to me."

Annie returned the smile. "Show me how to make this butter," she said, "and I'll help."

For the next several hours the two girls chatted and churned butter, taking turns lifing the paddle up and down until the cream thickened. When the butter was thick but not hard, they emptied it into a large bowl, salted it, and then packed it into molds, which they lowered into the dry well to keep cold.

While the girls worked, clouds gathered in the sky and now rain threatened. The temperature dropped suddenly, and Annie felt the cold wind bite through the thin cotton of her dress.

Molly straightened up and looked at the sky. "Let's run before we get wet," she shouted through the wind.

The girls ran to the tavern, reaching the porch just as the first heavy drops of rain fell. Soon it was coming down in a drenching flood, bending the branches of the trees to the ground, and washing down the hillside in little rivulets. The girls watched from the window, and Annie said, "Won't the militia be uncomfortable? I hope we hear news soon."

"We always hear the news at the tavern," Molly answered as she tied an apron around her dress and prepared to make dinner.

Her young visitor leaned back wearily in her chair. "I'm too tired to move," she said. "How can you start another job so soon?"

Molly laughed. "Because I'm hungry as well. And if I don't cook, we don't eat. You had better put on an apron too. There are potatoes to be peeled and onions to be chopped."

"Maybe I'll go back to Scotchtown," Annie said half-seriously as she rose tiredly to her feet.

Molly tossed a potato to her. "Tomorrow you can go home if you want—though you'll miss all the news. But tonight there's work to be done."

SUCCESS!

LOUD VOICES AND ROWDY LAUGHTER BROKE THE morning quiet. Turning over on her cot, Annie cracked her eyes to see if Molly was awake yet. Tangled bedclothes and a hastily tossed nightgown were evidence that the girl had been hurried out of bed.

As she stretched lazily, Annie wondered about the noise from outside the window. In the whole time she had been in Hanover, there had never been more than a few customers at the tavern. All the young men had gone along with the militia. Today, however, it sounded as if an army stood outside. "The militia!" Annie said, hopping from her bed as she realized what was happening. "They've come back."

Annie hurriedly dressed and washed, not bothering even to comb her hair. Her eyes danced as she skipped down the stairs and out onto the brick sidewalk. Scanning the crowd, she finally spotted her father engaged in a lively discussion with someone she did not know. She ran across the street and waited, just out of earshot of her father, until the conversation ended. Then she tiptoed up from behind and threw her arms around him. He turned, and when he saw his daughter, he scooped her up in his arms.

"Annie, Annie," he laughed. "How is the little tavern-keeper?"

"Just fine, Father. Molly has taught me so much. I've learned to milk, and churn, and properly make the beds, and wash. . . ."

"Sounds like you are set to become a perfect pioneer wife," Patrick Henry said, proudly. "Those skills will come in handy someday. And hard work never hurt anyone."

Annie smiled broadly. "What about the gunpowder, Father?" she asked.

"We had success, daughter. We caught up with Governor Dunmore's man in Doncastle. He promised to pay us 330 pounds for the gunpowder, which we can use to buy more gunpowder when we need it, and he sent that money on to Williamsburg. No shots were fired. And we showed the Governor that Virginians will stand up for the principle of self-defense."

"Now what happens, Father?"

"I am already late for the Continental Congress in Philadelphia, so I must leave tomorrow."

"Leaving again? So soon," Annie protested. "You aren't ever at home anymore."

"That is all too true, Annie. But I must go. As it is, I will arrive late for the Congress."

As they talked, father and daughter walked hand-in-hand to the tavern where they met Mr. Lewis on the steps. "Thank you for minding my Annie," Patrick Henry said, shaking hands.

"It has been my pleasure. Molly has been happy for the friendship. It is mighty lonely here since my wife passed away. And my daughter works too hard, but your daughter here has lightened the load and brightened the days for us."

"I think it has done Annie good as well. It's not good to grow up without knowing what it is to work hard." Then looking down at his soiled clothes and dusty boots, Patrick Henry said, "There's much I need to do here tonight. I'll require a room and a bath. And these clothes washed. Can you accomodate me?"

With his arm on Patrick Henry's shoulder, Mr. Lewis guided him into the tavern. "We always have room for you here, Patrick. Come, tell us about the gunpowder."

Annie hesitated at the door to the tavern, and her father noticed. "You may come in, child. As long as I'm here, you may come in."

Annie followed happily behind the two men as they took their seats at a table, and she waited expectantly as Mr. Lewis fetched two glasses of cider before sitting down.

"Well, it wasn't terribly exciting," her father began. "We marched out a week ago. The roads were dry, and we made swift time for the first two days. Then it began raining. The roads turned to thick mud, and the rivers swelled so much the horses couldn't cross. We had to use the ferry, which could cross only twenty of us at a time. It took us a day just to cross the river, and when we made camp on the other side, we had to sleep in the muck and mire."

"It sounds awful."

"Well, I confess that some wanted to turn back. They had gone with us as a lark. But when it proved to be more difficult than they expected, they lost heart." Then turning to his daughter, he said, "Your brother, William, however, proved himself a man. He didn't complain, and he stuck out the journey."

"That William is a good lad," Mr. Lewis agreed.

"By the time we reached Doncastle, we looked most disreputable. Our clothes were stiff with mud and our guns needed a good oiling. If the redcoats had chosen to fight, I'm not sure if we could have overcome them. But, Lord Dunmore's man didn't need any persuading. We surrounded the tavern where he was eating and called out to him. When he stood on the doorstep, his jaw dropped, and he quickly looked to see if he could make an escape. When he saw that he was surrounded, he asked me to have a cup of tea with him."

"Tea, Father?"

Patrick Henry looked apologetic. "I know we are boycotting tea, but since he offered and he was paying...and I was surely cold and damp. . . . Well, I accepted. And the tea tasted just fine," he said, laughing. "Anyway, we sat in the tavern with our pot of tea, and before you could say 'boo' he had agreed to pay the money for the powder."

"Not much courage there," Mr. Lewis said, a broad grin spreading over his face.

"I tell you, friend, the British have no stomach for a fight. We shall be victorious if we go to war." As Patrick Henry spoke, his face glowed with anticipation. "There he sat in all his fine scarlet garments, and we, in our torn and dirty work clothes, stared him in the face—and he backed down. And that's the story of the gunpowder. Once we made sure that the money had been sent to Williamsburg, we set off for home. Again it rained, but we rode our victory home and didn't mind the misery."

Annie looked at her father in his grime-covered clothes. Although he had washed his hands and face, the skin on his arms was gray with dirt. Before she could think, she said, "You aren't going to Philadelphia like that, are you?"

With a laugh, Patrick Henry shook his head. "No. I

will wash up here, but I need some clothes from Scotchtown. I think I will ask Mr. Thacker to bring some to me. Andrew is supposed to be meeting him here with a wagon shortly."

Mr. Lewis had gone back to the kitchen. Annie leaned toward her father and whispered, "Father, could I stay here a little longer? It is good to feel useful."

"How will Patsy manage without you?" he asked.

"I have nothing to do but feed my chickens. Elizabeth can do that," Annie said. "Besides, with Patsy just married, she doesn't need me around the house."

Her father nodded. Taking confidence from his reaction, Annie said, "Don't you think I could learn a lot by staying here? And didn't you learn a lot before you became a lawyer, when you were a tavern keeper, Father?"

Patrick Henry roared a deep belly laugh. "What I learned as a tavern keeper," he said, pushing his chair out from the table and standing up, "was to appreciate how much news you can hear in a tavern. That couldn't have anything to do with why you want to stay here, could it?"

Annie blushed. Her father always seemed to read her mind.

"Annie, an acorn never falls very far from the oak," he said, pinching her cheek. "There is nothing wrong with wanting news. In fact, even the Bible approves, 'Like cold water to a weary soul is good news from a distant land.'" He looked fondly at his daughter, seeing his own enthusiasms in her eager face. "I don't know. Let me think on the matter. Perhaps an arrangement can be worked out, but I make no promises. Now go and give a hand to Molly."

Annie found Molly in the kitchen, washing and drying the iron pots. The older girl looked up expectantly when her friend came in.

"What news is there?"

Annie returned her excitement with a glum expression. "Success. They were paid for the gunpowder."

"Then why so sad?"

"Father must leave in the morning for Philadelphia. He'll be gone again . . . for months this time," Annie said. "And I probably will have to go home to Scotchtown." But Annie had no sooner spoken when Mr. Lewis opened the kitchen door and waved for her.

"Your father wants you outside," he whispered.

There, on the dusty street, her father stood talking to Andrew Thacker, who had just arrived with his wagon. As Annie watched, Mr. Thacker joined them from across the empty square, a piece of paper in his hand.

"Doesn't this just beat all?" he said, waving the parchment in front of him. "The Lord Governor wasted no time."

Patrick Henry raised a questioning eyebrow, and Mr. Thacker noticed for the first time Annie standing next to the wagon.

"Come with me, Patrick," Mr. Thacker said. "I have something I must show you."

As they walked, the two men carried on a spirited discussion. Annie could see Mr. Thacker talk and her father shake his head. The piece of paper was passed back and forth, and the two men, grim-faced, headed back to the wagon.

"What has happened?" Annie asked.

"Nothing for you to worry about," her father said, making an effort to smile. "But I have decided to let you stay here for another week. I want you to ride home today with the Thackers. Have Patsy pack what I will need in Philadelphia. Then Mr. Thacker will bring you back tonight. Do you understand?"

"But Father," Annie began.

"Please don't question me, Annie. Just do what I say. I will see you later." Then, without another word, he returned to the tavern.

Annie stared after her father while Mr. Thacker loaded the wagon. Then, taking the reins from his son, he motioned the boy into the back with the young girl. They rode along in silence, the wagon bumping over the ruts and rocks that covered the road. Finally, she could stand the silence no longer. "Do you know what is going on?" she whispered.

Andrew shook his head. "I guess we will find out soon enough," he whispered back.

But Annie doubted that. Andrew might be told what

was going on, but she would be kept in darkness. She scowled and they rode the rest of the way back to Scotchtown in silence.

Their arrival threw the plantation into a flurry of activity. Patsy packed what clothes their father needed for the month or more he would be in Philadelphia. She made sure she packed an extra wig because he would pick at his hair until it looked worse than a bird's nest. All of his things had to fit in several packs that would be carried by a second horse. While she was there, Annie packed a few more things for herself. By late afternoon, they were ready and waiting for the Thackers to return.

Annie was surprised when Andrew arrived alone on the wagon. "My pa is coming by horseback," he explained.

As they bumped along the road to Hanover, Andrew said, "I found out what's going on."

"Then tell me," Annie insisted.

"Lord Dunmore has issued a proclamation—an official declaration. That's what Pa had in his hand."

"Well, what did it say?" Annie interrupted.

"If you'd give me a chance, I would tell you."

"I'm sorry. Go ahead."

"The proclamation says your pa is an outlaw. It accuses the militia of trying to stir up rebellion and says Patrick Henry and his followers have caused terror among the king's faithful subjects." Andrew spoke apologetically, sorry to be the one to bring bad news.

Annie's face showed alarm. "A traitor? But they can hang traitors," she said.

"That's why my pa and other men are riding with your pa to the Potomac River. He won't be alone as long as he is in Virginia."

"But your father. How can he be away from the farm for so long? Isn't this still the planting season?"

Andrew nodded seriously. "He says he is counting on me. If I get the crops in, then we'll eat. If I don't, then the winter will be hard on us."

"But Andrew, why would he do that?" Annie said with surprise. "You all could starve this winter."

Sitting up tall in the wagon, Andrew showed his annoyance. "Don't you think that I can do a good job?"

"Oh, Andrew, I didn't mean to insult you. But you have to admit, you aren't always the most dependable person. Remember the bees?"

"Well, my pa thinks I can do it. And I know I can. You just wait," Andrew said, his pride having been wounded. "Besides, Pa says this is one way I can be part of the war. I can't go fight yet, but I can keep the farm going if he has to be away."

The wagon rolled into Hanover, and Annie could see that there were many men still standing around. The stable behind the tavern was full of horses, and a neighboring farmer's boy had been put to work tending them.

Annie entered through the kitchen door. There she

saw her friend up to her arms in dishes. Molly's face was red and her hair curled in damp tendrils on her forehead, but she flashed a tired smile when Annie entered the room. "Have you seen my father?" the younger girl asked.

"He's in there, writing letters I think," Molly answered, pointing with her head. Annie hesitated outside the dining room. Mr. Lewis did not allow the girls into the public rooms because it wasn't a proper place for young ladies, but Annie needed to speak to her father.

As she stood there, twisting a lock of hair in her fingers, the tavern keeper walked by and saw her.

"It's fine to go in, child. Your father is the only one there. I haven't opened yet for lunch. Go speak to him if you'd like."

Annie curtsied. She crossed scrubbed, wooden floors to the table where her father sat hunched over his paper. She waited silently as he finished writing and set down his quill. He rubbed his eyes and then turned toward Annie, saying tiredly, "It has been a long week."

Annie stood behind him and rubbed his shoulders as he flexed his back. "Does this feel better?" she whispered. He nodded.

"You will be careful, Father. Won't you?"

Looking up at her worried face, he smiled. "Yes, child. I will be careful. But I know that my life is in God's hands, not my own. We must not worry."

AN UNWELCOME
VISITOR

WHEN PATRICK HENRY LEFT IN THE MORNING, TRAIL-
ing his packhorse behind him, he was accompanied by
twenty men on horseback. Their long journey to the
Potomac River was dangerous and involved crossing
many rivers, most without bridges or boats. All along the
way they would need to guard against agents to the king,
eager to have a hand in arresting the famous patriot.

Only two days had passed when Annie took sick. She
complained of a sore throat, and Mr. Lewis sent her to
bed. By evening, she burned with fever. There was little
Molly could do to relieve her suffering. She tried to lower
the fever with moist towels, but it didn't work. For several days the fever flared, until Mr. Lewis, fearing that
Annie might die, sent for Patsy.

That evening, John brought Martha, an elderly slave

woman who was also a skilled nurse, back to the tavern. She stayed at Annie's bedside, keeping the cool moist cloths on the sick girl's forehead. It was Martha who forced Annie to take sips of broth and herb tea between her dry, fever-parched lips, and it was Martha who combed her tangled hair and replaced one drenched nightgown with another.

When Annie awoke with a start from a fever-induced nightmare, Martha comforted her. Annie didn't remember any of this, but Martha told her afterward that she was so sick the family had thought she was going to die. But then, the fever broke. Annie awoke again, saw the soft morning light filtered through cotton curtains, and smiled.

Martha, sitting at her bedside, returned her smile. "We've been worried sick about you, child."

"How long have I been ill," Annie whispered.

"You've been in bed for a week," Martha replied. "At times, we thought we had lost you. But you'll be fine now."

She caught a glimpse of her arms on the white sheets and shuddered when she saw the rash that covered them. Closing her eyes, she drifted off to sleep. When she awoke again, a tray with hot broth sat on the bedside table, and Martha urged her to eat.

The broth tasted good, and Annie discovered she was very hungry. Soon Martha said she could eat eggs and biscuits, and before long she was devouring ham and cornmeal mush. As the girl regained her strength, the nurse allowed her to leave her bed and sit on the porch with a woolen shawl wrapped tightly about her shoulders. From that vantage point, the child watched the comings and goings of Hanover. Bewigged men in well-cut coats and breeches went in and out of the courthouse. Lawyers probably. Farmers and frontiersman, dressed in homespun and worn boots, came to town to gossip and buy provisions.

One day, there was no one but a skinny child whose job it was to tend pigs. The pigs he was minding had escaped from their pen and were rooting and squealing down the dusty road. They squealed and darted this way and that, and the boy, with more energy than skill, only managed to excite them further. When he drew near to the tavern, he noticed Annie sitting on the rocking chair, watching him. Sticking out his tongue, he stared back at her until the girl turned away with embarrassment. Then he went back to the chase.

Annie had been recovering for about two weeks when she asked the question that had been pressing on her mind, "Will I return soon to Scotchtown?"

Molly shook her head. "The fever has been bad there. Martha says many of the slaves have been sick, and she returned home to nurse your brother, Edward."

Annie's stomach churned. "Is he well?"

"Yes. He is recovering nicely, but your brother-in-law,

Mr. Fontaine, and Patsy thought it best if you stayed here until all danger from the fever has passed."

"But I have been such a burden on you," Annie protested, realizing with sadness the truth of her words.

The older girl shook her head. "That is not so. Martha did most of the nursing. And you ate very little."

"But what about my laundry. I know I have gone through piles of laundry."

Molly shook her head and would hear no more about it. "You weren't any trouble, Annie. But you could be a help if you would eat and get strong."

It was no longer spring, and the hot summer sun beat down on the hillsides of Hanover County. Annie was now up and about and able to help with the milking and churning, though Mr. Lewis still would not let her help with the heavy chores.

Everyday she waited for news from Philadelphia, but it was infrequent. Patrick Henry had arrived safely, that much she knew. And the men from Hanover had returned to their farms. There was news, also, about battles in far-away places.

In Massachusetts, minutemen—men pledged to go and fight on a minute's notice—fought the British at Bunker Hill. In Philadelphia, George Washington was appointed head of the Continental Army. He then traveled with other generals to Massachusetts to bring order to the army there. In Williamsburg, the royal governor, fearful of an uprising by the colonists, slipped out of town by night with his family and escaped to the battleship *Powey*, anchored off the coast of Yorktown. And in Hanover, Annie Henry had her eleventh birthday.

By August, Scotchtown was free of fever and Annie, wanting to see her family again, prepared to go home. Although she hated to leave her friend, who by now was like a sister, Annie couldn't wait to see the familiar house and her family. Mr. Thacker and Andrew brought the girl back by wagon. It was the first time that Annie had seen the boy since he had brought her to Hanover in the spring.

Already the fields were dotted with shocks of wheat. Before too long it would be threshing season. Annie wondered if Andrew had been able to get his crop planted. She hated to ask in front of his father, so she was relieved when Mr. Thacker took over the reins, allowing Andrew to climb back with her.

"You look well," the boy said seriously. "I heard you were awfully sick."

"They've been sick at Scotchtown, as well," she said gravely. "But God spared us all. Did you get your crops planted last spring?"

Andrew grinned broadly. "Ma had to help get the last of the seed in, but we finished. Got the whole thing planted before the heavy rains. And the fields look great. Even Pa says so."

"That's wonderful, Andrew," Annie said.

"There's more. Pa gave me a field—covered with trees—and said I could clear it and get it ready for planting. I've been working on that after my other chores are done."

When Annie looked at her friend, she no longer saw a boy. His chest had filled out and he stood nearly as tall as his father. His face had changed too. All the round curves had become angles, and he had the beginnings of a mustache on his upper lip. But it was his attitude that had changed most. He seemed responsible.

"Have you seen John?" she asked.

"Don't have much time for hunting and fishing," he answered with a touch of regret.

"Don't you come to school?"

"I just haven't had time. Ma helps me with my reading, and I can cipher. I don't need that Latin and stuff."

Finally, the wagon reached the top of a hill, and there, in the distance, Annie saw Scotchtown. It looked just as she remembered it: a long white house with eight large windows across the front, topped by a brown shingled barn-shaped roof. The summer gardens were in bloom with asters and coneflowers.

While Andrew unloaded Annie's things, the door was thrown open by Patsy who hurried down the stairs to greet her sister. "We've missed you so much, Annie. Thank God you are home," she said with a weepy voice.

Annie pulled back and said with surprise, "Look at you. No one even told me you were having a baby."

The older girl blushed and held her fingers to her lips, while she glanced at Andrew. He appeared to be busy at his task, but Annie could tell by the red of his ears that he had heard. It wasn't considered good manners to talk about having babies.

So Annie grabbed her sister's arm and pulled her up the stairs. "Now you can tell me about it," she said. "When is this baby coming?"

"Winter, I think."

"Maybe in time for Christmas," Annie said, full of excitement. "Wouldn't that be great if we could have a baby and Father home for Christmas?"

"Christmas would be a little early for the baby. As for Father. . . ." Patsy's silence and her sudden fidgeting with a locket sent a wave of alarm through Annie.

"Father is coming home?" Annie demanded.

Patsy shook her head, and tears sprang to Annie's eyes. For a minute she thought something terrible had happened to her father, but Patsy walked over to the little writing desk, picked up a letter, and said, "This just came from him. It says that he has been named commander in chief of the regular forces in Virginia. He went straight from Philadelphia to Williamsburg."

Annie was surprised. "But Father isn't a soldier," she said.

Her sister agreed. "I guess he wants to be one, and after bringing back the money for the gunpowder, he proved himself a hero."

"Does that mean he won't be back again?"

"I'm afraid it does. We won't see him this winter, I suppose."

There was silence as the two girls thought about a long winter without their father's presence. For Annie, the news seemed particularly bitter because she had already been away so long, but even this sad news couldn't spoil the young girl's pleasure in being home. She took endless walks across the fields and into the woods, thinking as the smell of dry leaves and wood fires filled her nose that there wasn't any place on earth as nice as her home. Though war might be waging in Massachusetts, and her father might be kept in Williamsburg, at Scotchtown all was well.

The feeling of well-being was shattered by an intruder one winter night. Something awoke Annie from her sleep. One minute she had been dreaming of her mother, and the next minute she was sitting up in bed awake, uncertain about what had disturbed her. She listened carefully but heard only the sound of raindrops falling softly on the roof. Pulling her comforter up under her chin, Annie snuggled back under the covers. She had just closed her eyes when she heard a distinct noise from outside.

She sat up in the dark and waited. There it was again, a loud pounding on the door. Surely someone would answer the door to see what poor traveler had gotten stranded on such a miserable, rainy night. Her father always made room for visitors. When no one answered, though, she wrapped her blanket tightly about her thin figure and shuffled out into the hallway.

Suddenly she heard a drunken voice yell, "Wake up you traitors. Get your lazy selves out of them beds. Get out here, Patrick Henry, before I come in and get you."

Annie heard heavy footsteps coming from outside the window. She whispered, "Thank you, God, that the shutters are closed." As the footsteps faded, she tiptoed from the hall to the parlor. There her sister sat, holding a lantern. Patsy held her fingers to her lips, warning Annie to be quiet.

"Who is it, Patsy?" Annie whispered.

"I don't know. Some fool who has had too much to drink. But why does he call father a traitor?"

Annie knew the answer. She remembered the parchment proclamation from Governor Dunmore. Apparently, no one had told Patsy—probably because of the baby.

"Where is John Fontaine?" Annie asked.

"He had to go to Hanover on business. And the boys are out hunting. They won't ever hear anything with all this rain. What should we do?" There were footsteps upstairs and the sound of whimpers. Elizabeth and

Edward, the two youngest children, had been awakened and were crying. Annie started to go up but then heard the soft voice of their nurse soothing them back to sleep.

As the sisters stood in the parlor, the pounding began again at the front door. "I tell you, come out," the wild voice demanded. "Patrick Henry is a scoundrel, a coward, a thief, and a traitor. And his family ain't no better. If there is a bounty on Henry's head, I mean to get it."

When Patsy heard the word *bounty*, her face went white. She slumped into a chair, cradling her stomach in her arms. Seeing her sister's fear made Annie angry, not at Patsy, but at the unknown man beyond the door. "I'm going to get the gun," she said.

What she would do with the gun, Annie didn't know. She had never shot it. She hadn't even ever loaded it. But she knew that holding it would make them both feel safer. The girl padded across the wood floors into the family dining room, where the gun hung over the fireplace. By pulling a chair over and standing on tiptoes, she was able to reach it. The powder horn and bag of musket balls hung on another hook.

Dragging her blanket behind her, Annie carried the gun back to the parlor. When Patsy saw it her eyes widened, and she said with a tear-filled voice, "You don't know how to shoot it, Annie. You'll kill us both. Put it away."

Her younger sister shook her head. "I've seen the boys

do it. It can't be hard. And if he comes in, we have to do something," she argued.

Before the older girl could say any more, Annie drew out a ball from the soft leather bag. Then, opening the gunpowder, she tapped a little into the musket's priming pan, as she had seen her brothers do. Her hands shook as she poured the gunpowder, spilling some on the floor. Next she poured a lttle more powder down the barrel of the musket, wondering as she did so whether it was enough. Finally, she dropped the ball down the barrel. It was at that point that Annie realized she had left the ramrod, a thin pole used to force the ball and powder deep into the barrel of the musket, in the dining room. Laying the musket down, she hurried to get it.

There was silence as Annie retrieved the ramrod, and she wondered if the man had gone. But the silence was shortlived. As she passed through the hallway, the doorknob began to twist. The girl froze, unable to move, but the door held. With a sigh, she went back into the parlor, where she found Patsy still in shock. Ramrod in hand, Annie held the gun tightly between her knees with the barrel up, and rammed the pole in. The musket was loaded.

Patsy had watched the procedure without speaking, but now that Annie had loaded the gun, she began to cry. The younger girl wanted nothing better than to throw down the gun and run into her big sister's arms. But she knew the time to comfort and be comforted would come later. Now was the time to fight.

There was a central hall that ran from the front door to the back, and Annie positioned herself on the floor halfway between the two doors. The hallway was dark; the candles had been blown out hours earlier, and Annie knew she didn't dare relight them. So she sat in the dark on the cold floor, where every sound seemed loud and where the frigid air cut through her thin nightgown, chilling her to the bone.

When her back grew stiff sitting one way, she shifted her position. All the while, she prayed, "Dear Lord, keep us safe," holding the heavy musket, ready to fire. Finally, she could stand the waiting no longer. She crept to a window, loosened a shutter, and peeked out. The night was still dark, but the rain had passed, and by the moonlight Annie saw two figures come towards the house at a run. Then she heard a yell, saw a flash of light, and heard the explosion of one musket followed by another.

From the parlor, Patsy screamed, and Annie aimed the musket at the backdoor. There was more pounding, only this time the voice that went with it was familiar. William! With relief, Annie ran to the door and swung open the latch.

William, water dripping down his hat and coat, brushed past his sister into the hall. "Are you both all right?" he demanded.

With a shaking voice, Annie said, "yes."

"Where's Patsy?"

"She's in the parlor," the girl answered.

William ran to the parlor, and found his older sister sobbing on the settee. "It's all right, Patsy," he murmured. "It's over. No one will harm you now. Try to get some sleep," he commanded gently, pulling the blanket over her and turning again to his little sister. "I have to go help John. You stay here with her, do you understand?"

Annie nodded solemnly. The boys were gone about thirty minutes when John returned, ashen-faced. As he removed his wet coat and boots, he tried to keep his face hidden from Annie, but she saw his shaking hands and red-rimmed eyes.

"Where did the man go?" Annie whispered.

William, who had come in behind John, said, "He won't bother you anymore. Tell us what happened."

Annie recounted the night's terrors as her brothers listened. William's face was grim, and he glanced several times at John who stared at the floor. Once, Annie thought her younger brother was going to speak. He lifted his head, but only a sob came forth.

"What's happened?" Annie demanded when she could stand it no longer.

"We saw him from the distance, but when we shouted, he turned and fired his musket. John fired back and hit the man. He's dead," William added.

For John, the effort to hold back his tears was too much. Rasping sobs shook his body, and he said over and over again, "I never meant to kill him."

William patted his brother's arm. "You did what was right, John. Father would be proud of you."

"But I killed a man," the boy sobbed.

"You were defending your family," William answered.

"Why couldn't Pa be here?" the weeping boy asked.

That's when William said softly, "Come, brother. It's been a long night. And tomorrow will be a long day. Let's see if we can get some sleep."

AN EARLY ARRIVAL

JOHN FONTAINE ARRIVED HOME TWO DAYS LATER AND found Scotchtown in confusion. The slaves had been put on alert for other trespassers, and John and William kept the house under close guard. William had even ordered a cast-iron bell to be hung near the porch so that his sisters could ring it in an emergency.

Patsy had taken to bed amidst worries that she might lose the baby. When Annie tried to cheer her up by talking about planning a party to celebrate the birth, her older sister shook her head. "There are more important things than parties," she said, echoing her father's words without realizing it.

The responsibility of protecting the household seemed to help John recover from that night, but Annie didn't have anything to take her mind off those nightmarish memories. She found herself afraid to go outside alone and jumpy if she had to cross from the house to the kitchen or her father's office. She hated the hours she spent alone because that's when she imagined what might have happened if her brothers had not come home.

Under John Fontaine's calm guidance, Scotchtown returned to order. One day, not long after his return, Annie found Patsy asleep in her dimly-lit room. Annie settled herself into a chair near the bed, feeling better just being in a room with someone else. That's when she saw Patsy's face tighten in pain and beads of perspiration dot her lip. After a few seconds, the pain seemed to pass, and her sister opened her eyes.

"Patsy," Annie said, "whatever is the matter? Is it the baby?"

Smiling wanly, Patsy said, "They've been coming like this for hours. You've got to find my John. Is he home yet?"

"He's home, but I can't leave you like this."

As the older girl lay there, her hand clutched the blanket and her jaw tightened as she held her breath through the pain and then relaxed. Opening her eyes, she whispered, "Please, Annie. Hurry."

Without waiting, Annie dashed from the room onto the porch. Desperately scanning the yard for her brother-in-law, Annie saw no one. Then she remembered the bell. She rang it furiously until one of the cooks appeared at the kitchen door.

"What's wrong, Miss Annie," she asked.

"The baby is coming," Annie answered. "We must find Mr. Fontaine and Martha, and I can't leave here." Annie heard her voice crack over the words.

"We'll find them. Don't you worry, Miss Annie. Go on and stay with Miss Patsy."

Annie hurried back to the darkened room where she found Patsy dozing fitfully. She prayed as she sat by the bed, knowing there was nothing else she could do. "Please God, let the baby be born well, and keep Patsy safe," she whispered.

The half hour before John Fontaine came seemed like an eternity to Annie. Every move that Patsy made, every groan, brought fears of immediate birth and possible death. But finally he arrived, and Annie said with relief, "You're here."

He stood awkwardly at the door, his hat in his hand, his farm boots still muddy from the field. "Is she all right?" he whispered worriedly.

"I think she's sleeping," Annie said softly. "Sometimes she groans, but otherwise she's quiet."

"Do you think she can hear me?" he asked.

"Come, sit by the bed and talk to her," Annie said. "I'll go and wait for Martha. Will she be here soon?"

"I don't know." John Fontaine sat gingerly on the side of the bed. He held his wife's hand and smoothed her damp hair back from her forehead.

There was nothing for Annie to do but wait. Finally she saw Martha making her way slowly across the yard to the house, weighed down by the heavy satchel that she carried in one hand. The girl ran to meet her.

"Will Patsy be all right?" she asked. "Isn't it awfully early for the baby to come?"

Wrapping one bony arm around Annie's shoulders, Martha said, "You let Martha do the worrying. I ain't lost a baby yet, and I don't intend to start now."

Annie looked at Martha's well-worn, wrinkled face, which spoke of many years experience and relaxed. Martha was in charge, not Annie. All would be well.

They had reached the house, and Martha released Annie. "Take my satchel inside and then fetch me some some water and rags." When Annie hesitated, Martha shooed her away. "Go on, child. Hurry. It will be hours before this baby comes, but we want to be ready."

Annie had been gone only a short time, but when she returned to Patsy's room, it looked different. Patsy was propped up by pillows in her bed. Sunlight flooded in through opened shutters, and a cozy fire blazed in the fireplace. John Fontaine had been sent outside to wait.

Martha busied herself in one corner, and when she saw Annie watching, she put her to work bathing her sister's face with a cool cloth. Throughout the day, Patsy labored. The pains came more frequently and with greater intensity, but still the baby was not born. Annie began to worry. Would the baby never come?

She whispered that question to Martha during one of the periods between pains, but the nurse just smiled. "Things are going fine, child. Now go see if you can't make Miss Patsy more comfortable."

Shamefaced, Annie returned to her sister's side. She mopped Patsy's forehead with a damp cloth and rubbed her lower back as Martha had shown her. Just then, Annie's stomach grumbled. She remembered that she hadn't eaten since breakfast, more than eight hours before. Timidly, she looked at Martha and mouthed the words, "I'm hungry."

The old woman nodded. "Go get some food. We don't want you to faint from hunger."

"I'll bring back something for you," Annie said.

She found her brother-in-law pacing in the hallway and reassured him. "She's fine, Martha says." Outside in the yard, her brothers were pitching horseshoes. They looked up when Annie came out. "Just getting food," she said. "Nothing's happened yet."

In fact, nothing happened until early evening. Annie did her best to make her sister feel comfortable, but still Patsy cried out with pain. Finally, there was a shout, and the nurse said, "Here it comes," and the next thing Annie knew there was a baby lying in Martha's arms. She wiped his face with a damp cloth, thumped his bottom, and out came a forlorn little cry. Then she lay the little boy on his mother's stomach.

He was the tiniest little thing that Annie had ever seen. His skin looked too big, and it hung in wrinkles around his ankles. With his feet tucked under him he looked no bigger than a hand. The minutes after the birth were full of confusion. Patsy laughed and cried as Martha washed her face and dressed her in a fresh nightgown. She looked delightedly at the little boy who now lay in her arms, wrapped in blankets. "Just look at him," she whispered. "Isn't he beautiful?"

Martha gave Annie a poke. "Don't just stand there, Miss Annie. Go tell Mr. Fontaine that he has a beautiful son," she said.

John Fontaine stood right outside the door. "I heard the cry," he said. "Are they both well?"

"It's a boy and they are both just fine," Annie grinned. "He's little as a peanut and red as a beet, but Patsy says he's beautiful, so I guess he must be."

John slumped down in a chair, exhausted. "Thank you, God," he prayed.

"Aren't you going to come see?" Annie asked.

"May I come now?"

"Martha said to get you, and whatever Martha says, goes," the girl said with a smile. "Come on. Patsy is waiting for you."

Annie felt out of place in the happy birthing room.

Being on the outside felt funny, as if she had just taken part in a miraculous event and then been shoved to the side.

"I'm being silly," she told herself later that night when the feeling came over her again. She had been lying in bed for hours, too tired to sleep. Everytime she shut her eyes, her mind would start working and then she'd be wide awake again. One minute she was reliving the night with the drunken man, the next she was feeling sorry for herself because Patsy was now the center of attention. As much as she tried to squelch the feelings, they kept popping up.

With relief Annie saw the first rays of the sun. Morning: now she wouldn't have to pretend to sleep anymore. She crawled from her bed and splashed her face with water from the wash basin.

Her brothers already were seated at the breakfast table. John speared a slice of ham as Annie came into the room. "'Morning," he said. "Cornbread's hot."

Annie took a seat at the long trestle table and looked without interest at the food. "I'm not very hungry," she said.

He smiled. "That leaves all the more for me," he said, stabbing another piece of ham. Annie grabbed a piece of cornbread and nibbled on it. She grew aware of William staring at her.

"Why are you staring at me?" she demanded.

"Just thinking."

"What does that mean? Thinking about what?

"About teaching you to shoot a gun," he said.

Annie looked with surprise at her brother. It wasn't usual for a girl, at least one who lived on a plantation, to know how to shoot. Afraid to show any eagerness, she asked, "Why?"

"Simple," William said. "We can't always be close to home. When spring comes, John Fontaine, John, and I will be off in the fields. Patsy will be busy with the baby, and we can't leave you unprotected in the house."

"But there are always people around," Annie protested.

"That's true. But Lord Dunmore has encouraged the slaves to revolt—to leave their masters and to join with the British. Our people seem loyal, but we can't be certain they will stay if trouble comes."

"Does Patsy know?" Annie asked

"How could she know? She's just had a baby. We aren't going to trouble her about something like this."

That made sense to Annie. John had kept quiet during the discussion, so Annie turned to him. "What do you think?" she asked.

He shrugged. "Shooting isn't everything, but sometimes it's necessary. Better that you know how, I guess, than to be defenseless. But Pa won't like it."

William looked impatiently at his brother. "Pa doesn't

have to know. Besides, he's in Williamsburg, and we are here. We have to do what we think is right."

Biting her lip, Annie looked at her big brother. "Will you tell Father what happened?"

He returned her glance, then turned away. "John Fontaine doesn't think it wise. What can he do? We will write and tell him about the baby, but that's all."

Annie could see the sense of it, but an uneasiness settled over her. There was sure a lot going on at Scotchtown that Patrick Henry didn't know about, but there wasn't much she could do about it. Eager to change the subject, she asked, "When do we start?"

"Today. Let's go to the woods, and we'll teach you to load this old gun," William said.

"But I know how," Annie protested. "Remember, I loaded it when the drunken man was here."

The brothers looked at each other skeptically. Then John spoke. "We think the gun was already loaded. When we get to the woods, you can show us how you think it works."

John grabbed the musket, and the three set off down the road to the woods.

THE LESSON

THEY FOLLOWED THE PATH THAT MEANDERED through fields, past slave cottages, finally passing through a tall beech woods. Upon reaching the woods, Annie stopped for a minute, letting her eyes adjust to the shadows. Turning toward her brothers, she held her hand out for the gun. "May I load it now?" she asked.

William and John stood and watched, prepared to tease their sister if she loaded it wrong. She sat down on a log, laying the gun over her knees.

"You don't sit down to load a musket," John laughed, but Annie ignored him. She made sure that the gun would not slide, then opened the powder horn and gently tapped its edge against the priming pan. When that was done, she sprinkled more powder into the barrel. Then, standing up, Annie leaned the musket against her leg while she bent to retrieve the ramrod. She looked at

her brothers who were watching carefully. With a flourish, Annie pushed a musket ball and some paper down
into the barrel with the rod.

When she had finished, she fixed a challenging stare
on her brothers. "Well?" she asked. "Did I do it right?"

John looked abashed, but William smiled broadly.
"That's great, Annie. Looked like a girl doing it, but at
least you got the job done." Then pointing at a tree, he
said, "Go ahead, Annie, shoot at that tree over there."

Annie raised the musket to shoulder level, trying to
hold the long gun steady. After sighting down the barrel,
she pulled the trigger and the musket came to life, throwing Annie back on her backside. John and William hid
their smiles behind their hands. "That's good," John said.

"Make sure you plant your feet," William added, wiping his eyes.

Annie picked herself up, brushing the dry leaves off
her skirts. She rubbed her shoulder and asked, "Did I hit
the tree?"

The boys grinned. "We forgot to look," William
replied.

John ran over to the tree. He searched the scarred
trunk of the old beech, but could find no evidence of the
musket ball.

Annie shrugged with disappointment, and William
patted her awkwardly on the shoulder. "That's fine,
Annie. It was your first shot. By the end of the day, you'll

be shooting like a drilled militiaman." Then scratching his chin, he said, "I have an idea. Sometimes people learn to do something best on their own without teachers hanging over their shoulders. John and I want to make you a challenge."

John looked at his brother curiously. He obviously didn't know about this plan. William continued talking. "No sense in wasting ammunition by shooting at trees. Maybe you should have to get us dinner. A couple of squirrels or doves, maybe an opposum or a raccoon. What do you say? You get us dinner, and John and I will admit that you are a good shot. Do you accept the challenge?"

Annie knew that William was laughing at her. But she took the challenge anyway. "Its a deal," she said. "I'll be back at dinner time—and I'll have something for dinner, or . . ." Annie paused, not sure what to offer if she couldn't bag any game. "Or . . . or I guess you'll go hungry tonight," she finished lamely.

"No. If you don't bring back dinner, John and I will think of some appropriate punishment. Come on John, let's leave Annie to her hunting."

Annie watched her brothers walk out of the beech woods. So much for shooting lessons. Now she was left with the problem of what to do. "Load the gun, you ninny," she scolded herself. After she had reloaded the gun she felt more confident.

The woods were quiet except for the occasional squirrel's chatter or bird's song. It made her nervous to be alone in the woods for such a long time. What if there were bandits or outlaws? What if there was another angry loyalist? She thought she heard a musket shot, then another. Each time she felt more nervous. Suddenly, the hours before dinner seemed endless and Annie wished she was back in sight of the house. Without thinking, she began to run, eager to put the shadows of the beech forest behind her. A noise! Were those footsteps?

She swung around, but saw nothing. Then, grabbing her skirt, she ran again. Behind her she heard the crackling of pine needles. Darting behind a tree, she turned to face her pursuer, but the woods were quiet. Annie could hear only her own rasping breath and the sound of her heart pounding in her ears.

It was not more than twenty-five paces to the clearing. Grabbing the hem of her skirt in her hand, she ran for the the light, not once turning to see who was behind her. Branches reached out, scratching her arms and a log rose up to trip her. She stumbled but did not fall. When she reached the field, the sun welcomed her, and she stood under its warm rays until her legs stopped trembling and she could catch her breath. It was then that Annie realized she still clutched the musket in one hand and her long skirt in the other.

She stared at the gun for a minute, then slowly brought it up to her shoulder. It felt too heavy and her arm trembled under its weight so that Annie could not aim it. Nonetheless, she stood facing the woods, ready, she thought, to shoot her pursuer. She stood there for a minutes until she heard a voice behind her. "What are you doing?"

Annie turned with a start. "Don't scare a girl like that," she yelled at a puzzled-looking Andrew Thacker. "I could have shot you."

The girl still held the gun to her shoulders, but now it was pointed shakily at Andrew, who held his hands up in front of his face as if to ward off a musket ball.

"Well, put it down, Annie. Don't you know guns are dangerous? Who gave you that musket anyway?"

Annie, breathing heavily, let the musket down to the ground. "I'm sorry," she said. "I didn't mean to point it at you, but there was someone in the woods."

Andrew looked as though he wasn't sure whether or not to believe her. He had heard the story about the intruder at Scotchtown as had just about everyone in the county, and now he figured Annie was imagining things. "You were just spooked, more than likely," he said. "I don't see anyone there."

Annie turned back toward the woods. "But I know there was someone there," she said. "When I ran, he ran. When I stopped, he stopped. I heard it with my own ears." She knew she sounded shrill, and she could tell from

Andrew's expression that he felt sorry for her. That only made her angry. "Don't be feeling sorry for me," she said.

"I've got to get back to work," Andrew said, pointing at the field behind him. "Will you be all right now?"

Still clutching the musket to her side, Annie nodded. Her eyes took in the field where Andrew had been working. It was pitted where stumps had been, and their remains littered the field. The oxen were chained to a stump where Andrew had left a long metal bar sticking up out of the ground. Still nervous, but not wanting to admit it, Annie tried to prolong the conversation a little longer. "What are you doing in the field?" she asked.

"Remember the plot of land Pa gave me?" Andrew asked with a grin. "Well, this is it. I guess it's part of the land we bought from you last year. Anyway, Pa said I should clear it and maybe next year it'll be ready to plant."

"Next year. Isn't that a long time?" Annie asked, amazed that it could take so long to get a field ready for planting.

Andrew grinned. "Feels like forever, but I can only work on it after I do my other chores. This field looked like those woods before I cleared it. Now I've got to remove all the stumps. Ain't easy," he said shaking his head. "I have to get back to work. Pa still keeps a pretty close eye on me."

"Go ahead. I'm sure whoever it was is long gone by now. I've got to get back to the house anyway," Annie said, all thoughts of bringing back dinner gone from her head. She walked along the edge of the woods, feeling safe because she knew Andrew could still see her. As she turned back to watch him, she heard a noise coming from the woods on the right. Before she could scream or raise the musket, her brother John stumbled out in front of her.

"What do you think you are doing, John Henry?" the girl demanded. "Was it you who was chasing me? Was it? 'Cause I don't think it was a bit funny."

Her brother looked at her sheepishly. "I didn't mean to scare you," he said. "I changed my mind about leaving you alone, but when I came back, you seemed so skittish I thought I'd play a trick."

Though his words sounded apologetic, Annie could see the beginnings of a grin forming on his face. She could feel a smile tease her own lips, but she was not willing to let him off the hook that fast. "You know I almost shot Andrew. I could have killed him, just because you scared me," Annie said.

"Well, you didn't," John replied.

"But I could have."

Annie began walking briskly toward home, and her brother hurried to keep up with her. "Don't you think I should get some credit?" he asked. "Didn't I come back?"

Annie turned on her brother, her face crimson with anger. "You scared me half-to-death, John Henry. That's what you did." Then she began to cry, which only made her angrier. She knew she looked ridiculous standing out in the middle of a wheat field with musket in hand, arms scratched and dress torn, glaring at her brother, who looked close to tears himself. She tried to nurse her anger just a little longer, but suddenly the situation seemed so silly that Annie began to giggle. What started as a small giggle grew into a roar, until she was bent double with laughter, and John was left staring at her with a worried expression.

Annie saw it and swallowed a new wave of laughter long enough to say, "I'm fine. Really. Everything just seemed so silly all of a sudden."

John gave her a questioning smile. "So you aren't angry anymore?"

Annie shook her head as she wiped tears from her eyes. Then she began to giggle again. "What am I going to do about dinner?"

Looking at Annie, the musket, and the empty game bag, John laughed. "I can help you there. Come on. Let me show you how to shoot that gun." The two walked in companionable silence, John pointing out the squirrels and Annie refusing to shoot them. When they were about 100 feet from a wheat shock, John turned to Annie and said, "Shooting isn't that hard. And you don't really have to be able to hunt in order to protect yourself. It would be better if you could hit a target like that wheat. Go ahead, shoot and see if you can hit it."

During the next hour, Annie practiced shooting and loading the musket until her shoulder was so sore she could barely lift her arm. She rubbed it and winced as her fingers touched her tender skin. Peeking under her sleeve, she saw an ugly bruise beginning to form.

Looking up at his sister, John noticed her pained expression. "I should have warned you about the gun's kick," he said. "That's why we wear a jacket or a vest when we're shooting." The sun was getting lower and the wheat began to cast long shadows in the field. "Time to get back," he said. "William will be waiting for you."

"But what about you. Aren't you coming back?" Annie asked.

"Not with you. William will think I'm weak if he knows I helped you. You'd better go back alone."

"A lot of help you've been," Annie reminded him. "I still don't have anything for supper."

John grinned. Reaching around his back, he pulled out his own game bag. In it were two squirrels. "I shot them before I came back to you," he said. "Thought you might need them."

Annie pulled back from the limp bodies which John held in his hands. "Poor things," she said.

"Oh, Annie," John teased. "God gave us these squirrels to eat, just like he gave us pigs. I don't see you giving up your ham and bacon."

"Well, you put them in my bag. I don't want to touch

them," Annie said, holding out the bag to John. Once the squirrels were in the bag, the two set off. John walked with his sister until they were in sight of the house, then he ran around the back way.

Annie went straight to the barn. There she found William, as she expected. She handed him the game bag without a word, turned, and marched out of the barn. John, who entered the barn just as she was leaving, winked as she passed by.

William must have seen the wink, because Annie heard raised voices and the next thing she knew, William was chasing John out of the barn. When he saw her, he turned and began to chase her toward the house. Annie ran quickly, but she was at a disadvantage because of her skirts. Besides, William was much bigger and stronger. He caught up to her on the steps leading to the backdoor and pulled her down until he had pinned her to the ground. Annie gasped for breath as William rubbed dried grass in her hair.

"Stop, stop," Annie shrieked. "Let me catch my breath."

Just then the door opened, and a deep voice said, "Since when do near-grown boys knock young girls down to the ground?"

William climbed to his feet looking shame-faced. "Mr. Dabney," he said. "We were just playing."

Scrambling to her feet and brushing off her skirt,

Annie felt her face burning with embarrassment, but the tutor was not looking at her.

"I think, Master William," he said with a touch of sarcasm, "you would be better served if you concentrated on your schoolwork. I know it is late—nearly dinnertime, I believe. But I'd like to see you in the schoolroom. Now." Then he turned and walked away, fully expecting William to follow.

William scowled before following the tutor to the classroom. John raised his eyebrows in an imitation of the tutor and said to Annie, in his best adult voice, "And you, my dear, would be best served by concentrating on dinner. I expect to see you in the dining room. Now."

With laughter, they went in to eat.

ON TO WILLIAMSBURG

THE BABY, BENJAMIN, GREW FAT OVER THE REMAINDER of the winter. No longer did his skin seem too big for him. He lost his baby fuzz, and the hair that replaced it was thick and curly. He had big brown eyes and a smile so broad it caused his cheeks to dimple and his eyes to squint. When Patsy was tired, Annie watched him. He couldn't yet crawl or sit, but he laughed when Annie acted silly, and she loved him.

But Benjamin was winter's high point. Otherwise, it was a lonely time. Patsy was devoted to her husband and her baby. She no longer sat around thinking about clothes and scolding Annie. Now she lived and breathed baby Benjamin and John Fontaine. John and William found endless ways to keep busy outside, and they made it clear that girls were not welcome.

Patrick Henry stayed in Williamsburg all winter. He

hadn't come home for Christmas, and, because of the baby being born, the holiday had slipped by without anyone taking any note of it, leaving Annie feeling sad and neglected. If only Father could come home.

That didn't seem likely. The letters from him were few and far between. One reason was the weather. It was harder for post riders to move the mail during cold and rainy weather. To Annie it seemed as though her father had forgotten them, and though she knew he hadn't been told about the night with the drunken man, she still felt like he should have known about it somehow. If he really loved her, wouldn't he know when she was in trouble? These were the kinds of thoughts Annie had during that long, lonely winter.

In late January, the weather broke. The temperature warmed to the sixties, and the air had the soft feel of spring. Stepping outside into the warm weather was like an invitation to play. Annie went to the stable and had Joseph saddle her horse.

As she rode away from home, Annie felt her spirits lift. For the first time since the drunken man had come and since the baby had been born, she felt free and unafraid. She rode further and further from the plantation, crossing the familiar pastures and fields, now brown and dead. A few scrawny cows grazed. An occasional deer, looking for food, crossed her path.

Annie wasn't certain when the idea formed in her

head. But she had been riding for little over an hour when she made up her mind. If Father would not come home, she would ride to Williamsburg to see him. The day was clear, the temperature mild, and her horse was full of energy. Nothing stood in her way.

As if the horse could sense her excitement, he picked up the pace, until Annie was flying over the fields. She let him run for ten minutes before reining him in to a trot. "Don't want to get tired, boy," she said. "We've got a long way ahead of us."

By noon, Annie's stomach began to growl, and she realized that she had neither food nor money. She felt a twinge of alarm, but it passed quickly. After all, she was Patrick Henry's daughter. It should be no problem getting a meal at any house she passed. Virginians were known for their hospitality. Annie could remember any number of travelers who had been fed and given shelter at Scotchtown.

Her stomach growled again, so Annie began to look for a house. Finally, on a small rise, she saw a cabin about the size of the Thackers. Annie walked the horse up to the front porch. She tied him to a post and knocked at the door. It was answered by a young woman, maybe Patsy's age, holding a baby in her arms. A blond-haired toddler peeked out from behind her skirts. The woman looked surprised.

"Hello," Annie said. "I was wondering if you might be able to give me a bite to eat."

Although Annie had heard many travelers make that request, she had never done it before. Somehow, it seemed embarrassing. It was like begging. She blushed and looked away.

The woman smiled and opened the door wider. Behind her was a single room with a table at one end and a bed and cradle at the other. Dried herbs hung from the beams, and a loft held barrels, probably filled with apples and potatoes. The table was set, and the smell of fresh-baked bread filled the room.

"My name is Abigail Byrd," the woman said. "My husband, Nathaniel, will come shortly for lunch." She paused and Annie realized, with embarrassment, that she was expected to introduce herself.

"Um, I'm Annie Henry," she said. "I'm on my way to Williamsburg."

"Williamsburg! Why, that's a far piece. And you're all alone?" Abigail exclaimed. She set the baby down on the bed and beckoned the girl over to the table. Then, picking the little boy up and carrying him over, she set him on the bench and placed a plate of dried apple slices and hot corn bread before him.

Annie watched while she performed these tasks. Abigail's mousy hair was pulled back into a simple coil at her neck. Her face was freckled as though she spent too much time outside without a bonnet, and her hands were rough from work. But she had a nice smile and clear gray eyes. She reminded Annie of Mrs. Thacker, except Abigail was younger.

Having settled the boy, Mrs. Byrd turned her attention to her guest. "I don't mean to be nosy," she said while urging the girl to sit at the table, "but what is a young girl doing going to Williamsburg?"

"I'm going to see my father," Annie answered.

"And he's in Williamsburg?"

"Yes."

"Does he know you're coming?"

Annie avoided Abigail's eyes. "Not really," she answered.

"Hmm," Abigail said. "Let me guess. Your father is Patrick Henry. He's been very busy, and he doesn't know you are coming."

"That's right," Annie admitted. "But he'd be happy to see me. He's been away for so long. I know he misses us."

"Of course he does," Abigail said. "But won't your folks at home worry about you?"

Annie felt a twinge of guilt. They would worry about her. She knew they would. Why hadn't she thought about that earlier? She chewed her lip. Just then the door opened. A stocky, bearded man came into the room. Abigail rose to meet him. He handed her his coat, which she hung on a hook next to Annie's. She whispered something to him, and Annie saw him glance in her direction. He was big, much bigger than Father, and seemed to fill the room. His hair had been blown by the wind, and it stood in unruly tufts on his head.

After he had removed his boots, he strode over to the table, where he towered over the young girl. Holding out his hand, he said, "I'm Nathaniel Byrd. Welcome." Then he sat down.

Abigail set the bread, dried apples, and ham slices before them. They prayed and began to eat. The man, obviously hungry, ate and ate. When he had finished, he leaned on both elbows and stared at his young guest. She blushed and looked away. He said, "Why don't you tell us about yourself?"

Annie took a deep breath and began. They were such good listeners that she found herself telling them about the past year, about her mother's death, her father's absences, the drunken man, Patsy's baby, and the lonely winter. While she spoke, Abigail moved to a rocking chair where she nursed the baby and put him to sleep in the cradle. She cleaned up the little boy and lay him on the big bed before slipping back to the table.

Finally, Annie finished speaking. "That's quite a tale, Miss Henry," Nathaniel Byrd said. "I know, as a father, that I wouldn't want a child of mine to go to Williamsburg on her own. It's dangerous."

Annie started to speak, but Nathaniel held up his

hand. "I ain't got the authority to stop you but at least spend the night here. I know its only midday, but there's rain coming, and the creeks can get riled. It wouldn't be safe to go on tonight. This way, you'll have a dry place to stay and can leave at first light."

Without waiting for a response, Nathaniel rose to his feet. He nodded at Annie, kissed his wife, and pulled on his coat. "It was a pleasure to meet you, Miss Henry. But I have to get back to my work," he said. "Stay as long as you like with us."

"Thank you," Annie said.

When he had gone, Abigail cleared the dirty dishes. "Let me just run out to get some water from the well," she said. "You rest for a minute."

The couple was visible outside the window. Mrs. Byrd lowered the bucket into the well and pulled it up again, dumping the water into a kettle that she had carried out with her. Nathaniel joined her and they talked, glancing at the house. Then Annie saw Abigail nod, and Nathaniel walk away. In the west, a line of gray clouds appeared, and the wind began to pick up. A dead leaf, pushed by the wind, skipped across the dry ground.

When Abigail returned to the house, she said, "Nathaniel took your horse around to the barn and gave him some oats. The rain is coming up fast. You will stay, won't you?"

Annie sighed. "I guess I'd better. Do you know how much farther to Richmond?"

Abigail picked up some sewing from her basket and began to work, glancing up at Annie from time to time as she sewed. "It's several hours in the best of weather. With this rain, it could be longer. The roads will be muddy and the rivers swollen. One river has no bridge or boat. You'll have to cross on horseback."

"Then it must not be deep," Annie said.

"That's true," Abigail admitted, "except when there's rain. Then the river swells terribly. Takes hours to drop. That's why Nathaniel wanted you to wait." She turned her face back to her sewing.

Annie felt jumpy. Sitting still was hard to do. She wanted to go, but she knew that wouldn't be wise. She walked over to the the window. The sky was dark in the west, but the storm still looked to be miles away. Should she try to get to Richmond before the storm? Annie didn't know. She came back and sat down in front of Abigail.

"From Richmond, I just follow the river to Williamsburg, right?"

"That's true, but if the water's high you won't be able to follow the river very closely. There'll be flooding."

"Well then, I could take a boat," Annie said, remembering all the boats she had seen docked in Richmond.

Biting her thread as she peered at Annie, Abigail nodded. "Yes, there are boats. But have you ever considered the kind of man who is likely to be on a boat? They are often rough and uncivilized. They spend their time on the sea, without people about. They aren't to be trusted."

"But last year a very nice captain helped me in Richmond," Annie protested.

"Oh, I'm not saying there aren't nice and decent boatmen. But they are rare. And what if you get on board with one who isn't so nice?"

Annie chewed her lip, as she often did when she was nervous. If what Abigail said was true, then she shouldn't go on to Williamsburg. But she had come so far. How could she turn back now?

Abigail must have seen her indecision because she said, "I'm not trying to discourage you from seeing your father. But you've bitten off a big mouthful, and we'd hate for you to get hurt."

"I know you mean well," Annie said. "But now I don't know what to do. I feel like if I don't see Father I will explode. I just have to go. I really can't wait." She ran out to the barn.

Abigail came after her. She wanted to stop Annie but, seeing the determination in her young face, she said, "At least take some food and a coat. If it rains, you will be cold. And come back if you have difficulty."

Annie nodded. Now that her mind was made up, she wanted to leave. While Annie saddled her horse, Abigail fixed a bag with food and water and brought out the coat.

"I wish you would stay," Abigail said. "Won't you?"

The woman looked so worried that Annie hugged her tight. "I'll be fine, really," she said as she mounted the horse.

It was a cold wind that nipped at the girl's cheeks as she rode. Glancing over her shoulder, the Byrd farm grew smaller and smaller, and the lone figure of Abigail Byrd, faded. Annie felt tears come to her eyes and her throat burned. She let the horse run, not caring that the wind was raw against her tear-streaked cheeks.

Annie came to a river. She reined in the horse and surveyed her options. The river was too wide at this point, so she explored the bank in both directions. Finally, she found a place where the river narrowed to about twenty feet. She edged the horse down the sandy bank. He put one hoof into the water and stopped. She urged him forward into the swirling water with gentle pressure from her knees. Immediately, her skirts were wet, and the icy coldness of the water took her breath away. Still, she urged the horse on. Reluctantly, he stepped forward until he reached the middle of the river, where the water came to his shoulders. Then he stopped.

Despite Annie's urging, the horse would not go forward. He moved nervously in the water until Annie, in frustration and cold, kicked him hard. The horse reared back, tumbling his rider into the water. Although the creek did not appear swift, there was a rapid current under the surface, and Annie could feel herself being pulled along. Her skirts and leather boots, heavy with water, weighed her down. The numbing cold of the water made her sleepy. "If I could just close my eyes a minute," she thought.

Then she felt the strong body of the horse next to her. Rousing herself, Annie reached out an arm and grabbed the rein. She struggled to keep her head above water as the horse pulled her back toward the bank. At last, feeling the solid ground under her, she scrambled up the bank and flopped on the ground.

For a long time she lay there, too exhausted and scared to move. Finally, though, she roused herself enough to look around her, then fell back in frustration. The horse had taken her back to the near bank of the river. She still had to cross it if she wanted to go to Williamsburg. She began to cry.

Red-eyed, she wiped the last tears away. Using the wet skirt of her dress, she blew her nose. Then she mounted the horse and turned back toward the Byrds. The wind blew fiercely in her face. It pressed Annie's sodden dress against her like an icy skin. She kept her head down, letting the horse pick his way back. Soon, she felt the first pin-pricks of rain. Each icy drop felt like a needle jab. Reining in the horse, Annie pulled on the oil cloth coat that Mrs. Byrd had lent her. It kept the rain off her dress but couldn't do anything to make her dry and warm. On they traveled until, in the distance, she saw a light.

As if sensing warmth, shelter, and oats, the horse picked up his pace, galloping the last fifty yards through the mud. Annie prayed that he wouldn't twist a leg or fall. The Byrds must have been expecting her. As soon as she arrived the door was thrown open, and Nathaniel carried her into the cabin.

While he took care of the horse, Mrs. Byrd removed Annie's wet clothes, wrapped a warm towel around her, and put a cup of herb tea before her. "You silly girl," she said in a voice that was comforting, not scolding. "We were worried sick about you."

Too tired to speak, Annie took the tea and drank it gratefully. Then Mrs. Byrd dressed her in a nightgown that had been hanging by the fire. Its toasty folds of fabric warmed the girl's skin as she lay down on the bed to sleep.

FATHER RETURNS

WHEN ANNIE AWOKE, SHE FOUND HERSELF IN A strange bed in a strange house. She looked around and saw the plain, well-scrubbed trestle table and benches, the empty crib, and the herbs hanging from the ceiling. Yesterday's memories came flooding back.

Outside, the sky was a deep blue, but moisture on the window meant it was cold. Annie quickly slipped into her dress, which she found hanging near the fire. It's fabric felt stiff, but it was warm and dry, and that's what mattered.

She found Abigail in the yard and the two children bundled under a bear rug in the wagon with only their faces exposed to the sun. She turned when she heard Annie, and a broad smile spread across her face.

"Good morning, Annie. How are you feeling today?"

"Much better, thank you," Annie said, glancing over the bright landscape, her eyes taking in the startling blue sky and the iced-over wagon ruts and hoof prints. Abigail's cheeks were rosy, and her eyes glowed with good health. "I'm sorry about yesterday," the young girl said. "I didn't mean to worry you."

"We know that," Abigail reassured her. "Sometimes we all let our hearts rule our heads, but I should have done more to stop you."

Kicking at a skim of ice with her toe, Annie sighed. "Do you think life will always be like this until England gives us our freedom?"

"I don't know. But the wisest thing is to remember what St. Paul said, 'I know both how to be abased, and I know how to abound; every where and in all things I am instructed both to be full and to be hungry, both to abound and to suffer need.'"

"What do you mean?" Annie asked

"I mean that we can't wait for circumstances to be perfect in order for us to be happy. You've been born to a family that is blessed in many ways, but your father is gone a great deal of the time. You can't say, 'I'll be happy when Father comes home,' because you don't know if he'll ever be home all the time. You need to be content right now."

Annie turned her back so that the older woman wouldn't see her wipe away the tears that trickled down her cheek. "I just want father to be home. I want a family like yours," Annie said.

Abigail hugged her. "And if you had our troubles,

you'd want something else," she said softly. "You'll have to learn that you can't find happiness by getting something. It comes only when you trust God to supply what you need. Now come along to the barn with me. Nathaniel's there, with a visitor you'll want to see."

Annie followed at Abigail's side, hoping the large man would not be angry with her. It took her eyes a minute to adjust to the dim light of the barn. When they did, she saw Nathaniel cutting a piece of wood with a saw. Another man sat on a bale of hay nearby, talking quietly. As she drew closer, her heart stopped. The man looked up, saw Annie, and rose to his feet, but before he could stand, she had thrown herself on him.

"Father," she cried. "You did come home."

Nathaniel and Abigail left the two Henrys alone in the barn. Patrick Henry said in a soft voice, "You worried the whole family, child. What were you thinking?"

"I just wanted to see you," the girl whispered. "It had been so long, and you hadn't come home. And everyone is so busy. . . ." she let her voice trail off.

Pulling her close, he said, "I'm sorry, Annie. I have been away too long. Too long for me and too long for you."

"But how did you get here?"

"Nathaniel rode over to Scotchtown to tell everyone where you were. I had just come home. If only you had been a bit more patient, child."

"I'm so sorry," Annie said, hiding her face behind her hands.

"It was foolish, yes," Patrick Henry said. "But good came out of it," he added, his eyes twinkling.

"How?"

"I was beginning to think I was expendable at home."

"What's that?" Annie asked.

"Not needed or necessary," her father replied with a stern expression.

"Oh Father, that's not true," Annie said.

"I know that now, but I had been thinking it. Is Scotchtown being tended to?"

Annie nodded.

"Are you eating meals regularly?"

Again, Annie nodded.

"Doing your schoolwork? Getting new clothes? Going to church?"

Annie looked embarrassed.

"Well then, you see, I figured I wasn't needed," her father said with a regretful sigh. "But now I know better. Come, Annie. We need to say good-bye to these good people and go home."

As they rode back to Scotchtown, Annie listened to army stories. Patrick Henry described the tents set up in rows behind the College of William and Mary and the men—farmers mostly—learning to drill for the first time. But the worst of it was the boredom. For months the army did nothing but drill as they received battle reports from Massachusetts. "Army life is one thing for General Washington," her father said. "It's quite another thing for those of us here in Virginia. And for your poor old father, military life was nothing but training. I never met the enemy, never engaged the British, and now I've been relieved of my command."

When he said that, Annie's eyes flashed. "What happened?"

"The Continental Congress reorganized the armies. There are no more independent Virginia regiments. Maybe it is not my calling to be a general."

Annie pondered this news. "Does that mean you'll be home more?" she asked finally.

"Yes, unless God has some other purpose for me."

"Won't you miss being a leader?" Annie wondered.

"I love Scotchtown," he answered. "My heart is never so happy as when I'm home, under my own fig tree, tending my own land, and in the company of my own family."

They rode together in silence, then Patrick Henry said, "You know, Annie, war is inevitable. The king will not swallow his pride and let us go easily. And it is too late for us to change our minds. We have grown used to making our laws, worshipping our God, leading our lives without interference from the king. He wants to make us a little London, but our ancestors risked their lives to escape that corruption and build a better country here. They came for liberty. Do you understand?"

There was an urgency in Patrick Henry's speech, a passion that Annie recognized, which both excited and repelled her.

"The thought of war scares me, Father," she admitted. "Last year it seemed like an adventure, but now it seems too close."

"Annie," he said, "I wish we didn't have to make these choices. But we know now that keeping our liberty is hard work. It takes diligence and sacrifice. The Henrys have had our share of sacrifice, and God may call us to sacrifice even more."

Finally, Scotchtown came into view. They walked their horses around the house and tied them to a post. Together they walked to Sarah Henry's grave.

"You remind me so much of your mother," Patrick Henry said. Annie nodded, her eyes filling with tears, and he drew her close. "I miss her. And yesterday, when I wondered what had happened to you, the thought that you were in danger was almost more than I could bear. But I have learned that God is able to comfort us in our trouble. Have you learned that, Annie?"

Annie shrugged. She had worked so hard to be strong and brave. She had done so many foolish things. Now she was just confused.

Annie looked up and saw her father watching her, a

sad expression on his face. She longed to comfort him, but the words stuck in her throat. Instead, she fixed her eyes on a cluster of boulders near the grave.

She could feel the weight of her father's arm on her shoulder. She heard the gentle tones of his voice as he said, "The only thing that has sustained me throughout this year is the knowledge that God, the creator and sustainer of all things, knows me and cares for me. What a comfort to know that although He knows my sin, my pride, and my anger, he is still my friend and my redeemer."

There was a struggle inside Annie. Part of her wanted to throw herself on her father's shoulder and weep until there were no more tears. But at the same time, Annie wanted to pull away. She wanted to say, "I'm fine. Do we have to talk about this?"

For minutes they sat on the bench, neither one speaking. Then her father told her stories about her mother, most of them stories Annie had never heard. As he talked, Annie's own memory conjured up images, long suppressed, of Sarah Henry before she was ill. She fought to hold back the tears, but that only made her throat ache, and the tears came anyway. She cried on her father's shoulder until she couldn't cry anymore.

When the tears stopped, Annie rubbed her eyes. Her father said, "You can't deal with problems by pretending they aren't there, Annie. Take them to God, because He is your only comfort in life and death."

Annie felt tired, so when her father said he had to go to work, she just nodded and watched him walk back toward the house. Then she prayed.

That night Annie understood for the first time the story of the Prodigal Son. Instead of scolding, she received hugs. That evening, after a feast, when the remains of a half-carved roast and a small ham sat on the table, Patrick Henry looked around at his family.

"I heard an interesting tale as I rode home this trip," he began. "It was about a family hiding a terrible secret. Something about an intruder and a death."

As Patrick Henry spoke, he looked deliberately from one to another. Annie squirmed uncomfortably under her father's stare, but she didn't speak.

At the other end of the table, John Fontaine cleared his throat. Annie saw Patsy squeeze his hand and nod encouragingly.

"Father," he said, "you have heard correctly. We did have trouble a while back, but it seemed at the time the best part of wisdom to keep the knowledge from you. I thought that the news would distract you from your other duties, but I was wrong. Please forgive me."

"Thank you," he answered. "There is no duty more precious to me than the duty to care for my family. If by my absence I've conveyed something else, then please forgive me." Then, breaking the somber mood, he pulled out his fiddle. "Let not our hearts be troubled. This is a joyous night. We are all together, and tomorrow we'll have all the time in the world to talk."

THE BIRTH OF LIBERTY

IT WAS MAY, A YEAR AFTER THE GUNPOWDER INCIDENT. Annie was nearly twelve. Early one morning she walked down to the barn to go riding. There she found John in a panic. Joseph, the slave who tended the horses, had taken the wagon into town. Marie, the gentle saddle horse that had belonged to Mrs. Henry, had been in labor all night and was about to give birth. She lay heavily on her side, her belly bulging with foal. Tiredly, she picked up her sweat-soaked head and strained before dropping it once again to the straw-covered ground.

"What's wrong?" Annie asked. Even her hushed voice seemed too loud.

"The foal is in a breech position," John said. "Feet first, and the cord is wrapped. They'll both die if the foal doesn't turn." John crouched by the horse's head, sponging her off with a warm wet rag. "Come on, girl," he whispered to the horse. "Come on, girl."

With every contraction, the foal was thrust more firmly into its deadly position. All that was visible were the tips of the foal's hooves struggling without success to be free.

Annie felt herself cheering on the mother. "You can do it," she whispered. But the horse had no strength. The mare groaned, a shudder wracking her body before she fell still. John knelt over the animal, listened for a heart beat, then rose wearily to his feet and said, "I'm afraid she's gone. She just plumb gave up."

Annie started to cry, but then she asked, "Isn't there a way to save the baby?"

John, suddenly energetic again, said, "We could try." After a moment's hesitation, he looked at Annie, saying sharply, "Get a knife, a sharp one."

Annie quickly came back with the knife. Then she watched, unable to look away, as John sliced open the mare's belly and removed the still-breathing foal.

Annie watched as John moved swiftly to remove the bloody mucous from the foal's nose and mouth. He looked up, a bleak expression on his face. "He's not breathing."

But Annie didn't want to give up. "Keep rubbing," she urged him, grabbing a rag and rubbing the back and legs of the colt. Tears streamed from her eyes until she could not see, and yet the two continued to labor over the colt. Then Annie felt a shudder. She wiped her eyes and saw the colt's chest heave, his head shake, and then he came to life, struggling to stand on his spindly legs.

"Yes!" Annie cheered softly. John rose wearily to his feet, wiped his bloody hands with a rag, and grinned at Annie. "We did it," he said. "We really did it."

Together, they watched the colt take his first tentative steps. He looked like brown velvet with white boots and a white blaze marking on his head.

"If only Father could see you now," Annie said proudly to her brother.

John blushed. Then he looked at the dead mare. "Let's cover her up," he said. They found an old cloth in the barn and placed it over the mare. They then turned their attention to the colt.

"How will we feed him?" she asked.

"We'll have to bottle feed him," John said. "Unless we can find a mare who will adopt him." His face brightened. "I think the Thackers just lost a foal. Maybe their mare would do. I'll go ask Andrew after we fix up a bottle."

"How will we make a bottle?" his sister asked.

"You get a bottle from the kitchen. A tall narrow one," he added. "I'll see if I can't find a piece of leather to make a nipple."

Annie brought back the bottle, which they filled with fresh milk. They then took the piece of leather, tied it to the bottle, and poked a hole in the end. Annie held the make-shift bottle up to the foal. Clumsily the colt nudged the bottle, unable to grasp the nipple in his mouth. As he butted the bottle with frustration, it wiggled back and forth, always just out of reach. Annie wanted to give up, until she remembered what she had learned about milking cows: You can't blame the cow if the milker is clumsy.

Her brother frowned. "Annie, you must hold the bottle still. Put it between your body and your arm. Like this," he said while demonstrating. "Then it won't move on the colt."

Annie tried again, wedging the bottle against her body with her elbow, the nipple jutting forward. Gently, John nudged the colt forward, guiding his head until the colt, smelling the milk, grabbed the bottle in his mouth. Annie felt a tug, but she held on tight. The colt played with the leather nipple for a minute until he got the hang of it, then he drank thirstily.

"He's drinking," Annie smiled. "He's really drinking."

"That's fine," John nodded. "You're doing real fine, Annie. Do you think you can do this several times today until I get back from Andrew's with the mare. That means you must stay right here for the colt," he said, fixing a serious glance on her.

Without hesitation, Annie nodded. "I can do it," she promised.

"Let's move the colt," he said, nodding towards the

dead mare. "We'll put her at the other end of the barn." Annie led the way, using the milk bottle to encourage the still wobbly colt forward.

When the colt had finished the bottle, John took it from his sister. "You must wash the bottle before using it again or else the sour milk will make the colt sick."

Annie nodded solemnly. When he had gone, she settled herself on the hay near the colt. "You'll need a name," Annie said to him. "It could be something like Brownie or Butterscotch. But those names are so ordinary. You need something special." For the moment, though, Annie couldn't think of anything.

It was past noon when Andrew finally came with the mare. Annie had nursed the colt three times and was tired, but she had not left. Andrew spoke softly to his horse, rubbing her chestnut mane with his one hand while he tightly held the reins in the other. He urged the mare over to the colt, and Annie gave the foal a push toward the mare.

For a minute the two horses sniffed each other curiously. Then the foal smelled the mare's milk and began nuzzling until he grabbed onto a teat and began to nurse noisily and hungrily. Annie grinned, and Andrew, seeing that the mare had adopted the colt, let go of the reins.

"They'll be fine together," he said as they walked from the barn. Annie nodded. For a minute they were both silent, then the boy let out a whoop.

"What's that for?" Annie asked, staring at her friend. "You look like the cat who swallowed the canary."

The boy had a pleased expression on his face and a look of pent-up excitement. He didn't answer but kept looking at Annie as if to say, "I know something you don't know."

"Come on, Andrew," the girl urged, "Tell me. What's going on?"

"Race you to the house," he said. "If you win, I tell you. If you don't, you'll have to hear the news some other way."

Annie took off running as soon as she heard the word "race." She could hear Andrew's heavy step right behind her, but she kept running, swinging her arm to the right to keep Andrew from passing.

She reached the back stairs of the house a half step ahead of him and sat down with a plop, saying, "Now tell me."

He sat next to her, breathing heavily and laughing. "You cheated. Tried to trip me with those big skirts of yours."

Between breaths, Annie said, "I have to run with them. All you have to do is run around them. Now tell me."

"The reason I was so late getting the mare over was that Pa had me go into Hanover to pick up something at the tavern."

"And that's the news?"

"No, silly. The news is what I heard when I was there."

"So what was it?"

"You are kind of impatient, Annie. Don't you know that patience is a virtue."

Annie glared at Andrew, then burst into laughter. "Okay. You tell me when you are good and ready. I have all the patience in the world."

"That's better. Well the news is . . ." Andrew spoke softly until he came to the punchline. "VIRGINIA HAS DECLARED HER INDEPENDENCE FROM ENGLAND."

Annie's eyes grew wide. "Are you serious? Is this true?"

"Yes, it is true. And there's more."

"What?"

"Your pa is the new governor—governor of the independent colony of Virginia."

Annie gave Andrew a hard stare. "My father. Governor?"

"Yep," her friend answered with a grin. "Patrick Henry, governor of Virginia. And in a few weeks the Continental Congress will do the same. You'll see. They'll write a Declaration of Independence, and then we'll be free."

Looking about at the home she loved, its white walls standing in gleaming contrast to the green fields all around, Annie shook her head. "We won't be free," she said. "But our fight for freedom will have begun."

Annie thought about these changes with mixed feelings. Patrick Henry would be distracted from his family once again, but the job had to be done. Patsy now had a baby, Andrew had made a field, John had birthed a foal, and she was growing up too.

Then shaking off the serious thoughts she smiled. "I now know the name for the colt . . . Father said we would see the birth of liberty, and I guess we just did. Liberty. That will be his name."

5/r

DATE DUE

NOV 12 1988		NOV 20 1988	

D1019973

VICTORIAN OLYMPUS

THE GARDEN OF THE HESPERIDES
by Lord Leighton, P.R.A.

VICTORIAN OLYMPUS

by
WILLIAM GAUNT

JONATHAN CAPE
THIRTY BEDFORD SQUARE
LONDON

VICTORIA COLLEGE
LIBRARY
VICTORIA, B. C.

FIRST PUBLISHED 1952

Dewey Classification 759.2081

PRINTED IN GREAT BRITAIN BY
WESTERN PRINTING SERVICES LTD., BRISTOL
BOUND BY A. W. BAIN & CO. LTD., LONDON

CONTENTS

ILLUSTRATIONS

SOURCES AND ACKNOWLEDGEMENTS

THE standard life of Lord Leighton is that by Mrs. Russell Barrington. *Lord Leighton of Stretton*, P.R.A., in the Makers of British Art series, by Edgcumbe Staley, and *Frederic Leighton* by Alice Corkran are also informative. Biographical and critical studies and memoirs of other artists of the period include *George Frederick Watts* by M. S. Watts; *Sir Edward Poynter* by Cosmo Monkhouse (*Art Annual*, 1897), the only complete biographical outline, however, being the article in the *Dictionary of National Biography*; *L. Alma-Tadema* by H. Zimmern (1886), also *Sir Lawrence Alma-Tadema*, O.M., R.A., by Percy Cross Standing; *Albert Moore, His Life and Works*, by Alfred Lys Baldry; *The Richmond Papers* by A. M. W. Stirling; *Giovanni Costa, His Life, Work and Times*, by Olivia Rossetti Agresti; *Marcus Stone* by A. L. Baldry; *Luke Fildes* by D. Croal Thomson; *Briton Rivière* by W. Armstrong; *Thomas Armstrong*, C.B., *a Memoir*; *Frederick Walker* by Claude Phillips; *William de Morgan and his Wife* by A. M. W. Stirling; *The Herkomers* by Sir Hubert von Herkomer; *The Reminiscences of Frederick Goodall*, R.A.; and *An Artist's Reminiscences* by Walter Crane. The preface by Mrs. Richmond Ritchie to *A Week in a French Country House* gives reminiscences of Adelaide Sartoris; *From Friend to Friend* by the same author, also. *Memories* by Lord Redesdale has some interesting sidelights on Leighton; so too *The Notebooks of Henry James*, edited by F. O. Matthiesen and Kenneth B. Murdock. *Time Was* by W. Graham Robertson has interesting memories of Albert Moore. On relevant aspects of architecture and design, *Fifty Years of Public Work* (the autobiography of Sir Henry Cole, K.C.B.), *Richard Norman Shaw*, R.A., by Sir Reginald Blom-

7

field, R.A.; and *The Conscious Stone* (the Life of Edward William Godwin) by Dudley Harbron have matter of interest.

Lord Elgin and his Collection by A. H. Smith, M.A., F.S.A., deals fully with the removal of the Parthenon sculptures. *The Autobiography and Journals* of Benjamin Robert Haydon and *Nollekens and his Times* by J. T. Smith are useful in contemporary comment. *The History of Modern Painting* by Richard Muther is valuable as a general survey of nineteenth-century art; for late nineteenth-century art in Britain, *The English School of Painting* by Ernest Chesneau (English translation with introduction by Ruskin) and *La Peinture Anglaise Contemporaine 1840–1894* by Robert de la Sizeranne. *The Royal Academy* by Sir Walter Lamb is also useful.

The author is indebted to Sir Hugh Poynter, Lady Markham Knel, Mrs. G. L. Thirkell, Mr. C. H. Gibbs-Smith of the Victoria and Albert Museum, Mr. C. H. M. Gould of the National Gallery, and Mr. Humphrey Brooke for their help or suggestions on various points; also to the Directors of the Guildhall Art Gallery, the City Art Galleries of Manchester, Sheffield, Leeds, and Burnley, and of the Lady Lever Art Gallery, Port Sunlight, for valuable information. He would also like to thank Mr. H. G. Massey, Chief Librarian of Kensington, for facilities accorded at Leighton House.

VICTORIAN OLYMPUS

HOW THE GODS CAME TO BRITAIN

Two thousand and nearly four hundred years ago a supreme masterpiece was planned—the temple of Athena Parthenos on the citadel rock, the Acropolis of ancient Athens.

The noble Pericles, chief magistrate of the city, great alike in war and peace, pupil of renowned philosophers, whose words were as thunder and lightning, who was called, like Zeus himself, Olympian, commanded that it should stand on the site of that former temple of Athena which the invading Persians had destroyed.

Ictinos, renowned also for his temple of Apollo at Phigaleia, was the chosen architect. Pheidias, distinguished even above the great Polycleitos as the sculptor of gods rather than of men, rose to the height of his powers in its adornment.

Of that statue he made of the Athenians' patron goddess, daughter of Zeus, the many-named Athena, who is sometimes called Minerva, who was known as Parthenos because of her virginity, there remains only a small copy—or 'souvenir'—but the original towered, superb and immense in the temple interior, forty feet, plated in ivory and gold. The more than human composure of the features, the eyes of lapis and the golden hair of the proud being, goddess of war who yet created the olive, symbol of peace, who held in one hand the image of Victory and rested the other on a mighty shield, carved with scenes of battle against giants and Amazons, filled beholders with awe.

Many a sculptor whose name is unknown worked with Pheidias and to his plans, but it seemed that the spirit of genius was upon them and in every detail was a wonderful beauty. Beautiful were the pediments, west and east, which celebrated the birth of Athena, sprung full-grown from the brain of Zeus, and her contests with the sea-god, Poseidon. Beautiful was the frieze which showed the Greeks assembled to do honour to their patron; on which the Panathenaic procession moved in the jubilance of high holiday, the gods looking on, the maidens swaying to the sound of flutes, the young athletes mounted on horses and riding bareback, their garments fluttering in graceful folds, as if the sweet breath of Zephyrus rippled the marble.

Complete four hundred and thirty-three years before the birth of Christ, the Parthenon was a wonder of the world. Its serenity was undisturbed by change in the affairs of men. Conquerors, solemn, hard-featured Romans, came in due time to admire and set down on their tablets statistical description. The centuries drifted into disorder but the Pentelic marble was still perfect as it had ever been. It survived the plundering Goths. It was converted from a pagan temple into a Latin church in the drowsy days of the Byzantine Empire (staggering through time in its interminable decay), yet suffered no hurt from religious zeal. There came the Turks, advancing westwards after they had taken Constantinople in A.D. 1453. They crushed the Greeks but spared the temple, being so indifferent to the beauty of architecture and sculpture that they did not take trouble to destroy it. Perfect still, in the seventeenth century of the Christian era, the Parthenon gleamed in the Mediterranean sun, though the bright red and blue with which it had been painted had long worn away and the figure of ivory and gold had vanished from the sanctuary to be replaced by the tubs of gunpowder which the Turks stored there. And then, in 1687, came calamity at last. That which nor the gnawing tooth of time; nor that earthquake of the fourth century which shattered one hundred and fifty cities of Greece and Asia; nor the savagery of the Goth, the superstition of the Frank, the rage of the Turk; could previously contrive—the ruin of the exquisite fabric—was caused by one unlucky shot from a Venetian engine of war.

The poet of ancient Greece would have said that the sea-god

Poseidon, whose feud with the daughter of Zeus had no end, whispered in the ear of the Venetian gunner and guided the cannon ball he aimed. It may well be that the Venetians declaimed against the atrocious act of the Turks, who, in using the temple as a powder magazine, had clearly invited its destruction; while the Turks must certainly have been angry at the loss of much valuable explosive. The fact was the same, that after two thousand years the glory had abruptly been dimmed.

For a century the Acropolis lay waste. The defenders of Western civilization had gained a temporary victory and stayed in Athens some time, but they were too busy fighting the Turks to think of restoring the city they had occupied; and soon the Turks were back again, more cruel to the Greeks than before and just as indifferent to the splendour of their past.

Athens was now a small and squalid town, enclosed by a ten-foot wall put up by the Turks. Straggling allotments stretched between the wall and the Acropolis. The stones of the Parthenon lay where they had fallen or else were ground into dust for use as mortar. A ramshackle mosque occupied part of its floor space. Around it was a huddle of mud huts and military debris of various kinds. Such was the regrettable scene which, in the year 1800, met the disapproving eye of a British visitor to Athens, Thomas Bruce, the seventh Earl of Elgin.

The Earl, a man of thirty-four, was a diplomat of already considerable experience. His diplomatic career had taken him from Vienna to Brussels, from Brussels to Berlin, had transferred him in 1799 to Constantinople as envoy to the Sublime Porte, the central office of Ottoman rule: but his heart was in classical antiquity and he was visiting the Turkish province of Greece as antiquarian rather than as ambassador.

Elgin was a man of culture typical of his age and country. An enlightened fashion had of late directed the attention of British amateurs to Athens even more than to Rome. Greece had been the mistress of the arts. Greece, too, was the ancient home of freedom and democracy and thus invited the sympathy and interest of a democratic island. Yet, less easy of access than those of Rome and

Italy, its treasures were imperfectly known and knowledge the more eagerly sought.

Between the age of Pericles and the age of George III the Society of Dilettanti constructed its own amateur bridge. Its periwigged connoisseurs surrounded themselves with classical heads and torsos, with Roman copies of lost Greek originals. They paid the expenses of architects and draughtsmen to make measured studies of buildings and sculpture on the actual site. They sent out, for this purpose, James (subsequently known as 'Athenian') Stuart, with a fellow architect, Nicholas Revett, and in 1762 the first volume of their *Antiquities of Athens* gave a model for further serious research. In the prevailing atmosphere of learned enthusiasm, Elgin determined to turn his appointment to the service of art.

It was quite usual for a nobleman to take an artist with him on his travels abroad. Elgin thought of employing the brilliant young painter, J. M. W. Turner (which would have been a service to art, though not, perhaps, to archaeology), but Turner wanted too much money, and indeed, as serious research was in question, the aid of a painter, however accomplished, was not in itself enough. The architect, Thomas Harrison, had pointed out to Elgin that casts from the sculptures were obviously more useful than drawings. The logic of the enterprise demanded a technical staff, and in 1800 the Earl was not only the head of an embassy but the leader of an expedition.

It consisted of a chief of staff, an Italian topographer, Giovanni Battista Lusieri, who was picked up in Sicily, a man conscientious and persevering in art and conduct. Under him, a figure artist was needed, and one Feodor Iwanowitch, a 'Tartar and native of Astracan', who became known as 'Lord Elgin's Kalmuck', was chosen in Rome. Rome also furnished two architects, Vincenzo Balestra, 'an extremely deformed hunchback', a pupil of his, Sebastian Ittar, and two *formatori* or moulders of casts, Bernardino Ledus and Vincenzo Rosati. In addition, the embassy personnel was of an antiquarian mind. There was young William Richard Hamilton, Elgin's private secretary (and an Harrovian as he had been), who threw himself wholeheartedly into the business. No less keen was the embassy chaplain, Dr. Philip Hunt.

Once the ball was set rolling it was pushed vigorously forward. By degrees an idea took shape. How much more satisfactory it would be to remove a few sculptures rather than to rest content with casts or drawings. To a scholar like Dr. Hunt, who dreamed of poring at leisure over certain stones bearing inscriptions, this was the real consummation of their effort. It was Hunt who obtained a 'strong firman', an order addressed to the Voivode, or governor of Athens, and the Disdar or commandant of the citadel, designed to protect the expedition from too much extortion or capricious hindrance. It expressly permitted them to 'take away any pieces of stone with old inscriptions or figures thereon'. Possibly the indulgence was due to the political circumstance of the moment. Napoleon had occupied Egypt and consequently the Sublime Porte was, for the time being, on the side of Great Britain and Russia against him. The British envoy was a person to be indulged, and if those few old stones (the *qualche pezzi di pietra* of the firman in its Italian version) from the 'Temple of the Idols', carved in some disgusting infidel fashion, could win British favour, why then the Sublime Porte was happy to part with them to the Christian dogs.

Elgin and his company were inclined to place a liberal interpretation on the permit. With that miserable scene on the Acropolis in mind who could say what new damage and disaster war and neglect might not bring about: more statues pounded into mortar by the Turks; more noses and fingers chipped off and carried away by irresponsible travellers; worse still, the rival spoliation by French connoisseurs. You might say that of right the Parthenon belonged to the Greeks, but then the Greeks belonged to the Turks. Did not this supreme masterpiece belong to civilization? And where was civilization if not in the secure centre of London?

The result was that they began to cram into packing-cases all of the Parthenon which could be transported—the mutilated sculptures of the pediments, the metopes, the great inner frieze, a caryatid from the neighbouring temple, the Erechtheion (of which Dr. Hunt was especially fond). A sort of frenzy seized on the party. They all worked like blacks.

There is no need to tell here of the many adventures and mishaps of the next few years. The epic story is related in detail in the *Journal of Hellenic Studies*, vol. xxxvi, 1916. Two transport ships, loaded with precious marble, were wrecked and salvaged with difficulty. During the brief truce of Amiens, Elgin visited Paris, and, as war broke out again in 1803, was there arrested, spending three years quietly, perhaps not unhappily, as a prisoner at Pau in the Basses-Pyrénées. Meanwhile his agents went steadily on. Money was paid out freely on his behalf (sums which made Turner's original demands seem absurdly small). Finally the wonderful works of art were conveyed to the shores of Albion by Nelson's men-o'-war, together with other glories of ancient Greece which the cultivated zeal of Count de Choiseul-Gouffier, former French ambassador to the Porte, had prompted him to bear off to France, and which had been rescued from his predatory hands by British tars. Thus it was that the gods came to Britain, and many there were, and of them many artists, to applaud their coming.

They were removed from Plymouth to the Earl of Elgin's house in Park Lane, and from 1807 when they were there first on view their fame spread far and wide. The merit of the Parthenon sculptures was to begin with a matter of some doubt, but John Flaxman, the 'Yorkshire Pheidias', recognized their quality at once. His lordship's museum was better than 'anything that Paris can boast', and to a young painter, Benjamin Robert Haydon, who came soon after, it was a revelation.

What a Periclean Greek would have made of Benjamin Robert Haydon it is hard to say. No one could less conform to the classic precept of 'nothing too much'. He was excessive in all things, excessive in ambition, excessive in anger, excessive in devotion—a volcano of feelings, simmering ominously, furiously erupting. He was then engaged in an agonizing duel with a canvas depicting the death of L. Sicinius Dentatus, a subject 'historical' in that he got it from the *Roman History* of Hooke, who had taken it from Livy. One day as he was fretfully painting in the figure of the ambushed warrior and despairingly rubbing it out again his young Scots friend, David Wilkie, called.

Wilkie was a Fifeshire lad, with no leanings like Haydon towards 'high art'. He had won success at the Royal Academy of 1806 with his *Village Politicians* and was content to follow this vein of homely sentiment; but he had an order to view 'the Elgin Marbles', as the sculptures of the Parthenon were now called in tribute to their protector, and, indifferently, not knowing what he was going to see, Haydon went with him. He was struck, as if by a thunderbolt.

In a 'damp, dirty penthouse' the marbles were ranged round. Haydon's heart thumped. He saw first a wonderful feminine wrist, in which were visible the radius and the ulna; the elbow, with 'the outer condyle visibly affecting the shape . . . the arm in repose and the soft parts in relaxation'. And then the Theseus—'every form . . . altered by action or repose', one side stretched, the other compressed 'with the belly flat because the bowels fell into the pelvis as he sat'. The Ilissus, with the belly protruding, from the figure lying on its side. The 'fighting metope' with the muscle under one armpit shown in 'that instantaneous action of darting out'. Here was the ideal combined with a perfect knowledge of nature. Haydon thanked God he was 'able to understand'. A 'divine truth' had 'blazed' in his mind and all the way home he excitedly chattered to the alarm of Wilkie, who tried to soothe him. Wilkie was insensitive to classic beauty. He could not read Pope's *Homer* 'because of its evident prejudice in favour of the Greeks', and was to earn Haydon's contempt by talking of 'a capital subject' for a picture as he stood before the Marbles—the subject being some boys playing with a garden engine, laughing and squirting water at each other—to Haydon, an idea which was low and common as could be.

Haydon now became a fiery propagandist for the Parthenon. Describing the Marbles to Henry Fuseli, the Keeper of the Royal Academy, he excited in him something of his own ardour. They positively ran to Park Lane. The journey itself was epic. They fumed as they were held up by a coal-cart drawn by eight horses, blocking the Strand. Again the way was stopped—by a flock of sheep—Fuseli darted this way and that through the flock 'swearing like a little fury', said Haydon. At last the goal was reached and Fuseli was convinced. He exclaimed, in the accent of Zürich, 'By Gode! De Greeks were godes! de Greeks were godes!'

Permission to draw from the Marbles was not easy to get, but Haydon managed it through the influence of his patron, Lord Mulgrave. He drew, in his excessive fashion, ten, fourteen, fifteen hours at a time—until midnight, holding a candle in the damp penthouse close to the serene and godlike figures.

In due course he was joined by the President of the Royal Academy, old Benjamin West, not too well pleased apparently to find Haydon already installed. 'Hah, hah! Mr. Haydon, you are admitted, are you?' said West. 'I hope you and I can keep a secret.' Then, to Haydon's horror, he sat down before a large canvas and began making fancy compositions from Greek history, introducing —and restoring to completeness—the statuary of the pediment ('I have ventured', West explained to the Earl of Elgin, 'to unite figures of my own invention with those of Pheidias'). Later, in 1808, Sir Thomas Lawrence also came to admire and to copy: and until after the battle of Waterloo the penthouse in Park Lane was a place of artists' pilgrimage.

Though he declined to act as curator, Haydon haunted the spot. He had, wrote Keats, in his sonnet to Haydon of 1817, accompanied by a sonnet on the Marbles, 'beheld the Hesperian shrine of their star in the East and gone to worship them'. He got leave to 'mould some of the Elgin feet'. He had pupils who made copies, and a set of these was ordered by Goethe. After the visit of the Grand Duke Nicholas, he presented a number of casts to the Imperial Academy of St. Petersburg. When Antonio Canova, famous sculptor in the antique style, was sent in 1815 to recover works of art taken by Napoleon from Italy he visited London, and Haydon met him. Canova, he related in triumph, said that the Marbles 'would produce a great change in art'. 'It's Haydon's damned French', observed Wilkie, 'that makes him think he said so.'

There were some dissenting voices in the chorus of praise. Artists of repute might approve. The group known as 'the Fates' might so 'rivet and agitate' the feelings of Mrs. Siddons, 'the pride of theatrical representation', as actually to draw tears from her eyes; but there was criticism too. Firstly, there was the ethical question involved. Had Lord Elgin any right to the Marbles? The young Lord Byron,

Greek in patriotism as in profile, fresh from Grecian travels, during which, like the ancient Leander, he had swum the Hellespont, indignantly denied the right. In *The Curse of Minerva* (1811) he attacked Elgin as a 'spoiler worse than Turk or Goth', with all the gift of vituperation which he had already shown in *English Bards and Scotch Reviewers*:

> Meanwhile the flattering, feeble dotard West,
> Europe's worst dauber and poor Britain's best,
> With palsied hand shall turn each model o'er
> And own himself an infant of fourscore.
> Be all the bruisers cull'd from all St. Giles
> That art and nature may compare their styles,
> While brawny brutes in stupid wonder stare
> And marvel at his Lordship's stone shop there.
> Round the throng's gate shall sauntering coxcombs creep
> To lounge and lucubrate and prate and peep,
> While many a languid maid with longing sigh
> On giant statues casts the curious eye.

Byron accused the object of his satire (which was withdrawn and not published until after his death) of having made 'the state receiver of his pilfered prey'. Yet it seemed reasonable that, if the masterpieces were to be in Britain, they should be public property, and the negotiations, which began in 1811, were less concerned with the poet's imputation than with the value of the objects to be bought. The Earl of Elgin claimed to have spent more than £70,000 on the business of removal. The State proceeded to that difficult equation of aesthetic and monetary values by which an acquisitive society makes its appraisal of art. What was the worth of the gods and godlike beings in pounds and pence? Were they as valuable as the works which hitherto had been considered the supreme triumphs of the ancient world, the Laocoön or the Belvedere Apollo of the Vatican?

On this point too there was criticism. Richard Payne Knight of the Society of Dilettanti was perhaps envious, and certainly contemptuous, of Elgin's efforts. 'You have lost your labour, my Lord Elgin. Your marbles are overrated. They are not Greek, they are Roman of the time of Hadrian.' This pronouncement annoyed

Haydon very much indeed and he made a violent onslaught on Payne Knight in a letter to Leigh Hunt's *Examiner*.

Yet on the whole the artists and connoisseurs of early nineteenth-century Britain, invited by a Committee of the House of Commons to give their opinion on the merits of Pheidias, were in his favour. Bow-legged, ugly, miserly little Mr. Nollekens, restorer of antique fragments by the addition of limbs which he stained with tobacco-juice to give the appearance of age—whose knowing leer has been immortalized by Rowlandson—said the Marbles were 'the finest things that ever came into this country'. The Panathenaic Procession was 'in the first class of the art'. He was not sure of their date. He admitted he had never been to Greece, though he had 'seen all the fine things to be seen at Rome'. He could not put a value on them, but he was sure of their quality and further remarked that 'fine things are not to be got every day'. John Flaxman, the sculptor Francis Chantrey, Sir Thomas Lawrence, famous alike as portrait-painter and connoisseur, the lesser Academicians, Richard Westma-cott and Charles Rossi, all expressed the opinion that these sculptures were in the first class of art, refusing at the same time, to the puzzlement of the Committee, to put a price on them. The aged president of the Royal Academy, Benjamin West, of whose moderate abilities Byron spoke so unkindly, submitted (being unable because of his years and ill health to attend in person) a written statement in which he gave preference to the 'Theseus' and the 'Ilissus' as compared with the Belvedere Apollo or the Laocoön because they were not 'systematic'—by which he seems to have meant 'conventional'—but were supreme 'in truth and intellectual power'.

Richard Payne Knight, though still reluctant to praise, became cautious in disparagement. He assigned the collection 'to the second rank', though he agreed that the frieze was in the first class of low relief—what there was left of it: it was very much mutilated, he added. His view that the sculptures of the pediment were of the time of Hadrian was, it appeared in cross-examination, taken from a seventeenth-century antiquary. He had worked out a price list with care, and not, it is to be hoped, with any prejudice against the

Earl of Elgin, and arrived at the figure of £25,000. This was his estimate of the Marbles' value as tending to form 'a national school for art'. 'They would not sell as furniture; they would produce nothing at all.'

William Wilkins, architect, was also lukewarm. Some of the sculptures he thought were 'very middling'. Parts of the frieze were even 'very indifferent indeed'. William Wilkins, sad to say, detected in the work of Pheidias a 'mediocrity of style'.

The evidence was conclusive, despite these minority carpings; nor did the Committee dispute Elgin's right to make off with the Marbles. They were disposed to agree that it was a rescue: that Elgin had not taken advantage of his position as ambassador but had acted as any private individual reasonably might, given the possession of sufficient wealth and idealism. This view was generally held. In a parliamentary debate on the Committee's report, Mr. Croker observed that to send the Marbles back to the Turks 'would be awarding those admirable works the doom of destruction'. Both Greeks and Turks had helped to remove them and John Cam Hobhouse, friend and fellow traveller of Byron, related in the account of his Grecian journey that Athenian porters claimed to have heard the enchanted spirits of the sculptures crying out in pity for their fellow spirits still in bondage on the Acropolis. However one might interpret the cry of a caryatid for her mates, it could be argued at least that the Greeks did not object to their removal.

So the Elgin Marbles were bought for the nation in 1816 at about half of the Earl's estimated expenditure and transported to the British Museum at a cost of £798, the Earl being consoled for monetary loss by appointment as Museum Trustee.

The report of the Committee had given several judicious observations on the importance of art, in comparison with which 'the memory and fame of extended empires and of mighty conquerors' are so transient. 'No country can be better adapted than our own to afford an honourable asylum to these monuments of the school of *Phidias* and of the administration of *Pericles*; where secure from further injury and degradation, they may receive that admiration and homage to which they are entitled and serve, in return, as models and examples to those, who by knowing how to revere and appreciate them, may learn first to imitate, and ultimately to rival them.'

Admiration and homage were prompt to come, not only from art but from fashion and athletics. The Marbles prolonged a classic vogue, already evident in the Greek simplicity of women's clothes. In 1814 was advertised 'Ross's newly invented Greek volute headdress from the true marble models brought into this country from the Acropolis at Athens'. Shortly after the Parthenon frieze was placed on public view at the British Museum (if J. T. Smith, Nollekens's biographer, is to be credited) a 'gentlemanly-looking person' was seen to stand rapt before it for an hour. He was accompanied by a number of young men to whom he pointed out the ease and elegance of the seat of the mounted Greeks, without saddle and stirrup as they were. The gentlemanly-looking person was a riding master. The youths with him were members of his academy and he was commending to them the study of ancient horsemanship in order that they might cut a better figure in Hyde Park.

The fame of the Marbles, the awakened interest in Athenian antiquities and eventually the Greeks' own struggle for independence helped towards a classic revival in architecture. Thurs William Inwood in 1819 was inspired by Athens in his design for the new church of St. Pancras in London. He has the curious distinction of being the first British architect to design a Christian church in the form of a Greek temple (or temples, for he utilized two). The steeple was adapted from the Tower of the Winds, though of course surmounted by a cross instead of a triton of bronze. The vestries were supported by caryatids copied from the Temple of Poseidon, surnamed Erechtheus, which stands by the Parthenon. Many a traveller, hurrying to or from the stations of Euston, St. Pancras, or King's Cross, has started in astonishment at the sight of these lugubrious maiden pillars, their classic grace smudged over with London grime.

Two years before Greece was again a nation—in 1830—came the Athenaeum Club designed by Decimus Burton (classic even to his first name). Two of the Club's founder members were among those who gave evidence in favour of the Elgin Marbles—Sir Thomas Lawrence and Francis (by now Sir Francis) Chantrey—and it is easy to understand how a body designed to represent the learned professions and the arts should place itself under the aegis shield of Athens, goddess of the liberal arts, war and wisdom, whose statue, not by Pheidias but by Edward Hodges Baily, the pupil of Flaxman, presided over the building.

If a church and a club, why not also a railway terminus inspired by ancient Greece? To Philip Hardwick, R.A., is due the Great Hall and the Gateway of the old London and North-Western at Euston. The Doric entrance of huge proportions, incorporating blocks of stone which weighed as much as thirteen tons, dates from 1847. In its startling immensity, its magnificent irrelevance to place or purpose, it partners, with a sympathetic unlikeness, the Venetian Gothic of the St. Pancras Station close by.

In painting, the process of imitation and rivalry to which the parliamentary judges of the Elgin Marbles had looked forward flowered at last during the latter half of the nineteenth century in a glow of splendour and success. By diverse routes (of which the masterpieces now in the British Museum were one main road) the classical world made a new appearance in the land of the factory and the steam engine. There came Olympus again—a Victorian Olympus—on the summit of which sit beaming and powerful figures, living in golden houses, girdled by a gleaming world: a godlike race which is still the astonishment of less-aspiring mortals—though it may not escape that envy and that distaste for perfection which mortals too often display. How this race of favoured beings grew and flourished it is the purpose of this history to relate.

OLYMPIANS AT SCHOOL

§ I

'I KNEW that they would at last rouse the art of Europe from its slumber in the darkness.

'I do not say this *now*, when all the world acknowledges it, but I said it then, when *no one would believe me.*'

It was 1854. Eight years previously, Benjamin Robert Haydon, despairing and outraged by neglect, had shot himself. His last ambitious works, *The Banishment of Aristides* and *Nero Playing while Rome was in Flames*, had unfortunately been shown in the same building and at the same time as the dwarf, 'General Tom Thumb'. Only 133 people had been to see the pictures, 120,000 had flocked to view the dwarf. This signal defeat for 'high art' had been more than the painter could bear.

Yet his impassioned voice still resounded. His *Autobiography and Journals*, edited by Tom Taylor, had been published in 1853. From this edition, in 1854, a young student of architecture in Rome was reading aloud to a painter-friend in the latter's studio. The reader was George Aitchison—his friend, Frederic Leighton.

The excited words beat on the tranquil atmosphere. '. . . torture and hope' '. . . a fever of excitement . . .' 'Why, in a succession of ages, has the world again to begin? Why is knowledge ever suffered to ebb?' 'How much we had lost, despite our moral principles, since those beautiful forms were created.'

Leighton went on calmly working. He stood absorbed in front of a large canvas, though not so absorbed that he was unable to listen and take in the stammered, fiery phrases in which Haydon had declared his admiration for the Parthenon and its sculptures, his sense of the injustice of things which made ancient times superior to the new.

Leighton was twenty-four years of age and singularly handsome in appearance. He had a finely cut, aquiline nose, wide-set eyes, a sculptured curl to his lip and fair hair which fell about the temples in curving wings. His dress proclaimed, or rather exquisitely suggested, the artist, for he wore a velvet coat and about his neck was a flowing tie, though they had nothing of the carelessness which might be called Bohemian nor of the ostentation which might betray the amateur or the charlatan. He was, as an artist, exactly right, and if there was any departure from the usual in his attire, there was also a sober suggestion of superlative quality.

This moderate and yet distinctive elegance reflected something of his character. There was nothing of the Byronic youth about him, no wild and smouldering fire in his eye, no sign of restlessness, brooding melancholy or impatience with the world. On the contrary, he was calm and thoughtful, even stately. A well—a perfectly —balanced young man, he considered the problem of Haydon with composure and a deprecation of the extremes to which that unfortunate being had gone.

Poor Haydon! His was a tortured soul, worshipping the classic spirit he did not possess. How much better he would have been, thought Leighton, without his mordant gift of satire and his devouring thirst for ink. How unclassic was his career, embittering enemies and estranging friends, cuddling phantoms and committing the final extravagance of angrily taking his life. These were errors to which Leighton could not imagine himself to be liable. The classics themselves had produced distorted images on the troubled surface of Haydon's mind. He had been, so sadly, an inferior, bewildered and demented in the presence of the superior beings with whom he knew he could never be ranked; whereas Leighton, young though he was, and certainly regarding them with admiration, felt in their presence no embarrassment at all. He could think of Pheidias without self-torment and approach any great master, indeed, with a courteous and well-bred familiarity which his own gifts and the nature of his education had already made mature. If Servius Tullius, king of ancient Rome, had recognized solely the claims of gifts and education in his division of society, he would, had Leighton lived then, surely have placed him among the *classici*, the first order of citizens. In this sense, the young man was formed in classic mould. He had been habituated from his early years to the idea of excellence. He must become familiar with all that was best; must also be so trained and disciplined that by his own efforts he might reach the highest standard of attainment; and this was in accord with the tradition of a distinguished family.

The Leightons were able, one and all. Frederic's grandfather, Sir James Leighton, had been court physician to the Tsar of Russia. Frederic's father, Frederic Septimus Leighton, who followed Sir James in a medical career, foreshadows the ability of his son. He had, for instance, the gift of languages, learnt Russian in six months, and astonished everyone by passing his medical examination in Russian at St. Petersburg, with the highest credit. His flow of conversation was copious and there seemed to be no end to his reading. Part of each day was set aside for the study of Greek and Latin classics, but he never failed to read also the latest reports of scientific and medical discovery. He was a true Victorian, precise and methodical, active and energetic, resolute and serious both in business and recreation. Frederic's mother had the gentler virtues. She loved music, had some talent for drawing and was devoted to her family.

There were three children: two girls, the elder, Alexandra, godchild of the Empress Alexandra of Russia, the younger, Augusta (affectionately known as 'Gussie'); and Frederic, the only surviving son (his younger brother James dying in infancy). As the only son he received much attention, and Dr. Leighton (in this respect also, typically a nineteenth-century man) set himself to form the boy's mind and show his affection by subjecting him to an austere routine.

This routine was the more strictly carried out because Dr. Leighton withdrew from medical practice. After the birth of two daughters in St. Petersburg (Fanny, who died young, and Alexandra) Mrs. Leighton's delicate health made a return to England necessary and so Dr. Leighton did not succeed his father as the Tsar's physician.

The family fortune had grown in Russia: the gossip of the time hinted at some special reward for some not very clearly defined service to the Tsar, though history can say no more than that the Leightons were rich enough to do what they wanted and live where they liked. Back in England, the family made a stay at Scarborough, and in the bracing air of that resort Frederic Leighton in 1830 first drew breath.

From Scarborough they moved to Bath, but Dr. Leighton was not long in practice there. He grew deaf, and the disability which cut him off from his patients turned him increasingly to the world of books and ideas and gave him ample time in which to train his children and in particular his only son. Like the utilitarian philosopher, James Mill, he was both parent and schoolmaster, and as James fostered precocious learning in his son, John Stuart Mill, so did Frederic Septimus in the young Frederic Leighton.

At the age of ten the boy was well grounded in Greek and Latin and knew more of the legends, the poems, and the history of the ancient world than he would have been likely to gain at a school. An untoward event now became the means of making his education still more exemplary and of pouring into the small vessel all the wonders of Europe.

In 1840 Mrs. Leighton had an attack of rheumatic fever and as a result the family again began to travel abroad for the sake of her health. They had never really settled down, and had moved from Bath to London in 1832, living first in Argyll Street and then in Upper Gower Street. They now went to Germany and Switzerland and away from winter to Italy. They visited Berlin, Frankfurt, Dresden, and Munich. They wandered, in affluent nomadism, from one Italian city to another—Milan, Florence, Bologna, Venice, Rome, Naples—and Dr. Leighton did not overlook, as well as the beneficial effects on his wife's constitution, those on his son's mind.

Frederic was introduced to all that was beautiful and interesting in the European capitals—the historic buildings, the great works of art, the varied customs of different peoples. He was taught, in the most natural and effective way, by actual conversation, the living languages of Europe. At the age of twelve he was fluent in French and Italian, in a year or two more in German too. Meanwhile he began to show a strong bent for drawing and painting, and this Dr. Leighton encouraged, without being at first aware of it.

He wanted the boy to be a doctor, for this was the family calling. Therefore he gave him careful instruction in anatomy. He taught him the names of the bones and muscles, described them in action and repose, and insisted that they should be drawn from memory and without mistake. Anatomy was as useful to the student of art as of medicine, and at fourteen Frederic Leighton knew more about the structure of the body than an academy would have taught him.

Dr. Leighton was disappointed when he found that Frederic wished to be an artist. There was so much that was inexact and uncertain about the career, so much that was alien to his scientific mind; yet, if this was to be his son's choice, then, obviously, the best masters must be employed, the most eminent practitioners had to be consulted. The expanding scheme of Frederic's education had already called for special tutors, among them a Roman drawing master, Signor Francesco Meli; but before Dr. Leighton sanctioned art as a main study he took the advice of a then noted sculptor, an American living in Florence, Hiram Powers, sculptor of *The Greek Slave* (and incidentally a Swedenborgian and a spiritualist).

The judgement which Powers gave on the drawings Dr. Leighton brought to him was emphatic.

'Shall I make him a painter?'

'Sir,' said Powers (Americans then had the Johnsonian habit of thus prefacing their remarks), 'you cannot help yourself; nature has made him so already.'

'What can he hope for?'

'Let him aim at the highest. He will be certain to get there.'

Excitedly, Frederic waited for the return of his father, the sound of the carriage wheels crunching on the drive. A smile reassured him. The doctor had accepted the specialist's report and permitted Frederic to go to the Florentine Academy, where he studied under the celebrated professors Bezzuoli and Servolini, upheld by Italians (though posterity has not endorsed their opinion) as the Michelangelo and the Raphael of their day.

Greek, Latin, French, German, Italian, history, the classics, mathematics, painting, sculpture, architecture, and travel, these were the elements of a truly Olympian education. On one of less than Olympian fibre it might have had an overwhelming effect. It might, by its richness, have caused a blank and confused state of mind. Time passed in a whirl of impressions—Roman priests droning Latin verses, German tutors expounding Meierhirsch's *Algebraische Aufgaben*, the journeys—fleeting visions of the Round Pond at Hampstead and the British Museum swiftly merged into and replaced by the sights and scenes of the Continent, of Brussels, Florence, Frankfurt, Paris, and Athens.

As it was, there were many times when Frederic was unwell—he was never completely well—when he became dizzy and had 'blots' before the eyes. Yet with him, the system worked. He was neither cowed nor bewildered by cramming, and the youth who went to the Accademia delle belle Arti was already a paragon. He had good looks, charm, friendliness, and an evident ability to draw. He spoke pure and idiomatic Tuscan and this made his other qualities seem the more agreeable to his fellow students. An account of his leaving Florence in 1846 suggests that gift of being popular which was later so notable among his many talents. As the diligence moved off, the Florentine art students ran behind it shouting, 'Come back! Inglesino! Come back.' Just as some bright immortal might have shone in their midst and then withdrawn into the divine ether, so he left behind a woeful sense of loss.

It was his own wish to leave Florence: not because he did not love the beautiful city on the Arno—it was always to be his favoured resort—but because the Academy of Bezzuoli and Servolini did not satisfy him. He was not convinced that these masters were in fact a Michelangelo and a Raphael—and as his father had insisted always on 'the best' it was natural that he should do so on his own account. At his age he needed some anchorage, less of place than of the mind, some person he could attach himself to in a way both friendly and devoted, a master who would be worthy of his disciple. The quest took him back to Germany and Frankfurt, the master was found in the Nazarene painter, Jacob Eduard von Steinle.

§ 2

It was like going home: was, in fact, going home, for Dr. Leighton had bought and furnished a house at Frankfurt which had thus become the Continental headquarters of the much-travelling family. There was something, too, in the German character which found a response in Frederic's own. The Germans were thorough—and he had been trained to appreciate thoroughness. They were in earnest as he was, precise in all they did, and punctual—a quality which many journeys had already taught him to value. Thorough, earnest, precise, was Steinle, in addition an idealist and a leading member of a school of painters which, in the course of forty and more years, since about 1800, had grown famous. These painters were called 'the Nazarenes' or German Pre-Raphaelites, but if Steinle was a congenial master, he had like his fellow Nazarenes a temperament which neither an English boy nor an Olympian in the making could be expected to understand—in which there was a deep-seated and pathological disquiet: for the Nazarenes were full of yearning, doubt, and complexity. They were, one might say, men fighting desperately for their souls, engaged in an intense spiritual struggle on which even national existence might depend.

To be a nation a people had to have a culture; and what was culture but a patriotism, a religion, a form—or forms—of art which made expression possible, without which it was not possible? Thus the opposition of 'classic' and 'romantic', which might otherwise seem, as far as Germany was concerned, a mere local skirmish in a battle of barren definitions, had become urgent and vital.

For a long time Germany had been half repelled and half fascinated by that classic civilization to which it had never historically belonged. 'The sole means for us to become—ay, if possible, inimitably great—is the imitation of the ancients.' So said the Prussian archaeologist and historian of ancient art, Johann Joachim Winckelmann, in the eighteenth century. He had exhorted German painters to study Greek sculpture and thus attain to 'the most sublime conception of beauty'. The attempt had been a failure—the work done in rivalry of the ancients cold and insipid—and the aggression of a, first, revolutionary, then imperial, France had helped to cause a revulsion of feeling. France had looked to ancient models. The Antique was the ideal of Germany's national enemy. It was possible to contrast French paganism with German faith, to regard the pagan cult as un-Teutonic. The painter, Overbeck, in this belief, denounced the director of the Vienna Academy, Friedrich Fuger, because he was 'given over to the service of Jupiter and Venus'.

So the source of inspiration must be looked for in Germany's own past—in the Middle Ages—but here again the ways diverged, a fresh difficulty of choice appeared. The Middle Ages were either fabulously 'romantic'—a world of magic and legend, of dark and secret forests, of storm and bedevilment, of paganism, indeed (without its mollifying deities); or they were religious, a world of Gothic churches and monasteries and Christian discipline. Yet that old Christian Germany had been Catholic. Between it and the present there interposed the bulky Protestant form of Martin Luther. Was it not necessary then to be a Catholic (or a sort of Catholic) in order to recover the best of what that old German world had to give? Was it not necessary to go again to Rome, not the Rome of the Caesars or of revised classical splendours but the Christian city of the Middle Ages?

Such was the nostalgic train of thought which had impelled the Nazarenes, 'Patriotic—Religious—Romantic—Art Catholic' as they were quite accurately called, to make Rome their centre since 1800. Under the leadership of Johann Friedrich Overbeck (the 'apostle John') and Peter von Cornelius of Düsseldorf they had lived, though they were not monks, in a monastery, adored the old painters of Italy for their religious spirit and averred their hatred of Raphael as the symbol of a corrupt age. Followers had come from all quarters: Pforr of Frankfurt, Veit of Berlin, Vogel of Zürich, and Führich and Steinle of Vienna.

Steinle, who was born in Vienna in 1810, was too young to have shared in the first fervour of the movement, to have lived the monkish life with 'apostle John' and the rest in the convent of San Isidoro on the Pincian Hill from which Napoleon had evicted the Italian and Irish Franciscans; but when the monastery had reverted to the monks after Napoleon's fall the Nazarenes remained in close communion, there was still Overbeck to inspire them, and Steinle had entered fully into the pious spirit which still prevailed.

He had worshipped Overbeck, a spare, saintly figure with long hair hanging down in unclipped waves from under a black skull-cap, a long cloak hanging in straight, sombre folds about him, his face carved in emphatic planes by earnestness, his lips firm-pursed with the habit of self-discipline.

He had haunted as they all did the cloisters of St. John Lateran, and when the sound of many bells clanged on the metallic blue of the evening sky and the cypress trees, dark and solemn, were etched upon its surface, he had shut his eyes to the pagan ruins and Renaissance palaces and revered the beauty of Christian Rome.

Some of Overbeck's anguish Steinle was spared. Steinle was a Catholic born in the Church of Rome, with no need of that self-searching which preceded the conversion of Overbeck, a North German Protestant by origin, offshoot of a line of Lutheran pastors in Lübeck; yet Steinle seemed to have derived from his artist brethren some of their sectarian melancholy. About them hung an air of being persecuted, even if the persecution consisted only in an absence of sympathy like that of Goethe. Swinging treacherously round, the author of *Faust* had become the disciple of Homer, had turned against the Gothic spirit of his own early productions and asserted that 'Art has once for all been written in Greek'. 'I made devils and witches but once', he confided to his friend Eckermann in 1826. 'I was glad when I had consumed my northern inheritance.' He had jibed at the new 'German Religious Patriotic Art'. 'Why,' asked Goethe, 'because some monks had been artists, should all artists be monks?'

Nevertheless the Nazarenes had triumphed, at least over those unrepentant pagans who sang:

> Des Deutschen Künstler's Vaterland
> Ist Griechenland, ist Griechenland.

Overbeck stayed in Rome but most of the devout self-exiled patriots eventually returned to Germany; some acquired positions of influence and were missionaries of the Nazarene creed and manner of painting—in Munich, Düsseldorf, and Frankfurt. Philip Veit, noted for his fresco *The Introduction of Christianity into Germany by St. Boniface*, became the first director of the new Staedelsche Kunst Institut at Frankfurt, founded by a rich banker, Herr Staedel, after whom it was named. It combined a museum with an art school of a strong Nazarene tendency. Veit's successor was Jacob Becker, also one of Overbeck's followers. After him Steinle had been appointed. It was to the Staedel Institute that Frederick Leighton came for tuition on leaving Florence in 1846, and it was Steinle who gave him the friendship as well as the teaching he desired.

Their liking was mutual and their friendship was to last many years. It was, in some ways, the liking of opposites, as of a young Apollo and a sad middle-aged monk. A gentle, ascetic man, with the severe dress, the long hair, the meek obstinacy and the pious aim of the Nazarene, was Steinle. He painted austere religious pictures and sometimes the clustering turrets, the romantic castle-life of medieval Germany, but Leighton admired most of all his zeal, and sense of high purpose, while Steinle had the greatest confidence in his pupil's ability. What an admirable result it would be if the brilliant boy were in due time to become a German genius, to remain in Frankfurt, to strengthen and add lustre to the Nazarenes' patriotic striving.

Yet it was here that a danger lay: for there was a fatal weakness inherent in this German school. Perfection stiffened under the earnest touch into ice. The stern passion which they felt so intensely died as it was transferred to their canvases and frescoes. That loftiness of thought which rejected all earthy and material things seemed hostile even to the material and earthy nature of painting itself. They scorned fat and juicy pigments—Cornelius, rejecting the means of expression he had elected to use, declared that 'the brush is the enemy of painting'. The Ideal, triumphant, imprisoned and destroyed the human body in harsh and unrevealing folds. In Steinle, as in the others, there was lacking something—a merely sensual vigour—a delight—a necessary imperfection—and art was crushed beneath the burden of an unrelieved solemnity. There was a subtlety in the matter—a subtlety which Dr. Leighton can hardly have foreseen.

How could one foresee that men of the highest principle and wholly admirable industry, men as renowned and respected in their chosen walk of life as any eminent doctor might be in his, could lack the prime secret and mystery of the occupation in which many believed them to excel? The scheme of universal education had its pitfalls. To consult all the great doctors of art seemed so reasonable a plan, but it implied a certainty as to their merits which none could guarantee. To be trained at Frankfurt under a famous master was well, and yet from the vantage point of a later century it may seem that young Frederick Leighton now breathed the atmosphere of a tortured and impotent escapism. In his educational travels from country to country he saw, there is no question, many a glorious masterpiece but also many a work which, acclaimed then, has in the course of time come to be looked on as one of those curiosities in which the nineteenth century was so strangely and exceptionally prolific. Olympus might fear for young Frederic in Germany, fear also on seeing the eager youth seek out the 'best masters' of Brussels.

It is true to say that Frankfurt was the Leightons' base for six years, from 1846 to 1852; that, broadly speaking, Frederic spent these years under the guidance of Steinle; but the family was still constantly on the move. In 1848 the Leightons visited Brussels, and here Frederic had a studio for a time and was introduced to an art which in contrast with the ascetic restraint of the Nazarenes had an immense and appalling exuberance, was proudly and furiously bad. He visited the nightmare workshop of the famous Antoine Wiertz, for whom, two years later, the State was to build the huge studio subsequently to be the Musée Wiertz.

Wiertz, the son of a Belgian gendarme, held the paranoiac belief that he was greater than any of the old masters, and, moreover, that it was within his power to reform society by means of painting. His picture *The Suicide* was meant to deter young men from reading books on Materialism and blowing their brains out. *The Novel Reader* warned girls against the erotic ideas which they might derive from the romances of Dumas *fils*. His *Thoughts and Visions of a Decapitated Head* was intended to bring about the abolition of the guillotine, and *Buried Too Soon*, in which a clenched fist reached out from the coffin, was a plea for cremation.

The Belgians went in for size. Another painter whom Frederick Leighton met in Brussels was Louis Gallait, the author of vast historical works, whose twenty-foot-wide *Abdication of Charles V* the young man had admired. Shades now, in the gloomy depths of nineteenth-century art, seem Gallait and Wiertz, yet in 1848 they were men of fame with whom it was gratifying to be acquainted and whose praise was assurance of merit. They praised Leighton and would perhaps have detained him in Brussels, but the powers which ruled his destiny put it into the mind of his parents to continue their travels and, like one raised from the nether-world dominion of Orcus, he is seen in the clear air of Athens in 1850, while in 1851 the magnet of the Great Exhibition drew back all the Leightons once more to their native land.

Praise might have detained him in London, for Royal Academicians were gracious to him and prophesied great things. In the handsome and talented artist of twenty-one, trained by the united skill of Italy, Germany, and Belgium, they divined a future glory of British art. He gave a speech at an official dinner and surprised everyone by his eloquence. Struck by his fluent delivery and the happy turn of phrase which brought round upon round of applause, Frederick Goodall, R.A., remarked to his neighbour that here, without doubt, was a future President of the Royal Academy.

What would he do next? His parents, at last, had had enough of travel and decided to settle at Bath. Was it to be England or Germany for Frederic? Neither. In spite of his affection for Steinle he made up his mind to leave Frankfurt, and the country to which he wanted to go was Italy again.

It was a sad moment for the Nazarene master. The pupil who might have become so great a German was slipping from his grasp, but, if he had to go, then surely it must be to Rome. There were the many bonds which linked the Germans with Rome. Overbeck was still living there. Steinle's pupil would gain the benefit of that Nazarene association which had inspired Steinle himself; and perhaps as Steinle had done he would one day return to Germany, the better for the experience. It is probable that, reluctant to part with him at all, Steinle contrasted Rome favourably with Florence and persuaded him to follow in the Nazarene footsteps by going there. At all events in 1852, alone this time, Leighton set out for Rome, after an affectionate leave-taking with Steinle who pressed on him an introduction and many messages of respect and devotion to the celebrated Nazarene, Johann Friedrich Overbeck, commending Leighton as almost a German and the most promising student of Frankfurt.

Rome disappointed young Leighton at first. The capital was not as beautiful as Florence. There was some difficulty in finding a studio; but once that was settled, the attraction of the city began to grow upon him. The life of Rome was picturesque. Shabby though they might be, the rococo coaches of the cardinals which paraded through the streets accompanied by footmen in cocked hats, gave it an air of fanciful magnificence. The peasants who lounged gracefully on the steps of the Piazza di Spagna, natural and practised models, pleased his artist's eye. Carnivals agreeably varied the never-ending ceremonies of the Church. There was a fascination in the long decay which had established a comfortable relation between the splendid and the popular. The Forum had not long ceased to be a cattle market with the title Campo Vaccino. A person of distinction might live grandly in palatial rooms over a pastry-cook's shop. Within the sixteen-mile circuit of the city there spread, widely, fields and vineyards, parks and gardens. It is true there was malaria in summer, but then the visitor could find delightful retreats in the mountains so near at hand. There was a certain amount of political uneasiness in the atmosphere, made visible in the presence of a French garrison, but the Papal States, which Macaulay, incensed by an earlier Pope (who hated gas lamps, railways, and liberalism), once called 'the worst-governed in the civilized world', had not yet lost the placidity of that condition and the uneasy sway of Pius IX in no manner interfered with the pleasures of a brilliant and cosmopolitan society.

The Nazarenes, however, were not much in evidence. Steinle's account had led Frederic to expect that they were the very heart and centre of artistic life in Rome, that he would at once consort with kindred German spirits. One of the first things he did after finding a studio was to hang up in it a picture by Cornelius and one or two of Steinle's—'to animate myself', as he said, 'by dwelling constantly on an *idea of excellence*'—but in 1852 the monastic brotherhood was fading into a memory.

Naturally, he went to see Overbeck as soon as he could, presenting Steinle's messages and letter of introduction. He found a sort of ghostly hermit, a man of sixty-three, tall and emaciated, his locks, still long but thin and grey, struggling from under a black kerchief. The monkish ideal had become the fixed habit of the solitary. Overbeck seemed to bear, with Christian resignation, the weight of sorrow and suffering beyond words. His art had produced an obsession. He was like some persecuted Christian in the time, and city, of Nero. He looked, said one of his visitors in those days, 'like a timid prisoner who dreads to see a spy in every corner'. Stooped under the load of an habitual martyrdom, Overbeck glided among the huge cold cartoons in his bare, cold studio, whispering tortured explanations, and the faint smile with which he acknowledged a comment was forced and full of pain.

He was courteous, and not only that, he looked with interest at Frederic's drawings and praised them highly, yet Frederic was disappointed. Liking Steinle personally he had accepted Steinle's precepts without question, but Overbeck, in whom as a person he could not become particularly interested, made these precepts appear less attractive. Surely art need not be such a miserable business. The complexities of faith and patriotism in which Overbeck had enwrapped himself were foreign to his brisk and genial nature. Even praise sounded hollow coming from one so entirely of another generation—of another kind. The gleam of pagan light shone critically for a moment on the Lutheran-Art Catholic clouds. Overbeck, Frederic decided, was 'pietistical'.

Anxious that they should get on well, Steinle wrote a letter to his pupil, reiterating that 'Overbeck is the purest and noblest man that I have ever met with: moreover, a genius'. Leighton replied with a marked absence of enthusiasm that he had found Overbeck 'a dear and estimable old man but naturally the difference of age and of aims is too great between us for him to supply your place. . . .' As for other Germans in Rome, poor remnants of the original brotherhood, such as Flatz and Rhoden, 'literal copyists of Overbeck's style', Leighton dismissed them as one would dismiss some disagreeable but altogether trivial thought.

The classic influence in Rome was manifestly stronger. Shrouded in history, as if by a sumptuous pall, Rome constantly incited its lovers to go back into the past, and its relics of the ancient world were the breeding-ground of revival. As the main repository of classical sculpture it had fostered one impulse of revival after another. The beginning of the nineteenth century had brought with it the attempt to make a new and more chaste product on the classic model. The Venetian sculptor, Antonio Canova, the Dane, Bertel Thorvaldsen, the Yorkshireman, John Flaxman, had 'purified' paganism, and Flaxman's outline illustrations to the *Iliad* and *Odyssey* had been the talk of Rome. At the apex of the Roman art world in 1852 was the sculptor John Gibson, the successor of Canova and Thorvaldsen, whose pupil he had been.

It was inevitable that Frederick Leighton should come to know Gibson, even though he stood in a camp opposed to Overbeck and the Nazarenes. The son of a Welsh market gardener, Gibson was entirely Greek in devotion. He habitually carried with him three packages, because the Greeks (or 'Grecks' as he pronounced them) had a great respect for the number three. He was steadfast in refusal to dress the contemporaries he sculptured in frock-coats and trousers, and draped the statue of Sir Robert Peel in Westminster Abbey with classic garments. His fame was crowned, not only by his statue of Queen Victoria for the Houses of Parliament, but by the *Tinted Venus* of 1850. A man of sixty-two when Leighton met him, he lived with his brother Benjamin (who was, it was said, a 'walking classical dictionary', and fed him with serviceable titbits of classical knowledge). He was celebrated for his vagueness about the world he lived in as well as for his art. He was apt to arrive at the wrong stations when travelling by railway, and on one such occasion was so incomprehensible that the porter asked, 'Are you a foreigner?' to which Gibson answered, 'No, I am a sculptor'. 'A god in his studio', remarked his friend, Harriet (Hetty) Hosmer, the American sculptress, though she added with native forthrightness, 'God help him, out of it'.

It is tempting to see, in such a god of the studio, the influence by which Leighton became a 'classic' in painting and was weaned from the Nazarenes. It was not, in fact, so. That critical spirit which he had begun to display, the first assertion, rather, of the nascent Olympian, revealed imperfection in the sculptors as in Overbeck. Disillusionment had come on his way across Italy when he had visited Hiram Powers again at Florence. Into the eyes (black and glittering like those of a Red Indian) of the sculptor-spiritualist had come no flash of recognition. He was 'very polite in his own sort of way' but he seemed to wonder who the young man was, to have completely forgotten those emphatic words ('he will be certain to get there') in which he had assured Dr. Leighton of the genius of his son.

Sculptors, Frederic Leighton found, knew or cared very little of painting. Gibson, he said, knew of painting 'as little as a man well can'. It was not among the relics of a classic revival that Leighton began to develop as an individual but in the more generally cultivated society which Rome offered, the society of those who might truly be called Great Victorians.

There may be little need to inquire why so many of them came to Rome. It may be supposed that Victorians liked, and were as much entitled to like, a sunny sky as people before or since. Some went for the express purpose of buying works of art—Gibson grew wealthy on the commissions they gave; some, perhaps, whether they admitted it or not because Rome was un-Victorian. A great Victorian, or at least the great friend of great Victorians, in Rome was that remarkable woman, Adelaide Sartoris, and it was she who introduced Frederic Leighton into a circle at once of 'high art' and the best society.

Mrs. Sartoris, the wife of an art critic and amateur painter, concealed beneath her married name that of a great dynasty of the stage, the tremendous family of the Kembles, a race apart, it was said, 'like those deities who once visited the earth in the guise of shepherds and as wanderers clad in lion skins'. Magnificent 'lines', lofty sentiments reverberated through its generations. It was Adelaide's grandmother, the wife of Roger Kemble, who returned the majestic answer to her husband's cry 'Give *The Tempest*, madam. How can we give *The Tempest*? Who is there to play Prospero?' 'I', said Sarah Kemble, 'will play Prospero, sir.' Their youngest son, Charles, and his wife, Maria Theresa, a Viennese actress, were the parents of the superb sisters Fanny and Adelaide.

They had studied music and the drama together in Paris, and Adelaide counted herself fortunate that she had been to no other school—Shakespeare, she said, had given her far pleasanter thoughts than the rule of three. She had sung on the Continent, impressing her sister 'even more as an artist than a genius', her countenance lighting up 'with a perfect blaze of emotion'. Covent Garden had been crowded to hear her *Norma*. There was an occasion, after she had been singing at home, when Fanny's little daughter asked, 'How many angels have been in the drawing-room?'

She had renounced her dramatic career at the age of twenty-nine. In 1843, the year after her success at Covent Garden, she married John Sartoris in Glasgow. It was a serious step for the member of a family which lived for the stage. There were times when a wild longing seized her to go back to it, but this she resisted and found consolation in delighting her friends with recitation and song.

Adelaide Sartoris would not live in England. The darkness of the sky and the dullness of the mode of life, she said frankly (she always maintained that nobody said anything straight out 'except my sister Fanny and myself'), were intolerable. For that reason she and her husband had come to Rome and had acquired, said Fanny, 'something completely foreign in tone and accent'. An actress might be expected unconsciously to acquire the accent and tone of her surroundings. At the same time, the frustrated, or discarded, ambition of Adelaide Sartoris caused her to give histrionic majesty to the everyday affairs of life. Rome was a stage and she trod its boards with a stateliness and intensity which belonged to the highest forms of drama. From the artificial world of the theatre, she diverted an operatic genius to the real world about her. She was capable of making domesticity sublime, raising the small talk of the drawing-room to a serious pitch, welcoming visitors not merely to her home but to a superior plane of existence. Such a woman was truly classic —as opposed to those mediocre beings who simply imitated classical sculpture—classic in herself, modelled from the most elevated examples and scorning all that was not excellent, a Muse—the Muse Melpomene in a Victorian gown.

She was, in appearance, all that a Muse might be imagined. She was noble, with her classic brows and deep-set eyes, her turquoise eyeglasses and her grey satin robe with its great blobs of ornament. In her, stoutness was turned by the excellence of poise and gesture into an incomparable stateliness. There were some people who found this stateliness alarming, but Frederic Leighton was not among them. He admired her without reserve and frequented her Roman drawing-room with delight.

Leighton had been introduced to John Sartoris, in Paris, the year before coming to Rome, and his introduction to the critic's wife entirely reconciled him to the city. This splendid and sympathetic woman had the secret which an Overbeck, a Powers, a Gibson, lacked. A Muse indeed, she had a universality which placed her in harmony with all the arts—with painting as with music, books, and the theatre. She was, said Leighton, 'a true painter in her great feeling for art', and those were thrilling moments when she recited or sang. How charming the vivacity, how perfect the mimicry, with which, her face alight with fun, she impersonated the Abbé Liszt talking to Madame de Metternich:

'Avez-vous fait de bonnes affaires à Paris?'

'Madame, j'ai fait un peu de musique, je laisse less affaires aux banquiers et aux diplomates.'

Nor was it idle mimicry for it relegated business, banking, and diplomacy to their proper insignificance: but when the laughter died she soared into her own sphere, and her delivery of Shelley's *Good Night* with a low obbligato accompaniment on the piano held her audience enthralled and silent, brought tears to their eyes.

She was, perhaps, thirty-eight when Leighton first knew her—perhaps, because a question mark insinuates itself into biographical

41

reference, against the year of her birth, presumed as 1814. She may have been a little more than thirty-eight or a little less; while Frederic was definitely twenty-two. The disparity of age might preclude, apart from the fact that Adelaide was married, the thought of love between them: and yet there was an affection, no less tender because disinterested. Obviously, she was pleased by the good looks, the talent of the young man—and he, on his side, adored her as an ideal being. The age of each had its dangers. A motherly sentiment on the one hand and a feeling of reverence on the other were not absolute safeguards against a warmer emotion, but it would be an idle speculation to pursue this thought and irrelevant to their mutual recognition of a lofty and even abstract excellence. If Adelaide had been George Sand, it might have been another matter—but she was not George Sand, nor was Frederic of that tribe of 'ill-bred young men' who would lavish on such a heroine their 'caprices d'amitié'. Adelaide Sartoris 'brought him out'. She was 'a mother to him' not in things domestic but in the arts. She made him aware of his own qualities, of a way of life conducted at the highest level, and placed him in the company of the most illustrious visitors from Britain.

Eminent among these visitors were Robert and Elizabeth Barrett Browning. Although Florence was their favoured city they sought a warmer winter climate and tearing themselves away from the delights of their Casa Guidi, arrived in Rome in 1854 with their small son. Their first impressions of Rome were unfavourable for death greeted them. Their American friends, the sculptor William Story and his wife, had found an apartment for them and been there to welcome them, but immediately after, the Storys' two children had been taken ill with 'gastric fever'. One of them died. 'You will understand', wrote Mrs. Browning, 'how the ghostly flakes of death have changed the sense of Rome to me.' Both Brownings suspected the climate. 'My child, the light of my eyes,' said she, 'has been more unwell than ever I saw him.' She declared she had not a 'ray of sentiment' about the 'palimpsest city' and valued the company of English people the more. It was indeed the Sartorises who made Rome tolerable to them. 'We see a good deal of the Kembles here and like them both, especially Fanny who is looking magnificent still, with her black hair and radiant smile.' 'Mrs. Sartoris is genial and generous—her milk had time to stand and turn to cream in her happy family relations. . . . Mrs. Sartoris' house has the best society in Rome and exquisite music of course.' In this best society was the handsome young painter Leighton for whom they at once formed a liking. He visited them in their third-floor rooms in the via Bocca di Leone, where the two poets settled down to write, he *Men and Women*, and she *Aurora Leigh*. There Leighton listened with respect to the dominant baritone of Browning, red-faced and at this time clean-shaven (to his wife's grief he had committed the 'suicidal' act of shaving off his beard): his voice an effective foil to the lisping utterance of Elizabeth Barrett, a slight shy figure, timidly tucking pages of manuscript under the sofa cushion at the approach of a visitor.

They all went on picnic excursions, to the seaside and into the Campagna—the Sartorises, the Brownings, Leighton, old John Gibson Lockhart, Scott's biographer (who liked Browning because 'he isn't at all like a damned literary man'). 'Could anyone forget him,' wrote Leighton of Lockhart, 'with his beautiful clean-cut features so pale and fiery at the same time: those eyes of jet in a face of ivory.' There would often be a seasoning of foreign notabilities— M. Ampère, 'the member of the French Institute who is witty and agreeable', M. Goltz, the Austrian minister; and brilliant talk— 'almost too brilliant', thought Elizabeth Browning, 'for the sentiment of the scenery', though it harmonized with the mayonnaise and the champagne.

William Makepeace Thackeray was in Rome, too, and through knowing Mrs. Sartoris and Browning, Leighton came to know him. The novelist had come to Italy with his daughters and was writing *The Newcomes* and drawing the pictures for *The Rose and the Ring* in great vaulted rooms in the via della Croce (over Spilman's shop —famous for cream tarts), full of marble tables and gilt armchairs and swinging lamps and lanterns.

Thackeray and the Brownings were all studio habitués, know-ledgeable on the subject of visual art. Browning had many friends among artists—the sculptor Story, the painter Page (known as the

'American Titian') who painted Robert's portrait so much in the Venetian style that it was lost in darkness. As part of the social routine, they visited Gibson and admired his *Tinted Venus* ('Rather a grisette than a goddess', remarked Mrs. Browning). Browning himself had a taste for modelling little figures by way of relaxation, while Thackeray, amateur draughtsman, was something of an art critic. Both visited Leighton's studio and both were as much impressed by his work as they had been attracted by his charm of manner. Returning to London, Thackeray chuckled to his friend, John Everett Millais, 'Johnny, my boy, we always settled that you should have the Presidentship of the Royal Academy, but I've met in Rome a versatile young dog called Leighton, who will one of these days run you hard for it'.

In the warm sun of brilliant friendship, Leighton's qualities shone out brightly. He was, in Mrs. Sartoris's opinion, 'the most promising young man in Rome', as he had been to Steinle the most promising young man in Frankfurt. He earned, as he always retained, the title of 'Admirable Crichton'. Never had there been such a compound of excellences. He was handsome. He was gay and high-spirited. He was a model of courtesy and irresistible in charm. Then he talked so well, and so well in so many languages, and everyone admitted that he was marked out for a splendid career as a painter. It was bewildering. No sooner was one superlative quality noted than another of a counter and complementary kind appeared to balance it. With so many mental gifts was he not studious, stooping, averse from exercise? Not a bit of it. He was splendidly active, fond of exercise, an accomplished dancer. 'I don't know what he is like as a painter,' said a girl with whom he had danced, 'but I know he is the best waltzer in Rome.'

And then he had presence of mind and promptness of action. There was in 1853 that day of sport and festival on a farm in the Campagna when donkey races were part of the programme and the tethered animals waited the event. One of the donkeys kicked over a beehive and an angry swarm of bees buzzed round it. The party scattered, leaving the hobbled donkey at the mercy of the bees—all scattered, that is, except Leighton, and one other young man. It was the work of a moment for Leighton to slip on gloves, tie a handkerchief over his face and run to free the donkey from its hobble. From this moment dates another great and lasting friendship, with the young man who stayed, helped, and admired Leighton's promptitude. His name was Giovanni Costa.

Costa, four years older than Leighton, was an artist too. He was the son of a wealthy Roman family (his father owned a successful wool-spinning business). He had worked in the studio of the Baron Camuccini, a follower of David and the neo-classical school, and, though he turned to landscape, kept the scrupulous classic regard for form. He is not one of the famous figures of nineteenth-century art, though Corot had some words of praise for him and a picture of his hung next to Whistler's *White Girl* in the Salon des Refusés; but he was certainly a distinguished Roman and man of the time.

A patriot and revolutionary as well as an artist, he threw himself into the desperate and yet conventionalized struggle of Roman politics—conventionalized because however fierce it became, it was admitted by each side—or by all sides—that life must go on. There were fantastic plots and sudden outbursts and then everyone went to bed at night as usual; battles in which all was lost, after which it appeared that nothing had really happened at all; domiciliary visits and a reign of terror by which no one was very much frightened. There was a certain vagueness about it all which might, or might not, be the result of far-sighted political cunning. The Austrians moved here and there in a vaguely acquisitive manner. The French, whose aims were no doubt very deep, occupied Rome. Pio Nono's liberalism was as vague as could be, and liberators, idealistically republican, had some difficulty in choosing their enemies or recognizing their friends.

Full of the spirit of revolt, Costa had plunged with energy into this complicated situation. He had pulled down the coat of arms from the Austrian Embassy, had hailed Mazzini and cheered Garibaldi, had shouldered a gun and shot it off with a company of volunteers, and when the French arrived, had 'fled' into the Campagna, though only to return in a few days' time. Heroism having 'become a habit', he adjusted it to his other habits. He was a revolutionary in the morning, in the frock-coat which was the revolutionary dress, but in the evening he was the gay Nino Costa, a painter in a velvet suit, who took his ease in the Caffè Greco.

It was at the Caffè Greco that he had first heard of Leighton. Raffaello, the waiter, who kept an album of sketches by the artist customers, by Overbeck, Cornelius, François and the rest, had told Costa of the astonishing young Englishman who spoke every language, who had, incidentally, much admired Costa's contributions to the album. The affair of the donkey-race (which Costa won) sealed a friendship thus already foreshadowed. It remained constant as all Leighton's friendships did and showed how little inclined he was to stay aloof from the Latin Rome—or to confine his attention to Embassy swells, literary lions, and Anglo-Roman salons.

Through all these new influences on Leighton, the influence of Germany waned—though that influence is still to be seen in the first inportant work of his Roman years. He had decided that it must be important, and while everyone was talking of his promise he was intent on performance. The time had come when it was necessary to justify the message which had gone round, had been flashed across Europe to London, that, afar off but already bright, a new star was rising. The diploma piece of youthful mastery was due, and the subject he chose was in itself a praise of mastery—the triumphal procession of Cimabue's *Madonna* through the streets of Florence.

Perhaps it was his Nazarene training which caused him to turn to the early days of Italian painting and the work of a primitive master. He chose a Florentine theme because he had pleasant memories of his days in Florence; but during his stay in Frankfurt he had become interested in Cimabue and Giotto, in whom the Nazarenes found that Christian purity for which they yearned. He had then read Vasari's *Lives of the Painters* and had taken from that work his first subject-picture, *Cimabue finding Giotto among his Sheep in the Fields of Florence*. Giotto, the artist who had drawn a perfect circle as evidence of his skill, could not but appeal to a youth into whom the idea of Perfection had been so painstakingly drummed; at the same time the triumph of Cimabue, that thirteenth-century Florentine, who was Giotto's master, was very attractive. How vivid seemed, as

46

Vasari's words evoked it, the power which had for the first time given the appearance of life to the stiff Byzantine ikon, 'wherefore', said Vasari, 'Cimabue's *Madonna* caused so great a marvel to the people of that age by reason of there not having been seen up to then anything better, that it was borne in most solemn procession from the house of Cimabue to the church with much rejoicing and with trumpets and he was thereby much rewarded and honoured'. There was a prophetic ring to those tumpets. The ceremonial moment, the rejoicing and the display, projected the success for which Leighton himself was already prepared.

The picture had been in his mind before he left Germany. He had made studies for it then and had many earnest discussions with Steinle over them. Now he began to work steadily. Dancing was cut out—except for an occasional quadrille. Despite a weakness of the eyes caused by too much concentration on minute pencil drawings, he spent long hours each day on the many and laborious stages through which he considered it necessary that the picture should go.

Evidently, to reach perfection nothing must be left to chance. Every stroke must be governed by certain knowledge, every part must be perfect in itself and perfectly adapted to the whole. Already Leighton worked to a system of the most elaborate kind. First of all there was the general plan—the 'cartoon'—which he hung up so that it should be constantly before his eyes. Each figure had to be carefully drawn, first from the nude, then draped. There were studies of drapery to be made. The drapery had to be applied to tracings of the nude drawings. After that came the colour sketch (for the general scheme of colour must be as carefully planned as that of the form) and at last the tracing for the finished work.

To trace and enlarge, he fastened string in squares to the cartoon and other squares in exact proportion to the canvas. When the general plan had been thus transferred the figures were carefully drawn in the nude on the canvas and painted in monochrome. The draperies were then arranged fold by fold on the living model, just as they appeared in the detailed studies, and were also painted in monochrome. The whole picture being complete in tones of grey, there came the final stage—the application of colour.

It was during this lengthy process that Leighton's friend the architectural student, George Aitchison, read aloud to him those fiery passages from Haydon's *Journals*. They were somewhat irrelevant to the work on which Leighton was engaged. Disconcertingly even, they called up a vision of an earlier perfection beyond the admirable strivings of the thirteenth-century Italian painters, the beauty of pagan conception from which Leighton's German masters had recoiled with horror. If he was inclined to deprecate Haydon's unmeasured violence of worship, the unhappy artist's words, no doubt, had their effect or were set aside in his mind for further reference. They may have hastened the trend which already made Frankfurt seem so far away. Another splendid prospect had opened in this great world of art which had already revealed to him so many prospects.

Florence, however, not Athens, was his present theme, and as the processional figures took up their positions on the canvas one by one he was heartened by many admiring comments. Long before it was finished, the picture was famous. A visit to young Leighton's studio was as much a part of the Roman fashionable routine as a visit to Gibson's. Mrs. Sartoris was delighted with her protégé. Thackeray and Browning were both warm in praise of *Cimabue*. One day there came Peter von Cornelius, Overbeck's great ally in the early Nazarene days, one who had shared and taken turns in cooking the frugal monastic meals of San Isidoro and believed, like Overbeck, that 'the truest use of art is that which leads it heavenwards'. He was a brisk little man of seventy with dark bright eyes, and an impressive manner which made students quake and caused Ludwig of Bavaria to look on him as the equivalent in art of a field-marshal. He had reorganized the Düsseldorf Academy, was now director of the artistic destinies of Munich and was distinctly affable to the prodigy of Frankfurt. It was something that he should say that Leighton 'had gone further than any Englishman except Dyce'. It was much that he should see in him a future power. With all that earnestness, that sense of art's patriotic mission which belonged to the Nazarene, 'You can', he said to Leighton, 'do something very significant [*etwas bedeutendes*] for England'.

Nevertheless Cornelius put forward a criticism. The figures in the

STUDY OF DRAPERY
by Lord Leighton, P.R.A.

frieze-like procession of the *Cimabue* were, he remarked, too regular and similar in movement, the composition too even. Would it not be better, for the sake of variety, to turn the leading figures towards the spectator?

After all those carefully laid plans, the hundreds of detailed studies, here was horrid doubt indeed. Was it possible that through the complex system of inner and outer fortifications which had been built the more safely to guard perfection, to guard it by making imperfection impossible, that something essential—the drama of the event, the life of the picture—had contrived, by incredible means, to make its escape? Every gift had been lavished on the work, every precaution taken to ensure their happy union, and yet, as in the old fairy tale, the unexpected flaw, which might have been the wish of a wicked fairy, spoilt all that was good.

Had that pedantry to which German painters were sometimes prone crept on him unawares in his German surroundings? Had the lifelessness to which the Nazarenes in their idealism were liable insinuated itself into his studies made so carefully from the life? Whatever the subtlety of error, Cornelius had put his finger on the weak spot. The procession did not move and Leighton, though it was some time before he could bring himself to alter a painting now nearly finished, had to admit it.

To alter a painting may not seem to the lay person so tremendous a step. Its importance, in this case, is to be estimated by that importance with which *Cimabue* had become vested during the long period of its preparation. It was generally understood that it was to be an event, something really 'significant for England', for, of course, it would eventually go to the Royal Academy in London. To alter it at the last moment was drastic. Yet were there not occasions when one must be drastic? If the composition became rougher—still, had not Steinle said it was possible to be too perfect? He had said so when Leighton had sent him a drawing, smooth, highly wrought, and delicate, of the young Roman model Vincenzo, described as 'the prettiest and wickedest boy in Rome'. It did not quite please Steinle. 'A certain roughness', he remarked, 'is needed to bring out fineness. If everything is fine, nothing remains fine.'

The period of trouble and doubt came to an end at last. The decision was reached, the words spoken: 'I have made up my mind to alter the *Cimabue*.'

With a swift stroke of the brush he wiped out the left half of the picture. All of this had to be done again.

§ 3

The heroic decision was announced in the presence of a young fellow artist who drew a sharp breath as the stroke was made. His name was Edward John Poynter.

Poynter was six years younger than Leighton, but like him had already spent a considerable time out of England. He had been born in Paris in 1836, the son of a successful architect, Ambrose Poynter, who had had a practice in Westminster since 1821 and designed many buildings in London and the provinces, among them St. Katherine's Hospital in Regent's Park and the National Provincial Bank, Manchester.

The early days of Edward John Poynter were spent in Westminster and he had gone for a while to Westminster School, but he was a delicate child and his education was interrupted in consequence. His parents took him away from Westminster in 1849 and sent him to Brighton College. In the following year he went to the Grammar School at Ipswich (where his housemaster at Westminster had been appointed head). In the normal course of things he would have gone to a university, but his delicate health made it necessary to send him abroad. In the company of a tutor he set out for Madeira in 1852, at the age of sixteen, spent the winter there, in 1853 travelled to Rome and in Rome felt himself fortunate to make the acquaintance of the already celebrated Frederic Leighton.

His was a very different, an altogether scantier and more haphazard course of education than Leighton had been through. Poynter, certainly, had shown a leaning towards art. He had, it would seem, a few lessons in water-colour from his father's friend, Thomas Shotter Boys, the architectural draughtsman who is known for some excellent views of London and Paris; but nothing of the elaborate training, the range of knowledge of his friend. He made water-colour sketches of landscape during his winter in Madeira. It may be he inherited his leaning through his mother, for Emma Foster was the granddaughter of Thomas Banks, R.A., sculptor of the *Falling Titan* (which is to be seen in the Diploma Gallery of Burlington House), of *Thetis and Achilles* in the Tate Gallery, whose sculpture Sir Joshua Reynolds had praised for its 'classic grace', of whom Flaxman had observed that 'he studied nature diligently for himself and copied the antique to form his taste'. And yet it may be said that Poynter's real introduction to art was in Rome and under the wing of Frederic Leighton.

Leighton was twenty-three, Poynter seventeen. Very like a young god must the elder have seemed to the quiet, self-contained boy; so handsome, polished, and assured; so brilliant and so kind. Kind he was, without doubt, in addition to everything else. He allowed Poynter to use his studio freely, to work with him, to make drawings of the models and the folds of drapery which were the material of the great picture, like a master setting the apprentice on his course: 'The friend and master', acknowledged Poynter in 1879, in the preface to his *Lectures on Art*, 'who first directed my ambition, and whose precepts I never fail to recall when at work.'

This first association which left so permanent a memory of disinterested kindness lasted only a few months. Poynter left Rome for England in 1854, but he had made up his mind to be a painter, not a painter of pleasant water-colours but of grand figure subjects like that which his godlike friend in Rome had undertaken. His parents, belonging to the same intelligent, professional class as those of Leighton, made no dissent and straightway he enrolled himself in Leigh's Academy in Newman Street. It was disappointing after Rome—even squalid with a London squalor which was depressing to artistic ambitions kindled abroad. Leigh's Academy may have been a little better than the establishment of Mr. Gandish which Thackeray described in *The Newcomes*, with its professor who genially taught ''igh art' and the 'Hantique', but not, perhaps, very much better, and Poynter did not stay there very long. He painted for a while in the studio of William Thomas Dobson, an ex-headmaster of the Birmingham School of Design, who in 1855 won the approval of Queen Victoria with a picture called *The Alms-Deeds of Dorcas*; but Poynter did not stay long with him. He went to the Royal Academy Schools and, as they prescribed, drew a statue and made anatomical studies from it showing the position of bones and muscles, after which, with the application of a great many bread-crumbs, he stippled and smudged at charcoal drawings of antique busts. It was not inspiring, and once again Poynter felt the need to escape.

There was in London an antidote to the stale stuff on which he fed, a brilliant and exciting school, the one hope, as many thought, for British art—that of the Pre-Raphaelites. Very different were they from those Continental Pre-Raphaelites—among whom Leighton had been trained: they were alive, vigorous, full of challenge. The Brotherhood of 1848 had now fought its way to recognition, its members were in the flush of achievement. The Royal Academy itself admitted them, its exhibitions during the fifties were dominated by them. Young artists were spurred on by the example of Holman Hunt, John Millais, and Dante Gabriel Rossetti; and the *Academy Notes* of John Ruskin, fierce in praise and blame but always on the side of the Pre-Raphaelites, proclaimed their merits to the nation.

It would not have been surprising if a youth like Poynter had been attracted by the peculiar magnetism which the Pre-Raphaelites exerted. It may even be more surprising that he was not—for what other alternative in art did England offer to a deadly dullness? It is probable that his brief experience of the Continent had a glamour for him which made him disinclined to stay at home and experiment further. He went to Paris in 1855 to visit the Universal Exposition, and decided that the French artists were greatly superior to the English. He may not have singled out the best works for admiration—he especially liked the work of Alexandre-Gabriel Decamps, a painter not of the highest importance—but that was the general result. It was undeniable that the art of England, seen through French eyes, was reduced in lustre. 'Est-ce qu'on fait de la peinture en Angle-terre?' the French artists asked in surprise. The Pre-Raphaelites, to them, were hard to understand—the great Delacroix, though he had been in England and admired Constable, found them entirely incomprehensible; and the best that could be said by the critics in appreciation of Holman Hunt's *Strayed Sheep* was that it expressed 'l'esprit moutonnier'.

So Poynter made up his mind to study in Paris where evidently painters were trained in the right way. An uncle by marriage, the Baron de Triqueti, who was also a sculptor, advised him to go to the painter of classical subjects, Charles Gleyre, and without difficulty Poynter was taken on in the atelier which Gleyre conducted.

. . . . . .

The classic revival in France, of which Gleyre was a minor product, had a character of its own. It dated from the French Revolution. It did not arise as in Germany from a sense of deficiency in culture, but from a militant political theory. The revolutionaries had looked back for an example of republican virtue—to Rome before it was an Empire, to democratic Athens. Art must be as hard and stern as republican virtue. If an aristocracy was to be destroyed, it was logical to destroy with it the aristocratic art, voluptuous and trifling, which had been, with all its triviality, the servant and supporter of a régime.

The new classic theme had been propagandist—and the propaganda had been carried on most actively by the painter Jacques Louis David. David tried to arouse the zeal of his contemporaries by ancient instances of virtue, patriotism, and self-sacrifice. He avoided the graceful and salacious myths which had pleased the frivolous nobles and replaced them by heroic episodes founded on historical fact or tradition, episodes in which the country had come first and human weakness had been subdued to its purposes. *The Oath of the Horatii*, painted in 1784, before the Revolution, already pointed the lesson. The Horatii, three Roman brothers, pledged themselves to fight and overcome three members of the Alban family, the Curiatii. They were not to be put off because their sister was attached to one of the Curiatii, and the victorious survivor of the triplicated duel killed her when she reproached him, holding the reproach to be treason. Pointed also was David's picture of the republican Junius Brutus, implacable against the royal house of Tarquin, who vowed revenge over the ravished body of Lucretia and condemned his own sons to death because they had taken part in a royalist plot. In the spirit of those he painted, David voted for the death of Louis XVI and with remorseless hand drew Marie Antoinette on the way to execution.

In style David was as stern as in subject. His forms were severe, his colour joyless. He borrowed from both Greece and Rome. Objects found at Pompeii and Herculaneum provided him with details of furniture. The Greco-Roman wall-paintings of Pompeii suggested a technique the reverse of intimate, and Greek sculpture caused him to paint the heroic Spartan Leonidas with a marble coldness.

Exiled as a regicide after the Restoration of the French monarchy, David went to Brussels and died there in 1825. Classicism, as might be expected, now lost its revolutionary and political meaning; though it did not die out in France. With some painters it grew soft. The iron will of Brutus, the valour of Leonidas, gave way to the loves of Cupid and Psyche. Pierre Paul Prudhon and François Gérard found in the gentle allegory all the subject they wanted, and for them it was sufficient reason for classicism that they could draw human figures without clothes.

Yet the original severity lingered in David's great successor, his pupil Jean Dominique Auguste Ingres. Like David, Ingres grew into a species of dictator. He was as much concerned with a principle on no account to be corrupted, though his probity was not that of the republican but of the artist. A little man with an obstinate set to his chin, he was the tyrannous upholder of a beauty serene and passionless. He did not confine himself exclusively to ancient subjects. He painted The Maid of Orleans at Rheims as well as Oedipus and the Sphinx, The Vow of Louis XIII as well as The Apotheosis of Homer; but in ideas he was obstinately fixed. He was a genius who was also a professor, who announced orthodoxy as a kind of new movement, and when the Classics were assailed by the violent and emotional tribe of Romantics threw all his weight on the side of reaction.

Of the Romantics, Géricault and Delacroix, who were not interested in beauty but in wild and unruly feelings, he could say nothing good. They had turned away from the ancient inheritance of France to the barbarous confusion of the Teutonic and northern countries—could stoop to illustrate Goethe's *Faust* and Shakespeare's *Hamlet* and take pleasure in the castles and abbeys of Sir Walter Scott. '*Someone* has been here', he said of Delacroix, whom he saw in the distance one day at an exhibition. 'There is a smell of brimstone.' The Racine of the easel, Ingres, in the romantic decade of the eighteen-thirties, opposed to the fiery productions of his younger contemporaries the iron restraint of his celebrated *Stratonice* (1839). It showed Antiochus, son of Seleucus, king of Syria, who had fallen violently in love with his father's second wife, prone in despair on his couch, as his stepmother paced across the mosaic floor. It refrigerated this antique passion in the cold formality of columns, drapery, and studied gesture.

When Poynter came to Paris, Ingres was still a power in the land though advanced in years (he died in 1867 at the age of eighty-six). Among his adherents was the master of Poynter, Charles Gleyre.

Gleyre, in 1855, was a sad and disappointed man of forty-nine. His face was lined and wrinkled, pouched and bagged. His eyes were myopic from too much tropic sun. Illness and misery had modelled a mask which was gentle and morose. His career had somehow missed fire, and for long periods he had been entirely unproductive.

The son of a Swiss peasant family, he had received a simple rustic education in which the classics had no part—although it was the classic spirit which he admired. He went to Rome in 1828 and spent six years there, doing apparently very little but living in a state of privation. From this he was rescued by what seemed a stroke of good fortune.

Horace Vernet, at that time director of the French Academy in Rome, introduced him to an American who wanted to take an artist with him on his travels. He was going to 'the Orient'—that imprecise geographical term by which the French describe any country with a sun hotter than their own. It meant, in this instance, Egypt and the Sudan. The American is supposed to have behaved badly: to have claimed all Gleyre's drawings, to have treated him like a native or a slave. After two years of discomfort thus spent they separated, but with a characteristic lethargy Gleyre remained in Africa. It is possible, if such rumour as emerged from the African wild is to be credited, that he was detained at Khartoum by the charms of a young Nubian. Eventually he returned to Cairo, suffering from ophthalmia and dysentery. He was somehow conveyed, half-dead, to Beirut, where monks took care of him, and was shipped back to France in 1837, aged thirty-five, worn out, with empty pockets and impaired vision. 'I have recognized', he said, with the bitter satisfaction of one aware of every nuance of his own misfortune, 'the emptiness of everything without having possessed anything. Now like a dead branch I float where the current takes me.'

The current floated him into teaching. In 1843 the painter Paul Delaroche gave up his atelier to students, and Gleyre took it over. For twenty-seven years his morose wrinkled visage appeared each week in the big grimy room and bent over the drawings of his pupils, to whom he addressed some words of advice or criticism in a depressed undertone. Disappointment was still with him. It was his fate to be despised by the hero he placed above all others—Ingres, the master, the classic genius he could have wished most to resemble. He became aware of it in a cruel fashion. Through Delaroche, he came to the notice of the Duc de Luynes, who had commissioned a scheme of decoration for his château at Dampierre. The main part of the work was to be done by Ingres, and Gleyre was honoured by the task of painting the staircase walls.

There is no doubt that Ingres behaved badly—no more excusably because with an economy of ill will or distaste, indeed without speaking a word. A gesture was enough to shatter Gleyre's hopes. Ingres was asked his opinion of the painting on the staircase wall. He looked, said nothing, then covered his face with his hands. By this pantomime he conveyed an unutterable aversion, more damning than any amount of spoken criticism.

The gesture sealed Gleyre's fate. The commission was cancelled and his paintings were obliterated. He made no reproach and did not talk about the incident. Ingres was still his hero even though he had behaved disloyally to a confrère and admirer. Beauty as Ingres conceived it was still Gleyre's gospel. It consisted, primarily, in the perfection of the human form, though in an abstract sense which made it necessary to separate the figure from the human individuality inhabiting it. The nude was the triumph of pictorial art but had nothing to do with character or emotion. Thus Gleyre, while able to regard the female form as divine, had a great contempt for women, and his misogyny was the one thing which made him animated and even witty. 'Have you heard of so-and-so's misfortune?' he would say. 'Such a good fellow. Succumbed after a two years' struggle. Married at twenty-five . . . I can't bear to think of it.' Apropos of an old miser whom he considered justly punished by marriage, he was reminded of Job on whom every curse was heaped including, said Gleyre, the fact that God did not take his wife away from him.

Such was the master of Poynter, 'l'homme antique' as his pupil and successor, Léon Gérôme, called him in reference to his stoicism and principles. He gained some fame by his picture *Le Soir* (which later acquired the title of *Lost Illusions*) exhibited at the Salon in 1843. Here, a poet who has dropped his lyre sadly watches the dreams of youth—a boatload of young women—glide away in a classic barge. He subsequently drew upon mythology for many subjects: Daphnis and Chloe, Minerva and the Graces, the nymph Echo, Venus Pandemos—though he was never anxious to exhibit. 'Ah! mon Dieu!' he would say, with his mild bitterness, 'I might be refused or—decorated.'

In the history of French art, Gleyre has a paradoxical importance. Some of his pupils were incited by his example to work in a method opposed to it. From the atelier of this tired classicist came those who looked at the real world about them and discarded both academic principle and story subject—the Impressionists, Monet, Renoir, Sisley, and Bazille. The relation of master and pupil was, after all, slight. No doubt there were many to whom the large, grimy studio was simply a convenient life-class, its visiting master a vague phantom, yet to Poynter, Gleyre was a more impressive figure than he seemed to other pupils. Poynter worked for three to four years— from 1856 to 1859—in the atelier so entertainingly described by

George du Maurier in *Trilby*, and he was one of the 'Paris Gang', as the Anglo-Saxon students who figure in *Trilby* styled themselves: the 'gang' comprising du Maurier, Thomas Armstrong, Thomas Lamont, and James Abbott McNeill Whistler.[1] The English members kept themselves somewhat aloof from the noisy and mischievous rabble which frequented the Atelier Gleyre. For a while, Poynter shared rooms with Whistler. Then he, Lamont, Armstrong, and du Maurier drew closer together. They took up their quarters at 53 rue Notre Dame des Champs, a famous artists' street near the rue de Rennes with high garden walls on either side, a single gutter in the middle of the badly paved road, and earth sidewalks fringed with grass; and here they formed a British and a Victorian colony.

For Poynter it was pleasant to be thus a little insulated from the Bohemian student life. Paris with all its attractions was on a less dignified plane than Rome viewed from the vantage of Leighton's studio. Student life in Paris had a coarseness which was sometimes too much. He did not approve of the unpleasant tricks they played on newcomers, making them strip naked, hiding their clothes, confronting them with a 'master' who was really a student disguised. There were many types and many jokes he would have nothing to do with. Though Whistler was amusing with his droll American songs and witty sayings, he was not very fond of him, the company he kept, or the tricks he played. He thought Whistler was wasting his time—indeed, the whole group looked on the American as the 'idle apprentice'. Whistler was all for the new and revolutionary school of 'realists', led by Gustave Courbet, whom Ingres, as ever opposed to change, termed 'merely an eye'; but Poynter knew or cared little about the object of Whistler's enthusiasm, and his first ambitious picture, *Mercury with the Cattle of Apollo*, was derived from the classical dictionary, and not contemporary life. The title has a deceptive air of simplicity—deceptive because the ancient myths were never-ending in their chain of cause and effect. How explain in a picture that here was the infant Mercury giving early indication of his craft by stealing the cattle of Admetus, King of Thessaly, which were tended for nine years by Apollo during his

[1] See also *The Aesthetic Adventure* by William Gaunt.

banishment from heaven by Jupiter, incensed because Apollo had killed the Cyclops who made the thunderbolts which had been hurled at Aesculapius, Apollo's son, who had given offence by bringing the dead back to life? Whistler no doubt would have said 'Why attempt it?' or 'Why give such a title to a picture of a boy and some cows?' but this was art as Gleyre understood it, and to Poynter who loyally followed him a classical subject was as indispensable to the artist as easel and palette.

§ 4

It can hardly be said that Paris added anything to the education of Leighton, but he did come to Paris at last and there consorted, in his own exalted fashion, with the 'Paris gang' while renewing his acquaintance with Poynter. Meanwhile the first British laurels had been placed upon his brow. The revised group of figures in the *Cimabue*, including some ecclesiastics as was proper in a procession going to church, and wheeling towards the spectator so as to overcome that effect of monotony which Cornelius had pointed out, was finished at last. A frame ('which can hardly exceed twenty-five pounds') was ordered from Mr. Allen of Ebury Street, Pimlico. Five weeks before the opening of the Academy in 1855 the picture was sent from Rome to London.

Leighton was prepared for criticism. He was not merely steeled against it but able to put it in its place in advance with lofty contempt. He warned his mother to be indifferent to the 'scribbling of pamphleteers; the self-complacent oracularity of those *pachidermata* is rivalled only by their gross ignorance of the subjects they bemaul'. He knew 'à quoi m'en tenir'. He considered it well that he should come to the Academy *an unknown*, though unknown in a certain limited sense for he added that 'ces messieurs', by which he meant the Hanging Committee, would not be entirely unprepared for *Cimabue*. 'One thing is certain, they can't hang it out of sight—it's too large for that.'

The path of the Olympian, however, was smooth. The picture, far from being hung out of sight, was put in the place of honour, where it attracted immediate attention and gained universal applause. Applause came, not merely from the despised *pachidermata* but from the great critic, John Ruskin.

It was the year in which Ruskin began those *Academy Notes* by which he extended his sway over the world of popular painters, making it for some of them a positive reign of terror. 'Twenty years of severe labour' (Ruskin dated the period of study from the age of sixteen) 'have given me the right to speak on the subject with a measure of confidence.' Confidently indeed did he speak, opposing with dramatic effect the Bad to the Good. He found much that was bad in 1855: of two kinds, the 'weakly or passively bad' and the 'energetically or actively bad'. Actively bad, in Ruskin's view, was *The Wrestling in 'As You Like It'* by Daniel Maclise, R.A., the rollicking, handsome Irish painter, friend of Dickens and the most successful Academician of the day. His Orlando, said Ruskin, looked like a fashionable tenor in a favourite aria. Also, the details were 'all drawn wrong'. Sharply, Ruskin called attention to faults of perspective and cast shadow. Then there was the passively bad: *Lear recovering his Reason at the Sight of Cordelia* by J. R. Herbert, R.A. 'In the whole compass of Shakespeare's conceptions the two women whom he has gifted with the deepest souls are Cordelia and Virgilia'—and then, what a fall: 'in the midst of the Royal Academy Rooms in England and in the middle of the nineteenth century, this profile of firwood and buff'.

On the other hand—there were two pictures the merits of which were the more in comparison. Ruskin allowed one great picture— 'but *this* is *very* great'—*The Rescue* by John Everett Millais, R.A., which showed a fireman coming down a burning staircase with the two children he had saved, met by the grateful mother. Millais in this year married Euphemia Gray, whose previous marriage with Ruskin had been annulled. There could be no further friendship between the two men, but *The Rescue* was a matter of art and Ruskin could praise Millais still as an artist and a Pre-Raphaelite. Millais had shown his devotion to nature in his study of fire, had placed a burning brand on a piece of sheet iron in his studio and painted it amid suffocating smoke—and the result was so convincingly true that praise could not be withheld.

At length Ruskin came to *Cimabue*. It was 'a very important and very beautiful' picture, although, in his disconcerting way, Ruskin pronounced that this picture of Florence and of a Florentine master was 'painted on the purest principles of Venetian art'. He approved the rendering of Cimabue and the young Giotto who walked with him, though he said the faces were on the whole the worst of the picture. Dante (who was among the spectators of the procession) looked too haughty, not noble or thoughtful enough. Nevertheless, Ruskin concluded, Mr. Leighton probably had greatness in him, though he would have to do much better yet—or else he would not do so well.

The dictator's verdict then was favourable. It was not without its barbs, however, and if Leighton was fortified against them he was perhaps less prepared for a modified eulogy than for a denunciation. There was something just a little irritating in the 'great' applied to Millais, the 'important' applied to him. Little envious of Millais as he might be, it was hard not to turn over in the mind the difference between the 'great' and the 'important'. 'I wish', said the artist, 'people would remember St. Paul on the subject of hateful comparisons.'

But everyone talked of the picture by 'the new man living abroad'. It was like a challenge hurled from afar, and coming from afar, it aroused the greater speculation. The Pre-Raphaelites were agog with interest. 'The R.A.s', commented Dante Gabriel Rossetti in a letter to William Allingham, 'have been gasping for years for someone to back against Hunt and Millais and here they have him.'

What was to be the result of the tilt against those redoubtable knights? The unknown was victorious. The first lady of the land was to single him out for the prize of the academic joust. It seems in accord with his high destiny, in which there was nothing that was not superlative, that the *Cimabue* should be bought—on the first day of the exhibition—by the Queen herself.

For many years Queen Victoria, who was now thirty-six years of age, had been the patron of the Academy and its painters. As Princess Victoria she had attended the Private View of 1837, had visited the exhibition of the same year as the Queen, and addressed a word or two to each of the members, presented to her by the President, Sir Martin Archer Shee. She had sat to many of them, to Alfred Chalon, Sir George Hayter, Sir Edwin Landseer, Sir David Wilkie. Charles Robert Leslie had toiled long on the picture of the Coronation, putting up at the inn at Windsor, where 'good and plentiful luncheons' were sent out from the Castle—'the best wine in a beautiful little decanter with a V.R. and a crown engraved on it and the table-cloth and napkins with the royal arms and other insignia upon them as a pattern'. The work had been the 'picture of the year' in 1843. After she was married, the taste of Prince Albert directed and improved Queen Victoria's own. They went together to the exhibitions, together planned the decoration and chose the pictures for Buckingham Palace and Balmoral, and made some etchings of their own in happy collaboration.

They were happy in 1855, even if there were many causes of national anxiety. The Crimean War was dragging on and the deplorable conduct of policy and operations was heavily criticized, yet personally the Queen was delighted with her married life, proud of her Consort's successful activities in that world of art and industrial science which he managed so much more ably than the Ministers of the Crown managed the Russians. In the month before the Academy opened there had been warming contact with foreign splendour, the visit of the Emperor and Empress of the French. They had sat together at the Royal Italian Opera, had jointly received the applause of huge crowds at the Crystal Palace, and in the expansive and glowing mood left by these ceremonies the purchase of works of art seemed more than usually pleasant. Mr. Dobson's *Alms-Deeds of Dorcas* was one—an improving picture even if Mr. Ruskin said it looked 'like the work of a man of good feeling and considerable industry who had been forced to paint against his will'. The other, the *Cimabue*, had so much that was calculated to appeal to Prince Albert. It was an aspect of his discernment, of that spirit which links him with the German Nazarenes—and even with the English Pre-Raphaelites in their love of the Middle Ages—that he was an admirer of the Italian 'primitives', of the Cimabue and Giotto whom Leighton had painted. Perhaps also there was in the picture itself something, to the Prince, agreeably Teutonic, a savour of Steinle and Frankfurt, a feeling of that 'streben nach Wahrheit' which Germans had brought to Italy.

The work was bought at the Royal command for six hundred guineas. The President of the Royal Academy and Director of the National Gallery, Sir Charles Eastlake, wrote from Fitzroy Square to give the news to the painter in Rome. Leighton received it with no vulgar outburst of excitement, but with a characteristic gesture he 'celebrated' by a generosity which in its own way was royal. He bought a number of pictures from less successful artists, including a poverty-stricken friend introduced to him by Giovanni Costa— George Mason, who lived in Rome on a starvation diet of the thin porridge called 'polenta'.

§ 5

It was then that Leighton went to Paris. During the latter part of his stay in Rome he had felt a growing discontent with the German 'idea of excellence' and even with Rome itself. His letters to Steinle, though always affectionate, contained more notes of criticism, expressed not with arrogance but with the authority of an independent mind. 'Rome is the grave of art', said Leighton, and these were painful words in Steinle's ear, for to him Rome had been art's hope. Painful, too, was that cool analysis which led to the conclusion that the German artists were 'queer' and 'pedantic'. It seemed as if the roles of master and pupil had been reversed; as if Leighton lectured and the master must meekly listen. 'I am almost beginning to fear you', wrote Steinle in a letter which breathes all the Nazarene sadness. As he had anticipated, his pupil had slipped through his fingers. He had gone into some loftier region where Steinle could not follow. He might come back to Germany, but it would be as a foreign visitor and not as one destined to add lustre to German art. Steinle mourned the loss of the incomparable youth.

Leighton, as was becoming because of his triumph, paid a short visit to London in 1855. The Sartorises were in London too, and Leighton introduced them to his family (at last satisfying his sister Gussie's greedy desire to know exactly what Mrs. Sartoris was like).

Then, like Poynter, he was drawn across the Channel by the International Exhibition of 1855, found himself a studio in the rue Pigalle, for some three years made Paris his headquarters, and from time to time saw Poynter and the members of the 'Paris Gang'. He does not seem to have cared much for Paris, though Mr. and Mrs. Sartoris were there when he was (they could not stay in England), though he was on good terms with the 'gang' who reaffirmed his title of 'Admirable Crichton'. Poynter's respect for him was great. George du Maurier, not quite English, and the more attached to the English ideal, thought him a god indeed, and from those handsome features, that short curved upper lip, may have taken some hints for the classic male, later to appear so often in his drawings for *Punch*. If Jimmy Whistler was less inclined, either by nationality or temperament, to see young Englishmen as gods, he found Leighton a person of charm and not without taste, for Leighton admired and positively bought the American's early etchings.

Nevertheless he was not able to enjoy the Bohemian student life. 'Bohemianism', so suggestive of the loosely picturesque, of disorder in living and rackety pleasures, was a word without place in his vocabulary. He could not know those idle and dirty ruffians in whom Whistler took such an unaccountable delight. Nor could he care greatly for the frugal variant of Bohemianism which the other English youths enjoyed. An Olympian could hardly take part in the boyish exercises, that swinging on trapezes, that twirling of Indian clubs which they practised in the rue Notre Dame des Champs. His Olympian taste was little adapted to their home-cooked suppers, their chops and bottled beer; or to those discoveries of cheap restaurants where a bottle of wine, costing only one franc, washed down the economical meal. Magnificence was his proper element. His idea of pleasure was a ball under the glittering chandeliers of the Embassy or a visit to the Opéra in the connoisseur company of Adelaide Sartoris, and failing these diversions he preferred, having no taste for liquor and low company, forming apparently no random attachment for a girl or girls, to stay quietly at home with a book or to go to bed at an early hour.

He may have regretted Rome, for if it was 'the grave of art' yet it had greatness. There was greatness even in that political stress in which Costa had been embroiled, of which Costa had made him aware. One indulgence, however, Leighton could permit himself in Paris: that passion for knowledge of every method of practising art which his father's universal system had given him.

He made the acquaintance of many artists. They were diverse in character and some, it is to be feared, were positively bad. It is hard now, when French art in the nineteenth century has been pruned and adjusted in critical proportion, to realize how it might seem before the adjustment was made. To the modern view it has become a broad highway, a series of obvious steps leading logically one to the next. The Romantics, destroying formality, lead to the observation of the real. The path of realism, trodden out by Courbet, Jean François Millet and the landscape painters of Barbizon, moves inevitably forward to the great research of Impressionism; but in the middle of the nineteenth century the path did not seem so clear. There was Ingres, the formidable opponent of progress, the more formidable because of his genius, waving artists back. There were others who possessed, if not genius, at least the authority of success. Like lamps (now long extinguished) they shone with a dazzling and misleading effect, and if Leighton was not dazzled he was certainly attracted towards them.

There was Charles Hébert, one of the French painters whose spiritual home was Italy, who painted the fever-stricken peasants of the Campagna. He was of a classic turn of mind, for Leighton, wishing to give Hébert a present for his help in setting up the studio, asked his father to send him 'any Greek classic (if Homer all the better) in the same edition as my Brumek's *Anacreon* with Latin notes'.

There was the great success of the fifties, Thomas Couture, who had a cosmopolitan school and following. The son of a Normandy cobbler, a fat, little man with a walrus moustache, Couture was still basking in his triumph of 1847, *The Romans of the Decadence*, alternatively called *The Roman Orgy*, a painting which, with curious result, applied the austerity of David to a scene of licence. Couture's Romans quaffed their bowls of Falernian with stiff gestures, and the

E

amorous abandon of the couch had a stony propriety. If he was not a great painter, he had 'a method' and Leighton, always interested in methods, wished to know what it was.

'The name of Ary Scheffer is the one I remember oftenest mentioned by him', said his sister Alexandra (who became Mrs. Sutherland Orr and the biographer of Robert Browning). Scheffer, the Dutch-born painter whom Heine accused of painting with 'green snuff and soap', a 'sentimental classicist', whose maudlin tenderness and thin, lifeless technique is intolerable to modern eyes, was then rich and famous, with a detached house in the rue Chaptal, and two studios flanking the avenue which led to it, one for work, the other, beautifully furnished like a chapel, devoted to musical parties at which great singers and instrumentalists played. Scheffer was important enough to intend it as a compliment to Leighton that he mounted three flights of stairs to see him.

They were all cordial to Leighton. Nicolas Robert Fleury, the painter of *The Massacre of St. Bartholomew*, was cordial. So too was William Adolphe Bouguereau, another of those painters who have become the perennial butt of rebellious spirits. Ingres himself was cordial 'though sometimes', said Leighton, 'bearish beyond measure' —and especially since 1855, when the medal of honour at the Universal Exposition had not been given to him alone but had been divided into ten awards, placing him in the hated company of Delacroix, on an equal footing with Meissonier, Cornelius, and Sir Edwin Landseer. Another friendly meeting was with Léon Gérôme, the future martinet of a cosmopolitan school, who was to train a Verestchagin of Russia, a Harrison, a Boggs, a Dodge from the United States, a Yamamoto of Japan. Gérôme offered his own variant of classicism. He had been inspired not by legends of the gods but by a gladiator's helmet in the Naples Museum. It was clearly a challenge to the painter to reconstruct the warrior it fitted. 'Think', said Gérôme, 'of all the painters and sculptors who have been here and never thought of remaking a gladiator.' He remade them in his *Pollice Verso*, his *Ave Caesar te Morituri Salutant*, while his *Young Greeks Cockfighting* (1847) had shown another and popular aspect of a reconstructed ancient world.

Thus Leighton mingled with the orthodox and the academic. It is true that he went to Barbizon and admired the unorthodox Jean François Millet, but if Paris influenced him it was mostly through the still active classical men, in particular Ingres, and no doubt it was this influence which caused him to paint *The Triumph of Music* which he sent to the Royal Academy in 1856. Its sub-title was 'Orpheus by the power of his art redeems his wife from Hades'. It was no small task to depict that scene in the underworld palace of gloomy Pluto, where Orpheus played so magically that, as Eurydice strained towards him, the routine of Hell was interrupted, the wheel of Ixion stopped, the stone of Sisyphus stood still, Tantalus forgot the tortures of his thirst, and the Furies softened. The critics were taken aback by a subject so very different from *Cimabue*. It was presumptuous of a young man to depart so flagrantly from the recipe of success. The critics did not say this in as many words, but they fastened upon a single weak spot. Leighton had shown Orpheus playing on a violin, not on the lyre. There were, said the critics, no violins in the ancient world, or presumably in that other world which the ancients had imagined. In fact, as Mrs. Browning wrote to a friend, Leighton was 'cut up unmercifully'. Prior to *The Triumph of Music* he made an experiment in a more familiar vein of subject: *The Reconciliation of the Families of Montagu and Capulet over the Bodies of Romeo and Juliet*. This fared a little better but received only moderate praise when exhibited at the British Institution, and though it was sold, was sold in a 'slovenly fashion' displeasing to the artist. For pounds, not guineas. The dealer let it go for £400 instead of insisting on those extra shillings which in some mysterious way acknowledged the painter's prestige. Clouds were drifting across the sky and obscuring the rising star. There were some who thought the star was less bright, was already waning; but Leighton was not one to be cast down for long. He rolled up *The Triumph of Music*, put it away in a cupboard and out of his mind, and set off again on his travels.

§ 6

Meanwhile an artist of a different country was also making his way, by another route, towards the Olympian goal of Leighton and Poynter. His name was Alma-Tadema.

Lourens Alma-Tadema was Dutch. He was born in the flat lands of Friesland in 1836, at the village of Dronryp, between Harlingen and Leeuwarden, the land of those barbarians whom the ancient Romans called Frisii. He was brought up in poor circumstances in the village on the sea-threatened plain, broken only by the mound on which the church stood above flood-level. His father, a notary, died when Lourens was four, leaving his widow with five children and little money. Lourens showed an early inclination to art (he signed a drawing 'L. Alma-Tadema'—Alma being the name of his godfather—at the age of six), but it was decided, when the time came for him to go to work, that he should follow his father and enter a lawyer's office. He did not want to, but making the best of things, he got up before daylight and painted until it was time to leave home. In the days of his success he related how he used to tie a string to his big toe when he went to bed at night. The string communicated with his mother's bedroom; she gave it a tug at five in the morning to wake him.

Then his health broke down and he had to give up his job. Possibly he had worked too hard for too long hours. As it seemed unlikely that he would live he was allowed to study painting. His health began to improve at once and he worked even harder than before, but the Dutch art schools would not accept him, so when he was sixteen he went to Antwerp and his systematic training began at the Antwerp Academy.

.   .   .   .   .   .

The battle of the classics and the romantics was being fought out in Belgium as elsewhere. The influence of David, who had died in Brussels twenty-one years earlier, still lingered. He had set up his dictatorship as he had done in Paris. Inspired by him, Flemish painters had turned against their own great master, Rubens, against the exuberant, earthy, sensuous nature of his art. The classic régime was so firmly established that it is said a sculptor, commissioned to make the model of a wolf, could only conceive the animal as the she-wolf of Rome, and without being asked included Romulus and Remus with it.

Patriotic as it had been in France, classicism in Belgium was the opposite. An independent kingdom since 1830, Belgium became less and less interested in the republican virtues of the ancient world, more and more in the events of Flemish history, and a school of patriots who painted these events grew up under the leadership of Baron Wappers.

Gustav Wappers was a national hero as well as a painter. His picture of 'the Burgomaster van der Werff of Leyden, at the siege of the town in 1576, offering his own body as food to the famished citizens' had happily coincided with the declaration of independence in 1830. Who would prefer an antique Brutus to such a burgomaster? The King of Holland bought the picture, and in 1832 Wappers was appointed Professor of the Antwerp Academy.

When Alma-Tadema arrived in Antwerp in 1852 Wappers was nearly at the end of his tenure of office, but the young student had six months under him. After Wappers's departure, he worked under Nicaise de Keyser, another history painter noted for *The Battle of the Spurs at Courtrai, 1302*, in which there was a more than usual respect for accuracy of detail. The spur of the dying Comte d'Artois was, it was said, faithfully copied from the original, the only remaining spur of the seven hundred which had littered the battlefield. In this environment it was natural for the young Alma-Tadema to attempt historical subjects, and in 1858 he became the assistant of the most exact and learned of the patriotic Flemings, Hendryk Leys. Like Wappers, Leys was a national hero. He had returned in triumph from Paris in 1855, with his tenth share of the partitioned gold medal, to be greeted by fireworks, processions, and wreaths of gold; and his death in 1867 was mourned as a national calamity.

Leys required higher standards of accuracy than either Wappers or de Keyser. He admired the detail of Dutch and early German pictures. He wished to use such detail in order to make the past real, and he spared no pains in research in order to ensure that he was accurate as well as minute. A Gothic table, for example, had to be convincing both as a piece of wood and a type of design. Authorities were to be consulted for the design. The painter's skill must make it solid. When Alma-Tadema had to paint such a table for Leys's *Luther* the master observed in criticism, 'It is not my idea of a table. I want one that everybody would knock their knees against'. It was no excuse for the insubstantial to say it existed a long time ago. When Alma-Tadema painted his *Education of the Children of Clovis* Leys frowned: 'That marble is cheese and those children are not studied from nature.'

It was a severe discipline to work under Leys's directions on the six frescoes for the Antwerp Town Hall which were to illustrate notable events in the history of the city. What sort of clothes were worn for a particular occasion? What kind of a pike did a soldier carry? How was a table set or a bed made? These and many more questions constantly arose and could not be answered in the careless fashion of older painters or glossed over, vaguely, in view of the precise construction which Leys demanded. There was frequent recourse to Louis de Taye, the Antwerp expert in archaeology, and thus the pupil of Leys learnt the method of the archaeologist as well as of the painter. Had not the painter a new field as an archaeologist? One could not paint what historical characters said nor even very satisfactorily imply what they were saying. A professor of history at the University of Ghent reduced this to absurdity. He kept asking Alma-Tadema to paint the occasion when the Counts Egmont and Horne and William the Silent exchanged verbal thrusts. William was leaving the Netherlands to organize a revolt against Spain. 'Good-bye, noble Prince without a country', said the Counts. 'Good-bye, noble men without heads', returned William the Silent. How could a painter make this visible to the eye—or intelligible at all without a written explanation? Alma-Tadema was sensible enough not to attempt it.

At the same time there was an inexhaustible store of historical subjects—or pretexts for painting the costume, the furniture, the buildings of a past age, which could be made visible by knowledge and skill. There was a seam, rich and untapped, if one went back further than the sixteenth and seventeenth centuries which had so far been the patriots' favoured period. Enough, perhaps more than enough, had been done about this period by Wappers, de Keyser, and the rest. So Alma-Tadema staked a fresh claim in the earlier field of Merovingian history—the dark and turbulent age between the fall of Rome and the tenth century. 'Perhaps', says Gibbon, 'it would not be easy within the same historical space to find more vice and less virtue'; yet it was already Alma-Tadema's theory that externals differed more from one age to another than did human beings. It was not Merovingian vice but the coins and ornaments—the main, if not the only, antiquities of Friesland—which first aroused his interest. His reading of Gregory of Tours and Augustin Thierry's Merovingian history enabled him to find a subject in which there was pathos: *Clotilda weeping at the Grave of her Grandchildren*. Louis de Taye helped him with the archaeological details. Madame de Taye sat for the head and arms of the weeping Empress.

Did Clotilda really weep? Where, critics asked, was the historical authority? The painter had an answer ready. It was only human that Clotilda, whose ambitions were ruined by the murder of her grandchildren, should have wept, and this, being human, was historic. The characters of history, Alma-Tadema assumed (encouraged by this astute sophistry), were not strange monsters. They had certainly been human beings who laughed and cried and generally behaved pretty much as human beings always would. It was possible to reconstruct sentiment as well as architecture and to explain the past by its modernity. It was this thought which inspired his first success, *The School for Vengeance: the Education of the Children of Clovis*, exhibited at Antwerp in 1861.

It was not possible to indicate on the canvas that the uncle of Clotilda had caused her father to be stabbed, her mother drowned with a heavy stone round her neck, that now, after the death of her husband Clovis, the Frankish queen had dedicated her sons to the work of revenge. As a costume piece, however, it did not lack interest, and the fair, sturdy little boys, throwing axes with commendable accuracy at targets roughly painted on a wooden frame, might well appeal to parents little versed in Merovingian lore. Originally bought by the Antwerp Society for the Encouragement of the Fine Arts at the moderate price of 1,600 francs, it passed to the King of the Belgians and subsequently into the possession of Sir John Pender, the pioneer of submarine telegraphy. Engraved, it was to gain a world-wide popularity.

In the same rich, dark mine, Alma-Tadema continued to hew with his *Venantius, Fortunatus and Radegonda* of 1863 which won the gold medal at Antwerp and his *Fredegonda at the Deathbed of Praetextatus*. In this picture, Praetextatus, the dying Bishop of Rouen, mortally wounded by Fredegonda's hired assassins, hurls his curses at the Queen—though the anger of the bishop and the hypocritical concern of the lady are less notable than the timbering of the hall, the cloaks and armour of the attendant dukes, the ornamentation of the couch. If even the artist had to admit that the Merovingians were unpleasant people, he could still maintain that they were 'picturesque and interesting'.

Alma-Tadema was now a fairly successful young artist of twenty-seven, but a series of events combined to set him on a new course. His mother died in 1863. He married in the same year a Frenchwoman, Mlle Gressin de Boisgirard; and about the same time made the acquaintance of the powerful French art dealer Ernest Gambart.

Gambart was not one of those dealers of whom more recent times have furnished examples, who have held by some unpopular aesthetic principle and waited with faith and patience for many years until neglected masters came into their own. He was interested in those painters who were popular or might be made so without difficulty, and he placed on popularity the highest market value. He believed in the best-seller and he knew by experience that an historical subject, a high degree of finish, and a 'human touch' were prime among its ingredients. There was a vivacious roguery in the way he took his clients into confidence on these matters—making them, as it were, accomplices of the artist's bid for fortune—which was quite irresistible.

Gambart's position was very strong, because of his connexions on both sides of the Channel. He had a London house, 62 Avenue Road,

St. John's Wood. A London house was essential, for not only was the wealth of England enormous but there was a vogue for picture-buying; patrons were rich, enthusiastic, and easily persuaded. He was able to sell them the work of English artists and also of the Continental stars, in search of whom he made frequent forays abroad. He bought and sold pictures by the Pre-Raphaelites—paying the sensational sum of 5,500 guineas for Holman Hunt's *The Finding of Christ in the Temple*, although he was far from being exclusively interested in Pre-Raphaelitism.

A great friend of his, and the source of great profit, was the woman animal-painter from Bordeaux, Rosa Bonheur. Gambart made a very good thing indeed out of her *Horse Fair*, in which the horses were the more convincing because they were life-size. This equine wonder was exhibited all over England and was captured by Mr. Vanderbilt for New York (a smaller version eventually finding its way to the Tate Gallery). Another painter who contributed to Gambart's fortune was the immensely successful Meissonier, the son of a Paris grocer and druggist, whose painting *La Rixe* was presented by Napoleon III to his Britannic hosts. Meissonier appealed to English taste by the amount of action and incident he could put into a few square inches, by the passion for accuracy which caused him, when he came to paint the siege of Paris, to copy, from the original, Henri Regnault's greatcoat and Friar Anthelme's gown. He was the favourite artist of that wealthy milord, the fourth Marquess of Hertford, who bought his *Bravoes* for 28,000 francs, to whose interest the number of Meissoniers in the Wallace Collection, Hertford House, still bears witness. In proportion to the fabulous wealth of Meissonier was that of his agent, Gambart.

Such an agent could make an artist. Of this Alma-Tadema was aware, and he devised a clever little stratagem to lure Gambart to his studio. He heard that Gambart was in Belgium and was interested in the Belgian painter, Dyckmans. With the help of a friend he contrived that Gambart should come to his, Alma-Tadema's, studio, believing the address to be that of Dyckmans. Gambart arrived, and found himself confronted by an artist unknown to him and, on the easel, a piece of Merovingian history.

There may have been some irritable spluttering and gesticulation to begin with; but then, a painter who could plan this trick was obviously of a certain shrewdness, and one could make something of pictures like that on the easel. The subject was obscure, but that was not necessarily against it. Some buyers took pleasure in tracking down explanations in books of reference, in retailing them to their guests. They were stories to tell, making for conversation, and giving the host the pleasant feeling of being both a connoisseur and a man of historical learning. At all events here were the right ingredients, subject, human interest, and an amount of circumstantial detail worthy of Meissonier himself. The conversation was decisive.

'Is the picture on the easel painted for anybody?' asked Gambart.

'Yes.'

'Has the buyer seen it yet?'

'No.'

'Then, it is mine.'

Gambart came back to Antwerp for more. He arranged to 'take on' Alma-Tadema for a series of twenty-four pictures—paying progressively at a higher rate for each successive work. His second proposition was for forty-eight pictures in three categories of price, the first rising from £80, the second from £100, the third from £120. The commissions turned out well, so well that towards their completion Gambart gave a dinner to the artists of Brussels which Alma-Tadema attended (he moved to Brussels in 1865 and stayed there until 1869). Alma-Tadema found to his surprise that the dinner had been given in his honour. Wrapped in the folds of his napkin he found also a piece of paper which proved to be a cheque from Gambart for an extra £100 over and above the price of his most recent work.

.   .   .   .   .

The success which won this tribute, so delicately given and substantial in amount, was not due to pictures like that which Gambart had first seen. Soon after he made his contract, Alma-Tadema ceased to concern himself with the hag-ridden queens, sombre prelates, and brutal warriors whose complicated and hideous careers he had dredged from the depths of the Dark Ages. The change can be dated to 1863. In that year the little Dutchman and his French bride went on their honeymoon to Florence, Rome, and Naples. The light, the colour, the warmth of the Mediterranean had all that effect which they usually exert on the Northerner. Dark indeed was Merovingia by contrast. Then there were the museums of Rome and Naples which offered not only their famous examples of ancient sculpture but everyday objects—the more fascinating because they were every-day—which the ancient world had used: beds, chairs, lamps, wine jars, cooking utensils. As Gérôme had been fired by a gladiator's helmet, so was Alma-Tadema by the evidence of domestic life a thousand years ago.

And there was the marble—that cool substance which made the warmth of the sun more delightful, which suggested the luxury of palaces and the pleasures of the bath. Alma-Tadema was wont to say that he first acquired his passion for marble in 1858 when he visited the handsome, marmoreal smoking-room of a club in Ghent, but this was only a faint, modern reflection of that ancient club—the public bath; and marble to be seen in its glory must be seen in Italy. Alma-Tadema in Italy took pleasure in the quarries where marble was to be found in its native state; in the ruins where it bore the patina of age; in the new buildings where it freshly glittered. As he looked on the tinted columns, framed in foliage and set against the wine-dark sea, he exclaimed, 'And yet fools say that pale green and blue do not harmonize.'

He decided to take his subjects from this glowing Mediterranean world. They would probably be popular and they gave ample scope for applying his early lessons in archaeology. He was not the first popularizer in the field—in France there was Gérôme, not to speak of Louis Hamon and Gustave Boulanger, but they invited competition. In 1863 Alma-Tadema turned out the first of those recon-structions which were to have an extraordinary success. The subject was 'Egyptians Three Thousand Years Ago'. As his honeymoon journey was limited to Italy, as he did not actually visit Egypt until he was an old man, it may seem strange that he should select an Egyptian subject but, he explained, he was going straight to the beginning. 'Where else should I have begun', he asked, 'as soon as I had become acquainted with the life of the ancients? The first thing a child learns of ancient history is about the court of the Pharaohs.' He had, moreover, a friend and admirer who was an Egyptologist, Georg Moritz Ebers, later to become professor at Leipzig and to distinguish himself by the discovery of the medical treatise known as the *Papyrus Ebers*. The German scholar was a man after Alma-Tadema's own heart. He believed that the proper study of the archaeologist is life and was working on an historical novel *An Egyptian Princess*, published in 1864, which clothed the dry bones of learning with romance. It is possible that the scholar and the painter influenced one another. Alma-Tadema tried more Egyptian themes—*The Chess Players*, *The Egyptian at his Doorway*, *The Mummy*—and having got into the way of them, it was a short and easy step to Greece and Rome. Between 1863 and 1869 he painted *A Roman Family*, *The Honeymoon*, *The Preparations for a Feast in a Pompeian House*, and other works as accurate as possible in accessories and conveying that the people, despite their strange dress, were just such people as one might know.

That Gambart approved there is no doubt. Here was a new kind of history picture, minute as a Meissonier, and full of sentiment. It was Alma-Tadema's *Vintage Festival* of 1869 which brought the first series of antique subjects to a climax, which called for that banquet in the artist's honour at Brussels. The wreathed columns, the carved pedestals, the tripod fuming with incense, the cone-tipped staff of Bacchus, the white-robed maidens and vine-crowned men, the musicians with double flutes and clashing cymbals, made this glimpse into the social life and ceremony of the ancient world vivid and apparently truthful. Everything was there save the wildness of the Maenad, the madness of wine, the lithe animal vigour with which an Athenian vase-painter would have animated the scene. The cup was that decorous modicum which the Greeks called 'of good genius', the more palatable for that reason, as Alma-Tadema very well understood, to nineteenth-century taste.

II

THE WAY TO THE HEIGHTS

THOSE Egyptian and other pictures of the ancient world by Alma-Tadema came at a time when there was a widespread desire to travel on classic ground. The old Grand Tour was extended. Greece was an obvious addition to the itinerary once mainly confined to France, Switzerland, and Italy, and for this there was more than one reason. There was that reawakened interest in its antiquities which the Earl of Elgin (and the Continental connoisseurs) had encouraged. There was also the wave of sympathy aroused by the Greek struggle for independence. British people especially seemed to have a vital stake in the struggle, as admirers of the classics and lovers of freedom. Lord Byron had ratified an unofficial treaty of sentiment by his death at Missolonghi while serving in the Greek cause. After that the most insignificant British traveller to Athens was vested with the Byronic mantle and could enter the city with the pride of a vicarious liberator.

Wherever freedom was cherished the sympathy was the same. The French Romantics were as definitely on the Greek side as were the British, but in both there grew up a somewhat undiscriminating taste for the picturesque. It was undiscriminating because the Turks were picturesque too. They were to be hated as oppressors but they were fascinating in many ways. A love of the Greeks led to an interest in Turkish modes and manners, and as the Crusader, consciously or otherwise, copied the Saracen, so the nineteenth-century romantic and liberal delighted in Turkish curios and trophies, in yataghan and yashmak, fez and tchibouk, becoming, by an odd transposition, an Orientalist through classical leanings.

It was hard to separate the glamour of the 'Orient' from the glory that had been Greece. The 'inventor' of the Orient, as he has been called, the French painter Alexandre-Gabriel Decamps, originally intended to celebrate its eclipse. He was sent, that is, to the Eastern Mediterranean as assistant to the painter Garneray, to study the setting of the naval battle of Navarino, where in 1826 the British, French, and Russian fleets had destroyed the Turkish and Egyptian fleets. Decamps stayed for a while at Smyrna, returned to France after about three years, and lived on his memories for the rest of his life as a painter. Instead of commemorating Navarino he painted what he remembered of Smyrna's alleys and the popular life of the Asiatic Turk, inciting other artists to do likewise and those who were not artists to go where he had been.

It was easy to mingle ideas of antiquity with impressions of the contemporary 'near East'. It might well seem that the Mediterranean world was, and always had been, indivisible. The same sun beamed on all the lands which fringed this wonderful inland sea. The reader of the classics might as little distinguish between the ancient gods as the ancients themselves had done. Was not the Isis of the Egyptians also the Venus of Cyprus, the Athena of Athens, the Diana of Crete, the Proserpine of Sicily, the Bellona of Rome?

The interest in Greece consequently led to an interest in Egypt. The researches of Napoleon's savants on the banks of the Nile had drawn attention to classic Egypt, as Elgin's exploits on the Acropolis had done to classic Greece. There was the same savoury mixture of classic and exotic, and Egypt exerted its appeal by the mosque as well as the temple, by the tumultuous life of the Arab as well as the Tombs of the Kings.

The number of Grand Tourists rose to new proportions. If the scholars were few, the lovers of adventure were many and the taste for the picturesque took them into obscure places. There was no stretch of Syrian desert or wild Albanian mountain country but sooner or later a wandering Briton would appear, with his map, diary, copy of Homer, canister of tea, and all that confidence which the name of Lord Palmerston on his passport could give. As for the unadventurous—the family tourists—from the forties onwards the extending amenities of Thomas Cook (who had the same friendly and almost domestic relationship with them as had Mudie's library with the booklover) assured their comfort whether in the Nile Valley or the Peleponnesus. Progress brought safety with it, and Progress, represented by the Universal Company of the Maritime Suez Canal, busily at work between 1854 and 1869, also made for Egyptian travel.

Sometimes alone, sometimes in the company of patrons, the artists went with the tide. Gleyre visited the 'Orient' with his American patron. Edward Lear, in the serious role of topographer (and not as author of Books of Nonsense), made hundreds of drawings in Greece, Palestine, Egypt, Crete, Corfu. Léon Gérôme sailed down the Nile with Bartholdi, the sculptor of the *Lion of Belfort*, and at the Salon in 1863 showed a picture of contemporary Arabs instead of Roman gladiators. Frederick Goodall, R.A., who made his first visit to Egypt in 1858 with the aim of painting scriptural subjects, found the new departure a gold mine. Gambart offered him £5,000 for his travel sketches alone. He became one of Gambart's English favourites and his Egyptian paintings were hugely popular. The first of these works was sold for 1,000 guineas and the buyer, Mr. Duncan Dunbar, referred to it as his '100-guineas-a-foot picture'. Goodall's camels were highly praised by Sir Edwin Landseer, his *Hagar and Ishmael* (1866) by Mr. Gladstone.

.　　.　　.　　.　　.　　.

The existence of this vogue may help to explain why Edward Poynter's early success included some paintings of ancient Egypt. There exists no account of the early life of this reserved and self-contained man which gives a clue to his mental development. He went, we know, from Paris to Antwerp with George du Maurier. Was he then impressed by Alma-Tadema's work? Yet Alma-Tadema had not yet embarked on his scenes of ancient life. All it is possible to say is that during the sixties Poynter and Alma-Tadema proceeded on similar lines which were perhaps suggested by the same trend of popular taste.

Poynter settled in London in 1869, and his efforts to begin with were miscellaneous. His first Academy picture was a scene from Dante, *Heaven's Messenger*, showing the Angel crossing the Styx. It was rejected in 1860, accepted—and 'skied' in 1862. For a while he found employment in design and illustration; and as a designer of cartoons for stained glass and other decorative work, he assisted William Burges, architect of the cathedrals of Brisbane and Cork.

Thus he strayed far from classic ground, for Burges, 'Billy' Burges to his friends, was a medieval man. He was a 'Goth', as the supporters of the Gothic Revival were known, the pupil of Edward Blore who designed Abbotsford for Sir Walter Scott, the assistant of Digby Wyatt, and an apostle of the pointed arch. When Burges restored Waltham Abbey, Poynter decorated its ceiling with the Twelve Signs of the Zodiac, the Four Seasons, and the Four Elements. Then he took to illustration, as so many painters did at this time. The celebrated Northumbrian family of engravers, the brothers Dalziel, were planning an 'Illustrated Bible' to which many painters of note were invited to contribute. The Dalziels were first attracted to Poynter's work by a water-colour drawing of 'Egyptian Water Carriers' which they saw at a minor exhibition in Newman Street. He did in all ten drawings, a number of them illustrating the life of Joseph. In 1863 he was at work on his *Joseph before Pharaoh*, and perhaps this suggested to him a further exploration. In 1864, at the same time as Alma-Tadema was beginning to paint ancient Egypt, Poynter produced his *On Guard in the Time of the Pharaohs*.

Also like Alma-Tadema, he began to vary Egyptian with Roman subject-matter. In 1865 he painted that well-known picture, now in the Walker Art Gallery, Liverpool, *Faithful Unto Death*, with which he scored a real success.

Pompeii and Herculaneum, smothered in the eruption of Vesuvius in A.D. 79, disclosed since 1750 in a state of preservation which made real their normal life and their last tragic moments, were of intense interest. For English people this interest had been increased by Bulwer-Lytton's novel *The Last Days of Pompeii*, written in 1834 and after thirty years an established classic. Poynter had painted such a scene as Bulwer-Lytton described. The skeleton of a soldier had been discovered at the Herculean gate in full armour. It was to be

ISRAEL IN EGYPT
by Sir Edward Poynter, P.R.A.

assumed that with true Roman discipline he had remained on guard, 'faithful unto death', in spite of darkness, fire, and the panic of the inhabitants. Poynter depicted the sentry, erect and dutiful, while in the background could be seen the corpses of would-be fugitives, the gestures of the still living who crouched before showers of flaming rubble. To the Victorian mind it was an excellent work of art because it was a lesson—in fact, a whole series of lessons—in costume, history, and devotion.

Poynter's next effort was Egyptian again—a picture called *Offerings to Isis*. It was not so exalted in theme, but it played, with something of Alma-Tadema's skill, on the thought of youth fresh and charming in that far-off ancient world, a young girl going up the steps of a temple, taking a goose as her offering; and it was also well received and soon found a purchaser. Now Poynter embarked on an ambitious composition, the idea of which occurred to him at a meeting of the Langham Sketching Club where the members were in the habit of making sketch compositions of some stated subject. 'Work' was one of these subjects. It did not, as it had done to Ford Madox Brown some years before, suggest to Poynter contemporary work, but work in ancient Egypt, and he liked the rough sketch he made so well that he decided to turn it into a big picture.

Israel in Egypt was the title. To this, in the Royal Academy catalogue of 1866, was appended the quotation: 'Now there arose up a new king over Egypt who knew not Joseph' (Exod. i. 8). The Israelites in bondage were seen drawing along a colossal sculpture towards the gateway of a temple. In its frieze-like movement it recalled the procession of Leighton's *Cimabue*—though Poynter had avoided Leighton's initial error and broken the even motion by dancing figures. Never so thorough an archaeologist as Alma-Tadema, he had nevertheless taken great pains to make the buildings and sculptured reliefs look convincing, and like the Dutch painter he had been careful to include that agreeable touch of human feeling. He made a charitable Egyptian give a drink of water to a fainting Israelite beside whom an overseer hovered, impatient and threatening. *Israel in Egypt* was bought by Sir John Hawkshaw, the civil engineer who built the railways and bridges at Charing Cross and Cannon

F

Street. Sir John was interested in the feat of primitive engineering the removal of the colossal sculpture on a long truck with wooden wheels, hauled by man-power. He was interested also in Egypt having gone out some years earlier to report on the site of the Suez Canal. It was instinctive with him to calculate how much man power would be needed to move so large a piece of stone, and his critical comment was that Poynter's slaves were not enough for the job. The artist overcame this objection by extending the line of men to the very edge of the picture, thus allowing the spectator to add in imagination, as many more as might be thought sufficient. And all was well.

The attraction of ancient engineering encouraged the artist to follow up *Israel* in 1867 with the work which used to be so often reproduced in illustrated school history books: *The Catapult*. Once again he showed his ingenuity, in reconstructing the ball-throwing engine of the Roman army. The scene was again laid in Africa, but this time at the siege of Carthage—as indicated by the inscription on the side of the catapult: '*Delenda est Carthago*'. The picture ensured his election as Associate of the Royal Academy in 1868.

It was in this period of early success that Poynter married. During the sixties he became friendly with Edward and Georgiana Burne Jones and was greatly attracted to that devoted couple. Burne-Jones had some secret which Poynter did not feel himself to possess, the secret of that imaginative world in which the Pre-Raphaelites lived. He and Georgiana were as if touched by an enchantment which transformed life into a happy dream. Painting for him was a means of admission into it, of exit from the prosaic Victorian world, and though he had had no formal training he seemed to be wonderfully buoyed up by the inspiring influence of Dante Gabriel Rossetti and William Morris, enabled by it to take on successfully any enterprise and give to a picture, a piece of stained glass, or an illustration a strange and distinct quality. He could, said Poynter, 'do everything' and though a pupil of Gleyre could scarcely have the same views as a pupil of Rossetti, the difference was no bar to friendship.

When Poynter first met Edward and Georgiana they were in rooms in Great Russell Street, 'beautifully situated opposite the

Museum, with a clear view of the trees in Russell Square out of the top windows, and an easy walk from Tottenham Court Road and Holborn', and when the Burne-Joneses moved to Kensington Square, Poynter took over their former quarters. They visited him there and joked about the freedom with which he made use of 'our rooms', Edward, when the time came to say good-night, tramping upstairs as if to go to bed in his own house. He visited them in Kensington Square and made a water-colour sketch of their small garden, and he met Georgiana's sisters who often came to stay with them. There was Alice who married John Lockwood Kipling in 1865, and was to become the mother of Rudyard Kipling; Louie, who became engaged in the same year to Alfred Baldwin, and Agnes, the good-looking one of the family. It was Agnes whom Poynter married in 1866.

.   .   .   .   .   .

If that reading of Haydon's *Journals* in Rome, with all their passionate enthusiasm for the Elgin Marbles, had made Leighton think much of Greek art, it was not until he returned to England that his bent really began to show itself. He had undergone many temptations to belong to other nations. He might as a result of his universal education have been a German or an Italian—yet he remained an Englishman. He became 'classic' after an English fashion—through better acquaintance with the Elgin Room at the British Museum and through a love of ancient art fostered not by Gibson, nor Ingres, nor Couture, nor Gérôme, but by an island Olympian, George Frederick Watts.

They first met in 1855 when friends in Rome wrote urging Watts to go and see 'a delightful young painter called Leighton' who was then on a visit to London. Their meeting began a friendship which was to last for forty years.

Watts was then thirty-eight, thirteen years older than Leighton and already famous and successful. His success had been of an un-usual kind. He seemed to have stepped as if by magic from the struggle of Victorian middle-class life into a serene and ideal world. The son of an unsuccessful pianoforte-maker in Marylebone who tuned pianos and gave elementary music lessons for a living, he might, it would have been easy and incorrect to foretell, have been doomed to many years of poverty and hardship. He was not, however, a genius on the distressed model but of a type which belonged to an old and generous tradition. He had a sort of magnetism which gave him the run of houses and converted acquaintances into patrons. Like some favoured apprentice in old Italy, he was, as a boy, made free of the sculptor William Behnes's studio, first in Dean Street, Soho, and later in Osnaburgh Street. The young Watts watched the process of statuary making, the production of those portrait medallions in which Behnes (Sculptor in Ordinary to Her Majesty) did a thriving trade. Long informative talks with the sculptor's brother, Charles Behnes, a man of some learning, gave him a species of literary education.

He had found patrons early. There was Nicholas Wanostrocht, an Anglo-Belgian with a school at Blackheath, who played professional cricket under the name of Nicholas Felix and added to the literature of the sport a work entitled *Felix on the Bat*. For him Watts made a series of drawings showing the various positions of the cricket-player (which eventually became the property of the Marylebone Cricket Club). Constantine Ionides of the Greek merchant house in London befriended him, and in 1843 when he was twenty-six the State became his patron. In that year, with his cartoon *Caractacus led in Triumph through the Streets of Rome*, he won one of the £300 prizes in the competition for suitable designs with which to decorate the Houses of Parliament. He was thus enabled to visit Italy, made himself agreeable on the way to some English travellers who wrote favourably about him to Lord Holland, then the British Minister at Florence, was invited to lunch on arrival—and stayed. There were a hundred rooms in the Hollands' palazzo. 'Stay', said Lady Holland, 'until you find quarters you like'—but where else could there be such delightful quarters, and an extra person in a house so large was no burden. Indeed, the young painter who sat so quietly and ascetically at the rich table and sipped his glass of water while rare wines were passed round was a romantic addition to the household.

The days went by, they became months, the months became years and still Watts was there. He lived, as old masters had done, with nobles who were well satisfied merely with his presence. Coming back to London in 1847 he once again won an official prize, the subject being *Alfred inciting the Britons to resist the Landing of the Danes by encountering them at Sea*, the premium £500. 'A great fellow or I am much mistaken', said Ruskin, two years later, though it is not obvious why he should add 'and we suffer the clouds to lie upon him, with thunder and famine at once in the thick of them'. There was neither thunder nor famine at the Cosmopolitan Club, a circle of distinguished men of which Watts became a member, nor at Little Holland House where he went to live in 1850.

It was the Florentine palace in an English version, the same story of indulgent patronage. The quality in him which appealed to Lord and Lady Holland appealed as much to his new friends, Mr. and Mrs. Thoby Prinsep. He was a part of the family without belonging to it. He painted the portrait of the beautiful Miss Virginia Pattle, sister of Mrs. Prinsep, and it is said that Lord Somers who married Miss Pattle in 1850 fell in love with her through first seeing the portrait. It was Watts who introduced the Prinseps, when they were looking for a place near London, to the house previously occupied by Lord Holland's aunt and then to let—Little Holland House, a rambling historic building with gardens and paddock, an 'oasis' of beauty and peace two miles from Hyde Park Corner. 'He came to stay three days, he stayed thirty years', said Mrs. Prinsep. As in Italy with the Hollands so here with the retired Anglo-Indian and his wife, Watts lived on terms of affectionate intimacy and at the same time in entire independence.

There was something a little unreal in this mode of life which erased every ordinary problem of living. It was aloof and detached from the ways of other men, and yet Watts was little inclined to ease or indulgence. He worked hard and long although delicate and liable to bouts of illness and nausea. Perhaps because of his frailness he was singularly high-minded. The immunity from care which would have made some men soft and epicurean made him a philosopher of an austere kind. Set apart from the gross material world he cultivated abstractions, refined and intellectualized all his impressions. Symbols or symbolic figures—Love (in the most rarefied and spiritual sense), Justice, Hope—became of more meaning than real men and women. In painting portraits he looked for heads which were of the most spiritual type, and was sometimes inclined to credit his sitters with a spirituality which belonged to him rather than to them.

He was typical of his age and race in his wish to paint ideas and to point to moral lessons, and yet he looked on himself as the pupil of Pheidias. Although he visited Rome with Lord Holland and both viewed the mighty frescoes of Michelangelo with deep respect, Watts was unshaken in his greater respect for the Greeks. If he admired Titian and Veronese, if there is a soft reflection of their richness in his painting, he judged them still by the ancient standard of beauty. It was not really necessary, he maintained, to travel in Italy, when there were the Elgin Marbles in London, and the casts of the *Theseus* and the *Ilissus* from the Parthenon, which stood on his studio mantelpiece, were among his most cherished possessions. Leighton argued often with Watts on his too-great attachment to ideas, but was at the same time much impressed by a regard for the Greek perfection of Beauty which he was predisposed to share.

The close friendship between them dates from Leighton's return to London in 1860. For some years the studio in the rue Pigalle had been the merest *pied-à-terre*. He had kept on travelling. He would appear in Co. Donegal, in Frankfurt, in Algiers (winter, 1857-8), in Rome, Capri, Greece (winter, 1858-9). Somehow, in 1859, he managed to interpolate a visit to Vichy with Algernon Charles Swinburne and Richard Burton. He came back to a martial scene, and he and Watts were drawn together in the patriotic mood of the moment.

A warlike cloud was blowing up. Though a treaty of commerce was signed with France in 1860, with a view to 'drawing still closer the bonds of friendly alliance', all was not well between the allies of the Crimea. France had aroused dislike by interfering in Italian affairs, by demands for Nice and Savoy. Despite those bonds of alliance Lord John Russell told the House of Commons that 'we must be ready to declare, always in the most moderate and friendly terms, that the peace of Europe is a matter dear to this country'. The dockyards were fortified; a depot for arms and stores set up; to 'nationalize shooting' (Lord Elcho's phrase) a Volunteer Rifle Corps was formed. Earl Grey told the officers that it would depend on themselves whether the movement was to be worthy of England or to become a mere laughing-stock. The artists did their best to make it worthy. They rallied to the Artists' Volunteer Corps. They fought sham fights in Kent and Surrey, did company drill in Burlington House Gardens where the Royal Academy now stands, and spent the whole of Saturday on military routine.

Many a famous artist joined in—Holman Hunt, John Millais, Dante Gabriel Rossetti, William Morris among them. Watts in spite of his cloistered life could ride, and with his long silky beard blown first over one shoulder, then over the other, made a fine figure on horseback as the company galloped over Wimbledon Common. Leighton, who did all things well, excelled at these war games. 'I make as bad a soldier as anybody else', he wrote lightly to Browning, but this was modesty. He was an efficient and a keen soldier. The German habit of punctuality and thoroughness, acquired in his early days, stood him in good stead. In summer he was out at Wellington Barracks doing battalion drill with the Guards at five in the morning. He and Millais designed the jaunty grey cap of the Volunteers. He set up cardboard targets in his studio for extra shooting practice. In a short while he was a captain and, as he remained a Volunteer for twenty years, it is clear the duty was also a pleasure. No one was more generally popular in the corps. 'It's all right', said one, 'when Leighton's on parade.'

Yet the Volunteers included many Pre-Raphaelites, and the Pre-Raphaelites as he jokingly said were his 'enemies'—not in any personal sense but in respect of art and ideas of art. Though they all wore the same uniform he rode among them, figuratively speaking, like a horseman from the Parthenon frieze among King Arthur's knights armed cap-à-pie. He had after all freed himself from the influence of one lot of Pre-Raphaelites—the 'pietistical' Germans. There was not a very close similarity between them and the English artists who were also called Pre-Raphaelite, but enough to arouse his critical suspicion. They, too, were in love with the Middle Ages. They, too, loved less the beauty of the figure than the mystic melancholy of legend. If it came to a question of preference between Athens and Camelot, Leighton was all for Athens. The English Pre-Raphaelites had an advantage over the Germans in their love of nature. Here Leighton was disposed to agree with them. He had made some minute drawings during those sunny winter days in the Mediterranean before he came home, at Capri a detailed study of a lemon-tree which gained the admiration of Ruskin. It might seem that in this he approached the Pre-Raphaelite method, yet perhaps there was more of the spirit of rivalry in it than affinity. He wished to show that the precision of outline was not their monopoly, and in the completed *tour de force* there was less of the Pre-Raphaelite than of Leonardo.

Nor, in spite of the patriotic union of the corps, were the Pre-Raphaelites so commanding in influence as they had been. Already there were many rifts in the movement. There was little kinship left between Holman Hunt and Millais on the one hand and Rossetti on the other; while William Morris, it was clear, had little sympathy with the exclusive pursuit of painting, was taking his own way as a craftsman. There was room for a new leader—and Leighton had all the qualities of a leader, even though, in spite of his flying start, he had been slower than Poynter to arrive at a characteristic style or to 'settle down' (if at any time those domestic words could be applied to him).

During the sixties he was still feeling his way. The always strong influence of Italy led him to paint such themes as *Paolo and Francesca*, *Michelangelo nursing his Dying Servant*, and *Dante in Exile*. These pictures were not unsuccessful. Gambart paid a thousand guineas for the *Dante* (Leighton promptly invested £1,000 in Eastern Counties Railway Debentures at par, $4\frac{1}{2}$ per cent.). On the other hand they did not represent the mature Leighton.

He attempted some religious themes, but in these he did not show to best advantage. The dutiful dullness which lurked in the Nazarene association was somehow present in them. It appears in the fresco for Lyndhurst Church in the New Forest, *The Wise and Foolish Virgins*, which he offered to paint in 1862 when staying at Lyndhurst with his friend, Charles Hamilton Aïdé, the poet, novelist, and composer. The church was new, a product of the Gothic Revival, harsh in its red and yellow brick, curious in line, yet inviting to the decorator of the sixties. William Morris's 'Co.' devoted itself to the stained glass in which the hand of Burne-Jones, of Ford Madox Brown, and Dante Gabriel Rossetti can be traced. On the fresco under the east window (still in a state of passable preservation) Leighton worked for several years. It was a handsome gift—more famous than Burne-Jones's 'New Jerusalem' window or Rossetti's roundels—yet colder, with a coldness which recalls an Overbeck, a Bouguereau, an Ary Scheffer. Ruskin, with whom Leighton was friendly (though not intimate), expressed doubts of his efforts at religious painting in his own inimitable fashion. Apropos of the *Ahab and Jezebel*, which depicted the meeting with Elijah in Naboth's vineyard and was exhibited in the Royal Academy of 1863, Ruskin wrote: 'You know you, like all people good for anything in this age and country (as far as Palmerston), are still a boy—and a boy can't paint Elijah.' Still, 'the pretty girls', said Ruskin, referring to Leighton's other pictures in the same exhibition, *Girl with a Basket of Fruit*, *Girl feeding Peacocks*, 'are nice—*very nearly* beautiful'. At the same time Leighton had made a mistake about the number of eyes appearing in a peacock's tail. Ruskin excused the cheerfully derisive tone of his criticisms on this and other points, which he had apparently written in the morning, by saying, 'I'm always wickeder in the morning than at night because I'm fresh.'

Leighton varied these themes with portraiture. When he went home to visit his parents at Bath he made many portrait studies, especially of the children of friends and neighbours, fascinating his young models by whistling like a bird, singing songs, and telling stories. It is a sign of both his habitual generosity and his love of children that when one of them, John Hanson Walker, told Leighton that he also wished to be an artist, he made him a sumptuous present of artist's materials. They arrived in a big crate—plaster casts of heads, hands, and feet, drawing paper, drawing boards, pencils, chalks, paints.

In addition to religious pictures and portraits he made many illustrations—some of them for the Dalziel Bible on which Poynter was also engaged. The brothers Dalziel admired his *Cain and Abel* as 'one of the grandest examples of Biblical art of modern times'. He illustrated works by his friends, Elizabeth Barrett Browning's *The Great God Pan*, Adelaide Sartoris's *A Week in a Country House* (a prose sketch of French life), while his knowledge of Italy seemed to make him the ideal illustrator for George Eliot's historical novel of fifteenth-century Florence, *Romola*. George Smith of the *Cornhill* gave him the commission in 1862. He was to do two illustrations for each of twelve numbers, receiving £40 for each or £480 for the whole novel. He went to see the author 'Miss Evans (or Mrs. Lewes)', whom he found 'of a striking countenance'—rather like Charles Quint with her large face, deep-set eyes, aquiline nose, big mouth, and projecting under-jaw. A certain remoteness in her manner he attributed to short sight; it was a remoteness which he tried to overcome in his own brisk and efficient way. There were so many things he knew about Italy which she might not, and he was helpful on a great number of details, of speech as well as costume. George Eliot (with 'a tremulous sense of my liability to error in such matters') accepted the help. ('I am very much obliged to you for your critical doubts. I will put out the questionable "Ecco!" in deference to your knowledge.') She expressed her admiration of the completed drawings with a politeness adequate to the occasion but with no great warmth.

Thus Leighton was busy on many enterprises and a success in the material sense. If one could speak of a period of poverty, the comparative poverty represented by Dr. Leighton's allowance to him of £250 a year, that period was now over. A natural frugality as far as vulgar wants were concerned had always made it go far. 'He never contracted a debt,' said his sister, 'he never drank, he never smoked, then or afterwards except on social occasions.' It was true he had asked for an increase in the allowance, but mainly on the ground that it was occasionally necessary to take a cab rather than to ride in an omnibus in evening dress. Now his pictures were selling. He was elected Associate of the Royal Academy in 1864, and this date roughly marks the beginning of his classical period.

It was ten years since he had listened to that impassioned praise of the Elgin Marbles in Haydon's *Autobiography*, yet it was not surely without its effect. Not for nothing either in their long talks had

Watts dilated on the supremacy of Greek art. A period of travel in the lands of ancient deities must also be allowed its influence. The classic themes followed in close succession: in 1864 his *Orpheus and Eurydice*, suggested by Browning's *A Fragment*; in 1865, *Helen walking on the Ramparts of Troy*; in 1866 *The Syracusan Bride leading Wild Beasts in Procession to the Temple of Diana*, suggested by the Second Idyll of Theocritus, and showing the beasts calm under the influence of beauty. If the bride seemed to belong to Mayfair rather than to Syracuse, the picture was no less impressive in effect. The year 1867 saw *Venus disrobing for the Bath*, 1868 *Ariadne abandoned by Theseus*, 1869 a whole group of classical themes: *Electra at the Tomb of Agamemnon, Helios and Rhodos, Daedalus and Icarus*.

.   .   .   .   .

Somehow the production of these works must be reconciled with the time spent on many distant journeys. It is hard to keep track of all the comings and goings of this remarkable man. It would seem that one year he is at Orme Square in Bayswater where he first settled in London, busy in his studio, industriously experimenting with the Gambier-Parry method of spirit fresco (which he employed at Lyndhurst); but beyond a doubt in the same year he is roaming in the Eastern Mediterranean. We know that like any other traveller he went by railway and steamship; that it was possible to do much work in England in the spring and summer and still travel a very long way in the winter. Nevertheless there was something almost superhuman in the energy and speed with which he did travel: as if like some mythological being described by Homer he flashed from one place to another. It must be understood that if any date is given to his activities in London he may well have been just off to, or just returning from, Italy, Germany, North Africa, Syria, or Greece.

He confessed to being 'sorely perplexed' when asked by Mrs. Mark Pattison in 1879 to date his journeys. He could do so only by reference to his pictures. He was, he worked out by this method, in Algiers when he was making studies for *Samson Agonistes*. He was in Spain, 'the year of the cholera', having made what he called a 'raid' there from the South of France. The year after, he was in Vienna, Constantinople, Smyrna, Rhodes, and Athens ('the greatest architectural emotion of my life by far'). A visit to his friend Sir Richard Burton at Damascus was placed as 'a year before I exhibited *The Jew's House*'; a visit to Egypt in the year before the opening of the Suez Canal (he rode, he remembered, over the Salt Lakes with M. de Lesseps).

His moves can be followed in part from the letters which describe the prolonged Grand Tour of the late sixties in the course of which he acquired many of those objects of art which later were to delight and astonish visitors to his mansion. He was looking at Greece and the Grecian islands in the intervals of painting that bodily perfection which Greek artists had sought. Thus in 1867, the year of *Venus disrobing for the Bath*, he was at Rhodes and Lindos, where he bought much pottery—'beautiful specimens of old Persian *faience*'—consoling his father, who did not care for these things, by the consideration that 'I could, *any day*, part with the whole lot for at least double, probably treble what I gave'. He went on to Athens. The weather was bad and he could do little painting, but he had all the more time to give to the ruins on the Acropolis, and the Earl of Elgin himself could have expressed no greater enthusiasm. Well though he knew the photographs, the casts, the originals in the British Museum, his eyes were now newly open to 'the impression which these magnificent works produce when seen together under their own sky'.

Even Byron, in his opinion, had not done justice to the exquisite scenery. By comparison with Athens, Venice was artificial. His thoughts on the Acropolis were refined by the thoroughness of his education. It reminded him, he said, 'of the admirable words which Thucydides puts into the mouth of Pericles'.

He came back to London in 1868 and, announcing his arrival, expressed himself 'right glad to get home again'. Yet in the same year he was off once more and this time to Egypt where the circumstances of the expedition were of a splendour that was unusual and befitting. He had audience at once with the Khedive, not as a painter (even an illustrious painter) but as a friend of the Prince of Wales

A letter had gone out in which the Prince conveyed his wish that Leighton should receive all possible aid. The Khedive was at his palace at Abbassia, and if the military review which was then taking place was not for Leighton's benefit, it happily coincided with his arrival. The Khedive greeted him in an open pavilion overlooking the great array of tents in which five thousand men were quartered. He clapped his hands and pipes were brought, their amber mouthpieces encrusted with diamonds and emeralds. The health of the Prince of Wales was gravely and politely discussed. In a leisurely fashion they approached the purpose of the interview. The aide who stood at the Khedive's elbow, Colonel Stanton, threw out 'a little hint' that a steam-tug would get Leighton down the Nile with the desired quickness. A tug! It was obvious to the Khedive that only a luxurious steamer would give fitting accommodation to a friend of the Prince of Wales. 'It is the same to me,' he remarked, 'and you will be more comfortable.' Without doubt, Colonel Stanton put in, the Prince would be much gratified by this courtesy and in a short space of time, like the satisfaction of a wish in some tale from the *Arabian Nights*, the Khedive's own steam yacht was ready.

For Oriental life and manners Leighton had a certain sympathy, the sympathy which he extended to so many different races. It was possible for him to feel and talk, if the occasion required it, as an Oriental would. He had done so when his sister, Mrs. Sutherland Orr, had been helped to escape from Aurungabad, during the Indian Mutiny, by a certain Sheikh Boran Bukh. He had written to the Sheikh a letter exquisitely patterned with the appropriate floweriness of praise. 'From one end of this country to another, Englishmen have read the account of your loyal bearing and from one end of the country to the other there has been but one voice to praise and to admire it: for uprightness and fidelity are precious in the eyes of all Englishmen and honour and courage are to them as the breath of life. . . .' In a very similar style the Sheikh acknowledged his 'invaluable kindness' and the gift of a revolving pistol 'highly admired by all who saw it'.

Thus Leighton was well adapted to appreciate Egypt: with no tinge of the tourist's incomprehension, with the pleasure of a

specialist in manners. The frequent salutations, the laying of a han
on the breast and the forehead, were graceful without servility. H
never failed to be impressed by the dignity of the Arab at his devc
tions. Uneasy as he felt, he could constrain himself at a feast to ea
with his fingers, pieces of fat mutton heaped on his plate by hospi
able and greasy hands, to spoon out a sweet from the common bow

It was less easy to restrain his natural habit of punctuality, a hab
by no means Oriental. He told those servants of the Khedive depute
to attend him at his hotel: 'I shall be ready to start at two o'clock
the day after tomorrow.' He was at the boat on time, but the captai
showed him over it in a leisurely way, offered refreshments, an
evinced no inclination to start. Leighton looked at his watch, aske
why he was kept waiting. The captain explained that they had no
really expected him, that the Khedive's guests sometimes kept hi
waiting four or five weeks.

Yet once they were started everything delighted Leighton. How
fully capable he was of entering into the spirit of ceremonial custor
was shown when the captain, at one point of the journey, wished t
stop the boat in order to propitiate a holy man stationed on th
river bank. Leighton immediately agreed; and when the captain an
crew went ashore in a body to kiss the holy man's hand, a delicat
politeness detained him on board, for he would not on any accour
hurt the old gentleman's feelings by not kissing his hand.

He enjoyed the hubbub of processions, the drums beating, th
muskets banging, the crowd shrieking and shuffling in the dus
the women huddled and dark against the sky, looking on from th
housetops. He delighted in the fawn-coloured shores, varied wit
strips of brilliant green and wildly luxuriant gardens; the vibran
blue sky, the purple shadows complementary to the gold of th
sands by which the yacht quietly glided. Many were the vivid im
pressions he recorded in his diary. The muezzin tearing his falsett
from his throat with an almost intolerable plaintiveness. The crev
of the Arab boat which bounced in the rapids at Assuan, green witl
terror and praying loudly to the Prophet, while Leighton sat amon
them in Olympian calm. The 'little Fatima', aged five, who watche
him draw and exclaimed, 'Washallah! how well he writes'. Th

94

dancing girls in their gaudy dresses who performed what he called 'remarkable gymnastics'. It was all exciting and sensuously moving. The question was whether it stood the test of an artist's calm reflection. At every stage of the journey Leighton made comparisons, and these were ever more distinctly in favour of classic Europe.

The paintings in the royal tombs in the Valley of the Kings were of great interest, but mainly from an 'ethnographic point of view'. Poynter, he remarked, would 'have a fit over them' (meaning apparently of pleasure), but as paintings they were to Leighton merely barbaric. There was nothing, he admitted, to compare with the monuments of Egypt 'for the expression of gigantic thoughts and limitless command of material and labour'. And then—the image of the Parthenon came into his mind, 'infinitely precious' in the added glory of its sculptures, and in contrast with its candid perfection Luxor and Edfu seemed stolid and oppressive. As he fingered a nosegay of flowers presented to him by the governor of Esne, the smell of a leaf of basil took him back in mind to Lindos and Rhodes and 'that marvellous blue coast across the seas that looked as if it could enclose nothing behind its crested rocks but the Gardens of the Hesperides'. At the ancient quarries between Kom Ombo and Edfu he could not but think of the marble quarries of Pentelicus from which Ictinos built the Parthenon and Pheidias carved 'the Fates', and with all his admiration for the columns of the Temple of Karnak it was impossible for him not to reflect on the superior qualities of the Doric and Ionic orders. As a transposition of ideas had diverted other artists from Greece and Rome to Egypt, with him the process was reversed. His Egyptian journey confirmed and even increased his love of Hellenic subjects, so vigorously shown in the *Daedalus*, the *Electra*, the *Helios and Rhodos* of 1869. His course now was clear, and his *Heracles wrestling with Death for the Body of Alcestis* (1871) inspired Browning to write of him (in *Balaustion's Adventure*) as if he were indeed some great craftsman of the classic past.

> I know, too, a great Kaunian painter, strong
> As Hercules, though rosy with a robe
> Of Grace that softens down the sinewy strength,
> And he has made a picture of it all.

III

THE GOLDEN YEARS

THE eighteen-seventies and the eighteen-eighties saw the ascendancy and triumph of what amounted to a new classical revival. In the war of revivals it had come out on top, though not without an amount of opposition which throws light on the complex nature of the Victorian mind.

There was a religious element in this opposition. Ultimately it was necessary to define classicism as paganism or a sort of paganism, and therefore it was necessarily opposite to the Christian ideal.

It was a point on which Benjamin Disraeli acutely seized in his novel *Lothair*, published in 1870. Into his picture of an aristocracy of fantastic wealth and indeterminate aims he introduced an artist, modelled on Frederick Leighton and called 'Mr. Phoebus'. Disraeli's description of Mr. Phoebus's *Hero and Leander* might almost be that of a painting by Leighton himself.

'When the curtain was withdrawn, they beheld a life-size figure exhibiting in undisguised completeness the perfection of the female form, and yet the painter had so skilfully availed himself of the shadowy and mystic hour and of some gauze-like drapery, which veiled without concealing his design, that the chastest eye might gaze on his heroine with impunity.'

In the 'countenance aquiline and delicate' of Mr. Phoebus, 'from many circumstances of a remarkable beauty', it is possible to see the features of Leighton himself. The views of Mr. Phoebus served as a foil to the precepts of subtle priests trying to instil into the minds of their noble friends unaccustomed ruminations on religious faith and duty. If they were more arrogant than those to be expected from his prototype there are views not in substance unlike them in Leighton's own *Addresses*.

'Might I venture to ask', says Disraeli's wistful and doubtful young nobleman, Lothair, 'what you may consider the true principles of art?'

'Aryan principles,' crisply replies Mr. Phoebus, 'not merely the study of nature, but of beautiful nature; the art of design in a country inhabited by a first-rate race, and where the laws, the manners, the customs are calculated to maintain the health and beauty of a first-rate race. In a greater or less degree, these conditions obtained from the age of Pericles to the age of Hadrian in pure Aryan communities, but Semitism then began to prevail and ultimately triumphed. Semitism has destroyed art: it has taught man to despise his own body and the essence of art is to honour the human frame.'

This imagined discussion has its parallel in Leighton's Academy Address of 1883, which is at least equally concerned with the physical attributes of a first-class race. 'In the Art of the Periclean Age, of which the high truthfulness was one of its noblest attributes . . . we find a new ideal of balanced form, wholly Aryan and of which the only parallel I know is sometimes found in the women of another Aryan race—your own.'

The 'Semitism' on which Disraeli (and Mr. Phoebus) remarked, that concern for the soul which caused the body either to be despised as a thing of little consequence or feared as an enemy, made many a Victorian frown on painting. Churchmen pondered sadly over the reasons which led men so evidently respectable as Leighton or Alma-Tadema to give so much attention to the human frame. The Bishop of Carlisle wrote with misgiving, in 1879, to the portrait-painter George Richmond: 'My mind has been considerably exercised this season by the exhibition of Alma-Tadema's nude Venus.' There might, said the Bishop, 'be artistic reasons which justify such public exposure of the female form', but he himself could not understand upon what principle this exposure was permissible. 'In the case of the nude of an Old Master much allowance can be made'—for Old

Masters, it might be assumed, knew no better and had the excuse of greatness as well as age—'but for a living artist to exhibit a life-size, life-like, almost photographic representation of a beautiful naked woman strikes my inartistic mind as somewhat if not very mischievous.'

The Bishop's doubts were mildly and even apologetically put. It would place too great a strain on the meaning of a word to call them 'Semitic'. They were, however, doubts not limited to men of the Church but closely connected with the beliefs of those who looked back to the Middle Ages, the revivalists of 'Gothic'. John Ruskin was certainly on the Gothic side. 'Classic' to him meant what was 'senatorial, academic' and so far as it implied a contempt for Gothic 'illiberal'. It was quite right that the British public should be able to see the Elgin Marbles in the British Museum, but not that they should be unable to see sculptures like those of Chartres or Wells, unless they went to the Kensington Museum where, said Ruskin, with all his implacable hatred of the machine, 'Gothic saints and sinners are confounded alike among steam-threshing machines and dynamite-proof ships of war; or to the Crystal Palace where they are mixed up with Rimmel's perfumery'.

He adopted his most teasing, frivolous, pettifogging manner in his comments on pictures with a classical subject, such, for instance, as he made in 1875, on Poynter's Academy work entitled *The Golden Age*. 'The "Golden Age"', remarked Ruskin derisively, 'in this pinchbeck one interests nobody. Not even the painter—for had he looked at the best authorities for an account of it, he would have found that its people lived chiefly on corn and strawberries both growing wild; and doubtless the loaded fruit-branches drooped to their reach.' 'Mr. Poynter's picture' appeared to Ruskin to 'savour somewhat of adventitious gas-lighting'. The object, no doubt, was 'to show us like Michelangelo the adaptability of limbs to awkward positions, but he can only, by this anatomical science, interest his surgical spectators'.

Poynter was naturally irritated and in return devoted a lecture to Ruskin's views on Michelangelo. He assumed, he said, that when Ruskin spoke of the glory of nature and God's works, he excluded the human figure, both male and female, and referred to 'mossy rocks and birds' nests, sunset skies, red herrings by Hunt, robin redbreasts, anything you like, in fact, but the figure for its beauty. In Mr. Ruskin's opinion . . . the introduction of the human figure is only to be permitted in its "subordination", which as he explains it, means the place it occupied among ascetic painters and such as knew not how to give it its proper, much less its most beautiful, form and action.'

There was truth in Poynter's estimate of Ruskin's tastes. Ruskin, the admirer of the Middle Ages, had some of the medieval repugnance for the animal body (if it were not an inherited Calvinist repugnance). The 'Nature', the study of which he so strongly advocated, was inanimate, and the most important part of the human anatomy was the head, as being, ideally speaking, the least animal. Portraiture, according to Ruskin's reasoning, was a Gothic achievement. When copying Carpaccio's *St. Ursula* in the Academy at Venice he had found 'it was necessary on the whole to be content with her face and not to be too critical or curious about her elbows; but in the Aegina marbles, one's principal attention had to be given to the knees and elbows, while no ardent sympathies were excited by the fixed smile'. It was not an abstract beauty of proportion which Ruskin looked for but the evidence of humanity. He objected that 'you can get no notion of what a Greek little girl was like, though matronly Junos and tremendous Demeters and gorgonian Minervas as many as you please', and he was relieved when Leighton 'so far condescended from the majesties of Olympus as to paint a child'.

The attitude of Thomas Carlyle was not dissimilar. His aversion for the 'fixed smile' of Greek statuary was equal to that of Ruskin, and his way of expressing it no less individual. Carlyle sat to G. F. Watts for his portrait, and Watts, as he often did in conversation with his sitters, began to talk of Pheidias. Carlyle advanced a criticism which no one else seems to have thought of. He contended that among all the sculptured beings which the genius of Pheidias had produced there was 'not one clever man'. With the long upper lip of Ecclefechan obstinately tightened he declared that a short upper lip showed an absence of intellect. He stuck to his point even when Watts cited Napoleon, Byron, and Goethe as evidence against him. He added that the jaw of the Greek was not sufficiently prominent. 'Depend upon it,' said Carlyle, 'neither God nor man can get on without a jaw.' 'There's not a clever man amongst them all,' he repeated, 'and I would away with them—into space.'

Yet there were on the other hand reasons why the good Victorian should disregard the objections to the revived classical school of painting. The 'classics' were the means of education. They represented the power of thought and bodily discipline, as well as, in the most general sense, of art. If the race which cradled the philosophy of Plato and the Olympic games produced also naked statues, these too must be presumed to have in them the virtue of the race, and those who depicted a Venus or an Apollo to be as worthy of respect as the person of letters who was ready with a classical quotation or attempted the learned exercise of a classical verse. The scholar could thus approve, on principle, what he might not, as a matter of visual art, well understand or particularly care about.

It was so, perhaps, with such a good Christian and noble statesman as William Ewart Gladstone. He looked, it is true, at the ancient Greeks from a literary point of view. In his 'Temple of Peace', as he called the library of 9,800 volumes to which he retired for study, there were two tables: one for politics, this always claiming his first attention (for duty must come before pleasure), the other, the Homer table for his enjoyment. When politics were done with he would sit down to Homer 'with the avidity of a young man eager to obtain a double first'. Homer, for him, 'opened a large and distinct chapter of primitive knowledge'. The Achaean civilization was 'a wonderful and noble nursery of manhood', the Games a great institution.

Whether those brooding eagle eyes perceived what could merely be seen is another question. William Blake Richmond, who painted Gladstone's portrait, remarked on his taste for 'a facile and perfect manipulation of material'. Gladstone admired the Italian sculptor Bernini because Bernini converted marble into a soft and intricately folded garment unlike marble; the designers of Dresden china for the cunning twists and vagaries by which they could make mere

VICTORIA COLLEGE
LIBRARY
VICTORIA, B. C.

material assume any shape. 'But', said Richmond, 'I never heard him express delight over the severe and far higher beauty of the shape of an Etruscan or Attic vase or of the quiet and restrained art which is so forcible a factor of their surface adornment.' The static and unchanging element of form, the hard visual fact, did not mean a great deal to this artificer of interpretations; but looking not so much at, as through, a work of art, he was able to ignore its physical aspect and to find satisfaction in the flow of ideas it induced. It is possible that the classical subjects of Leighton and Richmond in this way heightened for Gladstone the pleasures of the Homer table.

The classical scholar might imbibe some of the prejudice which was not unknown even to antiquity. Thus Benjamin Jowett had a Platonic distrust of art. Schliemann's discovery of Troy failed to excite him, for he placed archaeology in the same suspect category; but in so far as art was a general idea he was prepared to countenance it, was inclined to agree with G. F. Watts (to whom he sat for his portrait in 1879) that Ruskin, 'excellent about clouds, forms of leaves, etc.', put small things in the place of great and that this was a misfortune and an obstacle to the highest art.

If on any side, the statesman and the scholar were on the 'senatorial, academic and authoritative' side. So, too, was a considerable part of the wealthy, picture-buying middle class of the time. It was a class little inclined to make severe aesthetic distinctions—an omnivorous class with a huge appetite—but for several reasons it welcomed the classical subject. It was an escape from the present, for one thing. It represented that world of cultured education which many a wealthy buyer, grown rich through manufacture and industry, had not known; and to some, maybe, it was a privileged peep behind the screen of clothes by which the human body was concealed. The main fact remains that despite all niceties of opinion the pictures were bought in profusion to furnish the mansions of the wealthy.

Admired, sought after, munificently rewarded, the artist (whatever label might be affixed to his style and subject) was a prince in the seventies and eighties, and none was more princely than Frederic Leighton, both in person and in his immediate surroundings. It was in 1865 that he planned the house, so much in keeping with the superlative nature of the man, which so many visitors have seen with amazement, so many agreed was beyond compare—a house which became one of the wonders of London.

Orme Square, Bayswater, where he had first settled, did not satisfy him. He decided he must have his own town residence. He enlisted the aid of his architect friend, George Aitchison, who was now in practice in London, though the house was to be built to Leighton's own ideas—for this universal being was learned in architecture as in the other arts, among the honours which he received later in life being the Gold Medal of the Royal Institute of British Architects (1894) for the knowledge evident in the architectural detail of his paintings. He scrutinized all that was done. 'Every stone, every brick, even the mortar and cement—no less than all the wood and metal work passed directly under his personal observation', said Aitchison. He climbed on the scaffolding and peered through the window-frames, carefully criticizing each ornament and detail of execution. When off on his travels, he left minute instructions with his architect as to what was to be done. These instructions referred not only to the building plan but also to the furniture of which the shape, size, and decoration were all specified. The scheme of tables, cabinets, bookcases, and doors, stained black with arabesques in white holly, varnished so that the effect was of ivory and ebony, was his alone. The house was ready for occupation in 1866 (on the artist's return from a visit to Spain).

It was situated in Melbury Road, Kensington, and had the advantage of being close to Leighton's particular friend, Watts, though in Melbury Road itself there was a lack of grandeur which some might have thought a disadvantage. It was a narrow back street with an untidy frontage of small cottages and stables. Leighton spoke of these laughingly and with a humorous deprecation.

'I live', he said, 'in a mews.'

There was grandeur even in the deprecatory phrase. It was manifestly absurd that an Olympian should live in a mews, yet the recognition and tolerance of a surrounding imperfection was in itself Olympian. Just so might Zeus in sport have turned himself into a mortal and lived among rude stablemen in some humble cot where anon his gleaming splendour would shine incongruously forth, evoking cries of wonder.

Yet there was little of the mews in the house which Leighton built. It was, to the exterior view, a stately and reserved mansion of red brick. The façade, calm and distinguished, like the outward aspect of an English gentleman, courteously disclaimed the assertion of merit or display of wealth. There was no attempt to create the appearance of a classic villa: it was no temple, proudly supported by great columns, with a sculptured pediment over the front door. Magnificence was withheld, but only that it might more effectively burst upon the sight of those privileged to go inside. The interior was, in a sense, a life work. Many years passed before it was really as its creator would have it, before its gems of art and design were all in place. To describe it adequately it is necessary to see it, not as it was when Leighton first went to live in it in 1866, but as it became in the course of the years.

You entered first a small hall—in itself unassuming, for magnificence was still at a remove from the street. It contained a Roman view by Steinle and a stuffed peacock on a cabinet inlaid with mother-of-pearl, and, during the eighties, was further distinguished by a single choice work of sculpture, the *Icarus* of the young Alfred Gilbert. This had its own revealing story of generous patronage. In 1884 the future sculptor of the fountain at Piccadilly Circus was a young and struggling artist in Rome with a wife and two children to support. There he met Costa and so was introduced to Costa's friend Leighton, who offered the young man a commission. The subject was left to him, but knowing the classical taste of his patron he made a statuette of the son of Daedalus, testing his wings, which won the Prix de Rome and excited the admiration of all who saw it. The hall with its statuette was a kind of hors d'œuvre to whet the appetite for the banquet which was to follow. A few more steps and you passed through a massive door of ebony blackness, picked out with its ivory ornament, into an enchanted place. The Arabian Court.

From Kensington you were whisked into the atmosphere of the

Thousand and One Nights. Visitors, overwhelmed by the first impression, declared that they would not have been surprised to see bevies of Oriental beauties reclining on piles of silk cushions in the alcoves, troops of nautch girls swinging to the weird music of bronzed musicians, an Aladdin entering with his sack of precious stones. Above was the Arabic inscription in beautiful flowing characters: 'In the name of the merciful and long-suffering God. The merciful hath taught the Koran. He hath created man and taught him speech. He hath set the sun and moon in a certain course. Both the trees and the grass are in subjection to him.' There was a great gilt dome which, when the sun shone, sparkled with a thousand broken hues.

Melodiously, a fountain, hewn from one solid block of black marble, in which swam Japanese goldfish, splashed and tinkled. In cusped recesses stood choice examples of Damascus, Persian, and Rhodian ware. Ornament and colour were everywhere: the wood-work of Cairene craftsmen, fretted into lace-like patterns, engraved plaques of silver and gold, carved scimitars, luxurious divans with their tables inlaid with mother-of-pearl, and, behind, the gleam of marble, alabaster, and tile. The astonishing and intricate display of ornament was not entirely Oriental, though its very diversity contributed to the fabulously Oriental character of the whole. In general conception the Arabian Court seems to have been inspired by the Saracenic palace, La Zisa, at Palermo, but the blend of East and West was subtly modernized by craftsmen of Leighton's own time and country. The capitals were carved with representations of rare birds by Sir Edgar Boehm, the Queen's sculptor. The blue tiles were made by William de Morgan, that disciple of William Morris who had been inspired by Morris's example to venture into the realm of lost handicrafts.

The manufacture of the tiles, designed to harmonize with original examples of Saracenic craft and commissioned by Leighton in 1877, was an arduous task. Many were the chances and disappointments. Glazes cracked. Colour which should have been brilliant became, through various technical factors, dull and mottled. Kilns proved unmanageable and caused fires. It was expensive, because the imperfect tiles must be firmly excluded. Much labour and time were lost through the unreliable temperature of the oven. When the work was done De Morgan estimated that he was £500 out of pocket. He did not say so to Leighton—who, there is little doubt, without a moment's debate or hesitation would have proffered the amount; and yet, if it had been paid, the collaboration of artists would have lost its fine quality of idealism. An idealist was De Morgan. Tiles were a faith to him, not merely a means of making money. He had visions of whole cities made of tiles, cities ever bright and clean, for, as he pointed out, tiles had the advantage of being washable. The purity of his ideals caused Poynter to refer to him as a wonderful man; one who never had an evil thought in his life; with his wife (Mary Evelyn Pickering, daughter of the Recorder of Pontefract, who painted in the late Pre-Raphaelite manner), 'two of the rarest spirits of the age'. In craftsmanship this idealism eventually produced a peacock blue which, it was generally agreed, was quite a match for the colour and glaze of the Orient and was one of the Arabian Court's best features.

Then there was the mosaic frieze, designed by Walter Crane, one of those devoted souls who, not without talent of their own, take on the impress of the stronger personalities with whom they come in contact. He was impressed on the one hand by William Morris and Burne-Jones, on the other by Leighton, and as a result his art was a delicate hybrid in which the Pre-Raphaelite and classic influences were mingled. He was at once a designer-craftsman, a socialist (faithful to the precepts of William Morris), and a painter of mythology. His *Renascence of Venus*, exhibited at the first exhibition of the Grosvenor Gallery, was a wistful tribute to a Botticelli seen with the nostalgic eye of Burne-Jones. At the same time, as a follower of Morris, he made socialist cartoons, in which the reality of events was conveyed through an antique style, and Justice, menaced by the upraised batons of mounted policemen, fell swooning amid her classical draperies in Trafalgar Square.

He became friendly with Leighton in Rome, early in the seventies, Giovanni Costa playing his usual part of intermediary. 'I am glad', said Leighton, 'to hear that you have made friends with my excellent Costa who as an artist is one in hundreds and as a man one in thousands.' Leighton was 'very kind in his princely way' and showed his kindness some years later in the commission for the frieze. Though he was not uncritical of Crane's work—'I don't like the Duck-Women' was his remark when Crane suggested that the Sirens should appear in the form accredited to them on Greek gems—nevertheless the frieze, like the tiles, was considered a great success.

The Court was added to Leighton's mansion in 1877, though for some time previously he had meditated a suitable assembly room for the treasures he had collected (many of them when visiting his friend Sir Richard Burton in Damascus). He asked Sir Caspar Purdon Clarke, the architect and archaeologist, who in 1876 was going East to seek objects for the South Kensington Museum, to buy for him certain tiles in Damascus. 'I had no difficulty in finding my market, for Leighton with his customary precision had accurately indicated every point about the dwellings concerned. I returned with a precious load.' It is characteristic that Leighton not only did not quibble about the price but even insisted on paying double, so scornful was he of 'picking things up cheap'. Sir Caspar Purdon Clarke, with all the authority of a Director of the South Kensington Museum (and eventually of the Metropolitan Museum, New York), later declared the Arabian Court to be 'the most beautiful structure which has been erected since the sixteenth century'.

It was, perhaps, extravagant praise, but the house suggested extravagant terms, was immensely copious in its reflection of the owner's grand scale of taste. In the study to the left of the entrance hall, over the low bookshelves, the orderly writing-desk, hung choice drawings by Alphonse Legros and Alfred Stevens. On the opposite side of the Court were more objects of art—in the drawing- and dining-rooms, both of which looked out on the cloistered garden—so quiet, said Leighton, that 'not a sound reaches me here save the singing of the birds'. On the Pompeian red walls of the dining-room, Rhodian and Damascus plates were arranged in circular patterns and vertical files from floor to ceiling; over the substantial oak fireplace hung the painting of a female figure by Gregorio Schiavone, fifteenth-century master of the Paduan school; on each side of the hearth stood seats of Oriental design with mirror-glass fitted into back and arms. Here too reposed the Satsuma plate and sword presented to Lieutenant-Colonel Leighton by officers of the Artists' Volunteer Corps in 1878. The drawing-room was filled with paintings. In the ceiling of the covered porch which led to the garden, set in a frame of gold was a study by Delacroix for the ceiling in the Palais Royal. On the walls of nut-brown were the four great Corots, *Sunrise*, *Sunset*, *Noon*, and *Night*, which had once belonged to Daubigny; a silver-grey river scene, also by Corot, which was one of Leighton's favourites; two Constables, one of Hampstead Heath, the other the sketch for *The Haywain*; a David Cox; a Daubigny; and a landscape by Leighton's unfortunate friend, George Mason.

Still there was an experience to come. You went up the stairs to the studio, always surrounded as you went by works of art—a copy of Michelangelo's *Creation of Adam*, an unfinished picture of Lord Rockingham and Burke by Sir Joshua Reynolds. You arrived at an antechamber, whence, through a screen of mosharabiyeh, you could see the fountain playing below. Here was a further profusion of paintings: the *Girl shelling Peas* by Sir John Millais who presented it to Leighton and received in return his *Needless Alarm*, a Tintoretto portrait, a head by Bassano, *A Corner of My Studio* by Alma-Tadema, *Chaucer's Dream of Fair Women* by Burne-Jones. The antechamber led to the great studio.

There were a hundred things to catch the eye in this magnificent workshop. Easels stood around, each bearing its work of art. Travel sketches by the artist covered the walls—sketches of Rome and Rhodes, Athens, Venice, Seville, Algiers, the Nile, of Devonshire and Donegal, of Scotland and Wales. On the precious Oriental rugs leaned mighty portfolios, stacked with the innumerable drawings of fold and figure which preceded each painting. You turned to one wall and saw a beautiful study by Gainsborough for *The Mall*, painted for George III; to another and there was an engraving of the Royal Academy Exhibition in 1777, autographed by the Prince of Wales. The engraving showed Sir Joshua Reynolds as President, convoying members of the Royal Family. 'Why,' said the future Edward VII, 'that is Leighton showing me round the Academy', and he had insisted on making the artist a present of the engraving.

If, elsewhere, the Oriental influence seemed to dominate, here in the studio was the most powerful influence of all—the Parthenon frieze, a replica of which ran round the southern end and was constantly before the painter's eyes as he worked on one or other of the six or seven canvases which he kept in progress at the same time.

This main studio was one of the two between which Leighton, like other artists of this opulent day, divided his activities. You passed through a corridor lined with pictures and books into the 'winter studio': the smaller one, designed for use when the weak daylight of London was not enough to fill the other. Here there were fewer paintings and drawings, but many of the 'properties' which recalled the classical world, the golden lyre Leighton used in his painting of *The Garden of the Hesperides*, the wreath of flowers and the tambourine which played their part in pictures of festival, even a stuffed antelope destined to appear in some re-creation of a golden age; while on an ebony table stood the orderly clumps of brushes in Oriental jars and the palette of lemon-coloured wood with its great sweeping curve—a projection in itself of its owner's personality.

Something—a little—of the splendour remains in our own much-battered age, though Leighton House was closed and shuttered during the Second World War, the exterior, damaged by bombs, shored up by baulks of timber. The studio, suffering from dry-rot, was stripped to the brick, though the section of the Parthenon frieze remains. The blue tiles of De Morgan are still in position, though some subtle flaw in the recipe blanches them at intervals to a milky pallor and makes necessary their resuscitation with special oils. The Arabian Court was to need much repair before some of its magic returned. It requires an effort of the imagination to see the house as the superb piece of still-life it was when Leighton inhabited it; another effort, though a necessary one, to see it thronged and animated by Society. Then, indeed, it must have presented a spectacle such as Disraeli loved to describe, glittering like an extraordinary jewel of interior decoration, a *tableau vivant* with the fabulous touch of the exotic which Victorian stage-managers gave to performances at Drury Lane.

It was a privilege to attend the Sunday receptions to which nobles

SELF PORTRAIT
by Lord Leighton, P.R.A.

and politicians, dignitaries of the Church, distinguished foreigners, and the merely wealthy, came, eagerly, for a view of the master-piece due to be shown in the next Academy. The musical occasions which Leighton regularly arranged (as Ary Scheffer did in Paris) were events of the season. On these evenings of festival the Arabian Court was more than ever wondrous. Hothouse blooms and droop-ing palms added the profusion of Nature's ornament to the Cairo woodwork, the De Morgan tiles. Women beautiful and aristocratic laughed, chattered, exclaimed in rapture at the sheer brilliance of it all. Then came a tremendous moment. The host threw himself down in a chair and uttered an impressive 'Hush'. A deep silence followed, in which the tinkling of the fountain again became audible—and then, the violins of Joachim and Piatti wailed on the heated and per-fumed air; the voice of Mme Viardot was heard in the *Divinités du Styx*.

Leighton in middle age was even more distinguished than as a young man. He had now attained a majesty of appearance which was in keeping with the Olympian character. It is well conveyed in his self-portrait of 1881 for the Uffizi Gallery in which the clustering curls above the serene brow give more than ever the impression of honouring laurel, in which, with consciousness of being the object of attention, the artist, full-face, calmly confronts all spectators. Nor is it to be overlooked that behind him, as it were in the closest association and co-operation with him, is a portion of the Parthenon frieze.

His varied gifts had been affirmed by the passage of the years—amazingly so his gift of languages, for not only did he remember what he had learnt in youth but he learned more. He could, as of old, speak at least three German dialects, and as many of Italian, though the purity of his Tuscan always astonished and delighted his Italian friends. Yet he was capable in his maturity of learning Spanish in six months, and on being introduced to a Spaniard conversed with the utmost fluency. 'Do say', said the hostess to the Spaniard on this occasion, 'that he made one tiny mistake.' 'No, madam, no,' replied the foreigner, 'not one.' He could make himself understood by Levantines with a patois of several tongues, and (to the astonishment of Robert Browning) spoke to his manservant, apparently a Rumanian, in a language which only he and Leighton knew.

Thus he was able to set instantly at ease any visitor who knew little or no English, and this by the choice of words and the appropriateness of courtesy which they conveyed as well as mere fluency —for he had that social gift also, exactly proportioned to his own pleasure in social occasions. He made English, French, German, and Italian guests feel equally at home. When they saw him, beaming welcome from the stairs, they knew they would enjoy themselves.

To his other perfections he added that of the perfect host. The dinners he gave were banquets of the most luxurious kind. It is related that on one occasion he called for one of two remaining bottles of some especially rare and exquisite wine; that a guest, who would seem to have been somewhat below the general level of Leighton's guests in tact and good breeding, blurted out: 'It's corked.' By no outward sign did Leighton reveal his natural repugnance for the incident. At once the bottle was removed and the last remaining rarity served in its stead. After such banquets, smoking their cigars, the male guests wandered in a haze through the Arabian Court, and it sometimes happened that, gazing round them entranced, they forgot the fountain and walked into the water.

The host himself took sparingly of the good things he provided for his guests. His frugality was marked in middle age as in youth. It showed itself in the Spartan fittings of his bedroom with its plain iron bed, so much at variance with the Arabian enchantments below. Magnificence was his element, but his pleasure was to see others pleased by it, to achieve a social harmony in which the guests and décor were at one. Not in the modern sense a snob, he delighted in the best society because he had been trained, and was by nature fitted, to appreciate everything of the best. Though wealthy, he considered the possession and use of wealth as a generous exercise of taste, and he had a lack of interest in, a dislike for, the method of its acquisition and for anything in the nature of haggling, bargaining, or money-grubbing. Pictures, he was aware, had to be bought and sold, but this was a vulgar business which should be confined to its own lower sphere, a regrettable necessity, from which the artist must detach himself. It was with incomparable loftiness that he once received a deputation of dealers at Melbury Road. 'Gentlemen,' he addressed them, with courteous distaste, 'you will excuse me, I feel sure. I have placed their titles and prices upon the canvases I am willing to sell. When you have made your selection perhaps you will kindly ring the bell and my servant will acquaint me with your decision. I wish you a very good morning.' But the dealers showed signs of wanting to talk about the transaction, to discuss the prices so precisely shown on the pictures, and this made necessary some plainer Olympian speaking. 'I never', added Leighton, 'enter into discussion about my pictures with gentlemen like yourselves. I have given you my terms—that is enough!' He was averse from allowing his pictures to be engraved, lucrative process though this generally was, for his dislike of vulgar contact extended to the dissemination of his works and he did not wish to see his pictures 'in every cheap print-shop in the country'.

His suspicion of the commercial world was offset by a conspicuous generosity to fellow artists in need. Finding that the sculptor, Thomas Brock, was in want of a holiday and money, Leighton asked for a piece of notepaper, scribbled on it an order to his bankers, handed it over and, with an expression of good wishes, hurried either because he wished to spare the other the necessity of thanks or because he was just off on a journey, was gone. When his unsuccessful friend George Mason died he took great trouble to sell Mason's work to the best advantage on behalf of the widow. This generosity was the cause of some anxiety to old Dr. Leighton, who watched Frederick's career with tender pride. 'You see, Fred never thinks of the future', the doctor said, and insisted on buying him an annuity.

Nothing, however, no social pleasure or friendly duty, obscured the primary importance of his work. There is a well-known story of a lady who praised to Whistler Leighton's many accomplishments, his gifts of conversation and oratory, his erudition, his facility in so many languages, his love of music, his charm, his ability in practical affairs. 'Yes,' Whistler said, 'paints a little too, I believe.' Whistler, no doubt, was ironic, but it is a matter of surprise that Leighton did paint, not little but so much. He contrived it by an exacting self-discipline and the old habit of punctuality. Like his friend Millais he was up early in the morning, and after breakfast and a glance at *The Times*, he went to his studio at eight-thirty and worked there until noon. He allowed half an hour for lunch, then continued to work until four. From four to five he occupied himself with his large correspondence, never leaving a letter unanswered. After five he made his calls, running in to see Watts, perhaps, at Little Holland House in order to discuss deep problems of art, though always with the air of one with a certain limited space of time at his disposal, after which he had to catch a train or keep an important engagement. An exact time-table enabled him to fit together his travel abroad and his working life at home with a satisfactory dovetail. Once, he wrote from Rome to fix an appointment two days later with a model in London, and so accurate were his calculations that he arrived with his bag at the front door in Melbury Road at the precise moment the model was ringing the bell at the side entrance.

Time to him was order and beauty. The figures which denoted the flying hours on the clock were of far greater interest than the figures which denoted sums of money. A disarrangement of schedule was more painful to him than a monetary loss. There was one occasion when the schedule, to his great uneasiness, was put out by three hours. Only his respect for Royalty could then detain him at a supper-party, given by Sir Coutts Lindsay, which the Prince of Wales attended. Leighton had ordered his carriage punctually for midnight, but the Prince showed no inclination to leave and as, according to etiquette, no one could leave before him, Leighton could only watch with silent dismay the time go by. It was three in the morning before the Prince chose to make a move: three hours had been lost. 'By Jove!' said Leighton as he stepped into the brougham. 'I've not done this sort of thing for twenty years and I shall have to pay for it.'

He was, he said, 'married to his art'—for one thing the great house in Melbury Road lacked, and that was a woman to control its domestic economy and share with its lord the glowing success of its social occasions. It would seem, at first thought, a surprising fact: for one so compact of excellence must certainly have been the object of the match-maker's calculation. He was eminently, in the vulgar Victorian phrase, 'a catch', and even his family was not disinclined to see him make an, of course, brilliant marriage. Like Mr. Phoebus in *Lothair* he can be imagined as saying, 'I made Madame Phoebus my wife because she was the finest specimen of the Aryan race that I was acquainted with'.

He would, unless some unaccountable law of opposites had come into operation, have required virtue, beauty, health, intellect, and charm combined in an exquisite proportion if the hypothetical woman were to be a fit mate for him. Was it a criticism of English womanhood that no such paragon appeared? Yet there were goddesses in Kensington, in those days: girls with the straight nose, the short, curving upper lip, the firm and rounded chin which seemed to derive by some subtle and almost uncanny process or imitation from the sculptured Greek ideal; able to ride a horse and not unskilled in water-colour painting, instructed in Homer and fluent in French, capable also of presiding with distinction at the most illustrious of tables. Although such paragons existed, Leighton had to admit that he had never met a woman with whom he could possibly spend his life, and of the goddesses available none was fit to play Juno to his Jupiter.

Many a female heart must have beat more rapidly against the purple velvet of his evening coat as he waltzed with his unequalled grace, have throbbed when he exerted the charm which no one could resist; many a mamma must have gazed at him with the excitement of an angler, seeing a fish of the largest size, near, and yet tantalizingly just out of reach or beyond the capacity of the net and rod; but the most cunning of snares was unavailing against the dexterity of his tact, and if Cupid's arrows were showered at him they glanced aside or fell blunted from the perfection of his armour.

Was the classic ideal itself the reason for this immunity? One recalls the strain of misogyny which appeared in Gleyre and led him to consider marriage as the direst of fates; that lack of belief in feminine qualities of mind and talent which made Léon Gérôme so bitterly oppose the admission of women students to the Beaux Arts.

'Surely, it would be a good thing', someone said, interrogatively, to him. 'Oh yes, it will be good', said Gérôme, '—for repopulation.' Albeit more cheerfully than Gleyre, Leighton chaffed his colleague with large families who found it hard to make both ends meet, and without the cynicism of Gérôme, certainly expressed his opposition to Votes for Women.

Perhaps the constant routine of figure-painting, which involved the appraisal in a disinterested fashion of so much human flesh and dispensed with the allure of mystery which comes of clothes, made women too familiar for tenderness. The painter, after all, did no worship their perfection: he corrected them, adding a rounded contour to a bony model, removing the roll of superfluous flesh from the adipose, converting the merely rough suggestions which they were able, physically, to give, into the ideal standard of proportion which existed in his own mind. The ancient Greeks, capable of making women so beautiful in marble, had been Oriental enough to segregate them in everyday life, and a little of that classic indifference may possibly have transferred itself to their Victorian disciples and emulators.

It is true that Poynter and Alma-Tadema were 'family men', with all that the phrase conveys of normal domestic existence—though both, it may be noted, were, from Leighton's point of view, imperfectly 'Hellenic'. They were, in spirit, if not in the trappings of subject, 'genre' painters who took pleasure in the homely details, the little human touches of sentiment, the circumstantial, rather than in the abstract quest of perfection. If Poynter admired the classic Poussin, his fondness was given also to the finish of Van Eyck while Alma-Tadema made the ancient world as bourgeois as a Dutch kitchen. He domesticated Greece and Rome and extracted from the distant classic spectacle the moral that even amid Corinthian columns there was no place like home. Melbury Road was not in this sense domestic, and in matters of sex Leighton gives the impression of a more than Olympian aloofness. For him there was not as for Jupiter, a Metis, a Themis, a Eurynome, a Ceres, a Latona, a Juno, any more than there was a Danae, an Antiope, a Leda, an Europa, an Aegina. When, in his kindly way, he interested himself in the career of one of his models whose ambition it was to go on the stage, 'gossip', his sister told him, was aroused, and his indignation was great that this should be so. He wrote to his sister in impressive and decisive words: 'But let me turn away from the whole thing, it has pained me more than enough. I implore you not to reopen it. On the only thing that matters you are absolutely assured if you believe in my honour. If you hear these rumours again meet them with a flat ungarnished denial. Let that suffice, it does for me.'

One cannot imagine him the victim of that temperamental weakness which impelled so many of his contemporaries, fundamentally detached as they were, into awkward explorations of the unknown land of love: unsuitable alliances like the fretful union of the Carlyles, the marriages ignominiously ended of Ruskin and Euphemia Gray, of G. F. Watts and Ellen Terry. He was, in contrast, of too 'Hellenic' a mind to feel their peculiarly Victorian tortures. If great men, making fools of themselves, could put a touch of genius into their folly, which made folly itself remarkable, Leighton could not tolerate in himself the admixture and the result. If he had embarked on marriage it should have been a success, and yet there was only one woman of great influence in Leighton's life—Mrs. Sartoris, and hers was a maternal and disinterested affection. While it is possible to compare her to the muse Melpomene, she resembles also the Homeric goddess who charged herself with a hero's fate, appeared at suitable moments to direct him and yet stayed in her own empyrean. The long and idealistic friendship of Leighton and Mrs. Sartoris was terminated, to his grief, by her death in 1879. No doubt one should rest content with the statement that he preferred to be a bachelor and, successful in this as in other determinations, contrived to remain so. It was not so unusual, especially in an artist devoted to work and travel, as to call for comment. It contributes, however, to that impression of aloofness which Leighton gives. He had no one to interpret him (except in so far as a sister could, or as he so magnificently interpreted himself), and his bachelorhood was one facet of an impregnable position.

On account of his aloofness some artists stood in awe of him, and yet he was so evidently the centre of their world that Melbury Road magnetically attracted them and became the nucleus of an artist colony (or very heart of Olympus) which in time was more prosaically known as the 'Leighton Settlement'. Its growth was a gradual process which continued all through those palmy picture-buying years. As they became successful and wealthy, artists 'graduated', so to speak, to Melbury Road, and though not all of them were classical men, the stamp of classicism (of a kind) was given to their satellite mansions by the architect Richard Norman Shaw.

Shaw, who has left so marked an influence on the architecture of Britain, who is possibly best known by the redesigned Quadrant of Regent Street, had been brought face to face, like other nineteenth-century artists, with the necessity of making a choice from the styles of the past. Born in Edinburgh in 1831, he may, as a boy, have begun to appreciate the classical beauty of the buildings by which the brothers Adam had made the city a northern Athens. When the Shaw family moved to London in 1845 he went to the Academy Schools and became the pupil of C. R. Cockerell, a man who thought, architecturally, in the idiom of Greece and Rome.

He could not, however, remain unaffected by the century's other nostalgia for the Middle Ages and, as a young man, caught the prevailing enthusiasm for the Gothic style, succeeding Philip Webb, the ally of William Morris, as chief draughtsman in the offices of George Edmund Street, the designer of the Law Courts; becoming by virtue of his post a 'Goth' (to use the description then current) as opposed in the great 'Battle of Styles', to the 'Romans'. But though he took sides he was only a lukewarm 'Goth'. He was no out-and-out medieval man like William Morris, with whom he seems to have felt little sympathy. He was prepared to take the whole of history as his architectural province and to adopt any style which might appeal to him. In the course of time he advanced from the medieval period to the English Renaissance—that is to Tudor times and later—and at the point where the Pre-Raphaelite drew back, scenting corruption, he went forward with undiminished appetite.

He had a natural taste for the flamboyant and the spectacular. He had a sense of the picturesque, designing a house as a painter might compose a picture, indeed as the painters of the time composed historical pictures. He was equally at home in the fifteenth, the sixteenth, or the seventeenth centuries, and he made use of decorative features which took his fancy whether or no they were structurally suitable to the work in hand. He was, for instance, fond of that practice, the results of which are often so drearily manifest in the English suburb, of sticking thin planks, resembling a solid timber framework, on buildings where they served no purpose. If a grandiose effect is to be called more simply a 'fake', Shaw was able, with a virtuoso's disregard of rule, to bring it off with brilliance. By skilful distortion he gave to villas the air of palaces. It was one of Shaw's main functions to devise a new type of studio-mansion, the symbol of union between art and wealth. Steeped in tradition, his houses were not like, or not to be mistaken for, any there had ever been in the past; and in this there was appropriateness, for never had there been a class like that to which his clients belonged. Every age had had its merchant princes but not artist princes, and these were people who, in the seventies and eighties, kept him steadily employed.

It was in 1870 that he built 'Graeme's Dyke' for the Academician, Frederick Goodall, a house situated in a hundred acres of the Harrow Weald estate which Goodall bought in 1856 from the Marquis of Abercorn. In the very name there is something of Shaw's whimsical genius, for 'Grime's Dyke' was the original name, an ancient earthwork on the property being so described by the Ordnance Survey. 'Grime's', at Shaw's suggestion, became 'Graeme's', and he pleaded for this distortion of the old title on the ground that ' "Grime's" sounded dirty'.

Goodall said, with satisfaction, that the architect bestowed on the house 'much thought to make it as picturesque as he could', and this, without question, it was. Its chimneys were immensely high, its entrance porch exuberantly arched, it was curiously and fantastically gabled, timbered, barge-boarded, weather-tiled. Goodall surrounded it with conifers and filled the grounds with the Egyptian sheep of the special breed which contributed to the verisimilitude of his paintings of Egypt. These mild animals lay about on the heaps of sand, while the grounds were being made, as if on the edge of the desert to which they were used, and fed from the hands of visitors who brought dates with them, for of these they were remarkably fond. 'Graeme's Dyke' was eventually sold to W. S. Gilbert of the comic operas, who constructed a bathing-pool in the moat.

During the seventies it became the fashion for artists to commission houses from Shaw, the more readily because in 1872 he was elected an Associate of the Royal Academy. He turned with ease from the lavish informalities of the country house to the classic dignity proper to the town, advancing for the latter purpose to the time of Queen Anne, though even the Augustan manner acquired his vivaciousness and of necessity the first-story windows, which indicated the studio rooms, shot up to unprecedented heights. He designed houses in Fitzjohn's Avenue for Edwin Long, painter of *The Babylonian Slave Market*, and Frank Holl, who grew rich, partly by portraits and partly by melancholy subjects designed, as he said, to 'bring home to the heart and mind of Mayfair the temptations to which the poor are ever subject'. Then there was Kate Greenaway's house in Frognal and, in 1876 and 1877, two notable additions to the architecture of Melbury Road for Marcus Stone and Luke Fildes.

At that date, these additions to the 'Leighton Settlement' were both comparatively young men, in their thirties, but fame and fortune came early then. Both had made a good start as illustrators of Dickens and already had a record of Academy successes. Marcus Stone's *Edward II and his Favourite, Piers Gaveston* had been the sensation of 1872. Luke Fildes's *Applicants for Admission to a Casual Ward* of 1874 was so popular at the Academy that it had to be railed off and a policeman set on duty to control the eagerness of visitors to see it. Sir George Holloway paid 2,000 guineas for this glimpse of the wretchedness of London's poor and later declared his readiness to have bid up to 4,000 guineas.

The illustrators of *Our Mutual Friend* and *The Mystery of Edwin Drood* were plebeian deities perhaps, but they had their niche on Olympus and were the near neighbours of Leighton. Luke Fildes' half-acre of garden adjoined the garden of the great man, and if the interiors of their houses did not quite reach the splendour of his yet with their walls of Pompeian red and golden bronze, their Chippendale chairs, Florentine sofas and plush curtains, their terraces of glass, supplementing the principal studio and allowing the observation of open-air effects, they were not unworthy of their position.

So the 'Settlement' grew. To Melbury Road came Valentine Cameron Prinsep, son of Watts's patron, Thoby Prinsep; he had been drawn as a youth into the circle of Rossetti and been one of the band which painted the walls of the Oxford Union, but had later found his own course, visited India in the seventies, and painted a thirty-foot-long picture of the Durbar at Delhi as well as portraits galore of Rajahs in their palaces.

In 1877 came Hamo Thornycroft the sculptor, building his great sculpture galleries (from which the roof of the Arabian Court could be seen). Came also Colin Hunter, the Scottish marine painter who cruised every year in search of subjects off the mouth of the Clyde. Princely one and all, they clustered together in their golden houses, and though the gardens of each were so beautifully cloistered that they gave the impression of being in the heart of the country, they were amicably close. 'Corky', Hamo Thornycroft's cat, leaping over Watts's wall had not far to go to take a partridge from Marcus Stone's larder or help itself to Val Prinsep's pigeons.

．　　．　　．　　．　　．　　．

Still another remarkable house needs to be chronicled, though later in date than those of Melbury Road, and in the northern sector of Olympus: that of Alma-Tadema in Grove End Road, St. John's Wood. It was not until 1869 that Alma-Tadema settled in England, although for some time it had been an obvious goal. Through the efforts of Gambart he was already popular there and he felt it would be useful to be in closer contact with his dealer-patron, pleasant to live in this wonderfully wealthy land, which he had already visited once or twice (meeting Leighton in 1866). The pictures he exhibited at the French Gallery in London, *Portico of a Roman Theatre* and *Roman Lady returning from making Purchases*, were well received, and when his wife died at Brussels in 1869 he made the decision to settle in England and came to London with his two daughters, Laurence and Anna.

With the thought of a sensational appearance in mind he had, in the previous year, painted *Phidias at Work on the Parthenon*. On a platform of scaffolding, scroll in hand, bearded and somewhat corpulent, stood Pheidias, while Pericles, magistrate of Athens, inspected the frieze, the learned Aspasia at his side, the martial Alcibiades, nephew of Pericles, among the noble company. Just so might some Academician receive into his studio the famous men and women of London, and no doubt Alma-Tadema consciously intended its atmosphere of the Victorian 'Show Sunday'. It might well have been the picture of the year, but the buyer would not let it be shown and Alma-Tadema's first Academy success was the *Pyrrhic Dance* of 1869 (in which year the Royal Academy moved from Trafalgar Square to Burlington House). It was a success (though Ruskin was very unpleasant about it at a later date), and Alma-Tadema settled down. For a while he lived in Frederick Goodall's town house in Camden Square, while Goodall was travelling in Egypt. In 1871 he married Laura Theresa Epps, a painter also, who had studied with him. They went to live at Townshend House in Park Road, Regent's Park, by the Regent's Canal, and for three years stayed contentedly there, gradually converting the house into something resembling a Roman villa, painting its ceilings with such classical subjects as *Venus and Mars* and *Bacchus and Silenus*. *Bacchus and Silenus*, sad to say, was ruined by the bursting of a water-pipe during the later occupation of the house by the dramatist, Henry Arthur Jones.

The Alma-Tademas were driven from Townshend House in 1874 by the explosion on the canal of a barge filled with high explosive, which did much damage to the buildings near. They then went to Rome for a while, and Alma-Tadema there painted his *Audience with Agrippa*. Though Townshend House was repaired, he and his wife now looked for larger premises and finally acquired and reconstructed No. 17 Grove End Road, which Alma-Tadema laboured to perfect as ardently as Leighton his mansion in Kensington.

A high garden wall surrounded it. You approached the door by a tessellated pavement under a glass awning, to be faced by a door-knocker of antique design, a mask of bronze with the Roman greeting '*Salve*' carved above it. You entered a house, conceived largely by its owner in a style as close to that of Pompeii as the nature and climate of London allowed—'a delicious blend', so it was described, of 'old Rome, old Athens, and the natural country'. While Leighton held the gorgeous East in fee, Alma-Tadema lived as nearly as possible in one of his own pictures. The dining-room resembled and was named after the ancient *triclinium*, though you would pass thence into the essentially modern billiard-room, enjoying with your host a cigar (for which, also, the classics offered no precedent). You would be taken to the *atrium* (Alma-Tadema's learned word for his library), a room lined with many a work on archaeology and classical antiquity—among others you might notice a much-used copy of Baring-Gould's *Tragedy of the Caesars*. At one end of the room was a fountain playing in a marble basin, on the edge of which were strewn some withered rose-leaves. These were the flowers, originally sent from the Riviera, three boxes full a week during four winter months, which Alma-Tadema painted in his *Roses of Heliogabalus*. He kept them, and the petals littered the marble like the dead vestiges of some ancient feast. In the *atrium* stood a business-like escritoire, softly lit by a window of Mexican onyx—a form of lighting which the artist seems to have been the first to use (it was adapted by Alfred Waterhouse, architect of the National Liberal Club, who placed two onyx windows at the top of its marble staircase). And now to the *conclave* or studio by a staircase of burnished brass. A writer in a German paper assumed (his error is pardonable when the princely state of artists in Britain is considered) that these stairs were of gold, and his description of so rich a detail of interior decoration brought a torrent of begging letters to Grove End Road.

The studio had walls of marble and cedar doors, a marble fireplace surmounted by a chimney in the shape of a silvered column with gilt capital and base, a gallery at one end, a domed apse to one side, the vaulted ceiling of a silvery aluminium tone. In the apse was the inscription '*Ars Longa, Vita Brevis*'. Over the door was the artist's favourite motto carved in letters of gold: 'As the sun colours flowers so art colours life.' A piano inlaid with ivory and mother-of-pearl stood on a dais, containing inside the lid, on a vellum lining, the autographs of the musicians, including Paderewski, who had been guests of the painter and played on the instrument. The numerous easels in the studio each bore a picture at some stage of completion, for like Leighton, Alma-Tadema was in the habit of working on several at a time. Though his output was immense and speed of execution remarkable, there was one he had in hand for as long as two years—so long indeed that he forgot what he had intended to put in the upper half of it, though as it was clearly a bathing scene this could scarcely be a serious difficulty for one so well versed in every phase of the Roman bath. On a marble bench where a Lesbia or a Calpurnia might have meditated there would lie a pile of photographs of Rome or Pompeii, for Alma-Tadema considered photography a boon to artists, especially in ensuring the correctness of historical accessories. From the gallery you came into a conservatory filled with exotics. From the studio you had access to the garden by doors plated with metal on which were etched an outline decoration of 'The Four Seasons'—these doors sliding into the wall during the summer.

In these surroundings Alma-Tadema painted the ancient world with unremitting industry while his wife in her studio-boudoir, decorated in the Dutch Renaissance manner, busied herself with the works of a less classical character which she sent regularly to the Royal Academy, bearing such titles as *Hush-a-Bye* and *The Pain of Parting*. As in Leighton's house, there were many pictures by fellow artists and friends—a series of long panels in the hall including *The Battle of Psyche* by Leighton, *A Temple at Philae* by Alma-Tadema's pupil, the Hon. John Collier, *A Bit of Old Hampstead* by Charles Green, to cite a few from the series of fifty.

The master of this impressive establishment was, in middle age, a plump active little man, with shaggy grey hair and beard, and pince-nez on his nose, bubbling over with good humour and geniality. He had been since 1873 a naturalized Englishman and his Christian name was anglicized to Lawrence but he still retained the guttural accent which, if foreign, enhanced his prestige rather than otherwise. He would talk with none of the English reserve—as he painted with Dutch care some minute detail he would remark, 'I love my art too much to see people scamp it; it makes me furious to see half-work and to see the public taken in by it and not know the difference'. 'The secret of my success', he would say, 'is that I have always been true to my own ideas, that I have worked according to my own head. To succeed in anything in life one must first of all be true to one's self, and I may say I have been this.'

At the same time he took a delight in his own astuteness in business matters, though he remarked with some regret and as a sign of comparative poverty that he did not make on the average more than £10,000 a year and that he did not sell a painting for more than £5,000. Poynter, who liked him, admired, even if he was also amused by, this lack of reserve on material questions, and it certainly did not offend Alma-Tadema's friends among the *nouveaux riches* who, he remarked, were 'the best picture-buyers of today'. He had a shrewd knowledge of his market. The buyers on whom such as he could depend were not the old aristocracy (though his *Roses, Love's Delight* was bought by the Tsar of Russia), but those who owned mines and factories and manufactured popular commodities: the still wider public who would buy, if not a picture, an engraving of a picture. The *nouveaux riches* were both English and Americans—the greater part of his work went to America, for the brownstone mansions were rising in New York and the walls must be hung with the best and most expensive pictures that could be found. With the *nouveaux riches* Alma-Tadema was popular, for he was a good 'mixer'. If the entertainments at Grove End Road were not of that superlative kind which Leighton organized they were as well attended.

.   .   .   .   .   .

On the guests at these great houses the décor no doubt made a great impression. It was slightly improbable, but there was a pleasure to be gained merely from witnessing the improbability. The magnificence induced the humble frame of mind in which a cheque would be reverently offered. The vast studios, filled with 'properties', were the evidence of professional efficiency, the guarantee of a genuine article. Like the doctor's consulting-room with its hint of technical appliances ready to hand, the lawyer's office with its calf-bound volumes and deed-boxes, the studio invited confidence by its singular architecture, its unlikeness to any other place of work. Then, too, it had, in a human sense, romance, for romantic to the average person was the artist's model, on whom the whole apparatus was from time to time concentrated.

It was the great age of the model. While the stream of smart carriages made for Melbury Road and Grove End Road, disgorging their load of wealth and fashion, the artist's mansions admitted also the models in constant procession. As the human figure had for the painter in the classic manner a special importance, as their compositions, moreover, contained so many figures, the demand for models was great.

Their status was respectable. Far different were they in these Victorian days from the jolly damsels whom the eighteenth-century artist had employed, like those for instance who danced the Milk-maids' Dance on Mayday on the street for the benefit of their patron, Mr. Nollekens. The spirit of this age of strict decorum—to put the matter on no other grounds—made the studio austere. If there were, still, artists content in a lax and easy fashion to paint their mistresses, they were not to be numbered among these superb professionals who hired models as they might domestic staff. The models, similarly, well understood the professional decorum. Venus disrobed for the Bath with a gesture at once chaste and mechanical, Phryne posed unclothed with a faraway look which indicated that her thoughts were on her course in typewriting. Sometimes the models would mix, without appearing in any way unusual, among a gathering of fashionable visitors and the artist would remark in a confidential undertone to ladies who commented on the good looks of an unknown: 'She's a model, you know, but, I assure you, perfectly respectable.'

As the ideal human was the classic aim, naturally the painter sought for those who in real life came nearest to it. The ideal was defined by G. F. Watts as 'that form which most emphasizes human characteristics furthest removed from suggestions of the inferior

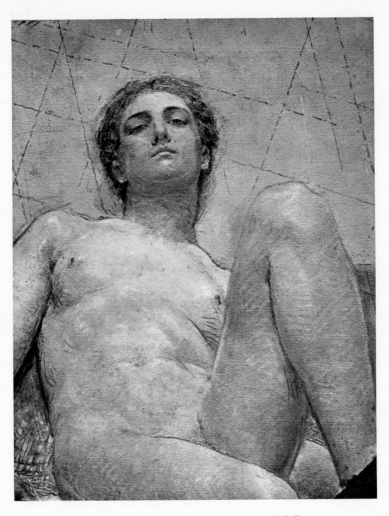

RECLINING FEMALE FIGURE
Drawing by Albert Moore

creatures—a principle so well understood and acted upon by the great Greek artists'. His verdict on English womanhood, judged by this standard, was on the whole favourable. 'The modern young lady', he said, 'is often of splendid growth and form such as probably the ancient Greek never saw', even though modern costume seemed designed to hamper it. Boots, for instance, were bad. The foot, Watts lamented, became too often a 'crumpled clump of deformity' on account of these 'abominations'. And again, corsets. The Greek would have shuddered at them. They were barbarous when compared with the loosely fitting, beautifully folded robe of the Greek maiden. It was this painful contrast which induced Watts to become a member of the Anti-Tight-Lacing Society.

Yet English models often posed more awkwardly than others. Leighton, on first settling in London, noted the difference and was inclined to be critical. 'As for your English models,' he observed, 'Tol! Lol!' It was generally agreed that Italian models were better in poise whatever 'suggestions of the inferior creature' they might give, and for this reason they were preferred.

They came indeed, unsought. The legend of the great city where artists dispensed so much money brought them streaming across Europe. Paris itself was only a stage on the way to London. Artists there, it is true, were more inclined to treat a model on a friendly and equal footing (as a human being and one who might even know something of art) than were the lordly painters of London. On the other hand, the pay in London was better. There were whole villages in the region of Naples which were, man, woman, and child, as familiar with Melbury Road and Grove End Road as with their own sunny district. They settled, some in the neighbourhood of Hatton Garden, some in West Kensington. Many a dark-eyed, olive-hued mother, dragging her bambinos with her, gazed with wonder amounting to terror at the strange splendours of Leighton's house, or with equal awe mounted Alma-Tadema's 'golden' stairs.

Many of the Italian girls were beautiful. 'Her grace was perfect', said Hamo Thornycroft of the slim Italian who posed for his *Artemis*, though (less romantic than that cold goddess, in Thornycroft's opinion) she married an ice-cream man. A great success was a slender beauty called Antonia Cura whom Leighton painted as a female juggler. Antonia was a favourite of Burne-Jones (who had a general preference for Italians because they seemed able to understand that an artist's work was serious and kept their appointments more conscientiously than the English). She seems to have inspired or modified the characteristic type of beautiful woman in his paintings.

The Italians supplied male models also, these being otherwise difficult to find. Some beery London loafer might serve the painter of contemporary life for his crossing-sweeper or Chelsea Pensioner, but not even by the aid of the artist's imagination could he be turned into Apollo. It was necessary to find a graceful Southern youth like Alessandro di Marco, 'a man', says William Blake Richmond, 'who seemed to stride out from Signorelli's grand frescoes, whom we all painted and drew from, a fellow so graceful and of such a colour, a kind of bronze gold, having a skin of so fine a texture that the movement of every muscle was not disguised, not a film of fat disfigured his shapely limbs'. No female models were permitted in Walter Crane's household, and Crane even adapted from di Marco's masculine proportions the central figure of his *Renascence of Venus*—this Venus retaining, however, a certain boyish leanness which caused Leighton when he first saw the picture to exclaim, 'Why, that's Alessandro!'

Then there was Gaetano Meo, presumed, from his Greek features, to be descended from ancient Greek colonists in Southern Italy, who had tramped across Europe from Calabria with his brother. They supported themselves as they went by playing harp and violin, and were performing on these instruments in Gower Street one day when Simeon Solomon, a painter whose eye for the antique had been sharpened by Swinburne, struck by Gaetano's handsome appearance, persuaded him to sit. Once introduced to the art world he became popular. Rossetti, Madox Brown, and Burne-Jones drew him. Leighton used him in the studies for his fresco at South Kensington, *The Arts of War*.

Such models often liked London well enough to stay, and sometimes developed a talent of their own. Gaetano was one of them. He took to painting pictures of remembered Italian scenes. He became the pupil of Henry Holiday, assisting him with designs for stained glass. He turned to mosaic, made the mosaic ceiling in the hall of 'Mr. Debenham's beautiful house in Addison Road' and worked with Richmond in his later days on the scheme of mosaic decoration for St. Paul's Cathedral. He was naturalized during the eighties, though his English remained quaint. 'Per Baccho!' he would say, when pleased with his work, 'I have superseded myself', or when he fell out with his employer, 'We have had sentences'. Richmond gives a pleasant picture of him in old age with fine silvery hair, features handsome still, happy with his wife and two beautiful daughters. Of classic mould were even the attendants of Olympus.

It was during the seventies and eighties that the upholders of classicism produced some of their most famous works: in 1876 that Leighton painted his *Daphnephoria*, considered to be his masterpiece. He loved processions, and the festival in honour of Apollo, celebrated every ninth year by the people of Boeotia to commemorate a victory, gave scope for the painting of figure and ritual march. Wearing a golden crown, clad in long garments, came the 'daphnephoros' or laurel-bearer, before him a beautiful youth, carrying a symbolic branch, adorned with globes and crowns; behind, a group of maidens and boys with the emblems of the Theban victory, while the 'choragos' or chorus-master, with upraised lyre, turned to encourage them on. The colour, the drawing, the composition were, as always, conscientiously planned and criticism, that 'narrow and unsympathizing spirit' which Leighton reproved, unable to carp at harmony or anatomy, could complain only of a certain absence of animation. 'If only', it was said, 'someone would pinch them or make them sneeze and jump.'

The picture by which Poynter is best known, *A Visit to Aesculapius*, was painted in 1880 and was exhibited in the Royal Academy, the title being accompanied in the catalogue by a quotation from the Elizabethan poet, Thomas Watson:

> In time long past, when in Diana's chase
> A bramble bush prickt Venus in the foot
> Olde Aesculapius healpt her heavie case
> Before the hurte had taken any roote.

The artist 'deduced' the sanctuary of the Argonauts' physician from ancient literature and monuments. It was a 'sanatorium' with open colonnades, a temple for the statue of the god and *ex voto* offerings, a spring of healing water and a cool grove. Aesculapius smiles indulgently as Venus holds out her foot for inspection, the nude group of which she is the main figure suggesting the Graces.

From legend Poynter turned to history again, and in 1883 painted another of those dramatic visualizations of an ancient event which created a strong impression, the *Ides of March*, in which Calpurnia warns Caesar of impending calamity.

The industry of Alma-Tadema was immense, though perhaps his work was only superficially to be classed with that of Leighton and Poynter. Ruskin, however strangely he expressed himself, was well aware of the possible and actual differences between the classic spirit and the representation of classic life—and his criticism of Alma-Tadema was very fierce indeed. 'Gloomy', 'crouching', 'dastardly' were the words he used of Alma-Tadema's *Pyrrhic Dance*, 'of which the general effect was exactly like a microscopic view of a small detachment of black-beetles in search of a dead rat'; and indeed there was in the black shields of the crouching warriors a curious similarity to Ruskin's image. But Alma-Tadema was popular. If some were stirred by the drama of *Ave Caesar, Io Saturnalia* in which Claudius after the death of Caligula is greeted with mocking respect as the new Emperor, others were delighted by the more intimate appeal of *Not at Home* in which the social mannerism of the eighties found its precedent in the coquettish Roman girl, 'out' when her lover called; or by the local interest of *The Emperor Hadrian visiting a Pottery in Britain*, where the Emperor stands at the head of a staircase not a little reminiscent of Messrs. Liberty's.

Leighton's *Daphnephoria* was sold to a private buyer for £1,500. Poynter's *A Visit to Aesculapius* was bought under the terms of the Chantrey Bequest for £1,050. The classic school was notable among the acquisitions of the provincial galleries. Manchester bought the *Ides of March*, likewise Leighton's *The Last Watch of Hero* and *Captive Andromache*.

Younger artists were moved by the powerful example of their

STUDY FOR HEAD OF ANDROMEDA
(from the model, Antonia Cura)
by Sir Edward Poynter, P.R.A.

seniors (and the still fermenting influence of the Elgin Marbles) to attempt similar themes. Here was the main inspiration of those who were students at the Royal Academy schools towards the end of the fifties: William Blake Richmond, Albert Moore, and Frederick Walker. The career of Richmond is a later parallel with that of Leighton, to whom he was junior by twelve years. He came of a dynasty of painters—his grandfather was the miniature-painter Thomas Richmond, his father the portrait-painter George Richmond, R.A. He was born in Beaumont Street, Marylebone, in 1842, and was christened William Blake because of his father's reverence for that great man. George Richmond had met Blake at the house of Frederick Tatham in Alpha Road, St. John's Wood (it was, he said, as if he 'had spoken to the prophet Isaiah'). It was George Richmond's worried remark that he could not work which had prompted Blake to ask his wife what they did in like circumstances ('We kneel down and pray, Mr. Blake'). William Blake Richmond treasured early memories of seeing Blake's followers, Edward Calvert and Samuel Palmer.

The spirit of Blake, in devious ways, descended on the Pre-Raphaelites, and as a boy Richmond saw them at his father's house. Millais and Holman Hunt came to an evening party when he was ten and they seemed to him like heroes, the handsome Millais 'like a knight of old'. Ruskin invited the boy to Denmark Hill (and lent him a drawing of Abbotsford by Turner and a study of mussel shells by William Hunt). It was from a Pre-Raphaelite environment that he went to the Royal Academy Schools in 1857. Ruskin would have been glad to look on him as a disciple ('if I would have decided to copy birds' nests, fruit, and primroses for the rest of my life'). He was not content to do so nor was he content simply to paint portraits, in spite of early successes which began with a commission from Queen Victoria—he was invited to paint a copy of Winterhalter's portrait of the Queen which she wished to present to the native ruler of Madagascar. He and his fellow students warmed to what he called the 'anarchy' of the Pre-Raphaelites—their defiance of convention. 'The old dodderers' of the Academy were 'vexed' by it, and this was pleasing to students with a fine youthful contempt for the 'sleepy old conventional school, so British in its narrow ways, so respectable in its absence of virile enthusiasm'.

On the other hand, it was not easy to paint like Holman Hunt, with that iron determination into which the first blazing enthusiasm of the Pre-Raphaelite Brotherhood had hardened. It was impossible not to admire the rival brilliance of G. F. Watts and the youthful Leighton. Richmond joined the Volunteers in 1859 as a boy of seventeen, and his personal contact with its classical members made a deep impression—deepened by the events of the next few years.

His student days ended, he toured the country houses as a portrait-painter, staying for some time at Oxford with Henry George Liddell, the Dean of Christ Church (then working on the Liddell and Scott Lexicon), and painting the Dean's daughters, Edith, Lorna, and Alice (original of Alice in Wonderland). In 1864 he married a beautiful girl, Charlotte Foster (she as devoted as he was to the arts), but his happiness was destroyed by her death a year after the marriage. Gloomily, he travelled to Italy. The gloom was a little lightened by the sun, the animation of Rome, and here, a cheering ray, Leighton came into his life again. As Richmond sat over his cup of coffee in the low-arched rooms of the Caffè Greco, thick with tobacco-smoke, noisy with many tongues, the handsome face of Leighton, back from Egyptian travel, beamed upon him; and with Leighton was 'a dark-skinned man of about forty, with eyes black and bright as diamonds, an enormous but well-shapen nose of true Etruscan type'—Cavaliere Giovanni Costa. Life was interesting again, not least because Costa, ever more deeply embroiled in political intrigue, made the young Englishman not only a friend but a fellow conspirator. If Leighton in his splendid aloofness was able to ignore Costa the rebel while consorting with Costa the artist, Richmond did not find it so easy. He shortly found himself holding compromising papers which concerned plans for a rising when the French garrison left. He buried them under a fig-tree in the garden at night—not too soon, for next day a sergeant and two Papal guards arrived with an order to search the premises. The search was thorough, but they went away disappointed.

Signor Narducci, Costa's brother-in-law, invited Richmond then to his estate in the Alban Hills, and here he found the life of a golden age in being. The house was an old fortified building like a castle with an ancient banqueting-hall. The cattle-drivers were picturesque in their goat-skins and scarlet waistcoats; the ploughs were drawn by twelve or fourteen oxen just as in the time of the Caesars. In March there was a rodeo, where the yearling cattle were branded, the cowboys dashed about on their rough little horses brandishing spear-like goads and the spectators watched from shelters screened with leaves.

Rome itself—and even more the sense of a link with antiquity given by the rural life of the Campagna and Alban Hills—turned Richmond to classic themes. Costa and Leighton both influenced him—he worked in the very studio in the via Felice where *Cimabue* had been painted and there began a *Procession in Honour of Bacchus* (exhibited at the first Burlington House Academy of 1869). This golden world was an escape—from all that was depressing in the life of Victorian England, from 'awful Clapham, hideous Charing Cross'. The classic myths came to hold for Richmond the same delight as did the Arthurian legend for the Pre-Raphaelites. A man opinionated, fastidious, and reactionary, he settled, on the outskirts of the metropolis and the land of his imagination, in a compromise which had its advantages. He set up house with his second wife—Miss Clara Richards (who had seemed to him 'like a Greek goddess') —at Beavor Lodge, Hammersmith; and if Hammersmith was not classic ground at least it was not yet built up and was less awful than Charing Cross or Clapham. The scent of hay came from the meadows across the river. Cows chewed the cud by the wall of the house. There were fields and market gardens still where the streets of Bedford Park, Acton, and Perivale have since grown up. Beavor Lodge stood alone in its high-walled garden with long flower-lined grass walks, two big Italian oil jars filled with daisies standing by its front door. Richmond was still living there when 'progress had taken place' and to his indignation 'monstrous additions' had been made 'to an already monstrous and ill-managed city'.

Like his father, he found it necessary to paint portraits, and he had a wide circle of sitter-friends. There was Browning, in whom Richmond perceived that 'private life' of which Henry James wrote, from whom he attempted to wrest 'the true Browning'; Darwin, modest, taciturn, sitting only a few minutes at a time: Robert Louis Stevenson, 'a sort of male fairy', talking beautifully, smoking constantly; Walter Pater, difficult and shy (Richmond designed the tablet to his memory in Brasenose College chapel). He painted both Gladstone and Bismarck, and was entrusted by the latter with a message to Gladstone. 'Tell him', said the Iron Chancellor, 'that while he is cutting down trees I am planting them.' The message was duly conveyed by Richmond, though Gladstone refused to see any double meaning in it or indeed any meaning at all.

Yet closely though Richmond observed these celebrities and interested as he was in them, his heart was given to Greece and Rome, and when he could he left Hammersmith to travel in Arcadia. Nineteenth-century Greece was, in his imagination, a living antiquity. The shepherds leaning on their crooks and playing reflectively on their reed pipes were the idyllic figures of Theocritus; the white-robed women of an Arcadian village with their whirring distaffs had stepped out of Homer. On Delos, Apollo's island, he travelled back in time. It was natural enough that he should paint the legendary events for which these scenes were so vivid a background, and thus in the seventies and eighties Richmond added his quota of classical subjects to those of Leighton and Poynter—a colossal *Prometheus Unbound* (sixteen feet high), *Ariadne deserted by Theseus on the Island of Naxos*, *An Audience in Athens during the Representation of the Agamemnon*, and many more.

.   .   .   .   .

Among Richmond's fellow pupils at the Academy Schools was a quiet boy, short and thickset with blue eyes and curly hair, speaking with a Yorkshire accent. His name was Albert Joseph Moore, and like Richmond he came of a painter dynasty. His father was the portrait-painter, William Moore of York; and his two elder brothers, John Collingham Moore and Henry Moore, were painters likewise. Albert was born at York in 1841.

His father gave him his first lessons in drawing when he was a small boy, but William Moore died when Albert was ten and in 1854 the family removed to London and settled in Phillimore Place, Kensington. Albert went to Kensington Grammar School and then to the Royal Academy Schools in 1858. In 1859 a visit to Normandy in company with the architect, William Eden Nesfield, who was collecting examples of French architectural detail, interested him in design as related to architecture, and with Nesfield's encouragement and help he began to get commissions for the design of wallpapers, tiles, and stained glass. He made a number of studies for the exterior sculptured frieze of the Albert Hall with its allegories of art, commerce, and manufacture—though these were not actually used.

After a short stay in Rome in 1862, he settled down in London to a life of quiet and secluded labour. He worked first in Berners Street and Fitzroy Street, from 1870 to 1876 in Red Lion Square, and from 1877 to 1891 in Holland Lane, Kensington. A confirmed bachelor, he wrapped himself up in his painting, and lived happily in a state of placid disorder and discomfort. He had a sitting-room in which there was nowhere to sit, for it never occurred to him that one might take one's ease in a chair and he was in the habit of squatting on the floor like a Japanese. Indifferent to his surroundings, he gave them just as much notice as would prevent them from bothering him. Whistler, visiting him one day with William Graham Robertson (Moore's pupil), was highly entertained to find him in the huge desolate room in which he painted, surrounded by numbers of spoutless, handleless jugs in each of which was a spiral of brown paper. 'Whatever can they be for? Do ask him', said Whistler, delighted by this Bohemian mystery. The question was put. 'For the drips', answered Moore. The roof leaked in several places, but it had not occurred to him that it might be repaired. Equally indifferent to his own appearance, he habitually wore a big ulster indoors and a broad-brimmed straw hat without a crown. Indifferent to society, he had as a favourite companion a dachshund called Fritz whose special attainment was to sit up and 'do George Eliot'.

In those days when Whistler was a close friend of Rossetti, he tried to bring Moore out and to introduce him into Rossetti's lively circle, but the effort failed. The quiet gentle man did not shine socially nor did he wish to shine. Rossetti, with less than his usual sympathy and unable to penetrate the reticence which Whistler appreciated as a mark of the artist devoted to his art, voted him 'a dull dog'. Nor did he seek or obtain academic honours. He was not one of those who lobbied and canvassed: not, it was said, one who would 'make the most of a patron and then in urbane and jolly good fellowship pass him on to a colleague'. Uninterested in fame and devoid of ambition, he minded strictly, in his own gentle way, his own business.

Yet to mind one's own business was a sort of definition, even if incomplete, of 'l'art pour l'art', that conception of the self-sufficiency of art which in these later Victorian years was gaining some ground in Britain. In Moore the classic tradition merged with the new 'aesthetic' trend. His ideal of beauty was founded on ancient Greece —in fact, as with so many others, mainly on the Elgin Marbles which he studied in the British Museum. He attempted, however, no subject drawn from either ancient mythology or history: no period reconstruction. He simply painted beautiful girls with the composed and regular features which belonged as much to Holland Park as ancient Athens. The rippling folds of their garments were inspired by the Parthenon, but it would be hard to say whether they reclined and meditated on the terrace of an ancient or a modern villa: Greek in pose and profile, they were almost photographically depicted as if a camera had been smuggled into the Golden Age. The intellectual effort of naming these pensive damsels 'Aphrodite' or 'Persephone' was not in Moore's line. They might indeed just as well have been English 'Rosemary' or 'Daisy', and his titles were, for the most part, as non-committal as *Midsummer* or *Reading Aloud*.

Founded as it was on Greece, his art belonged to the aesthetic age in its hybrid character. If the Parthenon gave him form, the Japanese prints which came into vogue in the seventies gave him his colour, subdued and mixed tones of salmon pink, old gold, and blue-green. Influenced by Whistler, no doubt, he mingled colour with music in some titles, such as *Harmony in Orange and Pale Yellow* or *Variation in Blue and Gold*; though his attitude to the naming of pictures is

THE DREAMERS
by Albert Moore

perhaps best expressed by his answer on one occasion to the question: 'What do you call it?'—'You can call it what you like.'

His method was as elaborate as that of Leighton. In succession came the 'thumb-nail' note; the general system of linear arrangement; the nude studies in black and white chalk on brown paper ('which might', said an admirer, 'have come from the hand of Apelles'); the black and white cartoon, the pricking and transference of outline to canvas with a pounce of charcoal dust; the detailed studies of drapery; the colour design; the final assemblage and welding of the whole. With all his deliberateness of method, however, Moore was a man sensitive to immediate impressions. The colour of some lemons on a piece of blue paper in a costermonger's barrow made the dreariness of a walk through Kensington tolerable to him; and this sensibility to colour, observed in his pictures, was admired by all those who professed a belief in 'art for art's sake'. 'His painting', said Swinburne, 'is to artists what the verse of Théophile Gautier is to poets.' To George Moore he was (with Whistler) one of England's two greatest artists, if not one of the only two artists England possessed. The friendship between him and Whistler was not simply due to their amusing one another, but to a real admiration on either side. Affectionate and at the same time critical, Whistler thought Moore might have been, in other circumstances— or another country—still better than he was. 'Albert Moore—poor fellow!' lamented Whistler. 'The greatest artist that in this century England might have cared for and called her own—how sad for him to live here—how mad to die in that land of important ignorance and bumbledom.' The lament was nevertheless a tribute.

.   .   .   .   .   .

If it was not exactly a classic 'school' of painting which thus came into existence and flourished in the seventies and eighties—for many were the differences between a Poynter, an Alma-Tadema, a Leighton, a Watts, a Richmond, an Albert Moore—it satisfied some at least of the conditions which make a school. These painters worked at the same time, in the same capital city, for the same people (or the same kind of people), on related themes. They had a common source of inspiration in the great Pheidias, the Parthenon frieze; and among them they engendered something of a 'style' which escaped from the limits of the easel picture and attached itself to the architecture of the time, thus playing its part in that Battle of Styles which is so conspicuous a feature of the Victorian Age.

The Battle of Styles reached its most acute point in the field of architecture. A product alike of the stubborn nonconformity and the sensitive yearnings of the period, it has a complex history, apart from the main course of this narrative. Not here is the place to tell in detail of the epic encounters of 'Goths' and 'Romans', of the internecine struggles of the Gothic faction, of the long-drawn and bitter fight between Lord Palmerston and Gilbert Scott to determine whether the Foreign Office should, architecturally, be Christian or pagan; yet something must be said of this diversity in building as the background against which part of the Olympian magnificence must be viewed.

The underlying issues were not dissimilar from those which disturbed the course of painting. The thread of tradition having been broken, it was necessary to go back to find it. Whither? You were compelled to choose between various forms of Gothic (or Christian) architecture or various classical (or pagan) styles. Realism—the exclusion of the past, the cultivation of the present moment, the extraction of a purely contemporary style from a contemporary problem—was as yet too daring a third alternative. It was left to the twentieth century to take Sir Joseph Paxton's Crystal Palace as a pattern of realism in architecture. The confusion which resulted from the rival nostalgias was great indeed. If there were several ways of being a 'Goth', from the austere English Perpendicular to the ornate Venetian, the massive Romanesque, there were as many ways of being classical, not only in the original Greek or Roman sense but in the adaptation of Renaissance styles, Italian, French, English; and any amalgam of these was possible according to the taste and fancy of the architect.

There was no knowing what a building would turn out to be, as Henry Cole, the reformer of art education and apostle of Design, remarked in a letter to *The Times* in 1872. While Lord John Manners was First Commissioner of Works 'the public were threatened with a period of Gothic'. This was the style accepted for the new offices in Downing Street, but the 'harlequin wand' of Lord Palmerston, First Lord of the Treasury, had turned them into a Renaissance palace. Captain Fowke, Inspector in the Science and Art Department, won the first prize in the competition for the Natural History Museum, South Kensington, with an 'Italian' design, but 'Mr. Cowper Temple, with delightful innocency, put the execution of it into the hands of a Gothic architect' and Lord John Manners, reappearing as First Commissioner, set it aside 'for a style of Gothic which it is difficult to characterize and approved by no one but himself. Some people', added Cole, 'call the style Byzantine and others Norman.'

These were the hazards attending the growth of what may be called the official Olympus of Kensington, the constellation of halls and museums, projected by the Prince Consort after the success of the Exhibition of 1851. If Cole himself, together with his friend Fowke, had not spent a holiday in the South of France in 1864, the great 'Central Hall of Arts and Sciences' which the Prince dreamed of, the Royal Albert Hall as it now is, would no doubt have looked very different from what it does today; but Cole was not immune from those whims he reproved in others. He and Fowke visited the Roman amphitheatres of Nîmes and Arles and were inspired by these ancient arenas to erect their like in London. Anything, they may have thought, would be better than Sir Gilbert Scott's proposal that the hall should incline 'to an early Gothic treatment with a tinge of Byzantine'. Its classic rotundities remain in strange contrast with the pointed and coloured canopy of the neighbouring Albert Memorial (on which Scott did have his own way), inflicting on the spectator an uncomfortable sense of ideological conflict.

In conflict also remain the South Kensington Museum (later to be extended and completed as the Victoria and Albert Museum), conceived in a more or less Italian style by Captain Fowke; and the Natural History Museum on the other side of the road in all the fretted splendour of Alfred Waterhouse's Gothic.

Thus, in Kensington, the battle of style was drawn: the classical side, however mixed and confused, had put up a valiant fight against the Goths, and though painters like Leighton and Poynter had no active part in the architectural fray, they were called in as decorators, sympathetic in spirit to the Albert Hall rather than the Albert Memorial, to the Italianate museum of art rather than the Gothic aisles of natural history. Their work on the adornment of the official Olympus was spread over many years. It began in 1862 with a frieze in glass mosaic for the South Kensington Museum. Mosaic —and terra-cotta—were two more of Henry Cole's holiday discoveries. He had become aware of their virtues when in Italy and, as the official advocate of Design, sought to plant them in Britain. To the frieze, Poynter contributed the figures of Pheidias and Apelles, while Leighton, *pari passu*, designed for it those of Cimabue and Niccolo Pisano.

The Museum's dining-room was assigned to their Pre-Raphaelite rivals, being decorated by William Morris's firm and containing panels painted by Burne-Jones; but in 1868 Cole invited Poynter to decorate the grill-room, and the painted tiles which occupied him for two years are famous in the annals of Victorian design. At Cole's suggestion Poynter went to Venice to study mosaic as a preparatory step to decorating the apse of the Museum lecture-hall. The project was not carried through, but in 1869 he had the important task of contributing to the classic frieze which circles the exterior of the Albert Hall—his subject 'The Four Quarters of the Globe bringing Offerings to Britain'. Whilst Poynter worked on this Leighton was beginning the frescoes for the Museum which (in 1868) Henry Cole had invited him to paint— *The Industrial Arts of Peace* and *The Industrial Arts of War*.

The Prince Consort had conceived these frescoes originally—as a kind of memorial of the Crimean War—and had talked of the project to Leighton. It was only fitting that Cole, acting in the spirit of that lofty discussion, and interpreting the wishes of the Prince, should, after the latter's death, invite Leighton to go on with the plan, which after some demur he consented to do.

'Demur' may not be the exact word, but 'exchange of views' hardly meets the case and 'argument' still less; a 'brush' perhaps it may be called. Henry Cole was an energetic, an able, a determined civil servant, used to having his own way. He had controlled and directed the inventiveness of Captain Fowke, bringing him on, from the design of such useful novelties as a collapsible pontoon, an improved umbrella with the ribs fitting within the stick, a machine for lighting a number of gas burners at the same time, to the more complex achievement of designing the Albert Hall. It had become natural for him to think of the artist as one who carried out his ideas, it was natural that in his zeal he should make some remarks on the style and treatment of the frescoes he commissioned. Yet admirable as he was in practical affairs, art was a strange thing to him, an artist of Leighton's stamp outside his experience. A merely human tenacity was now opposed to Olympian force. It was inevitable that Leighton should, magnificently, set him right, not in a vulgar way to triumph, but certainly with the result of delimiting their respective roles and incidentally exposing the distance between a painstaking official and one bred to greatness in the leading schools of Europe.

It was rash of Cole, in these circumstances, to attempt to impose his views as to whether the figures in the frescoes should be 'pictorial' or 'decorative'. The answer was long, and (though the aesthetic question involved may be technical and difficult to understand from the lay point of view) no one could fail to appreciate its tone of authority. In its invincible firmness, its courteous fluency, its occasional halt for the qualifying clause which would the more strongly reinforce the exposition, its placing of the issue on the broadest basis, it is a gem of the artist's manner and as such may be quoted at some length.

'I submit', wrote Leighton, 'that I have given reasons *why* the figures under discussion should not be pictures and that you, on the other hand, have not put forward a single reason why, a single principle on which, they *should* be pictures. You have contented yourself with adducing some precedents; as the question is entirely one of principles, precedent alone means nothing one way or another; if it were not so I should have opposed to you cases in which the, to my mind, sounder principle is observed.'

As the theme developed, one cannot say anything so undisciplined as anger crept into the rhythmic and flowing sentences, but certainly a note of Olympian reproof and an intimation that the matter so patiently and reasonably examined should not be again brought up.

'. . . you cannot propose upholding for admiration the mere fact that in old times picture and wall were sometimes one, but no doubt allude with just admiration to the harmony existing between them in the best examples and to the wise adaptation of one to the other. You, I submit, are attacking and attempting to subvert the very principles on which this harmony rests; my sole desire is to assert and defend them and I earnestly desire that, actuated, as I am entirely convinced you are, more by the desire to forward the truth than to triumph in argument, the views I have put before you may eventually commend themselves to you and deter you from further encouraging a practice which may be supported by precedent but cannot be made tenable in theory.'

It cannot be supposed that after this Cole had much more to say, and Leighton went ahead in his own splendid fashion. Dismissing Victorian officialdom, his mind went back to Greece. The work was to be carried out in the Greek spirit, as he explained in a letter to Steinle. 'I am by all means passionate for the true *Hellenic* art and am touched beyond everything by its noble simplicity and unaffected directness.' This truly classical spirit was to be sharply distinguished from that of the revivals which stemmed from Rome. 'The *Roman* or Napoleonic at its highest is antipathetic to me—I had almost said disgusting.'

It is not surprising, therefore—it was in key with the artist's temper—that the 'Arts of Peace' should not deal with subjects so un-Hellenic as the docks of London, the fuming chimneys of the Midlands, the kilns of Stoke and Hanley, but should represent beautiful women and handsome men in a Greek setting of temple and courtyard, the women preening themselves, the men going about such simple and dignified labours as were fitting to an ancient and idyllic existence. The artist made the scene Grecian 'partly out of sympathy', he said, 'and partly on account of the special beauty of the Greek ceramic and jewel work'.

Likewise the *Arts of War* had no heavy guns, steam battleships or breech-loading rifles, no parade of the Volunteers, but depicted Italian youth of the fourteenth century trying on its suits of armour and testing its swords and crossbows. The scene was placed in medieval Italy because it was there that in Leighton's view 'the conduct of arms seemed to reach its highest expression'.

That immense pains went into the work one would expect—and though Leighton was far from being exclusively busied with them, some part of the execution being entrusted to students of the Royal School of Art, they took many years to finish, were not complete until 1885. The preparation of the wall in itself was a lengthy task. It was washed with the specially prepared medium (to the recipe of Mr. Gambier-Parry) of gum and copal, elemi juice, white wax, and oil of spike lavender, coated repeatedly with a special compound of the purest white lead, gilder's whitening and turpentine intended to give the utmost smoothness. Even so the artist deplored that remaining roughness which made it like 'painting on a gravel path'. There were times when even he found the frescoes too heavy a burden. On one occasion, forgetting that he was on a ladder, he stepped back to survey the *Arts of War* and tumbled twelve feet to the floor. He could positively fall with aplomb, make light of his bruises, but the words were still rueful: 'South Kensington is doing its best to kill me. It may as well bury me too.'

Smooth, in spite of the roughness of the wall, the frescoes remain in the Victoria and Albert Museum, a little dulled by time, notable as evidence of that Victorian idealism, now so strange, which steadfastly excluded the contemporary world from art; yet this exclusion was approved by many contemporaries who wished to give their own houses a certain classic dignity and aloofness. Olympus by means of frieze, mosaic, and fresco deigned to be domestic, and the public works it executed were paralleled by private commissions which added a distinct element to the complexity of late-Victorian decoration rivalling the rustic chairs, the medieval tapestries, the cottage chintzes of Morris and Co., the Japanese screens and fans, the Oriental pots of the aesthetes.

In the mansions of the late Victorian age, the scheme of the

Parthenon found its echo. Leighton's architect, George Aitchison, together with Thomas Armstrong (of the 'Paris Gang'), devised a classical décor for the dining-room of Mr. Eustace Smith, M.P., at 52 Prince's Gate, the walls being gilded and a slightly indented pattern impressed on them, the dado consisting of inlaid designs of ivory, ebony, and mother-of-pearl. Two large pictures let into the wall and painted by Armstrong depicted somewhat limp maidens in a graceful dress of no precise period, while Leighton himself designed the frieze, as also the frieze, on the theme of Music, for Mr. Stewart Hodgson's drawing-room at 1 South Audley Street and the ceiling for Mr. Marquand's music-room in New York. During the seventies Poynter decorated the Earl of Wharncliffe's billiard-room with a series of subjects which included *Perseus and Andromeda*, *Atalanta's Race*, and *Nausicaa and her Maidens playing at Ball*, the series being complemented by a full-length portrait of the Earl in knickerbockers and carrying a sporting gun. In the same spirit Walter Crane designed many a piece of mosaic, many a vine motive worked in gesso in low relief. A lady who wished to have a classical firescreen asked Leighton to ornament it for her. He was not averse from such minor arts, but on this occasion he failed, if failure it could be called not to adjust his superb faculties to so trivial an undertaking. With all his habitual courtesy he requested the lady to accept a small oil painting as some recompense for having disappointed her.

Thus, though anything like a Greek architecture had come to a stop with the Greek revival in the early part of the century, the idea of things Greek retained its influence and those impressionable men, the Victorian architects, sought cunningly to introduce it—even as a flavour—into the home. They were men whose imagination was easily set on fire, to whom curious combinations presented no logical difficulty. By ingenious reasoning the 'Goth', Burges, was able to find a rapport between the Greek and Gothic spirit—which, existing between Herodotus and Froissart, Aristophanes and Rabelais, might, he considered, be found also in a building. In his own house in Melbury Road he brought Greek and Gothic motives together.

'The secret of all good architecture and all good furniture', pronounced Oscar Wilde with the effrontery of the aesthetic amateur, 'is to have the Greek line with the Oriental phantasy.' This curious and vague remark finds its explanation in the projects of Whistler's architect, Edward William Godwin, a man who in his time had designed Celtic castles and medieval country houses but was quite prepared to be Greek on occasion, or even Japanese—indeed, to arrive at a blend of the 'phantasy' of bamboo and the severe lines of the marble bench. It was Godwin who conceived a 'Greek' armchair, an imposing addition to the potted palms and the china-laden brackets of the interior of the eighties. The next step, one might argue, was to bring human beings into conformity with the setting, and even this did not seem too bold an enterprise.

The Olympian influence on dress or ideas of dress was an aspect of the late-Victorian dissatisfaction with the prevailing clothes and fashions—fashion being, in the words of Oscar Wilde, a form of ugliness so intolerable that it had to be changed every six months. It was natural that those addicted to the art of another period than their own should advocate its dress and that women's dress, as being essentially Fashion, should be the prime object of concern. Thus the women of the Pre-Raphaelite circle became medieval in appearance, their robes falling in long straight folds. On the other hand the classical faction would have them dressed in the Greek manner like the women on the Parthenon frieze whose garments hung loosely and gracefully from the shoulders. The Greek lady, remarked the Hon. John Collier (the pupil of Poynter), 'never supposed she had a waist. She often for convenience tied a string round her body, but only just tightly enough to keep the clothes in place, and then let folds of drapery fall over and hide the unsightly line.' This, he continued, was the noblest form of clothing ever invented.

The painter and the architect were interested, not only on the aesthetic ground that there is an art in everything, including clothes, but on the score of hygiene. G. F. Watts opposed the dress shown in the Elgin Marbles to the habit of tight lacing because it was healthier. The young women, heralds of emancipation, who boldly assumed a rational gymnastic costume and thrust eurhythmically with dumb-bells at the Health Exhibition in Kensington won the approval of E. W. Godwin, that incurable eclectic who was the pioneer of dress reform as of Greek armchairs, who had, it was noted, a life-size replica of the Venus de Milo in his rooms. It was from Godwin that Wilde, the 'Professor of Aesthetics', took the idea that 'over a substratum of pure wool, such as is supplied by Dr. Jaeger under the modern German system, some modification of Greek costume is perfectly applicable to our climate, our country, and our century'.

Society, however little inclined to be unconventional in everyday life, was all for dressing up on special occasions and for using some modification of classical costume (as well as of the Middle Ages) in the elaborate fancy dress balls and costume charades in which the eighties delighted. The ball of 1884 given to inaugurate the Royal Institute's new building in Piccadilly paid its tribute to Rossetti, to Leighton, to Alma-Tadema, in its choice of characters. Dante and Beatrice were there (Mr. Stock, R.I., and Miss Lisa Lehmann), Cimabue and Giotto (Walter Crane and his son). Mr. W. A. S. Benson, who made pieces of furniture for William Morris, was Niccolo Pisano, Mr. Forbes-Robertson was impressive as Virgil in a scarlet toga and with a wreath of laurel; and the spectacle was approved by the Prince of Wales and Princess Alexandra. In 1885 English girls, as classic in feature as any conceived by Pheidias, attended an Academicians' ball dressed as Grecian damsels. In 1886 Leighton, Watts, and Henry Holiday designed a series of *tableaux vivants*, illustrating Professor Warr's Greek translations. Leighton's favourite model, Dorothy Dene, was Cassandra, and in a pose which the artist may have taught, stood 'statuesquely', hands clenched to sides, her gaze 'riveted with intense prophetic emotion on Clytemnestra'.

It was but a short step to the stage performance. The classic drama was presented afresh, the classical plays of Shakespeare enjoyed a revival. E. W. Godwin prepared the settings and costume of a successful production of Sophocles' *Helena in Troas*, performed at Hengler's Circus in Great Pulteney Street. Oscar Wilde, who persuaded his wife Constance to appear among the supernumerary beauties, was enraptured when the stage curtains slowly divided and

Miss Alma Murray as Helen came forth from the house of Priam 'in a robe woven with all the wonders of war and broidered with the pageant of battle'. The handmaidens were posed in imitation of the Parthenon frieze, and their unbleached calico was considered to be surprisingly close in effect to the pentelic marble.

Alma-Tadema had a special delight in the living picture as a last triumph of archaeology, and took part in the festivities of the Institute of Water-Colour Painters as a classic reveller crowned with a wreath of bluebells. Sir Henry Irving and Beerbohm Tree leaned on him for guidance in their productions. 'No praise', said Irving, 'could to my mind be too great for Sir Lawrence's work for the stage.' The Lyceum productions of *Coriolanus* and *Cymbeline* were turned visually into Alma-Tadema paintings: for Ellen Terry, whose classic beauty had variously inspired Watts and Godwin, he designed the costume of Volumnia. Beerbohm Tree, during the rehearsals of *Julius Caesar*, came to Grove End Road so that the artist could help him with his toga, which Tree found a more intricate garment than it looked, and F. R. Benson, producing the *Agamemnon* at Oxford, found Alma-Tadema's knowledge of the chlamys and chiton invaluable. 'It was he', said Beerbohm Tree, remarking on the grand effect with which Alma-Tadema had brought ancient Rome to the stage of His Majesty's Theatre, 'who taught us the Roman handshake, the mutual grip of the wrist.'

A certain admirable element of simplicity in modern stage design, the dramatic simplicity which is so notable in the designs of Gordon Craig, may perhaps be traced back to Godwin's *Helena in Troas* if not to Alma-Tadema's *Coriolanus*. Only James McNeill Whistler could find in this high and solemn art of re-creation something risible. That, when seeing Wilson Barrett's *Claudian*—in which his friend Godwin, 'one of the most artistic spirits in England . . . showed us the life of Byzantium in the fourth century . . . by the visible presentation before us of all the glory of that great town' (to quote Wilde's enthusiastic review)—Whistler should rock 'to and fro in an agony of merriment' is of interest. Whether it was the play, the costume, or the acting which caused his mirth it is hard to decide. One may suppose it due to that realistic outlook which tied him so firmly to the present and made suspect the presentation of past glories: to the aversion of the master for those minor forms of art, which no artist in his sense of the word had produced. At all events he laughed, and so infectious is laughter that Godwin, however little he might appreciate its motives, seems to have found it difficult not to laugh too.

.   .   .   .   .   .

Thus in many ways the classic school made its mark. Leighton himself went on from strength to strength. In the abundance of his energy he was able to combine with painting, with travel, with the social occasions which also demanded their effort, those official activities which Ruskin would have described as 'senatorial'. The gift of ordering and organizing, administrating and judging, which came naturally to him was generally and gratefully recognized. He was an examiner and adviser to the South Kensington Museum. He acted on the Committee of the Society of Dilettanti which still, as in the eighteenth century, pursued its study and collection of antique art, even to the point of emulating the Earl of Elgin's triumph. It seems but fitting that Leighton should share the credit of a further splendid importation—when in 1870 two hundred cases of sculptures and carved inscriptions were brought, in H.M.S. *Antelope*, from Priene (famous among the twelve independent Ionian cities of Asia Minor) and presented to the British Museum.

Leighton's promptness and decision was as marked now as it had been in his youth. His friend Costa told of the occasion in Siena when a fire started in the Duomo and, causing general confusion, seemed likely to get quite out of hand. Clearing a way through the crowd came the alert, distinguished figure. His keen eye saw at once the mistake made by the firemen, who had opened windows and thus creating a draught had encouraged the flames. A few crisp words— in perfect Italian—and the windows were closed. Further instructions, in which there was all the efficiency of the Volunteer officer, were carried out without question. The fire died down, was put out. It was then that Leighton turned to the admiring Costa with one of those gestures so characteristic of him. 'And now', he said, consulting his watch, 'we have just time before lunch to look at the Duccios.'

It was only to be expected that he should, as so many had foretold, become the President of the Royal Academy. Millais rivalled him in fame, but Millais himself would have been the first to admit the greater claim of his friend, and these two were without rivals. Leighton was in Italy, at Lerici, with Costa in 1878 when the news arrived that the whilom President, Sir Francis Grant, was dead. Grant belonged to an earlier day. He was a painter of sporting scenes and portraits, a friend of Landseer, noted for his equestrian portrait of the young Queen, a man of respectable achievement whose death was to be regretted, yet an Early Victorian who scarcely represented the fullness of the age. 'The President is dead', said Costa and then, as he handed back the telegram which brought the news, and gazing significantly at Leighton, 'Long Live the President.'

Leighton stayed in Italy a while to finish the work he had set himself there. It would have ill become him to dash, as a lesser man might have been tempted to dash, back to London, to display some personal ambition, to show himself among the electors, to canvass votes. Yet the outcome was certain. Thirty-five of the forty votes went to him and it remains only a matter of wonder that any of the other five could have been given to an obviously lesser man.

Knighthood and other honours marked the accession as P.R.A. 'Monday', he wrote, 'I go to Windsor to be knighted.' 'Yes, I got a first-class gold medal for my sculpture' (his *Athlete and Python* exhibited at the Paris International Exhibition). 'I am believed', he added, with modest casualness, 'to have the "ruban" of an "Officier de la Légion d'Honneur"'; and this belief was, of course, correct. Congratulations too came in a shower. Steinle, who had for so long followed Leighton's career with deep, if sometimes anxious, admiration, wrote his joy. Robert Browning, Matthew Arnold, the Kemble clan, his natal Scarborough expressed their pleasure. There was a general feeling that, in the most superlative terms, the right man was in the right place.

Yet 1878 was a year of warfare in the arts, a crucial and important year. The great prophet of the Pre-Raphaelites, John Ruskin, had sounded alarm, had hurled insult and contempt at James McNeill Whistler who stood for a dangerous doctrine, 'art for art's sake', implicitly rejecting the social purpose and practical idealism which Ruskin insisted upon. If, as one might say, the Pre-Raphaelite and Aesthetic champions were in martial array, prepared to do battle in the lists of the Law, it might well be asked where the Classical faction stood, where Leighton himself?

Whistler would have had him give evidence in his famous libel action, for among the qualities of Leighton was Taste. He was not so narrow and prejudiced in his views as some of his fellow artists and friends. He had been one of the earliest admirers of Whistler's etchings and, as was his wont, had bought where he admired. He was one of those invited to inspect the controversial paintings in Whistler's studio before the case came on, but no comment by him is recorded and it unfortunately happened that the ceremony to which he was called clashed in date with that of the Ruskin–Whistler trial. He could not decline a knighthood in order to make an appearance in a law-court—and indeed was it fitting, in any case, that a newly elected P.R.A. should promptly stand in the witness-box, perhaps in the awkward necessity of opposing and contradicting some other Academic witness? There was here the possibility of many and great confusions, undermining the confidence of the public in all that was secure and settled in art, sowing the seeds of fresh professional dissension. Yet one cannot but feel a sense of disappointment, for he would have made a perfect witness. That he would have behaved with all his accustomed dignity is certain. It is the Olympian calm of his judgement that we miss in the jibes of the Attorney-General and the answering wit of Whistler, in the embarrassed and therefore over-emphatic testimony of the artists who actually figured in the case. He would not have shown the narrow prejudice of a Frith, nor any of the unhappy nervousness of a Burne-Jones. It is possible to see him setting everyone to rights, the Old Bailey firmly under his control, the issue placed on the highest possible level.

Then, the aesthetic and classical creeds had so much in common—in both there was a regard for Beauty in itself as an ideal distinct from other ideals—so much that Albert Moore, steeped as he was in the classical spirit, was Whistler's main partisan and spoke up on his side.

In default of his personal appearance it is necessary to turn to Leighton's Addresses to the Students of the Royal Academy for what, in conclusive settlement, he might have said at the Ruskin–Whistler trial. They indicate that he would have asked that the whole body of evidence be examined for an 'impartial conception' and a 'comprehensive view'. They give their warning against the fallacy of mistaking 'a coefficient for a primary cause'. In gist, though not in style, they are complementary to Whistler's *Ten o'Clock* lecture, to the underlying conceptions of *The Gentle Art of Making Enemies*.

The Addresses, seven in number, were given at two-yearly intervals in the period of fourteen years between 1879 and 1893. Biennially Leighton retired to Perugia in order to give care to fashioning them in appropriate surroundings. He poured into them all that knowledge of the art of Europe and the Near East which had been reinforced by constant travel. Even those who knew him well were astonished at the learning which he combined with eloquence and judgement—the luminous certainty with which he described the mysterious race of Etruscans, or Germany in the days of the Hohenstaufen; the way he appraised a Philibert de l'Orme or a Tilman Riemanschneider. His friend, Robin Allen, inquired, 'Have any of the multitude of men who love you ever called you Chrysostom?' for Leighton, like that saintly orator, might well have been termed 'golden-mouthed'. He spoke from memory and for this reason the printed version of the Addresses was insufficiently, though, as his sister pointed out, 'I need hardly say, never wrongly, punctuated'; but the sustained flow of language was both rich and correct. 'He would never', said Briton Rivière, 'get over a fault of grammar.' If, here and there, there was to be detected too insistent a note of pedagogy, this was due to his sense of a high mission.

'He could not be blind', says Mrs. Orr, 'to the exceptional merits of his work but he knew they were not of a nature to command general interest and appreciation. He often feared that what he had to say was beyond the immediate grasp of the students to whom it was addressed'—but a less serious treatment was impossible.

What was the aim of art? asked Leighton. Not to teach moral or religious truths. He abolished the 'didactic theory', by reference to Spanish art, where the most religious painters, 'a Juanes, a Luis de Vargas who wrought in the intervals of fasting, of prayer, and of self-flagellation were manifestly inferior to a Velasquez, the most mundane of painters'. The Italian Renaissance was supported by the scientific spirit which led to the study of anatomy and perspective. If there was a downward tendency in sixteenth-century art it was due less to 'the failings of religious faith among artists than to the excessive and too exclusive faith in Science'. He distinguished between the religions of Greece—the faith in a supreme God and on the other hand the 'joyous fellowship of gods and goddesses, loving and hating, scheming and boasting, founding dynasties upon the earth'. It was far-fetched to trace any ethical purpose or high religious character even in the subjects of Pheidias. Again, if the dignity of all human achievement depended on the moral sense, what became of Music? Was not to imply the dethronement of Music a *reductio ad absurdum*? 'What ethical proposition can Music convey? What teaching or exhortation is in its voice? None. Absolutely none!'

The language of art was not, said Leighton, the 'appointed vehicle of ethical truths', but there is a range of emotions to which Art alone has the key. Form, Colour, and the Contrasts of Light and Shade were its agents; but then, these emotions had an *ethos* of their own, conveyed notions of strength and repose, joy or sadness, languor or health. 'It is the intensification of the simple aesthetic sensation through ethic and intellectual suggestiveness that gives to the Arts of Architecture, Sculpture, and Painting, so powerful, so deep and so mysterious a hold on the imagination.' But if the artist was not a moral preacher, at the same time how steadfastly he must avoid the ignoble 'greed for gain', that poisonous taint fatal to all higher effort; or the vulgar thirst for noisy success, the hankering of vanity for prompt and public recognition; or the indulgence in a narrow, unsympathizing spirit, prone ever to carp and cavil.

Thus spoke Leighton, and if he might have set Baron Huddleston and Sir John Holker right, to some extent he set Whistler right also. If the Academy Address of 1881 was not so witty and amusing as Whistler's *Ten o'Clock* of 1885, it showed more learning and was free from the sketchiness of that famous lecture. Yet in many ways they support one another, a fact at variance with the relations of the two artists otherwise, for as clearly as Whistler stood opposed to the institutions of the age Leighton belonged to them. The Academy was his realm.

As soon as he was elected President in 1878, he began to display in his new office that unwearying and scrupulous attention to duty which was natural to him. He no longer had any time for soldiering, although he had been gazetted lieutenant-colonel in 1876. 'President of the Volunteers and Lieutenant-Colonel of the Royal Academy' was the Whistlerian quip. He finally resigned in 1883, gracefully explaining the pressure of his commitments—of the age itself ('we live in times so hustling and breathless')—though he was promptly made Honorary Colonel and received the Volunteer Decoration for long and distinguished service. As a President he was ideal. When the remark was made that he was the most distinguished holder of the office since Reynolds there were many who felt that this was but cold and half-hearted praise—that there could never have been any President like him. The paintings, the Discourses, the social abilities of Sir Joshua himself seemed to pale before the attainments of the Olympian. It did not seem possible that his like would ever be seen again. 'Leighton', said Watts, 'has made it impossible for another to follow him with *eclat*.'

Scrupulously he attended each council meeting, and his habit of punctuality caused him to be seated in his chair some minutes before the appointed time so that business might start on the very stroke of the hour. Each of the Addresses was prepared with the same care, in the temporary seclusion of Perugia. He took the keenest interest in the supervision of the students' training, and those who lectured to them were kept up to the mark by the example of his thoroughness and erudition. Professor Lanteri and Sir Edgar Boehm, discussing a lecture which the latter was to give on 'Bronze Casting', found gaps in their knowledge. What, for instance, were the dates of Niccolo

Pisano? They could not for the life of them remember. 'We must be careful,' said Boehm, 'or we shall have Leighton down on us.' The President would certainly have known, would have instantly detected a vagueness or inaccuracy which it was the duty of professors to avoid.

To all the ceremonies which attended the Annual Exhibition, the crowning event of the Academic year, he added his own grandeur. Gracefully he received the Sovereign and members of the Royal Family on the day of their formal visit before the opening. He shone at the Private View, the brilliant apex of the London season. In the National Portrait Gallery there is a group picture (by a little-known artist called Brooks), not, it is true, of this annual occasion but depicting the Private View of the Old Master Exhibition at Burlington House in 1888: except for the paintings, a similar scene. It is an impressive pictorial document of the time, crowded with recognizable portraits of famous and dominant personalities. Mr. Gladstone is there, and in the background John Ruskin apparently arguing with Holman Hunt, and little Alma-Tadema talking away vivaciously to his circle; yet of all there is one figure which captures attention by a singular beauty—Sir Frederic Leighton in amiable converse with Lord and Lady Wantage, with Lady Jersey by his side. There is such a crispness and purity of white about the beard that it might, you would think, have been carved by some Greek sculptor, something extraordinarily noble about the brow with its clustering curls. He alone in this typical late-Victorian assembly seems moulded by the genius of another and distant age.

At last came the Royal Academy Banquet, attended by the Prince of Wales, the Corps Diplomatique, members of the Cabinet, leading lights of the great professions, such a splendid gathering as could hardly be seen anywhere else at one time. The President rose and proposed the toasts: the Queen, the heir to the Throne at the board with other members of the Royal Family, Her Majesty's Ministers, the Armed Forces of the Crown. The Royal guest replied to the second toast, Mr. Gladstone or Mr. Disraeli or Lord Salisbury to the third, a Minister or warrior to the fourth; and then when the toast of 'The Academy' was proposed, the President rose to reply.

He was never at a loss for a word, for the right word: there was no hesitation for he learned his speeches by heart, being unable, he said, 'to think upon his legs'. Other practised speakers might have their criticisms to make. Lord Granville advised him, above all, not to be too long, but remarked, 'He did not take my advice'. 'Don't you think', said John Bright, 'there is rather much confectionery in your oratory—rather sugary, eh?' Yet in spite of these cavils, he was generously acclaimed. Then, when speaking was over, while the Royal Artillery band played, he tasted the full pleasures of triumph, though unwearying in courtesy and attention to his guests for the remainder of the evening. A wonderful man, they thought, and at the head of a wonderful institution, a bulwark of national life, the like of which was surely not to be found in any other land.

Great therefore was the pride of the Academician in the body of which he was member. It inspired love as well as loyalty, a happy feeling of brotherhood. John Millais belonged to it with all his heart. He had, he said, a friendly affection for every piece of furniture in it. No less was the affection of Leighton as its President. Its honour was dear to him. When, in the course of a House of Commons debate, the Sir Robert Peel of the time jibed at R.A.s as 'people of no very good taste', Leighton, in superb anger, consulted Lord Redesdale as to 'calling out' Peel and defending Academic taste with the duelling pistol. Identified with the Academy in every way, he enjoyed the smallest routine detail of administration equally with the great occasion. He was accessible, at an exact hour—generally nine o'clock in the morning—to the student with some problem to be solved. He answered with punctilious care the letters from parents and other relatives anxiously questioning some young man's talent and the chances of a painter's career. To one lady who thus consulted him about her son, he wrote: 'Let him have the education of a gentleman in the first place and if he should still have an inclination for art let him specialize.' His fellow Academicians placed entire confidence in him and their affection amounted to awe. Under the auspices of so eminent a man, all gained in prestige. Stronger than it had ever been was the Academy; the suspicion that those artists who did not adhere to it, or criticized it adversely, were but a fringe of eccentrics and incompetents took firmer root.

In the days of Leighton's Presidency, there was none who could or dared admonish, for Ruskin was now silent; and the satirical comments of Whistler were but the stings of a solitary gadfly. Rich, powerful, superbly administered, undisturbed by factions and generally respected, the Academy ruled the roost. Yet when its artists are enumerated and their work examined, there appear depths far below the Olympian height; departures from that lofty criterion which the President's Addresses uphold; painters who, it is to be feared, lacked aesthetic motives, had little feeling for or understanding of art. They were interested solely in subject-matter and they were interested in subject-matter as a manufacturer might be interested in his product—that is, in turning it out regularly and sticking close to a certain specified formula. It was in this formula and its commercial implications rather than the subject itself that the fault lay. To paint scenes of popular life was well: had not a Brueghel extracted masterpieces from such themes? To paint history was an enterprise which had its worthy precedents: to take a subject from literature was not unknown among the Renaissance masters; what these masters would have found it hard to understand was the sentiment —or sentimentality—which in these late Victorian works distracted attention from any quality they might possess as painting, a tempting irrelevance which lured the public into buying and ensured popularity.

It was, of course, impossible to suppose that everyone should paint like the President or possess a like combination of gifts. He could not by his single efforts make artists, nor was it his task to divert them from that which it was their nature to do. His position was not one which lent itself to an attitude critical to the point of being destructive. That belonged to such a man as Whistler who did not care about institutions, whose attempt to be the President of a society resolved in wordy and witty battle. 'The artists came out and the British remained', said Whistler of the end of his stormy reign at the Royal Society of British Artists. In Leighton's Olympus no such convulsion was possible. It was governed by tolerance, by dignified affirmation, and yet the skill with which the President steered the ship left much licence to the crew. His devotion to the Greek ideal gave a lofty definition to Academic art. At the same time it is hard to look with complacence or comfort on much that was produced during his term of office, and, in particular, on the purchases then made for the famous Chantrey Bequest.

It was during Leighton's presidency that the good intentions of Sir Francis Chantrey, R.A., were first given material form. Sir Francis had been one of those artists who had loved the Academy well. He had risen by industry and application from a small start in life as a grocer's boy in Sheffield to fame and wealth. He had painted and drawn portraits at from two to five guineas each; had found a mason to teach him stone-carving; had been employed as a wood-carver and, settling in London, had in due course become *the* artist to model a great man's head. He was R.A. in 1818, a Knight in 1835, a crony of Turner whose warm colour caused him to crack many a joke, for he was a merry fellow who would pretend to warm his hands before the glowing expanse of Turner's orange chrome. He shared with Turner the wish to benefit the art of the nation and the artists to come. The fortune he left at his death in 1841 (£150,000 in Consols) was bequeathed, subject to a life-interest for his wife, to the care of the Royal Academy. The annual interest accruing was to be devoted by that body to the purchase of works by British artists or artists living in Britain. It was assumed that sooner or later a national gallery would be built to house them. From these circumstances came the state of affairs which in the twentieth century has caused so much debate.

Where else should the Academy turn, save to the Academy, for those excellent works the purchase of which Sir Francis had enjoined? How many should be bought at a time? It was a sound principle that they should be few, seeing that the highest standard was prescribed; it was inevitable therefore that each should be bought for a very large sum. The Academy became possessed of a rich perquisite indeed shortly before Leighton was elected its President.

It seems fitting, in view of his many 'firsts', that a work of his should be the first purchase made under the terms of the Bequest, a piece of sculpture, the *Athlete struggling with Python*, which was exhibited at the Academy in 1877. A new departure for one famous for picture-painting, yet natural enough in one brought up on the classics. Indeed, when elected to the Society of Dilettanti, Leighton whimsically enrolled himself as 'sculptor, with permission occasionally to relapse into painting'. He had previously made some essays in sculpture, notably the medallion for the tomb of Elizabeth Barrett Browning in the Protestant Cemetery at Florence. If the Elgin Marbles could inspire the painter they were, nevertheless, in a different medium from his, and Leighton had long thought of rivalling on his own ground Polycleitos of Sicyon, whose athletes he so greatly admired. Similarly inspired, and by the same process of reasoning, his friend Watts had preceded him in turning to sculpture, but it was the general opinion that Leighton surpassed him, that in this as in other ways he was unsurpassable. That early knowledge of anatomy in which his father had so carefully drilled him, stood him in good stead. He chose the male form as the best for sculpture because the contours were more strongly marked, less softly rounded (though in painting he preferred the female form). Angelo Colorosi, the Italian, was his model, the bones, muscles, and sinews of the finished statue startling in their anatomical precision. 'Why, man,' said Alphonse Legros, at the time Slade Professor at University College, London, 'this is splendid; go on.' Seeing that he could thus excel in an art other than his own, a fellow Academician remarked that Leighton confounded the whole theory of division of labour. The *Athlete* was therefore bought for the considerable sum of £2,000 in 1879.

It would have been well if every Chantrey purchase had been of this kind, but there was many a steep descent to come—or at least what seems a descent to the critical eyes of a later generation.

There was Leighton's neighbour in Melbury Road, Marcus Stone, no longer the excellent illustrator of *Our Mutual Friend*, but the 'painter of sweethearts' who had made himself popular by the sentimental problem he posed year after year. Always there was a young woman and a young (or perhaps occasionally an elderly) man in Regency dress. They were meeting or parting, quarrelling or making it up, arriving at some cross-purpose in the game of love, and the painting itself was but an excuse for the sentimental mind to muse on the situation it suggested. Among the Chantrey pictures in 1882 was included Stone's *Il y en a toujours un Autre*. The title tells the story— in the presence of one lover the girl is manifestly thinking of another.

Then there was Hubert Herkomer, son of a Bavarian peasant family which had emigrated from Germany, first to Ohio, then settling in Southampton. Piety and sentiment had won him success. After some early illustrations for *Fun* and the *Graphic* he had made his hit at the Academy, and was able to settle with his parents at Bushey, near Watford, where he built that singular castle (called 'Lululaund') which still remains. His piety is marked by the Gothic towers ('Mother's Tower' he termed each) which he raised as a memorial to his mother after her death, in Landsberg, Bavaria, and in Bushey. The debt he said he owed to the England of his time was its having taught him that 'truth in art should be enhanced by senti- ment'. His sentiment appears conspicuously in the *Last Muster* of 1874, the pathos of which drew a spontaneous burst of applause from every member of the Academy Selection Committee of that year. The 'Master', for so he was known to, and long remembered by, the students who gathered about him at Bushey (where they had, as he remarked, 'the immense advantage of daylight through the winter months with good fresh air' and where, if one failed 'to reach the highest art, I shall endeavour to show him other branches, such as etching and mezzotint-engraving'), was noted for the energy and confidence with which he practised many crafts—though in his work it is hard for a later generation to find any trace of art. Far indeed does he seem from the classic criterion of Leighton, who nevertheless was able to write him letters of congratulation. With serious doubts we see him elected to the Slade Professorship at Oxford in 1885 in succession to John Ruskin—stilled at last was the voice of independent criticism. Without enthusiasm we note his Chantrey plum, *Found*—a Roman warrior wounded and fainting in the Welsh mountains is discovered by a wild British woman leading her flock of goats, with what mixed feelings of sympathy and fear the writers of the time were happy to describe.

From Scotland came some of the Chantrey men, such as John Pettie, pupil of Lauder, famed for his *Vigil* in which a young knight-to-be, evidently fatigued by his watch, holds up his sword in a gesture of dedication. Came William Quiller Orchardson, also of Edinburgh, achieving success with *Napoleon on board the Bellerophon*; Joseph Farquharson, too, with his all-too-joyless *Joyless Winter Day*; and from Philadelphia, Anna Lea Merritt, to win a Chantrey prize with *Love Locked Out*; from Massachusetts Francis Davis Millet, apt in humorous genre, whose Chantrey picture was *Between Two Fires*, familiar from many a calendar, in which a Puritan of the seventeenth century, sitting down to a meal at an inn, is embarrassed to find a damsel on each side of him.

It would be tedious to make a complete Homeric catalogue of the Chantrey winners in the days of Leighton's presidency, when the pictures destined for a national gallery which did not as yet exist began to pile up. They scarcely form an inspiring chapter in the history of British art. They were like a library, intended to be a set of the nation's best books, which turned by a deviation of taste into a collection of popular novels, tempered by one or two translations from the classics—for so one may look on the President's *Athlete*, on Poynter's *Visit to Aesculapius*. In contrast with these were the piquant anecdotes, the scenes which involved so much meditation on the psychology of the actors in them, the overpowering sentimentality, the large dull landscapes which in their wide gold frames were so exactly suited to the *salon* of a Podsnap or a Veneering.

That such pictures satisfied well the taste of a tasteless society is but, in the judgement of the severe critic, to lay an additional charge against them—a charge laid indeed at the time of their production by a William Morris, a McNeill Whistler. To Morris they were clear evidence of a social distemper, the idle nonsense produced by well-kept slaves to titillate the frivolous appetite of the ignorant rich. To Whistler their offence was not social but an offence against art: they were pictures that were no pictures, that had lost and made no pretence of attempting to speak the language of the masters. It took time for the weight of their criticism to make itself felt. Between 1878 and 1895 the Bequest was administered without hindrance, amid plaudits; a thousand guineas or more enveloped the most mediocre work in their golden haze and gave it a brief hallucinatory splendour. Then, at the end of the century, when the pictures could at last be seen together in the new Tate Gallery (that long-hypothetical national collection)—they were arranged by Poynter—the first chill of doubt crept into the air; as time went on it seemed necessary to relegate one, then another, and still another, to the basement. Gradually the basement filled up with works once enthusiastically acclaimed. With rueful dismay Posterity saw them once more assembled, perhaps for the last time, in the Chantrey Exhibition of 1949.

It is possible that in some ways later criticism has gone too far to its own extreme, has too arrogantly adopted the Nemesis rôle. If his sentiment be forgotten the qualities of a painter may be found submerged in the work of an Orchardson. There is a touch now and then of that always valuable period interest—when artists remembered their own period and were not obsessed by a fanciful Regency or Directoire; a little, not perhaps enough, of that 'social realism', admirable in its place, which Mr. Thomas of the *Graphic* had fostered. It would be of interest to consider again the earlier work of Frank Holl, which so largely consisted of 'starvation, coffins, and the dock'—the work of an artist who wished to bring home to the 'heart and mind of Mayfair the crime of poverty and the temptations to which the poor are ever subject'; who painted *Newgate: Committed for Trial*, an 'unpleasant' theme and a picture probably for that reason ignored. Yet it has become impossible to say much good of the Leighton Academy.

Did Leighton himself think it good? Was he satisfied with the men around him? There is irony in the conception of a Zeus surrounded by the deities of a minor and different mythology. Between the taste of his Addresses, which ranged so fluently and discerningly over the fields of great art, and the nature of the Chantrey pictures, there is a sharp division. He was like a superb conductor, meriting a classic orchestra, who found himself in the position of encouraging accordions to wheeze ditties some of which were intolerable to the ear. Yet as an administrator he had to make the best of the material at his disposal, and the claims of those many friends and neighbours of his to Academic honour were not lightly to be set aside. They were indeed not solely at his discretion, for Olympus was democratic, the vote of Forty was cast; yet we hear of no objection or demur on his part to the election of an Ouless or a Peter Graham, a Briton Rivière, a Frank Dicksee. Alma-Tadema, if not truly classic, must be admitted to the fraternity; if Marcus Stone, so too must Luke Fildes, especially after that extraordinary success *The Doctor* of 1891, in which, with an expression of intense concern, the medical man watches by the bedside of a sick child in a humble cottage. That the humble cottage, rafters, window and all, was positively built within the larger interior of the studio in Melbury Road so that the artist might paint it in its true rustic semi-darkness was in keeping with a spirit, at once opulent and attentive to detail, which demanded recognition. Then there was Frank Holl, who, advised by R.A.s to give up the 'coffins and starvation', had obeyed, had 'stuck' at their behest 'to heads'; was famous for the portrait of Mr. Gladstone painted at Hawarden, when the sitter, with all the immense endurance of Victorian greatness, had stood like a rock for five consecutive days for two and a half hours each day, and had at length exhausted the painter.

That Leighton conceived no prejudice against aims very different from his own may be partly attributed to that catholicity of taste which his early days of travel had helped to create. He had seen every variant of the nineteenth-century's academic art in every capital of Europe, had consorted on amiable terms with a Wiertz, an Ary Scheffer, a Bezzuoli. Yet his catholicity extended to artists who were not in the ordinary sense academic, some of whom, at least, if it had been possible, he would have introduced into the golden world over which he ruled. He sought, as ever, for the best; and if, for various reasons, it was not possible to draw Whistler to his side, at least he made every effort to have with him that distinguished Pre-Raphaelite, Edward Burne-Jones.

Here, however, another difficulty presented itself: that though one might seek the best, the best might prove unwilling, coy, elusive. It was an altogether benevolent conspiracy which in 1885 sought to bring Burne-Jones into the fold. The first intimation he had of it was a ring at the door and the news, brought by a servant, that a man was in the hall to say that Mr. Burne-Jones was elected into the Royal Academy. It seemed a joke, until the next morning's post brought a letter from the President, written at 10.30 on the night before, couched in the most friendly and elegant terms. An event had just occurred which filled 'him with the deepest satisfaction and with real joy'. A spontaneous act of justice had been done at Burlington House, 'the largest meeting of members I ever saw has by a majority elected you an Associate of the Royal Academy. I am not aware that any other case exists of an Artist being elected who has never ex-hibited, nay, has pointedly abstained, from exhibiting on our walls. It is a pure tribute to your genius and therefore a true rejoicing to your affectionate old friend, Fred Leighton.'

It was gratifying, undoubtedly. Burne-Jones had friends in the Academy, more friends than he thought. Poynter, his brother-in-law, wrote to tell him that a member he had never met, the animal-painter, Briton Rivière, had proposed him. G. F. Watts urged on him that he could 'help the cause of Art more effectually' by becom-ing a member than by 'staying outside'. Sir Joseph Boehm begged him not to refuse. All the same, for Burne-Jones it was a serious crisis—even, as he hated the necessity of important, practical deci-sions, a dreadful affair. Was there not a principle involved, the Pre-Raphaelite idea which had for so long stood out against the easy ways? What would his dearest friend William Morris say, Morris whose contempt for the golden houses and the artist-capitalist was so profound? Morris, in fact, showed his usual plain directness in a note to Burne-Jones's anxious wife. 'As to the Academy, I don't see why their action should force Ned into doing what he disapproves of since they did not ask him first.' Could it be, also, that the Academy had another design, that in luring Burne-Jones away from the Grosvenor Gallery, it sought to diminish the rivalry of that com-petitor, and the 'aestheticism' for which so many in these days admired it?

He explained some of his doubts in a letter to Leighton, but how difficult it was to resist the persuasiveness of his reply. 'I feel sure that whilst you would wish not to seem, even, to slight a body of men who have sought you out to do honour to your genius, you will be able to deal with an even hand between the two exhibitions. . . . I wish well to the Grosvenor Gallery and would not in any case wish it to lose the great pillar of strength which you are to it'—but—'It has long been my anxious dream that the Royal Academy should become a truly and nobly representative Institution including in its ranks and mustering on its walls all the best life of our country's Art.' If letters were persuasive, how much more so the President in person ('Don't say you have come to refuse it, Ned'). Burne-Jones could not say no, his acceptance was afterwards sent, albeit with the most melancholy foreboding. He may have thought that acceptance was a matter of form, that he could then forget about the honour—but soon there loomed the terrors of varnishing day and the Banquet, to which Leighton summoned him from Rottingdean in a note which had a certain authority as well as charm. 'I don't know how to summon up enough brutal courage to urge you to come up for the dinner (returning to Brighton by the 10.5 train that night).' It would never do for the newly elected to miss the great occasion. 'There are of course men who would say perhaps "See, even now he won't have anything to say to us—he won't even come to the first banquet".' Burne-Jones went; and yet he was, he said, 'particularly made by nature not to like Academies'. For some years he was a grudging exhibitor, a reluctant guest at the feast, and he resigned in 1893. With manly sorrow Leighton replied to his excuses. 'It was the one dark spot in the term of my Presidency as your election was its brightest. For your kind words to me individually', he added, 'I thank you very sincerely. I am not of those whose attachment to old friends easily fades away.' Yet the phrase implied that there was cause for such fading, and the dark spot remained.

The image of the 'bird in a gilded cage' which was undoubtedly in Burne-Jones's mind may add too much psychological importance to the incident. It could certainly not be applied to Leighton himself. No captive was he, but a King, though it may be that he was too constitutional a ruler of his realm, too much all things to all men. If some despotic whim, some bitter sally or critical stand had disturbed from time to time the unanimity of Olympus he might (as moods and doubts make people understood) have been easier to understand. Had he indeed an inner life, was there another and unofficial Leighton? As there has been no answer to this question, it is necessary to consider among his other perfections, the perfection of an enigma.

It was this enigma which Henry James looked at with the professional eye of the novelist. James was, of course, by nature inclined to enjoy an enigma, to construct a maze of the mind in which his readers would be led, tantalizingly, towards a centre difficult of access. He adopted this labyrinthine convention in describing Leighton and, the result being a work of fiction, it must not be considered too literally a portrait from life, but as, in its way, a humorous artifice for which the living person had given a hint. Yet, as the notebooks of Henry James show, the hint was taken from Leighton. The grandeur, which to Disraeli had seemed right and natural in a world where all grandeur must have a touch of the fabulous and unreal, aroused in the American writer a keen speculation as to whether, and in what way, it was unnatural. What was to be found behind it, what indeed if there was nothing to be found? Here was a problem to which interest was added by another and contrasting problem (though for the latter a solution was more apparent)—that of Robert Browning.

It consisted in Browning's being or appearing so very ordinary, when as a great poet he might well have been expected to be extraordinary. He was the normal man with an adequately commonplace stock of remarks and sentiments. The greatness then was hidden; it emerged, not in society, but when no one was about. It was the exact opposite of the quality of Leighton, and in the contrast, if there was something of comedy there was something also of the ghost story (in the Jamesian sense), the person invisible and indeed never to be seen.

All this was presented in the story *The Private Life*. Leighton, as the James notebooks confirm, was its 'Lord Mellifont' who was 'all public and had no corresponding private life'. Browning was 'Clare Vawdrey' who was 'all private and had no corresponding public one'. Vawdrey was 'loud, cheerful, and copious'. His opinions were 'sound but second-rate'. The real Browning, consequently, was for the world a shadowy form at a desk, indistinctly perceived through a window or even imaginatively discerned behind a closed door. How different was Lord Mellifont, in describing whom Henry James departs very little, except in a slight irreverence of tone, from the recorded impression Leighton made on most of his contemporaries. Mellifont was 'first—extraordinarily first—essentially at the top of the list and the head of the table'. He was 'almost as much a man of the world as the head waiter and spoke almost as many languages'. He 'sat among us like a bland conductor controlling by an harmonious play of arm an orchestra still a little rough'. As he 'leaned against a rock, his beautiful little box of water-colours reposed on a natural table beside him showing how inveterately nature ministered to his convenience'. Lord Mellifont's was always *the* chair—he 'made our grateful little group feel like a social science congress or a distribution of prizes'. He 'had never been a guest in his life'. He was 'the patron, the moderator at every board'. With the cheerfully turned phrases went the eerie feeling that another Mellifont could not, like the other Vawdrey, be occasionally glimpsed, that the disappearance, when he was not socially present, was entire. What, in fact, the fiction may lead one to inquire, did happen when Leighton went off on one of his periodical journeys? It is hard to see him in Scotland, staying with Millais, as anything but the grand figure of society he habitually was, beaming and genial, his geniality nicely adjusted to that of his fellow artist and friend; or in Italy with Costa, where his routine was ceremonial and exact as a royal tour and Costa remarked that he 'ran with him as on an iron rail'. It may be said that Henry James was superficial—superficial, that is, in withholding or expressing ignorance of the key. Perhaps there really was a key to Browning—in the defensive process which led him to reject any show of abnormality after the death of the wife he loved. Of any such crisis the life of Leighton offers no trace. Perhaps after all there was no key because no enigma and one must seek the man entire in the qualities so eminently and consistently displayed to general view; accepting those characteristics in which he does not seem quite human (in fallibility) as the sign of a classic excellence and, where he appears unconsciously fallible, recognizing also a certain perfection in this. 'Be', wrote Browning to him, replying to Leighton's letter of sympathy when Elizabeth Barrett was seriously ill, 'as distinguished and happy as God meant you should.' There is a certain distance in the kindly words—as of men living in two different mental worlds.

IV

THE OLYMPIAN TWILIGHT

THE golden day extended into a long mellow glow. Elsewhere there were plots and stratagems, discontents and rebellions, strange new portents, rumbles of thunder and lightning flashes as the century wore on to its end. Split into little groups, separated one from the other, overwhelmed by the age they found so uncongenial, desperately fighting, gallantly failing, like the barbaric heroes of Icelandic saga, the Pre-Raphaelites dropped one by one. Exotic and sultry, the aesthetic movement burst in astonishing crisis. It seemed at the time as if some artists wished to establish that Beauty itself was corrupt. There was a new race of classicists, in literature at least, who pointed to the wickedness of the gods and not their immaculacy, who even delighted in this wickedness. There were new artists called 'Impressionists' who, it was said, painted nature as if from the windows of a swiftly moving railway train—in broken, hurried glimpses; who would descend to the lowest depths in the perverse pleasure they took in sordid reality, who would paint, not the nude, noble and antique, but grotesque and animal nakedness, who celebrated, rather than the joyous festivals of wine, the sullen debauch of absinthe. Pert, irreverent in wit, cast in the Cockney rather than the Grecian mould, the nineties arrived with their passion for an outrageous novelty.

The world was changing round Olympus and yet Olympus did not change. The golden houses shone as brightly as ever, their inhabitants remained secure in their state, careless, if not of mankind, of those tales of little meaning told by artists outside their charmed circle. Rewards and honours were offered them in profusion. They lived to be full of years, and their later days were serene and authoritative. The last gleams of their sun, setting in slow majesty, cast their radiance into the twentieth century. Not supplanted or overthrown (though often surprised at modern folly), they quietly ceased to be, so recently that their nearness in time may surprise those who think of them as belonging to an epoch 'before the flood'. Sir Edward Poynter died only in 1919; Sir Lawrence Alma-Tadema, O.M., in 1912; Sir William Blake Richmond in 1921. Of the minor deities, Marcus Stone lived until 1921, Sir Hubert von Herkomer until 1914, Sir Luke Fildes until 1927, Sir Frank Dicksee until 1928. They knew —some of them—the days of sinking ships and flaming towns. They were still active when more startling innovations than Impressionism had made their appearance; though by then they belonged to another world—a world of art such as would never be seen again. It is fair to say that the 1880s represent the summit of their activity, but there was on the farther side the gentlest of slopes, so gentle that even as one century gave place to another they seemed still to be on the heights. The President, it is true, did not outlive the late-Victorian age, but if their stature was less there remained others who help us to keep our sense of continuity—or at least bring us to the very edge of the chasm from the hither side of which, in an air no longer touched with glittering magic, we see them well-defined still.

The career of that grave and industrious man, Edward Poynter, was crowned with many honours. He is indeed to be numbered among the great professors, officials, and connoisseurs, apart from his rank as a painter; a British Gérôme with the outward semblance of martinet acridity which seemed to go with the function. It was only an outward semblance, for he was a shy man and while the years hardened the shell of aloofness he remained, to those who knew him, generous and kind of heart. He had been a success in the four years of his office as Slade Professor at University College, London, from 1871 to 1875, and the lectures he had then given (rather against his will) were honest, unpretentious, and consistent. With a certain irony he remarked that 'in spite of the difficulties attending the subject I have come to the conclusion that it is much easier to write about art than to practise it, and am led to the further conclusion that as example is always better than precept, the more time I devote to painting in future and the less to public lecturing the better it will be for my art and those interested in it'. However this might be, he had spoken words which, if sober and phlegmatic, made sense. His theme was that work should be done well and that even the humble piece of craftsmanship well done thus attained the quality of art. He gave due praise to the designs and craftsmanship of William Morris, but he placed the study of the figure in the forefront, and it was for this reason that in 1875 he had taken arms against Ruskin and the 'curious spite' he had displayed against Michelangelo—the result, in Poynter's opinion, of Ruskin's never having cared to study the nude figure or appreciate its beauty. The pursuit of beauty was the counter to, the argument against, the 'realism' of the French school. He was typical of his age in criticizing the French interest in 'nature un-idealized', the 'cynical pleasure' with which they seized on the 'disgusting and horrible' for imitation, though as he named no names we can only speculate whether he referred to a Courbet or a Degas.

Yet it was the French system of art education which he advocated and introduced at South Kensington when he there became Director of Art in succession to Sir Henry Cole. Abandoned under his régime was the grubby curriculum of the old government 'Schools of Design'—that vague 'design' which some thought to be due to an imperfect translation of the French 'Écoles de Dessin'; those still vague intentions of applying art to industry which consisted in copying ornamental motives taken from many sources; the drawings from casts, stippled with chalk and smudged with bread-crumbs, which served as diplomas, won certificates, and took many months to do. He brought, in contrast, if not the atmosphere of *Trilby*, the methods of Gleyre's atelier to Exhibition Road. Under him students began to draw from the life, and this was his great reform. While Director of Art at South Kensington, in those days when museum and school still floated together in the splendid nebula thrown off by the Great Exhibition of 1851 and had not yet taken the distinct forms of Victoria and Albert Museum and Royal College of Art, he made purchases for the South Kensington Museum, which were approved as showing an excellent and catholic taste. He was, as a contemporary of his has said, 'a really great connoisseur in the old style'—no modern specialist, that is to say, in the work of some minor fourteenth-century Italian who, as far as facts are concerned, survives only in the list of members of a guild, but one with a thorough knowledge and appreciation of the great masters. Revering the Italians of the Renaissance, he could admire also the 'primitives' of Northern Europe, respond to a Goya, and recognize the merits of a Stubbs or a Cotman. He profoundly admired Poussin; his introduction to the first Italian volume in a series of handbooks on the history of painting has been highly praised; and his appointment as Director of the National Gallery in 1894 was amply justified by his earlier record.

He remained Director for eleven years—until 1905. It is no doubt unfortunate that his appointment coincided with the 'Rosebery Minute', a ruling which greatly curtailed the Director's power to buy pictures, and reflected the prejudice of Treasury officials against picture-buying as a needless extravagance. Yet even so his term of office saw the acquisition of many beautiful works—Mantegna's *Agony in the Garden*, Pisano's *Vision of St. Eustace*, the Flemish *Legend of St. Giles*, among them—and in this there was ample credit.

Yet this was not all. He followed Leighton (and, for his few months, Millais) as President of the Royal Academy. He and Sir Charles Eastlake are the only two artists to have presided over the National Gallery and the Academy at the same time; and he was President for twenty-two years, from 1896 to 1918. So close is Olympus to the present day.

During these later years he never stopped working. Every day of the week, including Sundays, found him in his studio at the Avenue, Fulham Road, except when he was on official business or away on holiday; and on holiday he spent his time in making highly wrought water-colour landscapes. Nor was there any lessening in his popularity, for at the time of his death there was no picture unsold in his studio. They went all over the world. The last of his large idealized figures, the *Diadumene*, a single life-sized nude, exhibited at the Academy in 1884, incurred some disapproval because of its nudity and was for a while unsold, but when a little drapery had been added it found a buyer in the United States. The *Visit of the Queen of Sheba to Solomon* (1887), which has been described as 'one of the biggest and most complex *machines* of its kind ever executed', went to Australia. His drawings were without number; some of them, excellent examples of the academic manner, are to be found in the British Museum.

Such a laborious career is almost of necessity without history in itself and insulated from outside happenings. The title of a picture, the bestowal of an honour, are its landmarks. The Poynter of 1896 is distinguished from the Poynter of 1902 by his progress from knighthood to baronetcy. There is little observable change in that erect and soldier-like figure. The reserved young student of the *Trilby* days has taken on a more authoritative reticence. The distinguished features with their not quite military cut of moustache are inscrutably senatorial. It is pleasant to think that they would relax now and then while Alma-Tadema lived, that he could laugh at the geniality and expansiveness of the little Dutchman, perhaps somewhat envying also these qualities; yet he seems to retain always that classic aloofness which Leighton, too, had, though in him it took a very different form. Contemporary events could have little effect on it. That strange exhibition of 1910 when the works of Cézanne, Gauguin, and van Gogh, of the 'Post-Impressionists', so horrified London, could have made no stir in that studio full of the remote atmosphere of legend; the inventions of the new age, the aeroplane, the cinematograph belonged to another existence, so did the war of 1914-18. The world had changed indeed around Olympus, yet so far was it from the present day. The place of Poynter is on those magically distant heights and slopes, on the other side of that gulf which is one of understanding as well as time.

The industry of Alma-Tadema was no less. There seemed to be no end to the possibilities of sentimental entertainment in its setting of marble. If the historian of the *Decline and Fall* had lived again at the end of the nineteenth century and paid a visit to Alma-Tadema's studio he might have rubbed his eyes in wonder, at the painter's dulcification of that grim spectacle he had described, of the crazy

THE SILENT GREETING
by Sir Laurence Alma-Tadema, R.A.

and paranoiac emperors, the toughs and thugs of the Praetorian Guard, the nobles and ladies alike full of lust and ferocity, the blood-mad populace screaming for death in the ring. Of this Gibbon would have found no trace; no trace either of those brutal and business-like heads, the heavy flabby flesh of old debauchees, the shifty and distorted leanness of the weak and corrupt, the predatory mouths of vicious matrons, which the genius of the Roman sculptor, unflinching in veracity, had recorded in his portrait busts. On the contrary, Alma-Tadema continued to represent the ancient spectacle as uniformly gay, innocent, and fair. The 'bloody circus' genial laws' were modified in his picture *The Coliseum*, exhibited at the Academy in 1896, by the presence of sweet and fresh faces—a stately mother's among them, a diadem of silver in her black hair, her peacock fan of gorgeous colours held up to hide her face from the view of the crowd. 'It is easy to imagine', said the critic of the *Athenaeum*, 'that in her noble spirit some thought of the victims of the amphitheatre arose.' The handsome young soldier in *A Silent Greeting* would, differently dressed, have excited no surprise in the most respectable of London clubs, the girl asleep amid silken cushions on an elegantly carved marble couch to whom he waves his 'silent greeting' would have been entirely conceivable in St. John's Wood. A laughing girl, we find in a written account of *Roses, Love's Delight* (a title which the *Anacreon* supplied), buries her lovely face in the soft and scented remnants of a ceremonial garland. Where, now, is this picture, bought by that admirer of British art, the Tsar of Russia; does it hang in some Soviet Museum, was it slashed by the hand of some revolutionary eager to deface and destroy the images cherished by the old régime? The celebrated line of Robert Browning, 'All's right with the world', gives a title to another picture if not the key to all. With an expression of delight a young woman on a gleaming terrace by the wine-dark sea, haloed by the blossoms of spring, inscribes on her tablets (rather like an expensive notebook bought in Bond Street) the beginning of a lyric or a love-letter.

No doubt such tablets did in fact resemble a modern notebook, and such things were small reminders of an implied transposition, helping to convey that late-Victorian Britain was but another aspect of a golden and classical age. It was ever the idea of Alma-Tadema that pictures should give rise to reflection. He had remarked that 'Art is imagination and those who love Art love it because in looking at a picture it awakens their imagination and sets them thinking'. That his pictures did so was gratefully acknowledged, and it seems fitting that in the general shower of knighthoods that fell upon artists in those days he too should become a knight. His name appeared in the Honours List of 1899 on the occasion of Her Majesty Queen Victoria's eightieth birthday. Charles I had knighted Rubens and Van Dyck; Charles II, Lely; William of Orange, Kneller; George I, Dorigny. Alma-Tadema was the next distinguished foreigner on the list.

The occasion called for a banquet, which was held at the Whitehall Rooms in London. Academicians were mustered in force to do the Dutchman honour. Onslow Ford, sculptor of the Shelley Memorial in University College, Oxford, presided over a gathering of a hundred and sixty celebrated men in the absence of Poynter (the P.R.A. being away). There was Benjamin Leader, painter of many a stark November landscape; Colin Hunter, that man of the sea; the Hon. John Collier, too, a Chantrey Bequest man he, who painted the explorer Hudson in an open boat in the Arctic waste; and Briton Rivière, in fame no less, whose polar bear surveying a brilliant sunset from the top of an iceberg, *Beyond Man's Footsteps*, had also won the coveted award. Connoisseurs were there; literature had its representative in Joseph Comyns Carr, critic, poet, and playwright, music in George Henschel. Onslow Ford paid his tribute, dwelling on the fact that since settling in England, Alma-Tadema had produced the grand total of no fewer than 273 pictures; and Sir Lawrence in reply said he was proud to think that the English and Dutch were brothers labouring in the same field; that the Dutch had been the pioneers of the great English school of landscape painting, and he recalled that when he sat next to Daubigny at the house of Frederic Leighton in 1870, the French artist had remarked that without Old Crome, Turner, and Constable, the modern French school could not have existed. So moved was one Academician that he left his seat to kiss Alma-Tadema's hand, was in turn embraced with Continental fervour. Something of the high spirits, the good-humour, the lack of reserve, of the guest of honour seemed to communicate itself to the whole gathering. Jollity bubbled, every face smiled and the proceedings became uproarious when the song which Comyns Carr had composed for the occasion, the 'Carmen Tademare', set to music by George Henschel, was sung. The room thundered to its chorus, in which all joined.

'Who knows him well he best can tell
That a stouter friend hath no man
Than this lusty Knight who for our delight
Hath painted Greek and Roman.
Then here let every citizen
Who holds a brush or wields a pen
Drink deep as his Zuyder Zee
To Alma-Tad—Of the Royal Acad—Of the
    Royal Acadamee.'

One might pause at this as at the supreme moment of 'Alma-Tad's' career, though many more years of happy labour were still to be his —the list of 273 pictures was to become a list of 400. There was still work for the theatre to be done, the designs to be made for Irving's production of *Coriolanus* at the Lyceum in 1901. Production by Sir Henry Irving, Incidental Music by Sir A. C. Mackenzie, Scenes designed by Sir L. Alma-Tadema. 'Three blooming knights,' said a Lyceum stage-hand, 'and that's about as long as it'll run.' It did not, it is true, run for very long, though the dramatic effect of the Senate House with its simple colour scheme, the red and white robes of the senators, the warm yellow of the interior, was highly praised. There was still a journey to be made, for the first time, to the Egypt he had so often evoked. He went as a member of Sir John Aird's party for the opening ceremonies attending the completion of the dams at Assuan and Assyut in 1902. He stayed for six weeks and as a result painted for Sir John the *Finding of Moses* on which he worked for two years, 1903–4—so long that, his wife pointed out, the infant Moses was 'two years old and need no longer be carried'.

King Edward VII visited Alma-Tadema's studio to see the picture, and soon afterwards the artist was honoured again by the Order of Merit, also bestowed in 1905 on William Holman Hunt.

For many years after his death in 1912 the house in Grove End Road retained its majesty. This too is now legendary. There came a day, no longer ago than in 1950, when the word '*Salve*' ceased to welcome, the classic front door with its knocker of bronze opened on a waste of cement puddles, gaps everywhere appeared in the fabric. The classic villa was being reconstructed as a block of ten post-war flats. The visitor, waved away by busy workmen, would find his way back to the lodge, where the word of parting '*Vale*', which to so many illustrious guests had been like a last cheery word from their host himself, now had all the melancholy of a final passing.

It was well perhaps that Leighton should die while the Queen still lived: before a slope, however gentle, appeared to lead away from the heights; while the blaze of glory still had its noontide fullness. Though it was so much the custom of the time to honour artists by a title or an order, the list of his honours outstrips the rest and is still astonishing in its profusion. It was a matter of course that he should be offered a baronetcy, and that he did not become the first artist-baronet was due to his own modest scruple. When Mr. Gladstone made the offer, it was typical of Leighton that he should put forward the prior claim of John Millais and G. F. Watts and propose to stand down in favour of his friends—a 'self-abnegation' of which the Prime Minister was appreciative. Watts was reluctant to accept, found it necessary to decline. Millais was first baronet of the brush; Leighton was content to follow shortly after in 1886. The universities vied in bestowing degrees. To the LL.D. of Cambridge, the D.C.L. of Oxford (1879), were added the Hon. Litt.D. of Dublin (1892), the Hon. D.C.L. of Durham (1894). Foreign countries paid their homage. The cities he knew so well made him Honorary Member of their Academies: Antwerp, Berlin, Brussels, Florence, Genoa, Perugia, Rome, Turin, Vienna (1880–9). In Paris his sculpture won the Gold Medal at the Salon of 1885, he was made Président du Conseil des Beaux Arts and Commander of the Légion d'Honneur. He was a Knight of Belgium and of Coburg in 1886; a Knight of the German Order of Art and Science in 1887; and architects paid tribute to his knowledge of their art by the Gold Medal of the R.I.B.A. in 1894.

The later years of Leighton were marked by all that energy which he had displayed throughout life. That he did not speak in public as many times as he was invited it is easy to understand. 'The reasons', he wrote to Mrs. Barrington, 'which have now for a good many years impelled me to decline any "public utterances" outside Burlington House have increased in weight and force as life and strength wanes, and as the demands on me grow in every direction. . . . Assent once is assent always—assent in half the cases would mean the *gravest* injury to my *work*, and I am a workman first and an official afterwards. Things have their humorous side, for those who press me most are sometimes those who on other occasions assure me that I "*do too much*". How tired I am of hearing it. I cannot but refuse.' Yet private, or semi-private, utterances he was still persuaded and even, when friends were concerned, ready to make. How superbly he gave his speech as chairman at the presentation of a Strad to his friend Joachim in 1894. The sentiments that had been expressed, he said, 'could not take a more fitting outward shape than that of the instrument over which he is a lord, this sensitive and well-seasoned shell, signed with the name of Stradivarius and, as I am told, worthy of his fame, flanked with a bow bearing the name of Tourte and once the property of Kiesewetter'.

There was much to take him away from his studio: many extra duties associated with those of President. He was, for instance, a Trustee of the British Museum. When the Marbles were rearranged in the Elgin Room it seemed only fitting that he should take a personal hand in their disposition, and his proposals were so full of reason as invariably to be accepted without question. It is surprising that he should find time for letters which were wonderfully copious even in refusal to extend his activities, less so that they should often finish with the words 'in haste'. He was, however, painting as industriously as ever. The celebrated *Bath of Psyche* in which the maiden, lifting aside white draperies, gazes dreamily into the still waters of the marble-rimmed pool belongs to 1890. *Perseus and Andromeda* and *The Return of Persephone* were painted in 1891. Eighteen ninety-two produced its classical theme in *The Garden of the Hesperides*, and a new departure is the cartoon designed for the dome of St. Paul's, *And the Sea gave up the Dead which was in it*. The decoration of the dome was a great artistic project of the eighteen-nineties; but something of the latent disharmony between the Christian and the classical standpoint appeared. The Cathedral Chapter ruled that Leighton's design was 'unsuitable for a Christian church'. Poynter, too, made his attempt and was very disappointed at being passed over. It was Richmond, more adaptable in style, who was finally entrusted with the commission, chose mosaic instead of painting as the medium (more than six million cubes of glass were needed), wrestled manfully for several years with the problems involved—the dimness of the cathedral lighting being one of the main difficulties—and was in the outcome much abused because the decorations were swallowed in gloom.

It was, perhaps, well that the President should be spared this laborious undertaking, so fraught with possibilities of disappointment. He was able to produce more of the ideal conceptions so typical of him—*The Spirit of the Summit* (1894), the *Flaming June* of the following year—but his health was beginning now to give way. He had never been exactly robust, though of actual maladies he had known little. It had been his regular habit to visit his physician. He saw, he said, 'Dr. Roberts every Sunday for him to tell me I am not ill'. Possibly on the Chinese principle that a doctor should be rewarded for his patient's good health, Leighton had once objected that Dr. Roberts's fees were too small and had urged him to increase them. Yet during the nineties the visits took on a more serious character. The first hint of physical fatigue comes in 1889. He was on a walking and climbing holiday with friends, and he wrote with envy of their greater ability than his to climb and walk. One of them, Sir James Paget, was seventy-three, the other sixty-five years of age, but Leighton, a mere fifty-nine, was piqued to find that they could cover with ease twelve, sixteen, eighteen miles a day to his one, and that they scrambled up mountain slopes without turning a hair, slopes which soon made him begin to puff. Such puffing may seem natural enough, the feats of his companions exceptional; but his own capacity for travel was still surprising. In the course of a lightning tour of Germany he was able to visit thirty towns in thirty days. 'A Yankee', he observed with pride, 'might be proud of such a record.' Eighteen ninety-four is an amazing year. He then took one of his sisters (Mrs. Matthews) to Bayreuth; returned to London; there completed his large decorative panel for the Royal Exchange, *Phoenician Merchants bartering with Ancient Britons on the Coast of Cornwall*, which in his magnificent fashion he intended as a gift to the City of London; went off to Scotland; later in the year was once more in his beloved Italy; even so, contrived to be back in London for the first popular concert of music at St. James's Hall.

It was too much. In the following year he was suffering from a dangerous heart trouble and it was all he could do to toil painfully up the steps of the Athenaeum Club. Whether or no it was the right prescription for this constant traveller, a visit to Algiers was advised. From every point of view it seemed the correct moment to lay down the cares of office at last. He wished Millais to follow him, Millais of whom people had spoken as the predestined President since his student days, much as they had of Leighton himself. 'My dear old friend,' he wrote from the Athenaeum, 'there is *only one man* whom everybody will acclaim in the Chair on May 4—a great artist loved by all—*yourself*.'

His colleagues were loath to let him go, would, they declared, cheerfully carry on, and distribute the duties in his temporary absence. Millais was doubtful whether a persistent hoarseness of the throat which now troubled him would in itself allow of his deputizing, but Leighton waved aside the objection. If it were a question of being heard at the Banquet—'it is quite immaterial whether you are heard all over the room'. Those close by would certainly make out his words; the reporter of *The Times* would be at his elbow and thus in due course they would be universally read and appreciated.

The end of March came and with it Show Sunday—but it was not the happy ceremony it used to be. There was the usual fashionable assembly, the usual exclamation of praise before the pictures, but the artist was sadly changed, nervous-looking and evidently not feeling well, though in spite of this—with an effort to make light of it—he

M 177

was even more than usually assiduous to his guests. He took Millais aside for a confidential and affectionate word: 'Come and see me quietly tomorrow, old boy. I go the day after.'

That quiet chat, no doubt with its imparting of tips as to the conduct of proceedings and the technique of their oratory, is left to the imagination. We follow Leighton on his last Mediterranean voyage. He remained a short while at Biskra, then cruised slowly round the Mediterranean and in its warm sun and by virtue of the enforced rest seemed to be somewhat better. He whiled away the time by reading—books which had a curious relation to and contrast with the nature of his own aims and ideas. Walter Pater's *Greek Studies* was among them with its subtleties of definition in which there was more than painting could express, its description of the myth as 'welding into something like the identity of a human personality the whole range of man's experiences of a given object or series of objects'. Leighton must certainly have been interested in Pater's 'Age of the Athletic Prizeman', but whether he would appreciate the bitter-sweet of the author's interpretations—'the sea-water of the Lesbian grape become somewhat brackish in the cup'—that sense of a sinister and perverse force sometimes counteracting and sometimes combined with an ideal of beauty, in the absence of his comments it is not possible to say—though there is, in his pictures, nothing to match the account Pater gives of the *Bacchanals* of Euripides. The realism of Arthur Morrison's *Tales of Mean Streets*, far as they were from Olympus, appealed to him, he thought them 'powerful stuff'. He was less attracted by Thomas Hardy, in spite of that classic spirit which others have discerned beneath the rustic disguises of Wessex. The characters of Hardy seemed to him merely 'talking dolls'.

He returned to painting with relief. In October he was in Rome again, once more in the company of the ever-faithful Costa, who watched him painting a study of fruit in the courtyard of the Palazzo Odeschalchi. It was set out on the top of a marble sarcophagus, and Costa was delighted to see the interest he took in it, in spite of his obvious ill-health—such interest perhaps a sign that he was indeed overcoming this ill-health; but, the study made, Leighton was anxious again to be on the move, must go once more to the

Vatican, to his well-loved cities, Siena and Florence. He was at Naples in October and, while there, with his usual forethought ordered his two seats for the November Wagner concert at Queen's Hall.

In the meantime, Millais had deputized for him at the Academy Banquet. Sir George Reid found him, as the guests were arriving, in a state of anxiety approaching despair. 'What am I to do?' Millais asked. 'I have no voice.' As the place filled he seemed to gain confidence, soon afterwards Sir George saw him smiling and talking to Lord Rosebery—even patting him on the back. Olympian indeed were the days when an artist might venture to pat a Prime Minister on the back. When he began to speak Millais was almost inaudible, but as he went on his voice grew stronger, his peroration was heard and approved by all. The Archbishop of Canterbury humorously commented on his 'geniality and eloquence when we could hear him, his perfect dumb show when we could not'. It was Lord Rosebery's opinion that the speech 'will help to bring back health to Leighton when he reads it'.

Though it could not do that it delighted the President, who wrote from the Hôtel de l'Europe in Algiers to say how glad he was to hear of Millais's success, how touched by the references to himself, how pleased too to hear of the purchase of *Speak, Speak* for the Chantrey Collection (the only purchase for £2,000 of 1895). He termed 'beautiful and impressive' this picture by Millais in which a young Roman who had been reading the letters of his lost love found her spirit, decked in bridal attire, looking at him with sad but loving eyes. Whether the spirit in fact appeared or whether the young Roman merely imagined that she did was a nice point which the artist was content to leave unresolved, and may have added to the fascination the picture held for his fellow artists. Herkomer adored its sentiment—he thought it would counter 'the fearful (and mad) wave of the modern tendency'. Richmond was haunted by its depth of 'modern thought'. The incorporeal, it is true, was not much in the President's own line, but the face of the spirit was that of the model (Miss Lloyd) whom he, as well as Millais, had painted, and he was able to do justice to a work he would not himself have been likely to undertake. Leighton's letter from Algiers then reverted to the sadder question which confronted the two stricken leaders. 'One of my reasons for writing to you is to urge you to give thought to the Swedish form of massage which Lauder Brunton and Broadbent both think highly of, and which did my general health immense good . . . do try. You can yacht afterwards all the same.' He (Leighton) was better—though thrown back by long railway journeys and bad food.

He was not really better, as his sisters and his friends saw by many outward signs, but there remained one signal honour to be offered and accepted; even in these last days we admire once again the quality which Henry James had described of being 'extraordinarily first'. The Barony. Queen Victoria, we are told, did not entirely approve of Leighton's style of painting, though in the now distant days there had been that purchase of *Cimabue* which Prince Albert admired. On the other hand it was impossible to overlook his many public services, his distinguished existence. The claim of Literature to the highest dignity it was in the power of a government to give had already been admitted by the bestowal of a peerage on Alfred Tennyson. That Painting and Sculpture should be put lower, ascending no higher than baronetcies, was hardly to be maintained. To place these arts on an equal footing with Letters was moreover to follow a policy which had been that of the Prince Consort himself. Leaving this important reason aside, there were others which claimed for Leighton his seat in the Upper House. Unquestionably in the first order of citizens was the administrator, the orator, the soldier, the person of beautifully rounded social attainments. The offer was made and was accepted.

How was he to be styled? His cousin, Sir Baldwyn Leighton, suggested 'Stretton'. Stretton in Shropshire had been in the four-teenth century the estate of the family known as Leighton of Leighton or alternatively of Stretton-in-the-Dale. In the fifteenth century a son of the house had, it would seem, migrated to York-shire and was supposed to have founded the branch from which the family of Dr. Leighton stemmed; but in these questions Leighton himself had little interest. Medieval Stretton was of

decidedly less import than ancient Athens, nor did the disguise
of nomenclature appeal to him. 'Leighton is a good name in
itself,' he objected, 'there were Leightons in Essex before the
Conquest.'

Yet his illness made him less masterful and clear as to his own
wishes than he might at another time have been. 'I haven't the least
idea what to do about my title. I suppose', he said wearily, 'I must
have a place in Shropshire'; and thus the title was gazetted, 'Baron
Leighton of Stretton in the County of Shropshire'. The motto was
'Dread Shame'. The official notice was issued on the day before his
death.

It may be a matter of regret that he never took his seat in the
House of Lords, although there was something splendid and dramatic,
regrettable though it was, in his final disappearance from the scene,
at the very moment when letters and telegrams of praise, homage,
and congratulation poured in upon him. After the elevation to the
peerage perhaps he himself would not have wished to linger. His
attitude to death was classic in the same way as his attitude to life.
He had always thought it deplorable to outlive full vigour of body
and mind, and though Dr. Leighton had lived to be ninety-two, his
son had no ambitions to exceed the age of seventy. His appreciation
of that which was complete and perfect in form caused him to
favour the allotted span, to distrust the shapeless and uncertain extension of old age and that impairment of the faculties which might
at any moment cloud it. He greeted the last dread visitant with all
the punctilious good breeding which he had always shown towards
his guests.

In those last days he was never heard to complain, and bore
stoically the periodic attacks of angina pectoris which caused him
great pain. Treating this mutiny of the heart with a proper sense of
proportion, he continued to the end to paint and draw, to answer
letters invariably of praise and sympathy with his accustomed
promptness. He showed a consideration for others which in one
instance almost recalls the self-denial of Sir Philip Sidney at the
Battle of Zutphen. At five on the morning of 23 January 1896 he
woke in terrible agony, but he would not ring for his valet. Believ-

ing him to be delicate, he thought it unfair to arouse and alarm the man at that early hour. It was not until seven o'clock had struck that he decided it was reasonable to summon aid. Composed and collected, he died on Saturday afternoon, 26 January, in the bedroom so spartan in its contrast with the singular magnificence he had created around him. His last words deserve to be chronicled among the famous last words of artists.

Turner, like Goethe, is said to have murmured 'Light, more light'; Gainsborough, 'We are all going to Heaven and Van Dyck is of the company'. The last words of Leighton were 'Give my love to the Royal Academy'. Thus, like Millais he affirmed the tie, not with an institution only but with a brotherhood, and of this there was further practical evidence when his will was read, for it was found that he had left unconditionally to the Academy the sum of £10,000.

It seemed to Edward Burne-Jones that 1896 was a fatal year for art —and artists. 'Such a lot of them have been going. Such a lot! Poor Alfred Hunt. Poor Millais—I grizzle a good deal over him, he was such a hero to me when I was young.' Now too he mourned Leighton, as later in the year he was to mourn more deeply still William Morris.

By that formal splendour which invested his life Lord Leighton of Stretton was surrounded in death. He was buried in St. Paul's Cathedral, as, so soon after him, Sir John Millais was to be buried. On the coffin, with its rich pall of crimson and gold, was inscribed the long list of his titles, degrees, orders, and distinctions. It was borne and attended by men eminent in painting and sculpture, in letters and science. Present at the funeral were representatives of the Royal Family, of the German Emperor, of the King of the Belgians, and a detachment of 450 members of the Artists' Corps of Volunteers marched with the procession. Fifty of them led the way through the dense silent crowds that lined the route along Pall Mall, by Charing Cross and the Embankment and thence to Ludgate Hill. As, with measured step, the slow advance was made into the church, the peal of silver trumpets was heard, and the solemn notes of Chopin's Funeral March. There was an immense pile of wreaths—

one from the Princess of Wales, who wrote on the card attached to
it (tied with ribbon of purple and white) in her own hand, the words

> Life's race well run,
> Life's work well done.
> Life's crown well won,
> Now comes rest.

Sir John Millais laid on the pile the laurel wreath from the Royal
Academy.

Tribute took many forms. Sir Charles Villiers Stanford, Director
of the Royal College of Music, composed not only the anthem sung
on the occasion but a Requiem, heard at the Birmingham Musical
Festival of the following year. Swinburne made Poetry's homage.
His own devotion to ancient Greece, his learned love of its literary
classics, had caused him to respect the painters of classic themes. Of
a picture by Watts he had said, 'So it seems a Greek painter must
have painted women'. In Albert Moore he had found that worship
of beauty in itself which had moved him to compare his painting
with the verse of Gautier. Of Leighton, it must be admitted, he had
not been uncritical. He had spoken even of a 'watery Hellenism',
though he had added balancing words of praise. Leighton, he
granted, was always 'laudable and admirable in a time given over to
the school of slashed breeches and the school of blowsy babyhood'.
Much was owing to him for the selection and intention of his subjects; and in 'Reminiscene' the words of praise were many. The poem
was called 'Reminiscence' as it recalled that visit to Vichy of Sep-
tember 1869, when Leighton and Mrs. Sartoris, Swinburne, and
Richard Burton (seeking in its waters a cure for an attack of hepa-
titis) had been in company together.

> A light has passed that never shall pass away,
> A sun has set whose rays are unequalled of might.
> The loyal grace, the courtesy bright as day,
> The strong sweet radiant spirit of life and light
> That shone and smiled and lightened in all men's sight,
> The kindly life whose tune was the tune of May,
> For us now dark, for love and for fame is bright.

The praises of the artist were sounded from the pulpit. Positively the Archdeacon of London, in a sermon in Canterbury Cathedral, could speak of form and colour and tone. Frederic Lord Leighton had taught 'us—the prosaic commercial Englishmen of the nineteenth century' to respond to these things and therefore more fully to appreciate the 'gloriously beautiful setting in which the Divine Mind has placed us'. It had sometimes been held that 'devotion to the sense of beauty must necessarily be sensual and lax in moral fibre'; yet here was this princely man, admirable in every respect, to show that 'the keenest enthusiasm for graceful beauty' was 'compatible with the purest idealism and absence of all that is base or ill-regulated in association'.

It was Thomas Brock, a friend from the old Paris days, in whose studio in Osnaburgh Street Leighton made his clay model of the *Athlete and Python*, who paid the tribute of Sculpture. He designed the monument in St. Paul's, with the reclining full-length figure of the artist in his peer's robes, on a bronze sarcophagus above a plinth of Sicilian marble. Painting with her palette and brushes knelt at the head, at the feet Sculpture with spatula and a model of Leighton's *Athlete awakening from Repose* (sometimes called *The Sluggard*) in her hand.

In 1897 the great memorial exhibition of his work was held at Burlington House. Now after his death the blaze of glory shot up in renewed brilliance. Gathered together were the characters of the ancient mythology he had evoked, the Psyches, the Andromaches, the Persephones, the Clytemnestras, the Helens of Troy, the paintings and sketches of many lands, the drawings of figures and draperies, the famous 'Lemon Tree' on which he had worked for a fortnight without pause, the sculptures of which it had been said that Pheidias could do no better.

Fifty thousand people came to see it. Every day the gallery was thronged, nor was there any falling off as the days passed. On the last there was a record attendance, and so fascinated were the visitors that it seemed they would never go. The crowded afternoon wore on, the light waned, the pictures dimmed yet still the spectators were as many as ever. Closing time came, the bell tolled, they

184

lingered still. It was a moment which could touch even the heart of the red-gowned Cerberus whose duty it was to see everyone off the premises. He was moved to petition for a half-hour more. It was an unusual request, but in the circumstances how could it be refused? The man, the occasion, were unusual, and the extension must be added to the number of tributes paid him, the final acknowledgement of a singular triumph, the moment indeed of apotheosis.

V

OLYMPUS AND THE PRESENT DAY

THE story of Leighton and that Academy over which he presided like Zeus for sixteen years is one of success, astonishing from the present-day point of view. The harmony and understanding which existed between the painters and the wealthy middle class in Britain's wealthiest time make an idyllic chapter in the history of patronage. The output of pictures as if the product of some great manufacturing industry, the vast revenue not confined to the exceptional individual but shared by the rank and file of moderate capabilities, the friendly and equal relations of artist-prince and merchant-prince, are alike impressive. The aims of the former are explained by the desires of the latter, which are almost identical with them.

Thus, the wealthy middle class wished to enjoy a world alternative to that which it knew. For the possessor of a fortune who had dealt with many harsh realities in gathering it up, it was desirable to escape from these realities into regions pleasant because imaginary or no longer existent, and useful because they held the secret of 'culture'. The extent to which artists were in sympathy with this longing creates a link between works which in other respects are very different—those of the Pre-Raphaelites who looked back to the Middle Ages and those of their rivals who looked back to Greece and Rome. As the Pre-Raphaelites lured Manchester and Liverpool into the realms of Arthurian romance so the academic faction played on the pleasurable aspects of the ancient world, or exploited a nostalgia for the aristocratic days of the Regency.

Yet though the works of Pre-Raphaelites and Academicians were often bought by the same people they were manifestly different in spirit. Something of that cleavage in beliefs and ideals which historically divides the Middle Ages from ancient Greece and Rome reappears in the Gothic and the classic revivals of Victoria's reign. There is a further distinction to be made between the anti-Victorian and the Victorian proper. William Morris and Frederick Leighton were not unlike merely because one was interested in Queen Guinevere and the other in Helen of Troy. While Morris was a rebel against the age and everything which separated it from an older England, Leighton was exactly conditioned to the age, had no word to say against it and indeed constantly praised in eloquent words the triumph of progress it represented.

It is a complexity in the classically inspired painters that, while their work forms one of the last episodes in the history of Europe's contact with the civilizations of the ancient world, it is at the same time so essentially a Victorian product. It followed naturally, as in previous revivals, from new discovery, the revelation of the past. The start of excavation had been a spring of the Italian Renaissance, the first splendid finds of ancient sculpture had excited the genius of a Donatello. The unearthing of Pompeii and Herculaneum in the eighteenth century made for another variation on the classic theme. The retrieval of the Parthenon sculptures from decay and neglect was stimulating to artists in the same way: there is, that is to say, a similar relation of cause and effect. It would follow that late-Victorian classicism is a part of the European story, one act of homage in a series to the Mediterranean fount of culture; yet British art was far from being hellenized. It would be more accurate to state that the Elgin Marbles adopted British nationality, shared in its isolation, and became less a glory of Greece than of the British Museum. The Greco-Britannic type, mysteriously found (to the surprise of Taine and Stendhal) in nature as well as art, was a result. Every fold of a garment in a picture by Leighton, Watts, or Albert Moore testifies to the influence of the Parthenon frieze, but in spite of the type they represented and the subject they chose, the spirit remains with a more than usual exclusiveness that of their own time and country.

It was this exclusiveness which most of all struck foreign observers of British art in the seventies and eighties. 'It would seem', said one, M. Ernest Chesneau, 'as though their studios were closed by a portion of the Great Wall of China. They keep up a continual Continental blockade but it is against themselves. European art is a sealed book to them.' They were, *per contra*, unknown to Europe except by their appearance in the International Exhibitions of the time, where they received none of that welcoming applause which had greeted Constable and others at the Salon of 1827 but rather a puzzled interest as of those who beheld something entirely strange to them and in many ways incomprehensible.

Here, no doubt, is one of the reasons for their immense success. They ministered to a similar exclusiveness in their patrons. If they went abroad, their works did not. They were produced for British consumption and they stayed in Britain—with the exception of purchases by Americans, at that time closely akin to the British patron in taste. 'Every nation', remarked Ruskin of this fact, 'is in a certain sense a judge of its own art, from whose decision there is no appeal. In the common sense of the phrase it knows what it likes and is only capable of producing what it likes.' Yet the insularity of the late-Victorian age was new rather than old, the insularity of a class; and to our French critics there was something monstrous in its novelty: the artists seemed strange animals rather than gods, created in the steaming jungles of the new riches, capable of life only in an economic temperature, a humidity of sentiment for which there was no earlier example—as there was to be none later.

Certainly in this hothouse atmosphere peculiarities grew large, one being that acute refinement in which late-Victorian art was distinct from that of Europe and also from the British art of an earlier day. If a Voltaire was able to term the 'Saxon genius' brutal and wild, M. Chesneau was forced to admit that 'the ancient fierceness of the Anglo-Saxon character' was wonderfully softened in the days when Leighton ruled over the English School, to judge by the works of art it produced. Refinement was a discipline which the middle class had added to its many disciplines and looked for in the works of its favourite artists. It was not desirable to look at ugliness, even though great artists of the past had found it abundant in interest. It was the merit of ideal beauty to be socially 'improving', in conformity with the general improvement of modes and manners. Classic, and academic art in a broad sense, were at one in this respect, thus the painter of contemporary life would so often depict not the poverty of London in all its hideousness but the spectacle of the poor made 'noble': an ideal poverty of beings who were handsome and dignified, albeit suffering. Though this did not materially improve the social system which made it possible, it gave that pleasing fillip to adversity which caused Luke Fildes's *The Casuals* to be admired by those huge crowds which it required policemen and a railing to control.

One peculiarity of this refinement lies in its effect on the subject picture, its suggestion of events which had no actual place on the painted canvas, of feelings to which it was hard to give any visual shape. In this delicacy of suggestion there was an element of mystery, a 'problem' to be solved by a mental communication between the artist and his public, to which the picture itself was a clue rather than a complete answer. Without the help of those animated gestures which are an obvious means of telling a story pictorially, the artist tried to set up a train of thought independent of the painting though provoked by its title. The *Last Watch of Hero* by Leighton has this mystery of a drama hinted at rather than told which the spectator must reconstruct from memory of legend or by reference to ti. Leighton was less liable to this than others, and yet here it is necessary to be equipped with the knowledge that Leander, the lover of Hero, has tried once too often to swim the Hellespont in order to be with her. In the night she has no doubt shown her torch as usual to guide him on his way but now the day has come and she stays, hoping against hope, at the window still, looking, it must be presumed, over the empty waters which do not appear in the picture. It would have been less refined to show Leander drowning, lifting eyes despairingly towards a distant light, a silhouetted figure, yet the picture might then have explained itself more fully. Torn garments and raised hands might have made it a physically comprehensible study of Hero's grief (and some antique master might have painted her thus), but in art, as in life, nothing was more repugnant to the late-Victorian than violent and unrestrained gesture. Leighton's *Hero* is still and tense, the meaning resides in whatever the title and the girl's frightened eyes may convey.

Descending, as it were, to Olympus below stairs, the modern observer will note that the 'problem' if not so lofty is in essence the same. What is the old gentleman thinking of in the picture by Orchardson entitled *Her Mother's Voice*? The clue is the presence of a girl at a piano, singing while a young man turns over the leaves of music. No doubt they are in love, but the title will not allow the matter to rest there. The girl must be the old man's daughter, her voice like that of a mother who is evidently no more, because the old man, sunk in his chair, seems to muse on the past. It is tempting to put into words the thoughts that may be passing through the head of that motionless figure: 'Extraordinary thing. Voice just like her mother's. Poor old Emily. We had some good times. Deuced sorry she's gone.' However much or little of poetry is imagined in the monologue, the challenge to sentimental musing remains. Sentiment, link between the painters of classic and contemporary themes, special product of the late-Victorian culture, upset the balance of form and content and on this score alone was unclassical.

In the hothouse atmosphere, weaknesses grew large; the 'success story' supports the modern apophthegm that 'nothing fails like success'—for that there was a failure can scarcely be doubted. It is possible—as William Morris did—to view that seemingly happy relation between art and riches as a bargain between ignorant plutocrat and obsequious menial, but only within limits, for it would be mere caricature to depict Frederick Leighton as the lackey of a Sir Gorgius Midas. It is possible to decry the interest in subject and the belief that the most important subjects must be remote in place and time; yet was it less reasonable for a late-Victorian to paint *The Return of Persephone* than for Titian to paint *Bacchus and Ariadne*? Further analysis is needed. Why, and in what respects, did Leighton fail? In some ways he confutes generalization. There was no 'Great Wall of China' round his studio. He was open to many influences outside Britain. He did not visit the galleries of Europe in that spirit of defensive contrast so well illustrated by Millais's remark to Frank Holl: 'Going to Spain? That's all right, my boy. Velazquez won't knock you down.' On the contrary he was of receptive mind, a man who understood the classic works he admired. Yet weakness there was, even of that subtle kind which consists in the apparent absence of weakness. Perfection itself (in that hothouse atmosphere) became an exaggerated growth. That observation of Steinle—'When everything is perfect, nothing is perfect'—has its application to him. The whole elusive question of that extra element which raises creative art above the product of skill, industry, knowledge, and intelligence is posed by the work of this singularly eminent person—so nearly the Sir Charles Grandison of painting. It is not easy to define that extra element save in such a word as 'temperament'—that spark of temperament which gives the Parthenon frieze itself more than dignity and measure—life, movement, its own reality.

In a somewhat different way the virtues of G. F. Watts prevented him from rivalling the Greeks he admired so much. The Parthenon sculptures inspired him with aims unlikely to have entered the head of Pheidias, made him wish to be a thinker in paint and stone, inciting others to noble deeds and resolutions. The Greeks may have intended to symbolize the conflict of lower and higher nature in the sculptured battles of men with giants and centaurs. They would scarcely have understood Watts's *Mammon* which gives, with all the Victorian refinement, a lesson on the misuse of wealth.

Still further from the classic spirit—its very negation, indeed—is the work of Alma-Tadema, in which the Victorian age smiles archly in fancy dress. In more than one fashion was the hope of the Committee on the Elgin Marbles frustrated. That the golden time of the seventies and eighties did not flourish into greatness is the conclusion of an age which has struggled hard to escape from Victorian dominance. Gone now is the Victorian Olympus as far, seemingly, from the twentieth century as it is from the fifth century B.C. Many of its productions have disappeared into that void which a radical change of taste creates. The golden mansions are a fable, the marble vestibules and fountains of municipal art galleries alone preserve the last influences of their splendour. Even sculpture breaks at last from its classic mould. It is perhaps a sufficient reason for turning back to it that it can still arouse wonder; yet also, as the classic ideal cannot die, the last effort to interpret it, however imperfect, may even today suggest other interpretations.

INDEX

INDEX

INDEX